LONI

Creative Texts Publishers products are available at special discounts for bulk purchase for sale promotions, premiums, fund-raising, and educational needs. For details, write Creative Texts Publishers, PO Box 50, Barto, PA 19504, or visit www.creativetexts.com

LONESTAR
by C.W. Wells
Published by Creative Texts Publishers
PO Box 50
Barto, PA 19504
www.creativetexts.com

ISBN: 978-1-64738-073-1

LONESTAR

by C.W. Wells

CREATIVE TEXTS PUBLISHERS
Barto, PA

To Jack MacMullan, a great coach and an even greater person.

TABLE OF CONTENTS

CHAPTER 1

Gale McClanahan heard the crunch of gravel and turned to the window. His daughter sat across from him at the kitchen table. She stopped drawing on a piece of spiral notebook paper and looked up.

Gale lifted himself out of his chair. Outside, he saw a black Cadillac Escalade parked next to his corrugated metal storage shed and saw two men climb out of the SUV. One was wearing a Stetson, a knee-length rancher coat and boots, and the other, a rust-colored sport coat and pressed jeans.

"Stay there, Tilly," Gale said.

He went to the door and stepped outside. On a Sunday afternoon in February, gray clouds swept over the sweep of plains and the wind was kicking up dust adding a chilled bite to the air.

"Gale McClanahan?" the man wearing the Stetson asked. He had one hand on his hat to keep it from tumbling away.

Gale nodded. The man looked familiar. Gale had seen him before. Somewhere.

"We need to speak with you." The man with the Stetson shook Gale's hand. His hands were large and veined. He looked at Gale through black, watery eyes, and his face was weather beaten and craggy. "Vernon Voss."

Gale's heart started to race.

"We need to talk." Voss pointed to the other man. "My colleague, Garvin Johnson."

Johnson reached out and shook Gale's hand. He was about the same age as Voss and had the same weathered look and thin, gray lips.

"You going to invite us in? Voss asked. "It's cold out here, Gale."

***

They sat at the dining room table in the small, cramped kitchen. Tilly sat curled on the couch playing with her mother's iPad. Voss put both his elbows on the laminated table and took a sip of the coffee that Gale had offered. Voss nodded at Johnson, who leaned forward, cleared his throat, and began.

"We've been following you for over a year," Johnson said. "We know more about you than you know about yourself. You're a hell of a coach, Gale."

Gale leaned back, puzzled. The conversation unfolding was surreal.

"You're the best high school football coach in Texas. You're going to be a great head coach in the League."

Voss and Johnson smiled.

1

"I don't understand," Gale said.

"We're offering you the head coaching job of the San Antonio Lone Stars," Voss said, his rheumy eyes boring into Gale's. "This is no joke, son."

"We think you can handle it," Johnson said. "We think you have what it takes, Gale. It's not too big a leap."

Gale felt a trickle of sweat on his forehead. He looked for an instant beyond the two men at Tilly, who was amusing herself with her mother's tablet. He wished Marybeth were home. She'd ask the right questions and make sense of what was unfolding.

"You're asking a high school coach in West Texas to coach the Lone Stars?"

"Not just any high school football coach," Voss said. "You've won seven state championships. You're 39 years old, and you're a fifth generation Texan, the son of a cattle rancher. You have what it takes. Besides, you played in the League. You understand the commitment."

Gale shifted in his seat. "You're crazy. I'm not qualified."

"We think you are," Voss said. "Besides, I've hired six different 'highly qualified' head coaches in fifteen seasons. Where did it get me? We haven't made the playoffs in years. We won one football game last year. I'm placing my money on a man who holds high respect in Texas. We're going to surround you with experienced coaches. We want you to be you. You're a winner."

"I don't get to pick my staff?" Gale asked.

Johnson smiled and looked at Voss.

"Now you're talking like a professional football coach, Gale . . . no . . . we have a staff in place from last year," Johnson said. "They're good men. The failure was at the top. Haden's gone. Their experience will be invaluable to you."

Gale had played two seasons as a back-up safety for Atlanta. When the team had cut him, he'd wanted to come home, take the money he'd earned in the League, buy a new pickup, place a down payment on a house, coach high school, and put a ring on Marybeth's finger, so that's exactly what he did. Under Gale's direction, the Kinney High School Lions had become a 2A-1 powerhouse. Gale didn't follow the League closely. His Sundays were devoted to studying tape and planning the next week's practices.

"We didn't come to West Texas to waste our time." Voss pulled a thick envelope out of his coat pocket. He laid the envelope on the table. He gestured to Gale. "Open it."

Gale reached over and unsealed the envelope. Slowly, he read the first page of the contract, trying to keep his hands from shaking.

"We're offering a one-year contract. Three million dollars with incentives. You turn the culture around and get the team pointed in the right direction, and we'll extend the deal."

Gale caught his breath. He made $68,400 a year to teach math and coach football. Marybeth made $47,000 working as a special ed teacher at the elementary school. The Lone Stars were offering more money than Gale would make for the rest of his life. Gale looked at both men. He thought about the stack of bills due at month's end sitting on Marybeth's water-stained desk, the roof which needed to be replaced, the decrepit boiler in the one-car garage, and the struggle to pay the mortgage each month. Over the last few years, a few influential Kinney boosters had approached Gale about a "special services contract" to keep him tethered, but he'd declined.

"Why one year?" Gale asked.

"We have faith in you," Johnson said after pausing and clearing his throat. "But one year's what we're offering. You prove you can win, and we'll pay you the premium rate. This offer will never come again. You have a chance to step into the limelight. They're only 32 of these jobs in the world. We're giving you the chance to have one of them."

"Think about it," Voss said, tapping his finger on the table. "Gale McClanahan, Coach of the San Antonio Lone Stars."

Gale leaned back. "How much time do I have to make a decision?"

"You don't," Voss said. "We need your answer before we fly back to San Antonio right after this meeting."

Gale looked perplexed. For a moment, he studied the contract resting on the table. "Now?"

"Take it or leave it. We're not interested in another indecisive coach. We have three other men in mind who I'm sure would be thrilled to seize the opportunity of a lifetime," Voss warned.

"I thought I was the only one," Gale said.

"We want you. You're our man. But we can't wait. We need to get this done before I fly overseas tomorrow. Understand?"

"I need to talk to my wife." Gale thought about Marybeth's reaction. She'd think he was kidding her. She grew up in the oil patch among roughnecks and wasn't easily duped. He was about to excuse himself and call her. His heart sank when he noticed her phone charging on the kitchen counter.

"Don't disappoint us," Voss said. "You say 'yes' and we'll be flying you to San Antonio in the morning for a press conference. This is going to move fast."

"I don't get to pick my own staff?" Gale asked again, confused, perspiration beginning to pepper his forehead.

"They're good men, Gale," Voss said. "It's a once in a lifetime opportunity."

Gale's heart pumped and his temples throbbed. He looked over at Tilly. She was focused on the iPad, oblivious to her father. What was Marybeth going to say? San Antonio was a world away from Kinney, Texas. Gale had tried to quell feelings of restlessness the past year. Despite his coaching success, he sometimes wondered, is this going to be it? The struggle to pay bills, the gnawing worry about money, and always the question if he could win at a higher level? With a stab of anger, he thought about his mother and father, buried in fresh graves under an empty, unforgiving West Texas sky, and the ranch, a family legacy, sitting in foreclosure.

He looked at Voss and Johnson, swallowed, and reached for the pen.

***

The SUV swayed in the gusts as Johnson and Voss drove to Midland. The flat, brown landscape spread out in front of them, the gray horizon stretching for miles. Dust whipped across the two-lane road and cold rain started to spatter against the Cadillac's windshield. Johnson had both hands on the wheel and turned to Voss.

"We got our man," Johnson said.

Voss smiled. "The poor sonofabitch."

***

Gale had asked a neighbor to watch Tilly before he drove to the Engle's house, which sat in a modest mid-century development on the outskirts of Kinney. Jack Engle met Gale at the front door. Engle and his wife, Barbara, had lived there for nearly forty years. Without a word, Gale entered the house as he'd done a hundred times before and heard Barbara in the kitchen.

"You okay?" Engle asked, inviting Gale to sit down in the living room. Engle had been Kinney's football coach for over thirty years before taking the principal position at the high school. Gale had been one of his best players. At the age of twenty-five, Gale had been given the head coaching position despite the objections of those who thought he was too young. In a few short years, Engle's instincts had proven right. Gale had built one of the most successful high school football programs in the state. The two men had grown close over the years.

Gale shook his head and handed Engle a copy of the contract. Engle turned to sit on a stuffed recliner next to the television set. Gale sat on the couch across from him.

Barbara came into the living room from the kitchen wiping her hands with a dish towel. She was petite and pretty with her gray hair cut short, straight nose, clear skin, and high cheekbones.

Barbara folded the dish towel neatly in squares and sat beside Gale. Her sunny expression changed when she noticed the concern on Gale's face and the confusion on her husband's. She asked, "What has Jack done to you now, Gale?"

Gale told them about the meeting that afternoon as the couple listened in mute astonishment.

Gale concluded by saying, "So, I guess you'll need to find a math teacher to finish the year. I hate cutting out on you, Jack."

Engle had announced in September he was retiring, and Gale hated to leave in his final year. A star fullback, Engle had met Barbara at Texas in the early 70's at

4

a sorority party, and she was married and pregnant six months later. Engle had played in the League for three seasons before a shredded ACL ended his career. He still walked with a slight limp, the unfortunate badge of a pro football player.

Engle leaned back in his chair. "Of course, but one thing's gnawing at me. Why you, Gale? I'm not trying to hurt your feelings, but have you asked yourself?"

"I'm still trying to figure it out."

"How can Gale and Marybeth turn down $3 million, Jack?" Barbara asked, sitting beside Gale on the couch. "We wouldn't, would we?"

"It depends."

"On what?"

"What I had to do to earn the money."

"Gale," Barbara said. "What does Marybeth think?"

Gale hesitated; his expression uncertain. "She doesn't know I took the job. She had to go to Midland to shop. She left her phone on the kitchen counter."

Barbara frowned and stole a glance at her husband.

"Can you find a math teacher to finish the year?" Gale asked.

Engle looked at Barbara. "I've got one right here, Gale. We're living under the same roof."

"You'll teach my classes, Barbara?" Gale asked. Barbara had taught high school math for years before retiring to chase grandchildren.

Barbara grinned. "I'll do anything for you and Marybeth, Gale. But I'm not sure I'd do anything for my husband. Jack's going to have to pay me a big salary."

"Looks like you have my replacement, Jack."

Engle nodded. He looked Gale in the eye. "I don't want you hurt."

Engle paused and let a few seconds pass before speaking again. "There's one thing I learned when I played for Dallas. There's no loyalty in professional football. You better turn the Lone Stars around fast. If you don't, they'll do what they always do in the League. They'll toss you on the scrap heap without a thought and find someone else."

***

Marybeth sat at the kitchen table holding Tilly in her lap staring at the contract Voss had slid across the table a few hours earlier. Gale sat across from her trying to gauge her reaction. Since he'd told her about Voss and Johnson, she hadn't said a word, but a cloud had crossed her face and her eyes showed a flash of anger. Gale had known Marybeth since high school, and he knew enough not to prod, but instead to let her process in silence until she spoke. Marybeth's deep hazel eyes remained cold as Tilly put her fingers on her mother's cheekbone and carefully traced the outline of her jaw.

"What does this mean, Gale?" Marybeth finally asked, her stare unwavering, as she looked directly into his eyes as she always did when she was searching to make sense of their lives.

"Besides the money?"

"Yes."

"An opportunity of a lifetime."

"I can't give everything up." She shook her head. "Kinney's my home."

"How could I pass it up? We can barely pay our bills. The house is falling apart."

Marybeth bit her lip and leaned back. "What did Jack say?"

"He told me to be careful." Gale reached over and picked up the contract. "If you asked me about all the things that could have happened to us, I never would have thought this."

"I hate they didn't give you any time to consider the offer. Why are they doing this, Gale? Is this the way the League works?"

"I don't know."

"Should we have had a lawyer look over the contract?"

"I didn't have time."

"I get the money, but why a decision now? If it wasn't the League, I'd say it was too good to be true."

Gale's stomach hurt, and he had a dull ache behind his eyes. He tried to look past Marybeth's anger. "What was I supposed to do? I get offered a job to be a head coach in the League, get paid more money than we'll ever see, and say, no?"

"You should have told them you needed more time. You took this job without asking me."

"I asked, but they wouldn't give it to me, and you left your cell phone on the counter," Gale said bluntly.

Marybeth went icily silent. Tilly pulled away from her mother and ran down the hallway to her bedroom.

Gale's voice softened. "Look, I'm sorry. But we'll be able to save and pay our bills without worrying every month how to make ends meet."

"Is it about money or ego?"

"Is that fair, Marybeth?" Gale shot back.

"Maybe not, but it doesn't matter at this point. It's a done deal."

"I can call them and tell them that I have buyer's remorse. I can quit."

"Sure. And blame me for the rest of your life for forfeiting your opportunity to coach in the League? Not a chance."

Gale shook his head and said, "I'm sorry you weren't part of the decision. I hate that part of this thing."

"I'm not picking up and moving during the school year," Marybeth said. "I'm not going to abandon my students. Besides, I never see you during football season anyway. After that, we'll see where we stand."

Gale felt a stab of guilt.

"I love you, Gale. But I'm mad as hell."

"I know."

"You never should have taken this job without talking to me." Marybeth rose out of her chair. "I thought our marriage was a partnership," she said as she walked out of the room.

CHAPTER 2

When Gale arrived at the corporate entrance to Midland International, he spotted a tired turbo prop sitting on the tarmac. He wondered when Voss' jet would arrive to fly him to San Antonio. The turbo prop was parked next to a row of single engine planes with their wings tethered to the ground to keep from careening into each other in the wind. The planes parked adjacent to the box-shaped cinder block hanger.

The night before had been a whirlwind. There were the calls to friends and co-workers, another conversation with Engle, the concern expressed for his players and students, all against the backdrop of Marybeth's iciness, and the uneasy reality of leaving the security of Kinney for the biggest challenge of his life. Gale had few regrets, but Marybeth's anger tore at him, and he wished he could have told his mother and father he was going to be the next coach of the San Antonio Lone Stars but the head on collision had killed them instantly years ago.

Marybeth had told her parents, who were retired and had moved to Colorado. The call had been met with silence and a few strained words of congratulations. Gale wasn't surprised. For years Marybeth's parents had been semi-estranged, as they were bitterly disappointed she'd passed on an opportunity to attend medical school to marry Gale. Even the prospect of her daughter being married to the coach of the Lone Stars didn't impress them.

And ever since she said them, Marybeth's words hung in the air. Was it about money or ego? At first, he felt certain of his answer, but now he was plagued by doubts.

Gale parked his pickup. He felt awkward and uncomfortable wearing the only suit he owned. It was charcoal gray, and he'd purchased it at Men's Warehouse in Midland. The last time he'd worn it was to Til's baptism. He wore a white shirt, a red tie, and dress boots as he climbed out of his pickup, grabbed his duffel, and went through the eight-foot security gate that ran around the airport's perimeter. He took a deep breath and gazed at the tarmac and looked up at the early morning winter sky, searching for the private jet that would wing him to San Antonio. Suddenly, a pilot popped his head out of the turbo prop's doorway and said, "Are you McClanahan?"

Gale nodded.

"Let's go," he said.

"This is the plane?" Gale asked, surprised, noticing the chipped paint on the plane's fuselage and black smudge streaking the engine cowling.

LONESTAR

"What'd you expect?" the pilot asked. "A Gulfstream? Welcome to the Lone Stars."

***

The Lone Stars' training complex sat next to an abandoned industrial site on the outskirts of San Antonio. The practice field stretched behind the squat, stucco building. Gale stepped out of the SUV in the light drizzle and was greeted by a smiling Garvin Johnson wearing a blue suit and Lone Star striped tie, who ushered him into the Complex.

Gale was struck by the shabbiness of the lobby. The thin-napped, beige carpet was worn and dirty, the pictures of former all-pro players were faded in their cheap metal frames, and the ceiling tiles were water stained. The leaves on a large potted plant in the corner were withered and brown, dead from neglect. A few abandoned, half-filled coffee cups sat on a glass top coffee table next to an ugly leather couch and two butcher block chairs. It was almost as if the shabbiness was fabricated, Gale thought.

"Can I ask you a question," Gale asked, following Johnson down a long, dingy hallway. "When was the last time this building was cleaned?"

"We put our money on the field, Gale," Johnson said. "That's Mr. Voss' rule. Makes sense, doesn't it? The press is waiting."

"Now?"

"You didn't think we flew you here to grab ass, did you?" Johnson laughed.

"I thought we'd have time to meet and talk about expectations and goals."

"The only goal is winning, Gale."

Johnson turned down a long corridor and pushed open a door. Gale blinked from the camera lights and heard the sudden hush of reporters sitting in a large conference room on folding metal chairs in front of a makeshift podium.

"I'm going to introduce you to the assembled jackals in a minute," Johnson said, smirking. "But first I want you to meet Sam." Johnson waved to a middle-aged man who was standing on the far side of the room. The man walked slowly over. He was bald, had a pockmarked face, and was wearing a baggy golf shirt and stained chinos. "Sam Lorenzo. He wears many hats, Gale. He handles the media and operations. A jack of all trades."

Lorenzo looked Gale up and down and didn't bother to shake his hand.

"Where's Mr. Voss?" Gale asked.

"He sends his regrets. He's flying out of the country this morning. A meeting in Dubai," Johnson said.

Gale shook his head. He felt all eyes in the room focused on him. He realized, despite the suit and tie, how nondescript he must have appeared. A strange face among seasoned reporters expecting a known quantity to be introduced as the Lone Stars' coach. He was a nobody, and they knew it.

9

Johnson moved past Gale and stood at the podium. He waited to speak until all eyes fell on him.

"I have the pleasure this morning of making an exciting announcement for the Lone Stars," Johnson said as the sound of cameras clicked. "Mr. Voss wished he could have been here, but he's got meetings to attend to in the Middle East. But he's thrilled, as am I, to introduce a young man who's going to turn things around here in San Antonio." He smiled at Gale. "He's a Texan, he's won multiple high school state championships, and he's no stranger to the League, having played for Atlanta. I'd like to introduce Mr. Gale McClanahan."

There was a murmur of disbelief in the room and one of the reporters in the back row laughed. Suddenly, hands shot up in the air, and Gale heard digital cameras clicking.

"Boys," Johnson said despite a few women reporters in the room. "I'm not taking questions. This is Coach McClanahan's day. . . Coach McClanahan."

Gale took a deep breath and stepped to the podium. A light from one of the video cameras nearly blinded him. When his eyes adjusted, he saw a sea of skeptical faces, sizing him up, looking for weakness. "I'm Gale McClanahan. I grew up in West Texas, and I'm going to give everything I got to win," Gale said in an unsteady voice, trying to control the growing anxiety. He breathed deeply to clear the lump in his throat and stop his hands from shaking.

He said nervously, "Mr. Voss has given me this opportunity, and I'm sure y'all are wondering why. I'm wondering myself." There was a ripple of laughter. "All I know is that life's about taking advantage of opportunities. I don't plan to let this one pass. I'm here to build a winning culture."

Gale paused for a moment. Johnson stood in the corner of the room with his arms folded and a thin smile written across his face. Gale took a deep breath and began. "It's no surprise winning starts with culture and high expectations. Mr. Voss didn't hire me to lose." Gale wiped his hand across the grime covered podium and held up a finger. "We're going to have high standards here, and the first person I'm going to hold to the highest standard is myself. . . questions?"

A reporter stood up. "What makes you qualified to coach in the League? Skeptics are going to say you lack the requirements for the job."

Gale paused for a moment. "Do you think the other former head coaches were more qualified? I did some research late last night on the franchise. The last 15 years, the team has been in the bottom of the League in team defense, points scored, penalties, turnovers and has lost 82 percent of the time to opponents in the game's last two minutes. No disrespect to those head coaches, but were they qualified? It may be high school, but my teams have always been disciplined and resilient. Those kids practiced hard, and they played harder. They gave me and the other coaches everything they had. We made ball security a priority and preached aggressive, penalty free football."

"With all due respect," said another reporter from the back of the room, "high school doesn't equate to the League."

Gale felt his throat tighten. "I disagree. Football is football."

"What offense did you run?"

"The Triple Option."

Laughter erupted in the conference room.

"Do you have any experience coaching the pro set?"

"I've never coached it."

"You don't plan to run the Triple Option, do you?" the reporter asked sarcastically.

"No," Gale said, feeling his palms begin to sweat.

"Will you get to choose your coaches?"

Gale looked at Johnson. Johnson smiled and shook his head as if to say, don't go there.

"As far as I know, last year's staff is returning."

"How do you feel about it?"

"I look forward to the opportunity to work with any coach who is dedicated to making this organization a winner." It was on this point that Gale felt most conflicted. He needed to be surrounded by seasoned coaches, but the thought of inheriting a staff that had only won one game the previous season bothered him. Like every other coach, Gale wanted to surround himself with coaches he knew and trusted.

"How do you think they feel having been passed up for the job for a high school football coach?"

"I don't know. You'll have to ask them."

"How familiar are you with the League?"

"I have a lot of homework to do."

"Do you know who Jerry Faust is?" a reporter asked at the front of the room. In the 1980's, Notre Dame had hired Faust, the coach of Moeller High School in Cincinnati. Faust had failed miserably.

Gale nodded.

"He couldn't make the jump from high school to college. What makes you think you can make the jump from high school to the League?"

"I've never failed at anything I've set my mind to."

"There's always a first time," the reporter muttered. "Will ownership have your back?"

"I wouldn't have taken this job if I felt otherwise."

A glimmer of approval washed over Johnson's face.

"How long have you been talking to Vernon Voss about the opportunity?"

Gale paused. He braced for the media's reaction. "Since yesterday."

"Yesterday?" the reporter asked.

"That's right."

C.W. WELLS

"How long was your interview?"

"I didn't have one. Mr. Voss offered me a contract on the spot."

There was a sudden rush of disbelief in the room. The reporter shook his head and looked up from his notepad. "I don't get this," he said, turning to Johnson. "You have a multi-billion-dollar franchise, and you hire an unproven, obscure high school football coach from nowhere. It's incomprehensible."

Johnson's expression turned to ice.

"No offense, Coach McClanahan," the reporter said, "but the whole scenario is ludicrous."

"Maybe I'll surprise you," Gale said.

Another reporter stood up. She had sunken cheekbones, her dark hair swept in a ponytail, and an aggressive, "gotcha" look on her face. "I googled you Coach McClanahan. In the 15 years you coached Kinney High School, you rarely punted. Is that a philosophy you're going to carry into the League?"

"Yes."

The buzz grew louder in the room. The media smelled more blood. Johnson broke into what appeared to be a weary smile.

"Did I hear you say 'yes', Coach?" she asked.

"You heard me," Gale said.

"Explain your philosophy on punting, please," she asked as cameras clicked and reporters leaned forward to catch every word of Gale's response.

"Statistically, punting makes no sense."

"How so?"

"David Romer proved punting is detrimental to a team's chances of winning."

"Who's David Romer?" she asked.

"An economist."

"Did you teach high school economics, Coach McClanahan?"

"No. High school algebra. But I understand statistical evidence."

"Why do professional football coaches punt?"

The conference room began to feel like the inside of a furnace. Sweat started to form on Gale's forehead. There was a still uninterrupted silence as the media waited for Gale's response.

"Coaches are conservative by nature, but the fact is that conservatism loses football games. Coaches just don't want to deal with the fallout of having a fourth down conversion fail. They don't want you guys all over them and having fans turn ugly. So, they protect themselves by punting when, on average, going for it more frequently leads to success."

"Will you carry a punter on the roster?" another reporter asked.

"I haven't made the decision."

"You're thinking about it?"

"Given roster numbers, I'm considering everything."

The female reporter broke in again. "Did Vernon Voss know your punting philosophy when he hired you?"

"You'll have to ask him."

"Will you have a say in who the team drafts?"

"I'm sure. I'm the head coach."

"It hasn't always been the case," she said. Gale glanced at Johnson and was met with a reassuring nod. "For years it's been a sore point for Lone Star coaches and scouts."

"Winning starts with collaboration," Gale said. "Voices need to be heard. I'm sure the scouting department and assistant coaches will work with me and Mr. Johnson to draft the best players."

"What about Mr. Voss?"

"I assumed he hired me to coach, not to do my job."

There was a sudden murmur in the room.

"How long is your contract?" a reporter asked. His gut hung over his belt, and he wore jeans and a San Antonio Spurs t-shirt.

"That's not public information," Johnson interjected.

Eyes turned toward Johnson. His expression didn't change.

"When are you meeting with your assistants?"

"Hopefully, right after this press conference," Gale said.

"How long do you think you'll last before you get fired?" the reporter with his stomach hanging over his belt asked.

Gale's eyes grew fierce. The day before, he was sitting at his kitchen table on a Sunday afternoon in Kinney, Texas, a highly successful coach in a town that worshiped high school football. Now he was surrounded by a pack of wolves and a growing sense of unease.

"I didn't take this job to suck air. I took it to win."

"That's what the last coach said," the reporter wearing the Spurs t-shirt remarked. "Haden was gone after two years. Sorry to say, I'm taking the under on you."

***

Garvin Johnson shut the door. Unlike the rest of the Complex, his office gleamed. The space had new carpeting, cherry wood paneling, an Espresso machine, a large screen television mounted on the wall, and a large monitor sitting on a sprawling desk. Scouting reports and several outdated League Directories sat on bookshelves along the walls. The nameplate on the office door said: Garvin Johnson, President and General Manager.

Johnson pointed to a stuffed leather chair. Gale's heart raced from the press conference. He was still trying to untangle what had happened a few minutes before.

Gale sat and Johnson took a seat across from him. Johnson's voice was fatherly. "Don't mind those media jackals. They've been on my ass for years."

Gale shifted uncomfortably.

"We have a lot of work to do, son," Johnson said. "We got to get you up to speed. Sam Lorenzo is going to take you for a tour of the facility before you meet the coaches. Where're you staying tonight?"

Puzzled, Gale said, "I thought the team would be handling my accommodations."

"There's a Hampton Inn down the street," Johnson said. "Perfectly fine. They have a free breakfast." He rose out of his chair. "Let's go."

Lorenzo was waiting for Gale outside of Johnson's office. His blank expression didn't change as he started down the hallway with Gale following. He pointed to a door down the corridor from Garvin Johnson's office. "That's the coaches' offices. We can go there later."

They continued down the hallway until they walked through double metal doors into the training facility. They stuck their heads into the locker room. The dressing stalls were empty and the player nameplates from the previous season had yet to be removed. A pile of dirty towels and crushed paper cups littered a stained thin napped, moldy green carpet. The white paint on the walls was flaking and chipping away. The room smelled stale, fetid, Gale thought. The stink was overpowering.

Lorenzo smiled for the first time. "Welcome to the Lone Stars."

Gale looked grimly at Lorenzo.

"Wait until you see the weight room," Lorenzo said.

They entered an area adjacent to the locker room and Gale looked in disgust. The first thing he noticed was unpainted concrete block walls, a couple of broken Cybex machines, a handful of worn-out treadmills and stationary bikes, and a weight training facility that made the Kinney High School weight room look like an Olympic training center. Weights were scattered in disarray across the frayed carpeted floor, and a few fluorescent lights hanging from the ceiling were burned out, others flickering on and off.

He was about to express his disbelief, but made a conscious effort to calm himself. "Who's our strength and conditioning coach?"

"We don't have one. He was fired a year ago and never replaced."

Gale's stomach sank. It was an absurd notion that a professional football team didn't have a strength and conditioning coach. Irresponsible.

"Where's the bubble?" Gale asked.

Lorenzo laughed. His ample stomach jiggled up and down as he rolled his eyes. "Bubble?"

"That's what I asked."

"Again, welcome to the Lone Stars. We don't have one. We're the only team in the League that doesn't have an indoor practice facility. Nothing like watching players burn-out in 110-degree heat."

Gale turned to Lorenzo, his eyes narrowing. "What do we have?"

Lorenzo smiled. "A high school coach with facilities to match."

"What do you mean by that?"

"Nothing."

Gale asked, "You're the Director of Media Relations?"

"Among many things."

Gale paused trying to control his growing confusion. He decided to change the subject.

"When can I meet the coaches?" Gale asked.

"In a few minutes."

"Is there anything I need to know?"

Lorenzo broke into a thin smile. "Everything. But you'll find out about your coaches soon enough."

CHAPTER 3

Rose Cutler barely lifted her head when Lorenzo abandoned Gale at his new administrative assistant's desk. In her sixties, Cutler's gray hair was cut above her shoulders, and her glasses rested on the tip of her aquiline nose.

Lorenzo left Gale standing in front of Cutler, searching for words.

"I'm Gale McClanahan – "

"I know who you are," she interrupted, focusing on the stack of paper in front of her.

"I'm supposed to meet the coaches."

"It's on your schedule." She held up a piece of paper and thrust it at Gale.

"Are you always this friendly?" Gale asked, taking the schedule.

Cutler leaned back in her chair and eyed him. "You're the fourth head coach I've worked for in seven years. What do you expect?"

"Courtesy."

"You came to the wrong place, Coach McClanahan. Courtesy is a rare commodity with the Lone Stars."

"Not for me."

"Well, then you came to the wrong team." She looked down again at the pile of papers on her desk. She lifted her head. "Don't get too comfortable. I wouldn't hang pictures. The last coach who hung pictures in his office didn't last a season."

"Good tip. Thanks for telling me," Gale said.

"You're welcome."

"Anything else I need to know?"

"Have you met Buddy Adams?" Cutler asked. Adams was the team's Defensive Coordinator and Associate Head Coach.

"No."

"Lucky you."

"How come?"

"Nothing I want to share."

"I can tell this is the start of a beautiful working relationship."

Cutler showed a hint of a smile. "Oh, we'll be fine Coach McClanahan, just as long as you do what I say."

***

The windowless coaches' conference room was empty and as shabby and grimy as the rest of the Complex. Over a dozen orange plastic chairs sat around a large, laminated conference table. Soda cans, plastic water bottles brimming with chewing tobacco spit, and pizza-crusted paper plates lay scattered around the room. Gale shook his head in disgust. Even cleaned up it would have all the charm of a bus terminal waiting room. He took a deep breath and leaned against the edge of the table waiting for his coaching staff to arrive. He thought of Marybeth and Tilly, their one-story ranch house resting on three acres outside of Kinney, and the security he'd surrendered with one swipe of a pen. Gale looked at his watch. He expected to have walked into the room and been met by a staff ready to make introductions and get to work. Instead, he stood in an empty room listening to an air duct rattle in the ceiling.

He was about to go back down the hallway and ask Rose Cutler if he had the right meeting room when a man wearing a faded Lone Star sweatshirt entered and reached out his hand. "Donta Jones, Special Teams Coach," he said. Gale winced as they shook. Jones' hands were the size of frying pans, and he stood nearly a foot taller than Gale. "I see all your friends are here." Jones broke into a smile. He had short graying hair and a white beard, which stood in contrast to his smooth ebony skin.

"Am I in the right meeting room?" Gale asked.

"You are."

"Where's everyone?"

"They left."

"What do you mean?"

"They walked out when they heard Voss hired you."

Gale frowned.

"Don't take it personally."

"How else am I supposed to take it?"

Jones smiled. "They'll be back. But not today. They went to a club near the airport to drown their sorrows."

"It's 11:45 in the morning."

Jones shrugged. "It's five o'clock somewhere."

"You didn't go with them?"

"Naw. The wife wouldn't approve. Besides, I was dying to meet the new head coach of the San Antonio Lone Stars."

"Well, here I am. What now?"

"How about lunch?"

"Does the Complex have a cafeteria?"

Jones laughed. "Did. But it got shut down last fall."

Gale looked perplexed.

Jones continued. "Sanitary violations."

"Where do players eat?" Gale asked.

"There's a bunch of fast-food options down the street. Team meals take place under the Golden Arches."

Gale shook his head. "Let's get out of here."

* * *

They had gone through the serving line at Grady's and settled into a corner booth. Jones rested his elbows on the table and stabbed a piece of meatloaf with his fork. A salad with bacon bits sat in front of Gale untouched. He had no appetite.

"We'll be lucky if we win a game next year," Jones said.

Gale looked up from his salad.

"Top to bottom, we got the sorriest roster in the League."

"We have a whole winter and spring of team building in front of us," Gale said.

"We got the smallest scouting department in the League. We haven't signed an impact free agent in three years, and the front office don't listen to us anyway. The scouts say draft this guy, and Voss and Johnson draft that guy. Unfortunately, 'that guy' has been a step too slow and a dollar short."

"I don't get it."

"Ego." Jones paused as he took a bite of mash potatoes. "They don't listen. They do what they want. Voss has run this franchise into the dirt."

Gale felt a growing pit in his stomach.

"No offense, but it seems like they hired you to prove they don't need an experienced coach. They can do it all by themselves, and they can do it on the cheap."

Gale turned and looked out the window.

Jones took a sip of iced tea. "Voss is one of those 'self-made' crazy bastards. Oil and gas. He has wells and leases all over North America."

"What can you tell me about Buddy Adams?" Gale asked, turning back to Jones.

Jones leaned back. "Should I be truthful with the new head coach?"

"Yes."

"He's the biggest asshole in the League. Unfortunately, he also happens to be my boss."

"I'm your boss."

"That's what you think."

Gale ignored the comment. "What's the deal?"

Jones laughed. "He's Voss' son-in-law."

"The hell." Again, Gale turned away in disgust.

"You got it."

"This job keeps getting more and more promising," Gale muttered. "What else do I need to know?

"Don't go near Voss' wife."

Gale's eyes clouded. He thought of Marybeth. "I don't plan on it."

"She's his fourth go-around and younger than his daughter."

18

After a few moments of silence, Jones took the last bite of his meatloaf and slid the check toward Gale.

"Split the check?" Gale asked.

"You got a lot to learn. The head coach pays. I'm a lowly assistant coach. You make the big bucks."

Gale smiled before his expression turned serious. "Donta, are you gonna help me turn this thing around?"

"Mission impossible."

Gale's eyes hardened. "That's not the right answer."

"I was young and stupid once, too."

"What does that mean?"

"You want to beat your head against the wall?"

"I want to win."

Jones leaned back and smiled. "Okay, Boy Wonder. You're serious, aren't you?"

Gale set his jaw. "Then we're all in?"

"I'm not sure what that means."

"It means we're going to turn things around."

Jones paused for a moment and shook his head. "For some crazy reason, I think you're serious."

"I am."

"Why should I attach my fading star to you? I'm 58-years old and this is my last stop. I've got my retirement savings and after years bouncing around this league, a shred of dignity."

"I've never lost. That's why."

"You got no clue of what you're up against. Do you?"

"Are you in, Donta?" Gale asked. "If not, then walk away. No hard feelings."

For an instant, Jones looked out the window at the cars streaming by the restaurant. He turned and said, "Find your office, get the coaches together, and stay the away from Adams. We need to start watching tape."

Gale grinned. "Then you're in?"

"I'm in, Boy Wonder," Jones said, shaking his head. "Neck deep."

"I have lots of ideas, Donta."

"I bet."

"I didn't take this job to fail."

Jones furrowed his brow and started sliding out of the booth. "Neither did the last coach."

***

19

Johnson didn't answer when Gale tapped on his office door. The conversation with Donta Jones had left Gale mystified. He headed down the hallway and found Rose Cutler at her desk, eyes glued to her computer. She barely looked up.

"The coaches' meeting?" she asked, ignoring Gale, typing on her keyboard.

"No one showed up."

"Not surprising," she said as she stopped typing and turned to Gale.

"There's not much sunshine around here."

"What did you expect?"

Gale's voice grew clipped and taut. He tapped his finger on Cutler's desk. "This is what I expect. You send an email to the coaching staff and tell them they better have their asses in the coaches' room at 6 a.m. sharp tomorrow morning."

Cutler rolled her eyes. "6 a.m.?"

"You heard me."

"It's the offseason. No one comes to work until 9 a.m. That's Mr. Johnson's rule."

"This is my rule. We start early and we work late."

Cutler smiled. "So, the Lone Stars have a new sheriff in town?"'

"You could say that."

"Well, then, I guess I should ask what else you want, Coach?"

"I need a laptop, email address, team directory, log in passwords, last year's playbook, and game tape by the end of the day. I want every single game from last season."

Cutler paused. "We lost the tape on Denver."

"What do you mean we lost Denver?"

"The file had a virus and infected every computer on the coaching and pro scouting staffs."

"Did your tech guy get it fixed?"

"We don't have a tech guy."

"Aw, hell."

"We have the TV tape of Denver."

"TV tape?"

"That's what I said."

"Why not call Denver? Tell them to send us another file."

"Can't do that."

"Why not?

She shook her head. "Because I can't. I'm not allowed."

"What do you mean?"

"Mr. Johnson and Denver's GM don't talk. They despise each other."

"Call the League office and have them send the game tape."

"Can't do that either."

"Why?"

"Because we didn't follow protocol."

"Protocol?"

"That's what I said, Coach McClanahan. Do you need to get your hearing checked?"

Gale stepped back and closed his eyes for a moment. His head hurt and his stomach ached.

Cutler continued. "There's game film protocol in the League, and we never follow it."

"What are you telling me?" Gale asked.

"We aren't in compliance. That's a quarter of a million dollar fine."

Gale sighed. "Send me what you have."

Cutler rolled her eyes. "You're just *full* of demands."

Gale was at loss for words. He pointed to a door. The nameplate had been torn off.

"That's my office?"

"It sure is. It's a dump."

"No surprise."

"Oh, and Coach McClanahan."

"What Ms. Cutler?"

"The keys to the Complex are on your desk. I need fifty dollars."

"Fifty dollars?"

"That's what I said."

"For what?"

"A deposit for the keys."

"Are you kidding me?"

Cutler leaned back in her chair, her glasses sitting on the tip of her nose. "Do I look like the kidding type?"

Gale shook his head.

"Everyone pays a deposit for keys. That's Mr. Johnson's rule," she said. "Don't lose them. I don't want to have to explain."

"What else do you need to tell me?" Gale asked.

"Nothing you won't find out for yourself," she said abruptly as she turned to her keyboard and began pounding away.

CHAPTER 4

Gale's office mimicked the rest of the Complex. The empty office stunk like cigarettes, the trash can overflowed with crumpled paper, month old half-eaten subs, Diet Coke cans, a couple of crushed pizza boxes, and an empty container of Tums. The metal desk was dented, and the bookshelves were empty but for a tattered and outdated copy of the League's Coaches Handbook.

Gale sat in one of the folding chairs scattered around the office and in frustration, picked up a Gatorade bottle on the floor and thought about hurling it against the wall when he spotted something move in the corner by his desk. The sudden movement startled him, and he realized he was staring at a mouse edging along the wall, looking for crumbs. In a swift motion, Gale tossed the Gatorade bottle at the rodent, and the mouse scurried across the floor by his feet and escaped under his office door into the hallway.

Gale sighed. He'd never felt lonelier. Instinctively, he reached for his cell phone and dialed Marybeth, realizing as he did so that he had no idea what he was going to say.

"Gale?" she said, her voice uneasy.

Gale sensed something wasn't right beyond her anger that he took the job without her consent.

"People are excited. The town's buzzing. You're a big shot now," Marybeth said, sounding hollow.

"And?"

"People are thrilled for you, Gale," she said.

"What's wrong?" He could tell something wasn't right. "Where are you?"

"In my classroom."

"Are the kids there?"

"No," she said.

"What's going on, Marybeth?"

"They're being horrible to you, Gale. Awful."

"Who?"

"ESPN. The networks. . . everyone."

"What are you talking about?"

"They keep showing the press conference over and over. They're mocking you, saying you're a joke and that you're not going to punt and that you're going to run the stupid triple option. They're saying on Twitter and Instagram that you won't last the first month of the season."

"Do you believe that?"

Marybeth met Gale's question with silence.

Gale's voice turned cold. "Turn off your laptop, Marybeth. Don't look at your phone. Okay? You and I both know this isn't going to be easy. It's the beginning."

"I know," she said, resigned. "You know I believe in you."

"I'm going to call you tonight. I'm trying to get my feet under me here."

"How have they been, Gale? Good people?" she asked.

Gale turned silent for a moment. "It's too early to tell."

***

A few minutes later, Gale stood over Rose Cutler's desk while she dug through a stack of files, doing her best to ignore the new coach of the San Antonio Lone Stars.

"Yes," she said finally.

"Where's the janitor's closet?"

She looked up and arched her eyebrow. "You'll get used to it."

"What?"

"The grunge. I stopped going to the bathroom in the Complex over a year ago. I don't want to catch typhoid. I go down the street to the Valero station. They clean their restrooms every 30 minutes."

"Where is it?"

"Valero?"

"The janitor's closet?"

"Really?"

Gale nodded. "Really."

Cutler pointed. "It's next to the team conference room."

Gale turned and started down the hallway.

"Coach McClanahan."

Gale stopped and looked back.

"You won't find anything in there. The custodians were let go after the season."

"You're kidding me?"

"We all take risks when we enter this building," she warned.

"I'm learning that."

"So far I haven't contracted typhoid."

"Lucky you," Gale said.

"Coach McClanahan. . ."

Gale took a deep breath. "Yes."

Cutler leaned forward in her chair and in a near whisper said, "By the way, you'll find the toilets are far from the dirtiest thing in this organization."

***

C.W. WELLS

The Hampton Inn sat down the street from the Complex. The new head coach of the Lone Stars had found himself without a ride to the hotel. He tossed his duffel over his shoulder and walked the half-mile in his suit and shiny boots. He passed a row of tired fast-food restaurants, a Home Depot, and a homeless shelter before checking into the hotel with his own credit card.

He was tempted to turn on ESPN to see what they were saying about him, but he had had enough for the afternoon. He was bone tired, his head ached, his mind raced, and he had a sinking feeling he'd made the biggest mistake of his life. He pulled his suit off and put on a faded Kinney High School football t-shirt and a pair of sweats. He climbed onto the bed and closed his eyes, feeling the walls close in, trying to make sense of how he was going to turn around the worst franchise in the League.

***

The king-size shopping cart was full of cleaning supplies, paper towels, sponges, rubber gloves, rolls of toilet paper, a broom, and a mop. When Gale had lifted his head up from the pillow in the early evening, the only place he knew where to start the reclamation of the San Antonio Lone Stars was Home Depot. Growing up on a hard scrabble cattle ranch, he'd never been a stranger to dirty, hard work. As a fifth-generation Texan, ranching was in Gale's DNA, and there had always been the self-imposed guilt that he chose coaching instead of working side by side with his father to keep the ranch solvent.

As a boy, Gale had a gift for horses and rode the junior rodeo circuit, an outlet for his athleticism and bullheadedness. He'd fought a temper and occasionally got into scrapes in elementary school. He'd hated bullies and found himself sticking up for the weak kid on the playground. Entering his freshman year of high school, Gale's father and Jack Engle had made sure Gale's temper and competitive nature were channeled onto the football field and wrestling mat. In his senior year, Gale had wrestled at 182 pounds and won the 2A-1 state championship.

Gale knew he looked absurd pushing the shopping cart to the Lone Star Complex, but there were too many items to carry. When he passed the homeless shelter, an old man smoking a cigarette outside the building warned Gale that the shelter didn't have any more beds.

Gale began in the locker room. He'd built a dynasty at Kinney High School by paying attention to detail, making sure the football program was a source of pride.

Gale remembered how his father had stacked firewood in neat rows by the barn and how he took satisfaction in fixing fences and keeping the ranch's heavy equipment in good working order despite the bank debt and losses piling up. Each summer in searing heat, Gale had worked with Mason Hayes, his father's longtime foreman, repairing fences and caring for livestock. Maybe if he'd devoted himself to ranching, his father and mother's fight to keep the ranch from creditors would have been different, Gale thought. Their struggles had made Gale even more determined to succeed.

Gale shook his head at the soiled towels strewn across the locker room and the trash scattered on the floor. The newly minted head coach of the San Antonio Lone Stars, making three million dollars a year, put on latex gloves, tried to ignore the stink, and went to work. He gathered the moldy towels and tossed them in trash bags. He picked up the trash on the floor and ran a vacuum over the stained, thin carpet, and pulled the player nametags off the locker stalls and tossed them away. He scrubbed the toilets, sinks, and showers with disinfectant and ran a mop across the tile floors. Afterwards, he moved to the weight training facility, if it could be called that.

He studied the weight room. It was shabby, cramped, and disorganized. He began by picking up the free weights off the floor and stacking them on the racks. He picked up several leather weight belts and hung them on hooks by the entrance and cleaned the smudged mirrors on the wall with Windex. He vacuumed, and before he finished, he made a note to call a technician to fix the Cybex machines.

He was about to leave the weight room when his cell chimed. It was Marybeth.

"Gale," she said.

He could tell by her voice she was upset. "It's been a terrible day."

Gale stayed silent.

"Til's sick."

Gale's stomach dropped. "What's the matter?"

"We got home today after school, and she started throwing up. She's got a 103-degree fever."

"Did you take her to the hospital?"

There was a sudden edge to Marybeth's voice. "Where do you think I am? I've been in the waiting room for an hour and a half. The poor child's miserable."

"I'm sorry."

"I wish you were here."

Gale was about to say, I wish I was, too, but held back. "Poor Til. I'm coming home this weekend to get my truck. When I get home, we can figure things out."

"We have a lot to figure out," Marybeth said. "I can't stand what they're saying about you."

"Forget the media, Marybeth. It's noise."

"I hate it, and you've only been the coach for one day. . . Jesus, Gale, one day."

Gale swallowed hard and heard a sharp cry, muffled sounds, and then Marybeth say, "I got to go. Til threw up all over me."

"I'm sorry, Marybeth."

"I am, too."

Gale put his phone in the back pocket of his sweats. He felt the gnawing worries of the day spread into an icy feeling of dread. When his parents had been hit head on during an icy January night and killed instantly, he realized all the planning, all the precaution, and all the prayers in the world weren't enough to keep bad things from happening to good people. He loved Tilly and Marybeth more than anything in the world. The thought of Til running a high fever and Marybeth upset made Gale want to go home, leave this shoddy place, and never look back.

Instead, he did what he always did to block out the fear and uncertainty. He lost himself in work scrubbing sinks and toilets, mopping floors, vacuuming, and emptying trash cans until the sun was nearly up. He even threw the dead plant in the lobby into the overflowing dumpster behind the building. While the Complex didn't gleam, it looked and smelled better. It was, he thought, a start to the Lone Stars' long, difficult road to respectability.

***

Donta Jones was the only assistant who showed up for the coaches' meeting at 6 a.m. Jones handed Gale a large cup of Starbucks and a blueberry muffin and said, "Payback for lunch yesterday. I thought you might need some caffeine."

"Where's everyone?" Gale asked, feeling a hot flush of anger on the back of his neck. He was tired. After cleaning the Complex, he hadn't gone back to his hotel room.

"They're giving you the middle finger."

Gale shook his head. "Go get your laptop."

"Why?"

"We're going to watch film."

Jones smiled. "I suppose it's going to be a long ass day."

Gale took a sip of coffee. "Don't plan on going home. I'll need to know what I'm looking at."

"By the way, did Johnson finally hire a janitor?" Jones asked. "I haven't seen empty trash cans in this building for weeks."

"I don't know. You'll have to ask him," Gale said.

"Cleaning this place must have been a bitch."

"Must have," Gale said, shaking his head and taking a large bite of muffin.

Gale wanted to rip his assistant coaches' heads off. What coaching staff in the League didn't show up when the head coach scheduled a meeting? In his anger, Gale wanted to fire the staff and hire his own people. He wanted Rose Cutler to send an email telling the coaches they were terminated. Gone. Still, Gale knew his first test was winning hearts and minds. Besides, Garvin Johnson had been emphatic: Gale wasn't going to pick his own coaches.

Gale figured the staff would expect the new head coach to go nuclear, so sitting alone in the coaches' room, he decided to take the opposite approach and made the decision to ignore them. Gale would go about his day, study tape with Jones, and avoid anything that smelled confrontational. He would do exactly the opposite of what the SOBs expected him to do in the hopes that it would confuse them and provide an opening. Besides, there were immediate obstacles he had to overcome.

Rose Cutler had still not given him a laptop, an email address, passwords, a playbook or game files. He had no tools and no staff. He hadn't slept and his head ached. Gale swallowed and tried to avoid the sinking realization he was riding a lame horse. And then there was Tilly and Marybeth.

CHAPTER 5

Jet lagged and even more ornery than usual, Vernon Voss found himself in his second meeting in Dubai in less than two weeks. He'd shuttled from Dubai to London, and now back to Dubai. He didn't want to think about the jet fuel he'd burned or the Gulfstream with its meter ticking and two pilots and flight attendant parked on the tarmac under a blinding sun. The negotiations had grown worse with each session in the Cayan Tower office of ESG Consultancy. Voss wasn't used to having a finger pointed at him. He hated the Swiss and the Saudi Prince's guts.

They sat in an elaborate conference room surrounded by glass and steel on the 73rd-floor overlooking Dubai's jagged skyline and the Arabian Gulf's blue, placid stretch. Voss had two skunks demanding immediate repayment of funds he didn't have. He'd accepted the terms when oil and gas prices had been their highest in decades. Voss Energy couldn't drill or borrow enough to fulfill its thirst for profit and had started looking beyond North America to West Africa and Sumatra. Then the bottom had fallen out. Here was Voss having to suck up to the neat and crisp Swiss banker wearing a tailored gabardine suit and the forty something Saudi looking like a Hollywood producer in his black V-neck t-shirt, designer jeans, and Gucci tinted eyeglasses, sipping Glenmorangie Single Malt Whisky at $1,000 a bottle.

"I need time," Voss said.

"That's what you said before," the Prince said in a British accent, leaning back, fingering his goatee.

"Cause I keep telling you it's true."

"You know the terms."

"I do."

"Therefore," the Prince said, his words clipped in arrogance as if he were still roaming the halls of Oxford, "we demand payment."

Voss looked angrily at the Prince. In his younger days in the oil patch, Voss would have ripped the bastard's head off. But here he was, in the Middle East, playing with fire. With energy prices at an all-time low, the debt repayment was staggering. Voss Energy's assets had been reduced to rusting drill equipment, expensive leases, and vast pools of natural gas and oil not worth harvesting.

"Give me six months."

"Impossible," the Prince said.

"You boys will get your money."

LONESTAR

The Swiss leaned forward in his chair. He looked trim and fastidious. His sandy hair was close cropped, and he was gray at the temples. "This is true. One way or the other."

The threat wasn't lost on Voss.

"We need assurances, Mr. Voss," the Prince said. "Not conjecture."

"I hear you loud and clear." Voss hid a bolt of anger as the Prince turned and smiled at the Swiss.

Voss knew he wasn't going to take it. He had learned growing up dirt poor in El Reno, Oklahoma with eight siblings and a mother and father who didn't graduate from high school that playing nice got you squat. He was a brawler. In the gas and oil fields, you had to be ruthless.

Voss picked his Stetson off the coffee table and rose out of his seat. He flashed a cold smile at the two men across from him. They stared at him with amusement, as if they had crushed an old, tired cowboy.

In a swift motion, Voss reached down and snatched the Prince's crystal tumbler of whiskey and flung the single malt in the Prince's face. He tossed the tumbler on the floor, the glass shattering.

The Swiss and the Prince looked stunned.

"Like I said, you'll get your money," Voss hissed before turning to leave. "In the meantime, you boys can go screw yourselves."

***

Jones and Gale started with the first preseason game against Houston. Jones plugged his laptop to the big screen on the wall so they could witness the Lone Stars' deplorable efforts. They watched plays repeatedly with Gale asking multiple detailed questions about schemes, play calls, and personnel. After nearly two hours, they still were looking at the first quarter against Houston.

By this time, Jones knew one thing for sure: the new Head Coach of the Lone Stars was relentless. Jones' inner voice was telling him Gale was different. There wasn't a question Gale was unwilling to ask. During one sequence, Gale demanded Jones rewind the play over a dozen times. The call had been a simple jet sweep that had turned into a debacle.

Gale kept shaking his head. "The play hasn't been coached. Look at it, Donta. I don't care if it was an exhibition game. It's a simple sweep. What was everyone doing during training camp?"

Gale's question was met with silence.

Gale rubbed his eyes and turned away from the screen. "If I didn't know better, I'd think this organization wants to lose."

"Don't tell the Commissioner," Jones said.

"Why have you stuck around?"

29

"This is my last stop. The train has passed. I'm trying to collect a few more paychecks before someone kicks me out the door."

"You know what really bothers me?"

"Tell me, Coach." Jones broke into a smile.

"Watch this."

Gale reran the play. "Besides no one knowing what to do, what else do you see?"

Jones studied the tape. "A broken play."

"More than that."

"Don't leave me wondering, Coach. What?"

"The tailback gets his ass kicked. He's alone out on the edge and gets decleated. Now look." Gale played the tape again.

"I see what you see. I see a running back get crushed," Jones said. "Kill the suspense. Tell me."

Gale turned to Jones. His face was red. "Not one single teammate helps the kid off the turf. Says it all." Gale lifted himself out of his chair. "I've seen enough for now, Donta."

"Where're you going?"

"It's about time I meet my friend, Buddy Adams. Let's go."

***

Gale and Jones stopped at Rose Cutler's desk. She was typing with abandon, banging furiously on her keyboard, her glasses resting as usual on the tip of her nose.

"I need a laptop, Ms. Cutler," Gale said, "and an email address, passwords, playbook, game film - "

"Take a chill pill, Coach," she said, cutting him off without bothering to look up.

Jones started to laugh.

"Chill pill?" Gale said in astonishment.

"That's what I said."

Gale bent down and looked Cutler in the eye. She lifted her head up momentarily from the screen and met his gaze without blinking.

"I won't ask for much. I promise. But if you ever tell me to take a chill pill again, you'll be looking for another job."

Cutler squinted. "Oh, really."

"Really."

"You know, Coach McClanahan. I spent the better part of yesterday afternoon trying to meet all of your demands. I was told you don't need a laptop and if you want one, you can buy it yourself."

"Who told you?"

LONESTAR

"Lorenzo."

Gale shook his head.

"By the way, you must have been busy last night. Where are the towels?"

"What towels?"

"The towels that were in the locker room."

"What about them?"

With a delicious smile, Cutler thrust a sheet of paper in Gale's hand.

"What's this?" Gale studied the sheet.

"A bill."

"Three hundred and fifty dollars?"

"Yup."

A confused look crossed Jones' face.

"Those were perfectly good towels, and Mr. Johnson's assistant wants reimbursement."

"They were full of mold."

"That doesn't matter."

"What else do you have for me this morning, Ms. Cutler?" Gale asked in disbelief.

"On a bright note, I didn't have to go to Valero," she said. "I peed right here."

"That's great news," Gale muttered.

"Cheer up. When you get fired as coach of the Lone Stars, there are plenty of janitorial openings out there."

"Good to know."

"So you know, the coaches are in the team room," she said, smiling. "Buddy Adams told me you're not invited."

***

Gale's phone pinged, and he stopped in front of the team conference room. He read Marybeth's text: *"Til's better this morning. Rough night. The flu. I'm staying home from school today to be with her. I was such a darn mess yesterday."*

Gale looked up.

"Everything okay?" Jones asked.

"Not everything. But the thing that matters most."

"You really want to go in there?" Jones eyed the team conference room door.

"No. But what else am I going to do?"

Gale swung open the door. The large, dingy room was built like a movie theater with stadium seating. Heads turned. The coaches wore disdainful looks, and after an instant, turned back to a man with jet-black hair and a blunt nose, which sat pugnaciously above a lantern jaw. He looked like an old Hollywood version of a prize-fighter. Buddy Adams leaned against an empty whiteboard at the front of the room.

Frozen, Gale met the man's glare. Jones followed.

Adams looked with disdain at Gale. His eyes darkened and his body went rigid. He leaned against the empty whiteboard with a "go screw yourself" look.

Gale stared back until Adams broke the silence. "Who invited you to the meeting? This is for the Lone Star coaching staff."

Gale shook his head feeling the hard eyes of the coaches glaring at him, daring him to pick a fight.

"I thought you'd invite me, since I heard a rumor I was the head coach."

"I hadn't heard that rumor."

"I bet," said Gale. He swept his eyes across the room and tried to make eye contact with the coaches.

"I didn't come here to pick a fight with you or anyone else." Gale ignored Adams and spoke directly to the other coaches. "The only fight we ought to pick is with the 17 teams we're competing against starting in September."

Gale paused and thrust his finger at the coaches. "If you're in, we'll meet in the conference room in fifteen minutes. I expect everyone to be there." He looked directly at Adams. "If someone has a problem, they can speak directly to me."

Adams broke into a thin smile. His eyes turned into slits. "I have a problem with that, Boy Scout."

The coaches smiled.

"Let's hear it," Gale said, ignoring the slight.

"You don't know nothin' about the League. You don't know nothin'. Head coach? Go back to West Texas and coach Pop Warner."

The coaches laughed.

"In or out?" Gale asked, staring hard at the coaches.

Jones looked grim.

Gale repeated, "In or out?"

Silence permeated the room. The coaches started to look away as Gale's eyes bored into them.

A few moments passed.

"You got your answer, Boy Scout," Adams said. "If you think the coaches don't want nothin' to do with your green ass, wait until the players show up."

"Any takers?" Gale asked.

He was met with silence.

"You got your answer," Adams said, beaming.

Gale turned to Jones. "Let's go."

Jones shook his head. He was about to say something but stopped.

They left the team room and faced each other in the hallway. "Nothing like a rebellion," Gale said. "Is Adams always that sweet?"

"Prick."

LONESTAR

"We can get mad or even. I say we get even." Gale studied the doors to the conference room. He noticed the lock under the crash bars. He reached over and with a snap locked the team room shut.

"What do you have in mind?" Jones asked, surprised.

"You'll see."

The night before, Gale had noticed the sprinkler system panel next to the entrance to the training facility. When he and Jones found the sprinkler system, he flipped open the box and ran his finger along the row of switches. He set his jaw. It was time for a statement.

"Here it is," Gale said.

"You aren't going to do that?" Jones asked. "They'll be hell to pay."

"Presto," Gale said as he flipped on the team conference room sprinklers.

Jones whistled. "Adams is going to love that."

Gale gave a hard look. "Those SOB's are going to wish they took up my offer, Donta."

CHAPTER 6

A few minutes later, Gale and Jones stood in the Complex's desolate parking lot under a clear sky. Cars raced past making a continual whooshing sound. The late morning sun felt warm on Gale's face.

"What now?" Gale asked.

"I don't suppose we go back inside."

"Let's wait."

Jones raised his eyebrows.

"How about lunch?" Gale said. "Grady's?"

Jones nodded.

"How about splitting the check this time?"

"I bought you coffee and a muffin this morning," Jones protested.

"If towels cost $350, can you imagine how much I am going to be out for flooding the building?" Gale asked.

Jones smiled and put his hand on Gale's shoulder. "That's if you still have a job at the end of the day, Wonder Boy."

***

Rose Cutler met Gale at his office door. For the second day in a row, Gale hadn't touched his lunch and Jones, not holding back, had eaten it for him while they'd sat in a corner booth.

Since arriving in San Antonio, Gale's only meal had been a Starbucks muffin. He had no appetite, and he figured he wouldn't have one anytime soon.

"We had a little mishap," Cutler said, raising an eyebrow.

"What's that?" Gale answered, trying to slide by her to enter his office.

"Seems the sprinklers went off during a coaches meeting. Mr. Johnson is very unhappy. Did you know there was nearly three inches of water on the team conference room floor?"

Gale shook his head. "Isn't that something? Someone's going to need to get that cleaned up."

"The doors were locked. I wonder how that happened? The coaches nearly drowned."

"That's terrible, Ms. Cutler."

"Guess what Coach McClanahan?"

"What?"

"We didn't have any towels because you threw them all away!"

34

Gale smiled thinly. "Did you get what I asked for Ms. Cutler?"

She folded her arms. "Demands. Demands. You've only been here two days and you're full of demands. Why don't you look in your office."

Gale entered his office and saw a new computer sitting on his desk, three large binders, undoubtedly playbooks, a stack of yellow legal pads, a package of pens and markers, an updated copy of the Coaches Handbook and Directory, and a neatly typed sheet with his email address and passwords.

He turned and stuck his head outside his office door. "Thank you," Gale said.

Cutler sat at her desk trying to ignore him, a faint smile crossing her face.

"I mean that," he said. "I know you're sick of me already, but I'm grateful."

Cutler looked up at him. "Actually, I'm starting to like you. By the way, Mr. Johnson wants to see you ASAP."

"Oh, really?"

"He's upset, Coach McClanahan. He said you threw out his favorite plant."

"It was dead."

"Doesn't that tell you something?"

***

Gale waited outside Johnson's office trying to avoid the glare of Johnson's assistant, who had a pinched face and suspicious eyes. Her frosted hair fell to her shoulders, and she seemed to have a permanent sneer. He stood with his arms folded, leaning against a wall, until the door swung open and Johnson motioned for Gale to enter.

Gale sat on one of the leather chairs and Johnson sat across from him on the plush couch.

"What's going on with Adams?" Johnson asked, his voice concerned. "I heard about the stunt you pulled on the coaches this morning. You're lucky I sent all of 'em home, including Adams. They'd rip your head off. We had to call Serve Pro to suck up all the water."

"You tell me."

"Buddy's a fine defensive coordinator, and I don't understand why you two can't get along."

Johnson paused.

"I want my own staff," Gale said.

Johnson leaned forward. After a moment, he broke into a fatherly smile. "You have a perfectly fine group of coaches. Good men."

"They won't work with me."

"Give it time," Johnson said reassuringly.

"What coaching staff refuses to work with the head coach?"

"I didn't turn on the sprinklers," Johnson said.

"We have the Combine coming up in two weeks, free agency, not to mention the draft, OTAs and training camp." There was urgency in Gale's voice. "Every hour I lose, I can't get back. You hired me to do a job, and I can't do it right now."

A concerned look broke across Johnson's face. He lowered his voice as if he were talking to a child. "We hired you to create solutions, son. Mr. Voss has given you a great opportunity. It's your job to find a way to get your coaches on board."

Gale sat back. He thought of Kinney and how simple and good his life had been. Now this . . .

"I need you to schedule a meeting with me and the coaches," Gale said. "Get us all on the same page."

Johnson shook his head, lifted himself up, walked across the newly installed carpet, and went to his heavy, cherrywood desk. He picked up two large binders and tossed them with effect on the coffee table in front of Gale.

"See those," Johnson said, pointing. "Scouting reports. One is for free agency. The other is for the draft. I run this entire organization. I haven't got time to referee spats between coaches." He shifted and his voice softened. "That's your job, Gale. Understand?"

Gale hesitated before he spoke. His head spun. "I need to speak with Mr. Voss."

Johnson paused for an instant.

"I don't want you troubling the owner with a small problem."

Gale shook his head. "You think the coaching staff refusing to work with the head coach is a 'small problem'?"

"I expect any coach worth his salt to be able to fix it." Johnson smiled.

Gale's hands tightened.

"Anything else, Coach McClanahan?"

"Nothing." Gale got up to leave.

"Coach McClanahan. How come you threw out the plant in the lobby?"

"It was dead."

"It's winter, son. The plant was dormant. Don't you know the difference between dead and alive?"

Gale shook his head and gave a thin smile before turning to leave.

"Oh, and one other thing." Johnson paused. "We didn't hire you to be a janitor. You need to focus on what's important. Remember, it's all about winning, Coach."

***

After Gale left his office, Johnson picked up his cell phone. He punched up Vernon Voss' number, and after a few rings, he heard Voss' gravelly voice above the din of traffic and honking horns.

"What do you got, Garvin?" Voss barked.

"Exactly what we want."

"That's good news."

"Where are you?"

"London."

"How was Dubai? Did you get a deal done?"

Voss went silent. After a few uncomfortable moments, he said, "Time's running out. Understand?"

Johnson sat back in his chair and felt a chill grow up his spine. "I understand."

"How's the kid doing?"

"Just as we'd hoped."

"Keep it that way. . . and Garvin."

"Yes."

Voss' voice turned to ice. "Keep an eye on my wife. I don't want her screwing anyone while I'm gone."

CHAPTER 7

At 4 p.m. sharp, Lone Star employees had cleared out of the Complex as if someone had called in a bomb threat. Gale and Jones found themselves in the coaches' room watching game film in an empty building, only halfway through the second preseason game against Arizona. Gale's apprehension continued to grow with every play he and Jones broke down. It wasn't only the lack of execution; it was the way the Lone Stars were overmatched. They were disorganized, slow, unskilled, and undisciplined. Even a high school coach could figure that out. In the past three seasons, Donta Jones had said Johnson had traded away the team's top draft picks for aging veterans, signed a handful of bargain basement free agents who were known around the League as journeymen, and had the lowest payroll in the League. Gale watched the Lone Stars' rookie undrafted free agent quarterback, Matt Abruzzi, take a vicious blindside hit, shook his head, and paused the tape.

Gale rubbed his eyes. He needed to get sleep and something to eat.

"I don't even know where to begin," Gale said, sipping a bottle of water.

Jones shrugged.

"I don't get it. How can a pro football organization be this bad?"

"Buyer's remorse, Coach McClanahan?"

"I've never quit in my life. I took this job. I'm going to see it through."

"You sound like a cowboy from West Texas."

"I am. I grew up on a ranch, and I didn't get raised to quit. How about you?"

"I've seen it all. I thought I'd have a championship ring on my finger by now, be a defensive coordinator, but it never panned out."

"How about head coach?"

Jones laughed and shook his head. "I had one interview for a head coaching position in all that time. The team brought me in to meet the quota. The League says you got to interview a minority when a head coaching job opens up. It was a sham. I knew the second I walked into the room the owner wasn't going to hire a Black man."

"How come you're in this room with me," Gale asked, "and not with Adams and the other coaches? If there's anyone who you ought to resent, it's me. Young, white, and unqualified."

Jones laughed and leaned back in his chair. "You are all the above, Coach. But I said to myself when I saw you yesterday wandering down the hallway lost and forlorn, this boy needs help. Besides, I like the underdog. It's probably the reason I ain't got a ring on my finger, and I'm employed by the worst franchise in the League."

Gale turned back to the screen. "Where do we go from here?"

"We keep watching film. I'll teach you the playbook since you have no say in that." Jones paused. "I'm going to start talking to the coaches, one by one. See if I can get them to start talking to you."

"Adams?"

"The man is evil, Coach."

"Why do Johnson and Voss keep him around?"

Jones smiled slightly. "You'll find out. Hang around long enough and you'll see things you never thought."

Gale's eyes clouded, and he turned back to the screen on the wall. He unpaused the play and wondered if Abruzzi would get up after taking a brutal hit.

He did.

Tough kid, Gale thought as the All-22 flickered. We better hope we find more like him. Otherwise, you can kiss my ass goodbye.

***

Lying in bed with the sound of the occasional car racing by the hotel, Gale thought back to his conversation with Johnson and played it over and over. It was the way Johnson had tossed the notebook binders on the table. Something about that struck a false note. It was almost theatrical, as if Johnson was acting out a role. The entire conversation seemed staged. If anything, it didn't make sense. But what did?

Gale arrived at the Complex before sunrise after four hours of fitful sleep. He wasn't the smartest kid, the best athlete, or the possessor of any special talent, but he had a capacity for getting things done. The reason he'd made Atlanta's roster was a combination of tenacity, willpower, and a fearless capacity for physical violence on the football field. As his first training camp had ended, he'd watched more talented athletes from bigger schools and with better pedigrees get cut while he had survived. Still, he'd known his time in the League would be short. He wasn't good enough to last. When Atlanta had cut him in his third year during training camp, Joe Barnes, the head coach, had asked Gale if he wanted to join the organization as a scout. Gale had declined. He had Marybeth waiting for him and a life in Kinney. It had been a simple decision.

Gale walked down the corridor to his office and spotted Jones coming towards him. Jones grimaced when he saw Gale.

"You're not going to like this," Jones said.

Gale could tell by the look on Jones' face it wasn't good.

"Your office." Jones shook his head.

When Gale opened his office door, he knew immediately he wasn't going to let this violation pass. On the carpet, sitting in front of his desk, was a neat pile of crap.

Jones said with disgust, "Worst thing I've seen in my career, Coach."

Gale fought to keep his hands from shaking. "I'm going to make the son of a bitch eat it, Donta."

"Easy . . . I don't want to have to bail you out of jail."

"You may be doing that," Gale said, his face reddening as he shut his office door.

***

In the mid-morning, Gale waited outside the coaches' conference room, trying to make sense of what he was about to do. He could hear the muffled sounds of voices and the occasional burst of laughter. A meeting was in full swing. Gale's anger had boiled into a rage. Jones stood next to him, his attempts to talk Gale out of an act of confrontation unheeded.

Gale opened the door and a hush fell over the room. Buddy Adams sat at the head of the table, and when Gale entered, Adams leaned back, and his eyes darkened.

"Can't you see we got a meeting in progress?" Adams sneered. "You boys are in hostile territory."

"The hell," Gale said.

"What do you want, Boy Scout?" Adams said, a slow smile spreading across his face.

"Don't ever, and I mean ever, mess with me again."

"Mess with you? How about the little shower you made us take yesterday?"

Gale took the plastic bag and tossed it onto the table in front of Adams.

"Eat it," Gale said.

Adams eyed the bag and sniffed. "I don't know what's inside the bag, but it don't smell good." He leaned back and smiled at the coaches before turning back to Gale.

"I said 'eat it'," Gale repeated.

Adams rose out of his chair. "Eat what?"

Gale took a step forward. "What you left in my office last night."

"Son, I didn't leave squat in your office."

Gale could feel his rage build. Adams stood in front of him with a grin.

"You ever mess with me again, I'll kill you."

"Did you hear that, boys?" Adams looked around the room smiling, his eyes turning black. "Boy Scout said he's going to kill me."

The coaches began to laugh.

Gale felt an intense burst of anger. In a sudden motion, he leapt forward and reached for Adams' throat.

***

LONESTAR

Sam Lorenzo heard the commotion in the conference room and broke into a grin. He fingered the neat roll of hundred-dollar bills and walked slowly to his office savoring the moment. It had been easy and had been surprisingly pleasurable. How many times does an employee get paid to crap in a head coach's office? After years of being maligned by higher ups, assholes who treated him like dirt, it was one of the highlights of Lorenzo's career. He knew if he played his cards right, crapping in Gale McClanahan's office was the start of better things to come.

CHAPTER 8

When Southwest flight 1237 circled Midland, Gale could barely turn his head to see the lights sprinkled across the vast and dark stretch of plain. His first week with the Lone Stars had been a train wreck. After he'd been pulled down before he could get to Adams, he could barely move his head without a sharp, knifing pain, and his left eye was swollen shut where one of the assistant coaches had struck him. The aftermath of the brawl had been even more of a mess. The meetings with Johnson, the recriminations, the threats, the increasing feeling of isolation and frustration, and the gnawing fear he would fail before he even had a chance. Fortunately, no one noticed him in the San Antonio airport, and thus far on the plane. Even though Gale was one of thirty-two coaches in the most popular league in America, he felt like a nobody. He wore his Kinney baseball cap tugged low, and even though it was nighttime, he wore his sunglasses on the plane to hide his bruised eye.

Marybeth held Tilly on her hip and stood apart from the swirl of travelers and greeted Gale by baggage claim. Til flashed a huge smile and reached out to Gale. He winced when he folded his daughter into his arms, feeling pains rippling up and down his neck.

Marybeth stood for a moment watching the scene oblivious to Gale's pain. "Sunglasses, Gale? Has the job already gone to your head?"

Gale slowly pulled off his sunglasses before putting them back on.

Marybeth's expression turned grim. "What happened?"

"I got pummeled."

"You're kidding me?"

"We have a lot to talk about, Marybeth. It's a long and ugly story."

***

It was after midnight and Gale and Marybeth lay entwined in bed. Despite the knifing pain in his neck, they'd been hungry for one another. Marybeth had softened, at least for the moment. Gale never grew tired of the way Marybeth felt, her soft, downy skin against his, and the smell of her freshly shampooed hair. From the moment he took notice of Marybeth his junior year in high school, he knew he was going to marry her. After years of trying to have a child and seeing specialists in Dallas and Houston, Marybeth had finally gotten pregnant and given birth to Tilly. It had been a miracle. Despite the worries of making ends meet, and the tug and pull and occasional chafe of marriage, life together in Kinney had been good.

LONESTAR

Lying in the dark, with streaks from an icy winter moon illuminating the bedroom, Gale told Marybeth everything. They found safe ground and talked into the early hours of the morning, recounting in disbelief how they had gotten to this moment. To Gale's relief, Marybeth had avoided recriminations.

Marybeth sat up with her head against her pillow and said, "Why are the coaches doing this to you, Gale?"

"I don't know," he said.

"I don't like it. It's almost like the team hired you to fail."

"No one hires anyone to lose."

Marybeth was lost in silence for a moment. "I've been thinking," she said. "It's been bothering me. We should have had Grayson look over your contract. God knows what's really in the document."

Grayson Wallace was the town attorney. He'd known Marybeth and Gale's families for years. He spent his time relishing being a small-town lawyer, drawing up wills, helping settle ranch disputes, and arbitrating oil and gas rights. Most of his generous income had come from lucrative oil and gas leases on a vast and undeveloped piece of property he owned outside of Kinney. He enjoyed sitting with his cronies every Friday night during the football season watching Kinney roll over another opponent and the next day sending Gale a long email critiquing the game.

"It's been bugging me, too. I would have had Grayson look over the contract with a fine-tooth comb if Voss and Johnson had given me time to make an informed decision."

"You need to see him in the morning."

"It's a Saturday."

Marybeth turned to Gale. He could see her outline in the faint light and the swell of her breasts beneath the blankets. "You're not a nobody. You're a professional football coach. The whole town wants to see you." She paused. "The contract worries me, Gale. I got a bad feeling about it. It's full of legal nonsense. I tried to read it again yesterday."

Gale closed his eyes for an instant, suddenly feeling exhaustion overwhelm him. "Let's see what Grayson says."

***

Grayson Wallace sat behind his oak desk with a steaming mug of coffee resting in front of him. When Gale had entered his office, Wallace had looked him up and down and had refrained from asking him about his eye, which was shut tighter than a bank vault. Wallace's diplomas hung on the wall collecting dust, and his wood paneled office, overlooking Main Street, was strewn with legal volumes and law journals. He sat back in his chair, reading the document carefully with an occasional grunt.

43

After nearly thirty minutes of wading through the contract, Wallace looked up and adjusted his glasses. He had a shock of white hair and gray stubble on his chin that had eluded his razor.

Wallace shook his head. "I've never seen anything like it, Gale. Convoluted. Disingenuous. Manipulative. Binding. Brilliant."

"All that?"

"And more." Wallace leaned back in his chair. "The most alarming is termination without cause. They refer to a provision I've never seen and can barely understand. It's cloaked in a dense tangle of legalese. You should have shown me this before you signed, Gale." With disgust, Wallace dropped the contract on his desk. "You quit this job; you owe them three million dollars."

"What?"

"I'll say it again. You owe them money you never made if you quit before the terms of your contract are completed."

Gale looked alarmed and confused.

"For instance, a standard claw back provision requires the employee to return earnings if he makes the decision to leave before the terms of the contract are fulfilled. In this case, if you leave before the contract is satisfied, you owe them the entirety of your compensation whether you collected the money or not."

Wallace pulled his glasses off and rubbed the bridge of his nose. He tapped his gnarled finger on his desk for effect. "If they terminate you before the contract is fulfilled, you owe them what you collected in pre-tax earnings."

Gale's face clouded. He was stunned.

"You can take this contract to arbitration. You can fight it. You can bring it on your hands and knees to the Commissioner of the League and the Supreme Court, but there isn't anything you can do about it. The contract is written in questionable faith, but it's a binding, legal document, and you signed it."

Wallace took a sip of coffee. "You want my advice?"

Gale nodded, feeling blood pounding in his temples.

"You better win and you better not spend a dime of what they pay you. Not a single penny until the day after this contract expires. Don't take any of the so-called 'perks.' They're all subject to tax and reimbursement. They're bogus, Gale."

Gale could feel a pit growing in his stomach. He felt embarrassed at how easily he'd been duped.

"Another thing. What happened to your eye?"

Gale shook his head. He winced from sharp stabs of pain racing up and down his neck. "I had an accident."

"It looks like you were on the receiving end of a fist."

Gale got up and stuck out his hand. Wallace rose and slowly shook it.

"Be careful," Wallace said as Gale turned to leave. "I don't want to see you and Marybeth and that daughter of yours hurt."

"Neither do I."

LONESTAR

"Don't trust anyone, Gale. Don't sign a thing without me reading it. Understand?"

***

The last of Gale's players filed into the locker room at Kinney High School. The room gleamed from fresh paint and the Kinney Lions' mascot stenciled on the wall in vivid blue and gold. The locker room stood in sharp contrast to the Lone Stars'.

A few minutes later, forty-seven high school players sat on stools in front of their lockers. They waited quietly for Gale to talk. Engle stood by Gale's side, calm as ever. Gale had wanted to tell Engle everything but was too embarrassed and angry. Engle had asked about Gale's eye, and Gale had said he'd had an "accident." Gale felt a lump grow in his throat. They were great kids. All of them. He needed this time to formally say goodbye. He'd planned the team meeting earlier in the week and now the players, his players, waited for him to speak. In the fifteen years Gale had coached the Kinney Lions, he'd never grown tired of the kids. Dealing with adolescents in a crazed football town like Kinney took energy, but despite the challenges posed by teenagers and their parents, Gale had mostly relished the experience.

The team laughed after Gale joked about his swollen eye. Gale grew quiet, trying to quell the sinking feeling that he'd left this world, his world, for the Lone Stars. He felt tears begin to well and cleared his throat. Before he could get a word out, he did something he hadn't done at his parents' funeral. He cried.

***

When Gale had pulled out of the long dirt driveway under a washed-out winter sky in his pickup, he could see Tilly waving and Marybeth's ashen face in the rearview mirror. After Gale had told Marybeth about his meeting with Wallace, she'd sat stunned at the kitchen table, unable to speak. With the threat of the Lone Stars garnishing Gale's back pay, they realized they would be living off Marybeth's teacher's salary. Wallace's words haunted Gale when he'd said, "Don't spend a dime." After arguing, Marybeth and Gale had stayed up late that night trying to figure out how to live on $47,000. It was Sunday, and Gale was about to make the long ride to San Antonio. He thought about driving to his family's ranch, now in the clutches of the First National Bank of Midland, but the pain of seeing the 1,223-acre property forlorn and empty was too much.

He was a coach without authority, without support, and unable to spend his earnings. As his anger rose on the drive past small towns and dusty cattle ranches, he knew for certain he had to win. Despite being ostracized by the coaching staff, not being allowed to play a decision-making role in free agency or the draft and being unable to spend a penny of what he earned, he grew more and more determined that coaching the San Antonio Lone Stars was not going to destroy his marriage and his life. He kept flashing back to the meeting where Garvin Johnson had tossed the two large binders on the table. The moment felt false, and Gale needed to know why.

CHAPTER 9

When Gale arrived in the early morning darkness, the Complex's parking lot was vacant. When he entered his office, he found an envelope on his desk sitting under a chipped glass football shaped paperweight. Gale set his cup of coffee down and pulled out the invoice. It was a $5,125 bill from Serve Pro to suck up the water that had rained down in the team conference room and to remove a damaged carpet. Gale crumpled the bill and tossed it into the trash can. He hesitated and took a deep breath and walked down the deserted hallway to Garvin Johnson's office. He tried opening the door, but it was locked. He started searching for keys. He dug through Johnson's assistant's desk drawers until he found a clump of keys wedged behind a stale package of Pepperidge Farm cookies and a box of Kleenex. Gale could feel his heart pumping. One by one, he tried each key until he found one that slid into the lock.

He hesitated for a moment, looked down the hallway and listened for footsteps, pushed the door open, flicked on the light, and began searching for the two binders Johnson had dropped unceremoniously in front of him during their meeting the week before.

Gale looked around the office until his eyes settled on the binders sitting next to Johnson's computer. He opened the binder with Free Agency written across the cover. He started flipping through pages with growing alarm. What he found shocked him. There wasn't a single free agent name, scouting report, or salary cap analysis. Nothing but blank pages. He opened the Draft binder. He found pages and pages of empty white paper. The Combine was less than two weeks away, where college players were scouted for the draft and the free agency signing period was around the corner, and the Lone Stars had done nothing to prepare for either. A sham.

He was about to put the binders back when he heard, "What are you doing?"

Gale turned, feeling his heart thump wildly. Standing in the doorway was Donta Jones, shaking his head.

"You scared me," Gale said. "What are you doing here so early?"

"Got to impress the new head coach." Donta smiled and leaned against the doorframe. "It's not always that you find someone breaking into the GMs office. You're beginning to worry me, Boy Wonder."

Gale pointed at the two heavy binders sitting on Johnson's desk. "Take a look."

Jones flipped open the Free Agent binder and skimmed through the pages. With a hint of sarcasm, he said, "Looks like Johnson's been busy. In true Lone Star fashion, he's been working his ass off."

"Look at this," Gale said, handing Jones the Draft binder. Jones flipped through the empty pages, shaking his head.

"It's a joke, Donta. The Combine is a week away, free agent signing in two weeks, and nothing. Not a single scouting report. What's college and pro scouting been doing?"

"I hate to tell you this, but it's no surprise. Pro and College scouting have been whittled down to nothing. They don't even travel anymore. They're scouting on tape. Last year, only Johnson and Voss went to the Combine. During the draft, Johnson and Voss didn't even bother to let Haden in the room. Imagine that. . . the head coach wasn't allowed to take part in the draft with the owner and GM."

Gale was about to tell Jones about his contract but stopped short. He was too ashamed to admit how he'd been misled.

"How can the League let this happen?" Gale asked.

"You think Mr. Spencer Tate III, the Commissioner, has any say? Think about it, Coach. The Commissioner works for the owners. Besides, someone has to be a doormat in this league. Why not San Antonio? It's not like we're in New York or Chicago. San Antonio ain't exactly a marquee town. We're the smallest media market in the League after New Orleans and Buffalo. I've seen more folks attend high school games."

Gale frowned and stepped toward the door. "Let's get out of here," he said, shaking his head. "It would be my luck that Johnson shows up and happens to ask why we're hanging out in his office at 4 am."

***

That afternoon, Johnson leaned back on his office couch and sighed.

"I've told you, Gale. You coach the team. I get the players. What don't you understand, son?" Johnson smiled reassuringly, staring for an instant at Gale's bruised and swollen eye.

Gale leaned forward. He wanted to tell Johnson he knew everything was a lie. The contract. Free Agency. The Combine. The Draft. But he held back. He made the decision to play his cards close. "I want to know who you're thinking about. I want the list of free agents you're wanting to sign and see the scouting reports for the draft."

Johnson shook his head. "What have I been telling you? That's not your job." He crossed his legs and leaned back.

"What is my job?"

"To win, Gale."

Gale sat back. "Any progress on what happened in my office?"

Johnson grinned and tapped his desk with his forefinger. "Don't you know a prank when you see one? Someone's having fun."

"You call that fun?"

"I call that not a big deal. It was a joke. Don't get your underwear in a bunch over things you can't control."

"Like the Draft?" Gale asked.

"Exactly."

"Who's going to the Combine?"

Johnson's eyes darkened for an instant. "I am."

"Who else?"

Johnson hesitated. "The college scouts are going to scout it on the League Network."

"What?" Gale heard his voice break.

"I know what I'm doing. There's no need to send a bunch of scouts to Indianapolis to chase women and run up bar bills."

"How about free agency?"

"I have my eye on a few players."

"Who?"

"You'll find out," Johnson said, lifting himself off the couch. "By the way, Gale," Johnson grinned. "Maybe I'll save your butt and draft a punter. The media is still buzzing."

Gale looked at Johnson in frustration.

"Do me a favor. Don't run the triple option, son," Johnson said, smiling. "Bronco Nagurski isn't going to be on our roster any time soon."

***

Gale and Jones had poured over the playbook and game tape until midnight. The Lone Stars' ineptitude the previous season had staggered Gale. As he'd watched each game, he'd realized the forces of mediocrity had made winning impossible. Missed blocks, poorly designed plays, penalties, and worst of all, lack of effort had resulted in a 1-16 season. On his way to his office, Gale had looked around the Complex in disgust. Trash cans were beginning to overflow once more, the floors were filthy, and the bathrooms needed scrubbing. Earlier in the day, he'd noticed Rose Cutler had once again started leaving the Complex to find relief at Valero. He made a mental note to clean the Complex that night.

Since the brawl with Adams, the coaching staff had further ostracized Gale. As Gale had passed coaches in the hallway, expressions darkened, and postures stiffened as the assistants did their best to ignore him. Gale had only run into Adams once, and Adams had grunted, before flashing a cruel smile when he saw the extent of Gale's damaged eye. It was nearly impossible to believe Gale had been the Lone Stars' coach for nearly two weeks and hadn't had a coaches' meeting. While he did his best to soak up as much as he could from Jones, it angered him that the coaching staff was not only dysfunctional but viewed him as a pariah.

After he and Jones had called it a day, Gale walked back to his office and unrolled the sleeping bag he'd placed behind his desk. He couldn't afford the Hampton Inn or an apartment, so despite Marybeth's concerns, he'd decided to sleep in his office. After a few minutes of trying to get comfortable on the hard, thin napped carpet floor, Gale fell asleep, exhausted and troubled, trying not to think about the unfolding nightmare.

***

At three in the morning Gale snapped awake. He heard a scratching sound near the foot of his sleeping bag. The cramped office was pitch black and Gale listened until he felt something brush up against his pillow. He bolted upright and realized a mouse was sniffing around his office, looking for crumbs.

He climbed out of the sleeping bag and switched on the lights. The only sign was mouse droppings in a neat line along the edge of his sleeping bag. Gale sighed. For the past few days, he'd watched the Combine on ESPN with Jones, taking notes on players who might make a difference to a team that had little talent. When Gale had told Jones they would be watching every minute of the Combine, Jones had shaken his head and said, "It's a waste of time, Coach. Just because you're the cook in the kitchen, it don't mean you get to pick the ingredients."

Shaking off his exhaustion, Gale checked his phone. There was an edgy text from Marybeth, and an email from a *San Antonio Express-News* reporter who wanted to write an in-depth feature on the newest coach of the Lone Stars. Gale noticed Sam Lorenzo hadn't been copied. After the initial press conference and buzz of Gale's hiring, the media attention had faded away. Until the email arrived from the *Express-News* reporter, there had been no more questions about punting on fourth down or about an obscure high school coach being hired out of a nowhere West Texas town. In the ADHD world of news, for now, Gale's story had run its course. San Antonio was a backwater, and despite the city's growing popularity, few cared about a small-market franchise that had a tradition of ineptitude.

Gale scrolled down until he noticed an email that caught his eye. It was an invitation to the Mayor's Charity Gala. The email was written in a swirling script, inviting the newest coach of the Lone Stars to the annual black-tie event at $500 a plate. Gale shook his head. He hated parties and had no patience for small talk. The thought of spending money he didn't have and standing among hundreds of people at a fancy event made him cringe. Besides, he didn't own a tuxedo, and he wasn't going to rent one.

In a swift motion, he hit delete.

***

Later that morning, when Gale walked by her desk, Rose Cutler paused from tapping away at her computer.

"Did you see the bill?" she asked, her voice stern and matronly.

"What bill?" Gale said, playing dumb.

"You know what bill, Coach McClanahan."

"Remind me?"

Cutler gave Gale a look. "For the sprinkler stunt you pulled. You owe accounting $5,125."

Despite Gale's worries, he couldn't suppress a smile. "I don't know what you're talking about."

"Yes, you do," Cutler said knowingly.

"You better go back to accounting and find out what's going on."

"I put the invoice on your desk."

"Never saw it."

"I bet. Mr. Johnson wants the bill paid."

"He can pay it," Gale said.

"He's going to be upset."

"I need to focus on football, Ms. Cutler. They hired me to coach. People seem to forget that around here. I asked two days ago for salary cap information and medical histories of all our players."

Cutler ignored him. "The bathrooms are getting dirty again."

"Get someone to clean them."

"That's your special talent, Coach McClanahan. You think the Lone Stars hired you to coach? I'm sure Mr. Voss and Johnson have different plans."

"I'm sure."

"$5,125 Coach McClanahan. I want a check written by the end of the day."

"Sure thing."

"By the way, the salary cap information and medical histories . . ."

"Yes?'

"They're on your desk," Cutler said, starting to type away.

"Finally good news," Gale said.

Cutler frowned. "Unfortunately, it's the only good news you're going to get."

"Why's that, Ms. Cutler?"

"Buddy Adams is looking for you."

Gale's expression hardened. "Why?"

"Who knows. But whenever that man shows up, bad things happen."

"Personal experience?"

Cutler grimaced. "Ask Haden. Adams did everything he could to get him fired."

"Mission accomplished."

Cutler leaned forward in her chair. "From everything I hear, he's going to get you fired, too."

"You think?" Gale asked.

"I know, Coach McClanahan," she sighed, her expression softening. "Sadly, you haven't got a chance."

CHAPTER 10

Buddy Adams sat at the head of the conference table with his arms folded across his chest, a toothpick dancing in his mouth, and a well-worn scowl. He had the look of a Hall of Fame coach. The granite jaw, the thickly bristled coal-black hair, the intense eyes, and the swagger. Except over the past four years his Lone Star defenses had been ranked at or near the bottom of the League. Before marrying Voss' daughter, he'd earned the reputation of being a malignant drifter, bouncing around the League's turbulent solar system.

Gale sat a few chairs from him, not wanting to get too close, as if he were edging up to a rattler. Gale's eye was still swollen, but at least the swelling had gone down enough that he could see.

"How's our boy from Kinney?" Adams asked half-amused, rolling the toothpick back and forth in his teeth. "That eye sure looks ugly."

Gale kept his mouth shut. He could tell Adams was relishing the moment.

"I bet you wish you were back coaching high school, educating those fine young men to be upstanding citizens. If I'm right, Boy Scout," Adams paused for effect, "then we'd finally be in agreement, cause me and my coaching staff sure wish your sorry ass was too."

Adams leaned forward, zeroing in on the kill. "But I'm a humane man. A dog gets hit on the road, and I'm gonna be the first one to stop to put that dog out of its misery."

Gale tried not to blink. He set his eyes on Adams.

"Since Vernon gave you a job you aren't qualified to do, I'm gonna throw you a lifeline and keep you from getting skinned alive every Sunday. This is how it's going to work." Adams thrust a stubby finger at Gale. "You can wear the headset, act like you're Vince Lombardi, preen in front of the camera on gameday, but you stay out of my way. I make the decisions. I coach the team. Understand? You can keep whatever self-respect you got and let me and my boys lead the Lone Stars."

Gale shook his head. He leaned forward. "Is that it?"

"That's it."

"Take it or leave it?"

"That's right, Boy Scout."

"If I leave it?"

Adams glared. He bit down on his toothpick. "You think you're a beaten dog now? Do you know what coaching is in the League? You don't gotta a clue. When the players report for OTAs, they're going to flush your ass down the toilet if we don't do it first. . . high school," he said with contempt. "On gameday, when eighty thousand people are screaming at your ass cause you screwed up, you're going to be pissing your pants, Boy Scout. You never felt pressure like that. I'm granting you mercy, son. Buddy Adams is trying to save you from yourself."

Gale fought a flash of anger but stayed silent.

"My momma always said, 'don't look a gift horse in the mouth.' Don't be a horse's ass. Take the deal I'm offering. We'll be a happy family. You can sit in your office all-day long picking your ass, show up for practice and watch it with those media boys, and collect your fat paycheck." Adams smiled as if he knew Gale's contract was a lie. "As long as you stay out of the way, we'll have a perfect marriage."

Gale felt his jaw tighten. He paused for a moment before striking. "What happened against Buffalo last year?"

Adams' eyes turned into slits.

"I'd like to know."

Adams stopped chewing on his toothpick and let it sit in the corner of his mouth. His eyes darkened.

"Tell me why you ran a safety blitz on fourth and 18 when the team's about to get its first win?" The play had resulted in a miraculous touchdown in the final seconds for Buffalo. When Gale and Jones had watched the play unfold on tape, Gale wondered if Adams was trying to throw the game.

Adams' face turned red.

"If I'd been head coach, I would've fired you," Gale said leaning closer. "How about against Las Vegas?" Gale continued. "Even a high school coach would have known to move from man to zone. You got your butt kicked."

"Fuck you," Adam said, the veins bulging in his neck.

"Against Miami when your defense had too many men on the field three times in the fourth quarter? Tell me about that? Or when you played Arizona, when your defense had 175 yards in penalties?"

Gale shook his head in disgust. "If you think I'm going to let you control the Lone Stars, you can screw yourself."

Adams slammed his fist on the table. "You're playing with fire."

"Maybe. But if I'm going down, I'm going down on my terms."

"You have no terms, son," Adams said, his hands balled into fists.

"You think?"

"I know. Vernon and Johnson had their heads up their ass when they hired you. A publicity stunt."

"Now you're going to be the hero and save the day?"

Adams grunted. "There's not an assistant coach on this staff who's going to work with you other than Jones. I can tell you that. I'm trying to save you from yourself, Boy Scout. Clear and simple."

Gale watched as Adams spit his toothpick onto the conference room floor.

"You heard my offer of generosity," Adams said.

"I did."

"You going to take it, Boy Scout?"

Gale rose out of his chair. "Not a chance."

Adams shook his head, leaned back, and folded his arms across his chest. His voice was suddenly calm.

"You think your life is hell right now?" Adams said. "It's only going to get worse. You're going to wish you kissed my ass today cause you're in for a world of hurt."

"Is that right?"

Adams pulled a fresh toothpick out of his shirt pocket. He unwrapped the plastic and tossed the wrapper on the floor. "You better listen to me, Boy Scout."

For a moment, Gale eyed the wrapper sitting on the worn carpet. His thoughts turned to his father, who was the most disciplined, principled man he'd ever met besides Jack Engle. His father had lived by small but meaningful principles: Push your chair in before you leave the table, pick-up after yourself, leave things better than you found them, pay attention to detail. Work hard. What his father couldn't foresee was a fourth-generation cattle ranch driven to bankruptcy by forces he couldn't control and a son who'd left the ranch to coach football and teach algebra.

Gale looked at Adams in revulsion. "Voss must love his daughter."

"What does that mean?" Adams shot back, taken off-guard.

"Otherwise, he would have fired an incompetent son of a bitch like you years ago," Gale said in disgust, shaking his head before walking out of the room.

***

"What are you doing?" Rose Cutler asked as Gale grabbed the corporate credit card out of her hand. Gale had tricked her into showing him the Visa card, which looked as though it had never been used.

"I'm putting it to good use," he answered.

"Oh, no you don't. No one uses that card," she warned.

"Who says?"

"You know who says," she said alarmed. "Now give it back."

"I promise I will after I come back from Home Depot."

"You already owe Mr. Voss money. You're going to get yourself in big trouble, Coach McClanahan."

"What have I got to lose?"

Cutler shook her head and gave Gale an ambiguous look. "You're lucky it's Friday afternoon and everyone's gone. Otherwise, I'd have to report this."

Gale smiled. "By the way, I won't tell anyone--I mean no one--where I got this card."

Cutler frowned.

55

Gale watched with amusement as she locked her desk drawer, switched off her computer, and grabbed her coat and handbag. "What are you looking at?" she asked, irritated.

"You have a good weekend," he said.

"If you're headed to Home Depot, I suspect mine is going to be a whole lot better than yours."

Gale turned and watched her leave, only slightly remorseful about the fact that he had no intention of giving the credit card back.

CHAPTER 11

Gale had never seen a collective work ethic as mediocre as the Lone Stars. The culture reminded him of the government bureaucrats he'd witnessed over the years, piling into their cars at the Kinney Municipal Office or the DMV as soon as the clock struck five. In the League, where every front office and coaching staff ulcerated to get the edge, spent hours and hours preparing, when there was never enough time, Gale looked at the Lone Star organization in disbelief. The offseason workday for employees was embarrassingly short, everyone scampering away from the Complex as soon as they could. Those included coaches, scouts, and the few front office staff who were left after years of cost cutting.

Worse, the free agency period had passed, and Johnson hadn't signed any players. Unsurprisingly, after his meeting with Adams, Gale still found himself in a tense standoff with the coaching staff. He spent his days with Jones watching film and feeling more and more isolated. While he was learning the League, studying the playbook, which even after a month, looked as poorly conceived and incomprehensible as it did on the first day he'd been forced to inherit it, he had growing fears about how he would approach Optional Training Activities or OTAs and training camp. Returning players avoided working out in the Complex, and the calls Gale had made to veteran players had been unreturned. Gale suspected Adams had not only poisoned the well with the coaching staff but had been drumming up trouble with the team.

Gale had only gone home to Kinney once since the meeting where he'd met with Grayson Wallace about his contract. He and Marybeth had spent much of the weekend arguing over finances and trying to regain the spark that had been wavering since their lives had been upended. Now, on a late Friday afternoon, Gale found himself alone without his family pushing a large shopping cart at Home Depot. He was filling the cart with buckets of paint, brushes, rollers, scrapers, and sandpaper. Before leaving the vast box store, he'd eyed several large rolls of thin, multi-purpose dark blue carpeting, the same royal blue that adorned the Lone Star helmets.

***

That evening, he and Donta Jones donned old sweats and torn t-shirts and began to breathe a semblance of pride into the organization. They started in the locker room. When they finally wiped the paint off their hands and cleaned their brushes and rollers after midnight, they gave tired smiles. While the locker room had a long

57

way to go, it was a start. The freshly painted walls sparkled. As soon as the paint dried, Gale and Jones would stencil the Lone Star logo on the wall and begin painting the weight room. After, Gale and Jones would cut the rolls of royal blue, multi-purpose carpeting Gale had bought from the discount rack and lay it in the dressing room and weight facility. While fresh paint and new carpeting didn't win football games, it helped establish higher expectations. Someone had to have them, Gale thought.

***

On Monday morning, Gale's office phone rang with an annoying buzz. It was Rose Cutler.

"There's a young woman on the phone, and she wants to speak with you," Cutler said, placing emphasis on 'young woman,' as if it was strange a woman other than Gale's wife would be calling. "She says she's from the Mayor's Office."

"Put her through," Gale said, pushing away a stack of play diagrams he'd been reviewing.

"Coach McClanahan," the woman said, her voice husky, businesslike, determined. "I'm Catherine Reiser, Chief of Staff for Mayor Andujar. I'm calling about the Mayor's Charity Gala. You never RSVP'd."

Gale shook his head.

"The mayor wants you and Mrs. McClanahan to be his guests," she said. "He's adamant you join him."

Gale's mind started spinning, trying to think of an excuse. How could he tell her he hated parties, chit-chat, and couldn't afford to attend?

"I'm honored," Gale said, "but–"

Reiser interrupted. "The mayor told me he won't take 'no' for an answer. He told me to tell you that you and Mrs. McClanahan will be sitting at his table. He also told me to tell you the night is on him. He's got all sorts of plans for you to help the community. He's calling it a gift in kind."

Reiser pressed on before Gale could think to respond. In a resolute voice, she said, "We'll see you Saturday night. I'm going to resend the invitation. We look forward to meeting you and your wife."

Before Gale could protest, Reiser hung up. He looked at the phone in his hand, sighed, and started calculating how much it was going to cost to fly Marybeth to San Antonio, rent a tuxedo, and stay in a hotel. There was no way Marybeth was going to sleep with him on his office floor, especially with the threat of a mouse hunting around their sleeping bags. His heart sank. Even worse than the money, he hated parties. He knew he'd be clinging to Marybeth all night, praying he wouldn't have to speak.

***

LONESTAR

The receiving line at the La Cantera Resort and Spa stretched to the lobby. Marybeth held Gale's arm as the line inched forward to the large banquet room where the Mayor and his wife were greeting guests.

Despite Gale's growing unease, he could barely take his eyes off Marybeth, who wore a black gown she'd borrowed from a friend, her grandmother's pearls, and her hair swept into a bun. She had the clearest skin Gale had ever seen, and after all the years together, he still was mesmerized by her eyes, now touched with a hint of mascara. Better yet, Marybeth had agreed to attend, and they had veered away from any talk about their dire finances.

When they had checked into the Marriott Courtyard that afternoon, despite their money troubles, and their growing dread, they had begun to kiss each other with intensity, and after finishing, had fallen asleep under the soft sheets and comforter. With Til staying with the Engles, it was the first time they had been alone in a hotel since her birth.

"This shirt itches," Gale said, as they stood in the receiving line.

"It's supposed to itch. I had it dry cleaned and starched," Marybeth said.

Gale had refused to rent a tux. Instead, he and Marybeth had driven to a men's clothing store when she'd arrived that morning in San Antonio and had purchased a black tie for Gale to wear with his white dress shirt and dark suit. As he entered the resort's banquet hall, he suddenly felt self-conscious being the only man without a tuxedo, but Marybeth had assured him no one would notice. "Besides," she'd said, "you'll be the most handsome man at the party."

As the line moved forward under large crystal chandeliers, Gale kept using his index finger to scratch beneath his collar. Finally, Marybeth shot him a disapproving look.

"Please behave, Gale McClanahan," she said, squeezing his arm. "People are going to think you have fleas."

CHAPTER 12

Mayor Mike Andujar greeted Gale and Marybeth with a warm smile and a firm handshake. Newly elected, he'd earned a reputation for being tough on crime, running on anti-corruption as a district attorney who had made his name taking down a drug kingpin with ties to a Mexican cartel. Despite public threats on his life, Andujar had pursued the case unrelentingly.

Andujar was in his early forties. He was handsome with penetrating eyes, wavy black hair, and a politician's gift for making people feel they were the most important person in the room. Already, there was talk that Andujar had his eyes on the Governor's office.

"I'm glad you could attend," Andujar said after he shook Gale's hand.

Gale nodded. He felt awkward surrounded by men in black tie and women in evening gowns and cocktail dresses, pearls and diamonds, sipping drinks, in casual conversation, occasionally tossing their heads back in laughter, seemingly at ease among the hundreds of partygoers. Gale thought back to Kinney where each summer, the fire department held a barbeque and dance at the high school to raise money. Occasionally, Gale would spot an old rancher wearing a bolo tie, but for most men it was pressed jeans, an open collared shirt, boots, and a Stetson. The women wore jeans and cotton shirts or light dresses. Nothing fancy. A local country western band would play. The crowd was casual, and for the most part, friendly.

"I want you to meet Catherine Reiser," Andujar said. Reiser stood next to Andujar holding a glass of red wine and a warm, yet businesslike smile. A pretty thirty something woman with strawberry blonde hair cut to her shoulders, a smattering of freckles on her nose, and tired, green eyes, she wore a black strapless dress and a world-weary look.

"We're not strangers, Mike," Reiser said to Andujar. "I had to convince Coach McClanahan to attend."

"Is that true?" Andujar asked.

"It is," Gale replied.

Andujar smiled and turned to Marybeth, who Gale promptly introduced.

"Welcome to San Antonio," Andujar said. Marybeth took his outstretched hand. "We have big hopes for your husband."

"I don't envy you," Reiser said, her eyes settling on Gale. "You have a big challenge."

Andujar said, "We have lots to talk about. I'm a huge football fan. Unfortunately, the Lone Stars haven't given us much to root for. That needs to change."

Gale hesitated before he said, "I didn't take this job to lose." He'd hoped he didn't sound defensive.

Andujar gripped Gale's shoulder and smiled. "That's what I like to hear, Coach. Let's talk football at dinner."

***

Gale and Marybeth edged toward one of the several bars in the cavernous banquet room. A few hundred people, all movers and shakers, had gathered for the annual event, which raised over a million dollars for local charities. The room was noisy with conversation and laughter as Gale and Marybeth clung together, navigating their way through the maze of people.

When they finally reached one of the white table-clothed bars with bartenders in formal dress mixing drinks in crystal glasses, they ordered tonic water and looked at each other in bewilderment. While Gale enjoyed an occasional beer and wished he could have one now to ease his discomfort, Marybeth frowned on alcohol. One of her brothers had spent the better part of his adult life in and out of rehab centers, and Marybeth still hurt from the pain his addiction had brought her family.

Gale suddenly felt a tap on his shoulder and turned. Vernon Voss stood with a whiskey in his hand next to a stunning young woman, looking bored and distant, holding a half-filled tumbler of vodka or gin in one hand and her phone in the other.

Voss, his black eyes watery and bloodshot, looked Gale up and down and smiled thinly. "Didn't you get the memo, Gale? It's a formal event. Where's the tux?"

Gale's face burned. He thought of Voss sliding the bogus contract across his kitchen counter. He wanted to lash out but kept quiet. What was done was done. Before he could reply, Voss reached over and took Marybeth's hand. "Vernon Voss. I presume you're Gale's better half?"

Marybeth forced a smile and shook Voss' hand.

"My wife Vanessa," he said, turning to the twenty-something icy pale blonde with searing blue eyes, sharp cheekbones set off by a shovel-shaped jaw and an hourglass figure. "Vanessa's not happy with me." She rolled her eyes. "I've been traveling too much. Haven't I darling?"

Vanessa ignored Voss, and for an instant, gazed coyly into Gale's eyes, exploring. He felt an impulse to look away, as if Marybeth would think he might be tempted.

"I hear you're dining at the mayor's table," Voss said continuing, sipping his drink, his watery eyes boring in on Gale.

Gale nodded.

"Be careful."

Marybeth's expression turned from unease to confusion.

C.W. WELLS

"That boy has it out for the Lone Stars. I don't want you hobnobbing with that SOB. Understand?" Voss' eyes narrowed. "I don't want anything to spoil our relationship, Coach."

Vanessa shook her head, her eyes lingering on Gale, and brushed past him to refill her glass.

"Vanessa doesn't like when I speak truth," Voss said after she left. "You both enjoy the evening," he said for Marybeth's benefit. Voss turned to Gale with a half-smile and whispered above the din. "Next time wear a tux. Remember you work for the San Antonio Lone Stars. You're not a high school coach anymore."

After Voss had drifted off in the crowd, Marybeth said, "What was that?"

Gale shrugged.

"I don't like him, Gale. He's horrible. His wife . . . she's young enough to be his daughter."

"An ice queen."

Marybeth looked at Gale. "I saw the way she looked at you. You stay away from her. She's trouble."

"There's no worry there."

"You better, Gale McClanahan," Marybeth said, pulling him close.

"There's only one woman in my life." Gale met her gaze and smiled.

"Who's that?" Marybeth asked, her face playful for an instant.

"Marybeth McClanahan," Gale said, relieved to see her mood lighten.

***

Andujar ignored the other guests at his table and locked his eyes on Gale. Gale sat across from the mayor and put his fork down. The filet mignon in front of him would have to wait.

"Why do you think Voss hired you, Gale?" Andujar asked in the curious way of a seasoned attorney. "It's not every day a high school coach gets picked to lead a professional football team."

Gale shrugged his shoulders. He glanced at Marybeth sitting next to him and saw she was holding her own with Andujar's wife, who had been a kindergarten teacher until her husband's political career took off. "I don't know," Gale said. "You'd have to ask him."

"I did. I called Voss the day the news broke. He said they had their eye on you for some time. He told me he wanted a new approach. He wanted someone with energy and enthusiasm who understood how much football means in Texas."

"I'm going to do the best job I can," Gale said, worrying again that he sounded defensive, almost naïve. Voss' warning about cozying up to the mayor was still ringing in Gale's ear. Gale could see Voss sitting a few tables away. How could he tell the Mayor of San Antonio he'd signed a contract without reading it and hadn't even been able to gather the coaches in the same room with him?

Andujar said, leaning forward and taking a bite of asparagus, "No offense, Gale, but I'm surprised by your appointment."

Gale took a sip of water.

"I'm not trying to diminish you in any way. You're a helluva high school coach. But the League?"

Gale eyed him and let his comment sink in. He felt embarrassed, and for an instant, overwhelmed. The banquet room was filled with people enjoying the evening, catching up with friends and business associates, comfortable in their formal wear and evening gowns. Gale had largely been ignored. A few attendees, out of curiosity, had spoken to him before dinner, but he realized he and the Lone Stars held little allure.

"Are you really going to go for it on fourth down? No punting?" Andujar smiled.

"It depends on the situation," Gale said.

"If it backfires, the armchair quarterbacks are going to have a field day."

"Maybe."

Andujar turned serious. "I'm worried about the Lone Stars, Gale. We're a growing, major-league city with a third-rate franchise. I've told Voss he better start investing in the team. I hear bills aren't being paid."

"You'd have to speak with the owner."

"I have. I don't like his answers." Andujar took a sip of wine, ignoring the guests around him and focusing on Gale. "Do you know about the attendance clause?"

Gale's mind began to swirl. He looked over Andujar's shoulder and could see Voss sitting next to a bored Vanessa, holding court a few tables away. Three seats away from Andujar, Gale noticed Catherine Reiser and caught her eye before looking away. As far as Gale could tell, she was unaccompanied. She appeared to listen intently as the large man sitting next to her with a flabby chin and an oily forehead went on and on about lack of funding for a municipal project, but Gale had the feeling she was focused on his conversation with the mayor.

"It's buried deep in the lease agreement with the city. Last year the team averaged 36,000 per game. Worst attendance in the League. That's supposedly paid customers who watched a bad football team. If season attendance drops below an average of 30,000 fans per game, Vernon Voss gets to skip town, move the franchise, and do a lot of damage to the city. I'm no genius, but it sure appears from where I'm sitting that he hired you because he wants the team to fail."

Andujar took a bite of salmon, and after a moment, continued. "Voss fired Haden because he was pushing back, starting to make too much noise about Voss and Garvin Johnson's meddling. I suspect Voss hired you because he figured you wouldn't give him trouble, and frankly, wouldn't know what you were doing."

Gale felt his cheeks burn. His suspicions were proving true.

"He raised ticket prices, too." Andujar lifted an eyebrow. "I'd cry from the rooftops that the whole situation is a charade, except," and he looked around the large banquet room before shaking his head, "no one cares about the Lone Stars. I'd put up a public fight, but there are reasons why I can't. At this point, the less said publicly, the better." Andujar's face clouded. "Put it this way, I got handed a bag of shit."

For an instant, Gale thought about what he'd discovered in his office and the brawl with Adams.

Andujar continued. "Voss has run the franchise into the ground and people are disgusted. They could care less about the team. But I have a vision for the city, and it includes a winning franchise."

Andujar paused and sipped his wine. "If I could, I'd have the city buy enough tickets to meet the attendance clause. But when it was suggested in a cabinet meeting, it was shot down, and rightly so. We have a large deficit, and we can't fund our schools. Imagine the city purchasing football tickets?" Andujar waved his hand dismissively. "I've had a couple of local heavy hitters tell me they approached Voss about buying the team, but he turned them down. Something's up. We need Voss to sell to a local buyer who wants to win. We get new ownership, and I can start pushing for a new stadium."

The Voss Energy Dome had been built in the early 80's and had fallen on hard times. A few weeks earlier, Gale and Jones had walked through the facility and found it dreary and dilapidated. He'd heard that numerous attempts to renovate the stadium had been abandoned by the City Council.

Andujar speared a piece of salmon. "I spoke with the Commissioner about the situation. He could care less about San Antonio. He didn't say it, but I could tell he wants the team somewhere else. Some bigger market to pad the League's pocket."

Gale felt like he'd been slapped. The sham contract, the confusing conversations with Johnson, the war with Adams and the coaching staff. All setting him up to fail.

Andujar continued. "It boils down to this. I need you to win, Gale. I need you to give fans a reason to attend games. I know I'm asking the impossible, but you can't lose. I don't want to see some mayor shaking hands with Voss, all smiles, welcoming the Lone Stars to a new city. That's unacceptable."

Andujar leaned back and sighed. "You do whatever it takes," he said, stabbing another piece of fish. He pointed his salmon-filled fork at Gale. "Don't let Voss get his way. If you need anything, call Catherine Reiser."

***

As Gale and Marybeth left the Gala after the band struck up and people began gathering on the dance floor, they walked to the parking lot on a chilly March night.

Gale had reluctantly told her what Andujar had said. As they approached his pickup, Gale could tell the excitement of the evening had drained from Marybeth.

"Oh, Gale," she said angrily. "What have we gotten into?"

***

Later that evening, Vernon Voss and Vanessa drove home silently from the Gala. The Mercedes S-Class sedan purred as Voss coldly focused on the road ahead. Vanessa stared out the passenger-side window, expressionless.

"I saw the way you looked at McClanahan," Voss said, breaking the silence. "Don't think his wife didn't either."

Vanessa turned to Voss.

"Is it a crime to look at a man?" she asked, her voice flat, emotionless.

"If you only looked."

She shook her head. "You're the most insecure man on the planet."

"I don't ask for much. Don't screw other men. Show up when I ask you. Try to stay sober."

She shook her head again and looked back out the driver-side window.

"Oh, is that all?" she asked.

"That's it."

"Sounds like a perfect marriage."

Voss turned to her, angry in the car's faint light. "You married me because I'm rich. I married you because you're eye candy. That was the deal."

"Except there's one problem," she said in a cutting voice.

"What's that?" Voss asked.

"I'm still eye candy and you're about to go bankrupt."

Voss grabbed her arm and squeezed. She winced. "Let's hope not. Because if I go down, you go down, Vanessa."

CHAPTER 13

Donta Jones reached over with his fork and speared several fries off Gale's untouched plate. Gale watched a crowd of chatty senior citizens pile into Grady's for dinner.

"You got that look, Coach," Donta said, dipping the fries into the gravy left on his plate from a hefty slice of meatloaf. "What's up?"

Gale recounted what the mayor had said at the Gala.

Jones ate the forkful of fries, leaned back in the booth, and shook his head. "Is it a surprise?"

"How are we going to win, Donta?" Gale's eyes narrowed.

"We aren't. We're outsized, outmatched, and outgunned. Every other team in the League's light years ahead of us. What pro coaches spend a weekend painting the locker and weight room?"

Gale shook his head and set his empty fork down.

"You haven't even met with the coaching staff. Maybe you shouldn't have given them all a shower?" Jones asked.

Gale ignored him. "We can't lose," he said, his jaw tightening.

Jones' expression turned sympathetic, as if he were speaking to a misguided child. "We're going to lose, Coach. I'm sorry to tell you."

Gale hesitated before telling Donta everything, from signing the contract to the meager earnings he and Marybeth were surviving on. Gale could tell Jones could read the desperation on his face.

"You're telling me you're going to owe them money for coaching the Lone Stars?" Jones asked, his voice rising, incredulous, placing his elbows on the table and shaking his head. An older couple looked over at their table, and after a few moments, turned back to their meal.

"Voss has me by the balls, Donta," Gale said.

"The only way out of this mess is if the team wins and we get attendance over 30,000?"

Gale leaned forward. "We have two big problems. The coaching staff and the roster. What's the answer?"

"You got me on both. I got no answers."

Gale stared off for a moment. "What happens when the players show up for OTAs and Adams pulls his stunts? Who're the players going to listen to? Me or Adams?"

Jones didn't hesitate. "Adams. He'll bully them with Voss' backing."

"The roster?"

"Voss and Johnson are going to fill training camp with undrafted free agents. Bottom of the barrel. Draft night's going to be a horror show."

"I've got to win over the staff, Donta. Somehow, someway."

"That's a tall task. They hate your guts."

"Do they?"

"Sorry to tell you, Coach, but one of them crapped on your office floor."

Gale paused for a moment. He said, "How do we get Adams out of the picture?"

Jones frowned. "You tell me."

Gale looked away. The line to the salad bar was slowing to a crawl with a clump of senior citizens trying to decide among the array of choices. "The problem is Adams is exactly who Voss and Johnson want to stir the pot. An egotistical a-hole."

"If Voss wants to lose, I don't get why he didn't hire Adams to be head coach? Something's up."

Gale shook his head. "Voss only wants Adams around to mess with us. We only have a few weeks until the draft, then the players report. The roster is the least of our problems. We have no control over that. But the coaches . . ." Gale's voice trailed off.

"I got no solutions for you. With everything you've told me, it doesn't look good. Maybe Adams will get hit by a truck?" Jones smiled.

"I'd like to arrange that."

"I could see the headline. New Lone Star Coach Places Hit on Defensive Coordinator."

Gale sighed. "To get rid of Adams, it would almost be worth it."

"Easy coach. I'm sure Mrs. McClanahan doesn't want her husband in Huntsville."

Gale shook his head. "No, that wouldn't go over well at home."

"Nope."

"Let's get out of here," Gale said, leaving chicken fingers and fries sitting on his plate. He began to reach for the check.

Jones beat him to it. He smiled. "It's on me, Coach. I'm not here to add to your growing list of woes."

***

As usual, Gale found the Complex empty in the evenings. The only sound echoing down the corridors came from an old, creaky HVAC unit pumping air throughout the building. Gale had run four miles on one of the few working treadmills in the training facility and was returning to the coaches' locker room to shower, dripping with sweat, when he noticed the door to the Draft Room was ajar. He stepped inside and gazed at the empty magnetized whiteboards mounted on the walls and the broken television set sitting in the corner of the room. Habits die hard in the League and teams still used vinyl covered metal strips to magic marker potential draft choices and place them in rows according to the player's draft position. Unlike the Lone Stars, the draft room in 31 other cities hummed with anticipation and displayed a hopeful and meticulous plan to draft the very best players. In the age of Google and smartphones, placing vinyl covered metal strips on a magnetized board was an archaic system, but like many things in professional football, a stubborn habit. The Draft Room was a sacred place – unless you worked for the Lone Stars.

Gale realized Garvin Johnson's gameplan on the rapidly approaching draft was a mystery. Like the empty binders in Johnson's office, the Draft Room gave no evidence anyone had done any preparation. Like everything else in the organization, its hollowness brought Gale near despair.

Gale left the room and went into the hallway. He started walking to the coaches' locker room when he thought he heard a sound coming from his office. He turned and walked down the hallway until he came to Rose Cutler's desk and peered into his office. He found Sam Lorenzo going through his desk drawer.

Lorenzo stopped, turned, and looked up, the blood draining from his pockmarked cheeks before his expression settled into a look of disdain.

"You always go through other people's desks?" Gale asked, with his arms folded, leaning against the doorframe.

"When they steal credit cards," Lorenzo shot back, breaking into a defiant half-smile, his yellowed, nicotine-stained teeth, flashing. He slowly closed the desk drawer.

"Steal?" Gale raised an eyebrow.

"That's right. You've made unauthorized purchases."

"The only evidence of stealing is you going through my property."

"Your property?"

"That's what I said."

Lorenzo shut the desk drawer. "Everything in the Complex belongs to the Lone Stars."

"That means you can rifle through my desk?"

Lorenzo nodded.

"What makes you think I stole a credit card?" Gale asked.

"Not think. Know."

"I'm curious. Who told you?"

"Mr. Johnson's assistant."

Gale shook his head. "What are you really up to?"

"I told you."

Gale stepped forward. His t-shirt was drenched from working out. He wiped sweat off his forehead with a towel he'd slung over his shoulder. "Open the drawer." Gale pointed at his desk.

Lorenzo stood motionless.

"I told you to open it," Gale repeated.

LONESTAR

Lorenzo gave a thin smile. "See for yourself." He slowly opened the drawer and stepped away.

Gale walked around the desk and looked. His wallet was open, and its contents were strewn around the drawer. The Visa card and lone twenty-dollar bill Gale had were missing.

Gale looked up. "Give the card and my money back."

"Not a chance. You've been stealing." Lorenzo pulled the credit card out of his pocket and held it up. "Imagine if this leaked to the media, it could end your career, McClanahan." Lorenzo grinned.

"That would make your day, wouldn't it?"

"As Media Relations Director, I'd hate to have to make a call to *The News-Express*."

"I bet."

"Imagine, a coach, making millions of dollars, stealing from an organization?"

Gale slowly shut his desk drawer. He could feel his shoulders tighten and his face flush. "Get out," he said, inching closer to Lorenzo.

"Watch yourself, Coach," Lorenzo said, backing away. "You don't want to make any more enemies than you already have."

"Get out of my office."

Lorenzo smiled. "I'm going to tell Mr. Johnson about our little conversation tonight. He's going to be unhappy, but most likely not surprised."

"Tell him anything you want," Gale said, shaking his head in disgust. "But make sure you tell him if I ever find you again in my office, that will be the last time."

"Like I said, I'd hate to see the headline," Lorenzo said before turning to leave. "Imagine, Gale McClanahan, charged with theft." He smiled slyly. "What a story…"

***

A few minutes later, Lorenzo climbed into his car littered with soiled fast-food wrappers and Dr. Pepper cans. The front seat was blanketed with cheap cigar ash. Lorenzo broke into a smile of satisfaction. The team credit card had been a convenient excuse. Lorenzo had been stealing money for years, from coaches, players, staff, even the security guards before they were let go to save money. Everyone was game. McClanahan's twenty-dollar bill would come in handy. It would buy Lorenzo a bottle of Smirnoff Red Label, his favorite. Stealing gave him a thrill, but what he'd overheard Johnson telling Voss that afternoon brought goosebumps. The football world was going to explode. He could only imagine the crush of requests he was going to get from the media. The upcoming Draft was going to put the Lone Stars in the spotlight. It was going to be a wild few weeks.

CHAPTER 14

Gale missed his family. He missed Marybeth and Til more than he thought possible. He missed bringing Marybeth her coffee in bed each morning and making Til her breakfast. He missed driving his daughter to the tiny pre-school in the basement of the Methodist church and kissing her goodbye. He missed the evenings when he would come home, and after putting Til to bed, sit with Marybeth at the kitchen table to grade papers and tests, and afterwards, sprawl on the couch with her to watch Netflix.

When Gale had made the decision to accept the Lone Stars' offer, he thought he was entering an exclusive world. What he found was a stark reminder the planet was full of sharks, and he would have to keep Johnson and Voss from devouring him and his family.

On Draft Day, when Rose Cutler reminded Gale that the only team officials allowed in the Complex that evening would be Johnson, Voss, and a handful of support staff, he shook his head and fought the anger building inside. The day before, a couple of tech guys from a local company had been setting up video equipment in the Draft room to live stream the event for ESPN and The League Network. On his laptop, earlier in the week Gale had watched Voss being interviewed on ESPN about the Lone Stars having the first pick. When the reporter had pressed Voss who the team would select, he gave a smile, shrugged, and said, "You boys will have to wait and see."

"Don't think you're the only one who felt this way," Cutler said, sensing Gale's frustration. "They didn't let Haden in the room either."

"You've told me that," Gale said.

"Quit feeling sorry for yourself."

"Who said I'm feeling sorry for myself?"

Cutler leaned back in her chair and peered at Gale over her glasses. She gave a half-smile. "I don't need these cheaters to tell you want a pity party."

"Pity party? You sound like my wife."

"The poor woman," Cutler said, shaking her head.

"Did you tell Johnson I wanted to see him?"

"Yes."

"And . . ."

"He said he was too busy."

"Doing nothing," Gale said under his breath.

"He's a very important man, Coach McClanahan. Hasn't he told you?" She leaned back in her swivel chair.

70

"Is Johnson in his office?"

"Remember I told you he's too busy."

Gale shook his head and started down the hallway.

"You'll be sorry," Cutler said. "Very, very sorry. I warned Haden, too."

***

Johnson's face turned calm when Gale burst into his office and shut the door.

"What now, son?" Johnson said, looking up from his computer.

"We need to talk."

"It's draft day, Gale. I haven't got time."

"That's unacceptable."

Johnson sat back in his chair and eyed Gale. "Unacceptable?"

"That's what I said. I'm the only coach in the League who has no idea what the GM is going to do tonight. We have the first pick in the draft, and you won't tell me anything. Even our scouts have no clue. I would call that unacceptable."

Johnson stood up. He smiled as if speaking to an angry adolescent, ever the diplomat. "Mr. Voss and I gave you a chance to coach. No one ever said you'd be involved in the draft."

"What's the game plan?"

"I get the players and you coach. I've told you."

Gale shook his head. His mind raced to all the game tape he'd watched. "We have multiple needs. Every position. We have seven picks, and they all need to count."

"You don't think I know?" Johnson's eyes sharpened before he smiled. "I was playing football when you were sucking on your mother's tit."

"How many games did we win last year?"

Johnson's face turned grim. "An aberration."

"In the past five?"

"It's challenging to win in the League," Johnson said.

"Especially when you're trying to lose." Gale knew instantly he shouldn't have gone there.

Johnson's eyes bore into Gale's. His amiability vanished. "This conversation's over, Coach. I'm going to try to forget we ever had it."

"I need players." Gale could feel his voice on the edge of desperation.

"Oh, you'll get players, son," Johnson said, waving the back of his hand. "You'll get the players you deserve."

***

C.W. WELLS

It was obvious to Gale the scene unfolding was surreal. The large TV above the empty bar flickered while the bartender cleared Gale and Jones' plates before asking if they wanted another beer. They nodded.

A world away in New York, the Draft was about to begin on the screen above them. Over the years, the League had turned the Draft into a primetime event during the "offseason." The reality was the League didn't have an offseason. The Combine, free agency, the Draft, OTAs, training camp, and the constant headline making tweets, posts, and stories kept the League front and center for millions of fans.

The dark, empty bar near the Complex was a hole-in-the-wall and Jones' favorite. Cheap food, cheap beer, and a place where people left him alone. He and Gale sat on stools while the bartender poured beer from the tap and put two mugs foaming to the brim in front of them. He ignored them and started to wash and rinse glasses.

"When was the last time you sat with the head coach and watched the draft in a bar?" Gale asked, his voice resigned.

"There's always a first," Jones said.

"I don't like Ward," Gale said, shaking his head. Ward was the marquee player in the Draft. A surfer-dude quarterback out of USC with exceptional talent and a penchant for throwing costly interceptions. Gale had watched hours of tape and surmised that Ward's make-up would be troublesome. "I'd rather develop Abruzzi."

The more tape Gale had watched, the more promising Abruzzi had become. It was rare an undrafted free agent, especially a rookie quarterback, could make an impression. Gale hoped Abruzzi would make a big leap in his second year.

Jones nodded. "We need help up front on both sides of the ball. Simon is the kid I would take." Simon was a stud linebacker from Alabama who had turned the SEC into his own personal playground.

"Or Singletary," Gale said. Singletary was an overpowering defensive end from Clemson.

Jones' eyes flickered as the commercial break ended and Spencer Tate, the Commissioner, strode to the podium in Radio City Music Hall wearing an open collar shirt, blue blazer, and khaki-colored slacks, trying to look like a man of the people despite his $57 million annual compensation. After giving an introduction, Tate smiled, and said, "The first pick in the Draft goes to the San Antonio Lone Stars. They're on the clock."

Gale took a deep breath and rested his elbows on the varnished oak bar.

The television feed switched to the Lone Stars' Draft room at the Complex. Gale felt a sudden rush of anger. Sitting next to Johnson and Voss with a smile spread across his face was Buddy Adams.

Gale turned away from the television in disgust.

"Look who they brought into the asylum," Jones said, his eyes clouding.

Gale turned back to the TV. "How am I going to explain?"

LONESTAR

"Tell the media the truth. You weren't invited to the party."

The TV feed switched back to the Commissioner, who stood at the podium, presiding over the most powerful and lucrative professional sports league in the world.

The ESPN announcer said, "The first pick is in" while the camera panned the crowd of boisterous fans before focusing on Tate, who slowly began to read the card in his hand.

"The San Antonio Lone Stars trade the first pick in the Draft to Seattle for a first-round pick next year and the following year."

For an instant, Gale put his head down and closed his eyes.

Jones leaned back and swore.

Gale's chest felt like a truck was sitting on it. He slowly blinked with recognition, and said finally, "I get it."

"What?" Jones asked.

"Voss and Johnson want to make sure we tank this year, so attendance keeps falling. Right? So next year, in a new city, Voss has a bright and shiny deal and a team loaded with draft picks."

"You think they'll have the balls to trade all of 'em?"

"Yup," Gale said, sighing, pushing away from the bar. "Let's get out of here, Donta. I can't watch this."

CHAPTER 15

Lorenzo smiled when his phone started chiming and pinging with calls and texts from media around the country. Trading a first-round draft pick wasn't unusual in the League, but the media had another question: they wanted to know why Gale McClanahan wasn't in the Draft room with Johnson and Voss.

Lorenzo slapped away at his laptop in his bunker-like office in the Complex. The statement was terse and led to a multitude of questions. He would show it to Voss and Johnson before hitting send and revel in the damage. Sowing discord was nearly as satisfying as that first burning hit of Red Label sliding down his throat, he thought.

After he finished typing, he read the statement with satisfaction. He pushed print, and after a few moments, pulled the sheet of paper from the printer and made the short walk down the corridor to show Voss and Johnson.

When he entered the Draft room, Johnson, Voss, and Adams were drinking whiskey and smiling from ear to ear. Voss had done what he wanted to do, and it wasn't over yet. There were two more days of the Draft and six picks to trade.

Lorenzo handed Voss the statement he'd written, and Voss slowly smiled, his sharp teeth flashing under the fluorescent lights.

"Send it, Sam," he said, handing him back the sheet of paper. "That boy won't know what hit him. The media's going to have a party."

Lorenzo smiled and silently reread the statement.

"For Immediate Release: There have been questions this evening as to why Coach McClanahan failed to be present for the first round of the Draft. Unfortunately, Coach McClanahan is handling a sensitive and personal matter. We wish him the best and pray that the serious issues keeping him from team activities will soon be resolved. Fortunately, the team has a well-regarded Associate Head Coach, Buddy Adams, to lead the Lone Stars until McClanahan's personal matters are resolved."

***

"Pray?" Donta Jones said the next morning, showing Gale the Lone Stars' statement on his laptop, which rested on the kitchen table. Raising an eyebrow, Jones handed Gale a cup of coffee and grunted. Jones and his wife, Yvonne, lived in a leased two-bedroom home in Shavano Park, a tidy, attractive suburb. The kitchen had granite countertops and stainless-steel appliances. A bowl of apples sat on the table. "I'd call the statement false and misleading," Jones said.

LONESTAR

Despite sleeping on a soft mattress instead of his office floor, Gale had found himself staring at the ceiling for most of the night. The evening before, he'd avoided the Complex and had taken up Jones' offer to stay at his home. Gale didn't want to risk running into Voss, Johnson, and Adams. He couldn't trust what he would have done if he'd seen them. His anger had skyrocketed, but after seeing the Lone Stars' media statement, his feelings had turned to hatred. He knew his pastor, a tall birdlike figure with a high-pitched twang, would object, because God professed unconditional love, but he despised Voss, Johnson, and Adams for what they were doing to him. Now this. A statement leading to endless speculation and further obstructing Gale's ability to coach. The coffee felt like jet fuel flowing through his veins. He sat at the table, gritted his teeth, and stared stonily out the window.

Yvonne moved from the counter and sat across from Jones and Gale. She had a kind face and deep, brown eyes. Her grandmotherly appearance brought calm to the scene despite a heavy silence among them. She was late for work but made it a point to sit with Gale and her husband.

"Do you have a good lawyer?" Yvonne asked. She was an accountant for a local bank, and after years following her husband around the League, understood the League's venom and mercurial ways.

"Not here."

"Then hire a good one."

Jones nodded.

Gale shrugged. "Slander's hard to prove."

"Yes, it is," Yvonne said. "But it's the principle."

"Have you checked your phone?" Jones asked.

Gale shook his head. He stared at his cell sitting on the table. He didn't want to look. A sense of dread washed over him.

"How'd you get yourself into this mess?" Yvonne asked, reaching over and putting her hand on Gale's arm.

Gale leaned forward in his chair. "I don't know. But at this point, it's not how I got into this mess, but how I'm going to get out of it."

"That's the Gale McClanahan I know," Jones said.

"You both be careful," Yvonne warned. "Those are bad people running the team."

"Bad . . ." Jones echoed.

"The only way out is to win," Gale said.

"You really believe we can?" Jones asked doubtfully, shaking his head. "Last night, we traded our top draft pick."

"It's all I got, Donta. But I'll tell you one thing," Gale said, before reaching for his phone. He noticed Marybeth had called. "I've never lost."

***

75

"Are you okay?" Marybeth asked. Gale stood in Jones' driveway in the light drizzle with his phone pressed to his ear.

"You saw it?"

"I walked into school and got hit with a barrage of questions. Then the Engles called. A sensitive and personal matter? A serious issue? They made you seem like you were diagnosed with cancer or you did something criminal."

"A blindside hit," Gale said sarcastically.

"Jesus," she said. "Those a-holes."

"It's open season, Marybeth."

"What should I tell people?"

"Tell them your husband has always had serious issues. What's new?"

"I want to laugh, but I can't," Marybeth said. "I'm angry, Gale. I want to scream or cry. I don't seem to know which."

"Tell everyone it was a misunderstanding. A miscommunication between me and the owner. Tell 'em I've never been better."

"That's it?"

"What else is there?"

Marybeth paused. Gale could hear her trying to catch herself. "Come home, Gale. Walk away. Please."

"I can't do that," he said. "You know that."

"These are terrible people. They're trying to destroy us for no reason."

Gale cursed under his breath. "I've got to go to the Complex and settle this."

"Come home."

"I can't walk away, Marybeth."

Marybeth's voice grew resolute. "These people are evil, Gale. This isn't about quitting. It's about survival."

Gale paused for a moment. He wasn't sure what was more terrifying. Dealing with predators or the effect that this mess was having on his marriage. He knew it wasn't in his DNA to quit. But he also realized the forces against him were growing more and more sinister.

"Let me see what's going on," Gale said, buying time. "If it's as bad as we think, I'll climb in my truck and come home and never look back. But we'll owe Voss money the rest of our lives."

"I don't care about the money."

"Yes, you do."

"What does that mean?" she asked.

"It means until the day we die, we'll be trying to scramble to pay debt. I saw my mother and father live that way trying to keep the ranch solvent. It killed them."

"A car killed them."

Gale went silent.

"I'm sorry," Marybeth said after a moment. "I shouldn't have said it."

"I need to try to straighten things out."

"Come home."

"Give me a little more time to try to find a way forward," he said. "I'll call you tonight."

"Gale . . ."

"Yes."

"I'm sorry about your mom and dad."

"I know."

"I loved them."

Gale swallowed hard. "I did, too."

***

"Stealing?" Gale said.

"You heard me," Johnson said, pointing his finger at Gale. Lorenzo sat in the corner of Johnson's office with a smirk.

"Sam here said he found the credit card in your wallet."

"He did. After he went into my office and rifled through my desk."

"The Lone Stars' desk," Johnson corrected Gale. "The media statement was kind, son. There are a whole lotta questions circling you. Sure, we don't want you in the Draft Room, but stealing? I'd hate for that to leak."

"I bet."

"You owe Mr. Voss nearly eight thousand dollars, and that includes the Serve Pro bill. We're going to garnish your wages until it's paid back."

Gale leaned forward. He could feel his face flush. "I bought paint and carpeting. Donta and I spent hours fixing up the locker room and training facility. I spent money to have the Cybex Machines repaired and buy new weight benches. Stealing?"

"Unauthorized."

"You would have said no."

"For good reason, son."

"I've been here for over two months, and I haven't found a good reason for anything."

Johnson ignored Gale and turned to Lorenzo. "Sam, what would happen if we put a press release out that Coach McClanahan stole?"

Lorenzo grinned. "The word "pariah' comes to mind."

"What if I told the media what you and Voss are up to?" Gale shot back.

Johnson's eyes grew dark, and he said, "That would be a shame, Gale. I'd hate to see you and the missus in trouble."

Gale focused hard on Johnson. "You're going to trade all the draft picks, aren't you?"

Johnson and Lorenzo glanced at each other. Johnson smiled and leaned back in his office chair.

"I'm going to coach a roster filled with misfits."

Johnson tapped his finger on his desk, gave a saccharine smile, and rose out of his chair. "It'll be your team, Coach. You'll own it. Quietly and graciously. This meeting's over."

CHAPTER 16

Seven picks, seven trades. Voss and Johnson had amassed a war chest of draft choices for the future and left the cupboard bare for the upcoming season. During the Draft and for a few days afterward, Gale had been bombarded with texts and emails from the media about his absence and had swallowed his pride and fury. He feared Johnson and Voss would paint him as untrustworthy, that he'd padded his own pockets with a team Visa card. Blackmail. Gale had explained his "personal issue" had been resolved and he'd returned to work. There had been no pushback from Voss or Johnson or an official team statement. The damage had been done.

Gale knew in the League, the moments after the Draft ended were nearly as vital as the Draft itself. Teams flew into a frenzy after the last pick in the Draft was chosen and hit the phones to sign undrafted free agents. Not unfrequently, undrafted free agents could turn out to be bonafide players who could make a significant impact on the field.

Gale knew from experience. Nearly two decades earlier, fifteen minutes after the Draft had ended, he'd received a call from Atlanta, and had agreed to a contract within minutes. He was 22-years old and had stood in his parent's living room while his mother and father and Marybeth had hugged him. For a kid from Kinney, Texas, it had been a life defining moment.

A week after the Draft, and barely two weeks before OTAs, Johnson hadn't signed an undrafted player. The roster stood at 48. Entering OTAs and training camp, teams carried 90. Gale's high school roster was nearly as large as the Lone Stars'. Worse, Gale's continual attempts to reach out to the players were met with silence. He'd heard a rumor Adams was meeting with players away from the Complex, as always undermining Gale's efforts to establish control. There were moments when Gale concluded that the only course was to relent, be a figurehead coach, a puppet, and let Adams have his way.

Gale turned off his computer and sighed. It was late afternoon, and he needed to go for a run, a long one, to try to shut out the incessant worries racing in his head. Gale walked out of his office and found Rose Cutler packing up to leave.

"I forgot to give you this," she said. "If you hadn't given me an impossible amount of work all day, I would have remembered."

Gale ignored her. "What is it?"

"Here." She thrust a file at him. "You have your team. Good luck."

Gale opened the file. There was a long list of names typed along the margin with a college or university beside each name.

"What's this?"

Cutler sighed. "Undrafted free agents Mr. Johnson signed."

Gale grunted and began to wander back into his office, studying the roster of players.

"Aren't you going to say, 'thank you'?" Cutler asked.

"For what?" Gale said, turning.

"For ruining your day." She hinted at a smile.

"Ruining my day?"

"I haven't watched a football game in twenty years, Coach McClanahan. I hate football. But I know one thing. That list of players is going to get you fired."

Gale looked at her quizzically. "If you hate football, why not find another job?"

"Another job?" Cutler leaned back, a horrified look on her face.

"That's what I said."

"Forfeit my League pension?"

"I thought it was only for players and coaches."

"Ha! Only a few more painful years, Coach McClanahan, and I've got enough of a nest egg to retire."

"Then what?"

She pursed her lips, suppressing a smile. "I've got plans."

Gale stepped back. His face began to redden as he read the first page of the report.

"I told you I was going to ruin your day," she said ominously, her glasses resting on the tip of her nose.

Gale shook his head and closed his office door, realizing that what Rose Cutler had said was true.

The list of signed undrafted free agents made Gale's heart sink. Most of the colleges he'd never heard of.

Jason Smith - Coe College

Javarious Dorsett – Springfield A&M

Devonte Briscoe – Eastern Mississippi Technical College

Morgan Fryer – Kingstown University

He closed the file and tossed it on his desk. He swallowed hard and thought of Marybeth and Til and the terrible mistake he'd made accepting Voss' offer. The guilt nearly overwhelmed him, pulling him deeper into despair.

***

The players were supposed to come from far and wide. Instead, they failed to report for OTAs. In a normal situation, Gale would have been stunned, but this was the San Antonio Lone Stars.

League teams used Organized Team Activities or OTAs to begin preparation for upcoming mini and training camps. OTAs were an opportunity to begin installing plays, teach fundamentals, and assess the mental and physical acuity of the players. There was nothing voluntary about OTAs. In the League, players knew attendance was mandatory. While a player might choose not to participate in OTAs to highlight a contract dispute, like everything else in the League, OTAs were part of a critical process of preparing for the most orchestrated and physically violent season in professional sports.

"I heard," Donta Jones said, standing in Gale's office shaking his head. "Johnson pulled the plug."

Gale folded his arms across his chest and leaned against his desk.

"It's par for the course," Jones continued.

"What's Adams saying?"

"Nothing. As big a prick as Adams is, he'll do whatever Voss and Johnson tell him. Rumor is after he plays a part in destroying your life, Voss is going to name him head coach next year in a new city, with a new team, and with a heap of shiny draft picks."

"No surprise. It's the perfect scenario. I get the blame for a terrible season and next year Adams gets to be the hero."

"Yup. I also heard he's getting a fat bonus for making your life miserable."

"I'm glad someone's getting paid," Gale grunted.

"I'm not kidding."

"Who told you?" Gale asked.

"Your friendly administrative assistant," Jones said, lowering his voice, turning to make sure the door was shut.

"The lady who loves me so much?"

Jones smiled. "That one."

"How'd Cutler hear?"

"Johnson's admin assistant."

"When does the League step in and end this farce, Donta? Canceling OTAs?"

"Think about it. They don't. OTAs are optional. There's nothing in League or Player Association rules mandating teams have to hold 'em. Besides, despite the media right now making the Lone Stars the biggest joke in sports, if you're the Commissioner, you'll put up with all the chaos so Voss can move the team."

"I guess." Gale closed his eyes for a moment and paused. "How am I going to get Adams out of the picture?"

"I don't know."

"He's got razor wire between me, the coaches, and the players. I texted and called every player on the roster in the last two weeks multiple times . . . nothing. I can't go into required practices with no authority, Donta. It's bad enough where I stand now. But when the players arrive ..." His voice trailed off.

"I've got nothin' for you, Coach. They have us by the balls."

Gale shook his head. "I can't accept it."

"Sorry, Coach."

"There's got to be a way."

"I'm not seeing it."

"Neither am I," Gale said, sighing, lost for answers.

***

Gale was reduced to digging change out of the nooks and crannies of his pickup. He ran his hand underneath the Ford's frayed bench seat and found two quarters and a nickel. Altogether, his search in the truck's cab had produced a couple of dollars, enough to buy a good cup of coffee. It was one of Gale's few pleasures. He liked rich, strong coffee and had existed too long on the stale, watery brew he found in the Lone Stars' Complex.

The parking lot at Starbucks was nearly empty, and Gale pulled into a space near the entrance. The coffee shop was tucked in a shopping center a few miles from the Complex. He climbed out of his pickup and inside, ordered. After a barista with a stripe of green hair, a nose ring, and tats on her neck and arms gave him his coffee, he sat down in one of the leather chairs facing the parking lot.

He was about to sip from the cup when a black Range Rover pulled into the lot too fast and came to a jolting halt in the parking spot next to his.

A woman opened the driver side door and with a reckless push, smashed the car door into the side panel of Gale's truck.

"Shit," he said under his breath.

The woman, wearing Gucci sunglasses, a denim shirt, and tight white jeans climbed out of the Range Rover. She had high cheekbones and ash blonde hair swept in a ponytail. Twenties. Stunning. She didn't even pause to check the damage. She shut her car door and glided into Starbucks. His heart sank. He realized the woman was Vanessa Voss.

Gale rose and confronted her near the entrance.

"Can you take it a little easier on my truck?"

Vanessa blew by him and ordered a skinny latte.

"Wait a minute," Gale said angrily, following her.

She turned, took off her sunglasses, and looked right through Gale with frigid blue, vacant eyes. She didn't blink. She gave him a long, searing look and walked out the door.

CHAPTER 17

The Manhattan skyline cast long shadows across Madison Avenue as the limousine edged its way through the long stream of morning traffic. Cursing, Vernon Voss shut the file and tossed it on the seat next to him. Voss Energy's balance sheet was upside down. Voss had weathered the perils of the oil and gas markets before, but this time plunging energy prices had him by the throat. He'd ignored the calls from the Swiss, who despite his prim nature, was growing more and more shrill on behalf of his Saudi client. Mike Andujar, San Antonio's incorruptible mayor was nipping at Voss' heels as well, threatening a lawsuit if the Lone Stars skipped town. Voss was increasingly aware Andujar wasn't going to give up without a fight.

Voss' thoughts returned to Andujar jawing away at Gale McClanahan at the Mayor's Gala. Voss had warned McClanahan but wondered what had been said. Despite his concerns, Johnson had assured Voss that everything was going to plan. Already ticket sales were dwindling. It was no surprise. There was more than buzz around town that the Lone Stars were going to leave, and the debacle Voss and Johnson had orchestrated at the Draft had kicked up a firestorm of protest from the few remaining Lone Star fans who cared. Canceling OTAs was icing on the cake. Fans were tired of losing. They were tired of promises to rebuild. All that mattered now to Voss was attendance falling below the threshold. Then he could make a deal and collect millions from the city. Salvation lay this way.

Thus far it had been a brilliant call to hire McClanahan. Hapless, McClanahan was on track to fail spectacularly. While Voss despised his son-in-law, being a prick came naturally to Adams. Adams had divided the team and cut McClanahan's balls off. It was worth the money Voss had been shelling out and worth the false promises. In the end, Adams would get screwed, too.

McClanahan . . . Voss shook his head. He'd seen how Vanessa had looked at him that night at the Gala. It had made Voss' blood boil. It was another reason to make certain McClanahan failed.

***

Spencer Tate greeted Voss in his mid-century furnished office decorated with a deep red oriental carpet and rare Japanese prints. Other than a silver Championship Trophy replica sitting on the Commissioner's walnut coffee table, there was no hint the middle-aged man with a white button-down shirt, a blue and gold tie, and a conservative, custom-tailored suit oversaw the most lucrative professional sports entity in the world. As dirt poor as Voss grew up, Tate came from wealth. His father had overseen one of the most venerable investment houses in Boston, and Tate had enjoyed the upbringing of the privileged. He'd attended Groton before matriculating to Harvard, and upon graduation, rose with lightning speed up Wall Street giant Stone Thompson's cutthroat ladder before finding himself sitting at the top at the age of 46. Tate had the easy social graces of a man used to summering on Nantucket and residing in a luxury penthouse apartment perched above the Manhattan skyline.

He took the Commissioner's position solely to feed his ego. He'd had little interest in football. He'd spent his childhood in Brookline playing golf and tennis at The Country Club. But congenial as he appeared with his full head of brown hair, thin, aristocratic nose, and boyish looks, he'd earned a reputation for being ruthless. The thirty-two owners he served knew Spencer Tate loved profit and power as much as they did. Tate had negotiated the largest TV deal in the history of professional sports, navigated brain injury litigation, expanded the brand into international markets, outmaneuvered the League's players' association at each turn, and had done so with an easy smile and a velvet hammer.

Overall, under Tate's leadership, the League had found itself in the strongest position it had been, except for the San Antonio Lone Stars, a team that had sullied Tate's reputation for having a Midas touch.

Voss knew it.

When Voss greeted Tate, the commissioner's congenial facade evaporated. Voss knew he was the ugly stepchild of the League. Despite hiding personal assets around the world, Voss understood it was only a matter of time before creditors closed the circle.

They sat facing one another in Tate's sunlit office. Voss could see a helicopter beating above the building tops, racing toward the Hudson.

"You caused quite a stir at the Draft, Vernon," Tate said, playing with one of his cufflinks.

Voss gave a thin smile.

"OTAs? First time in the history of the League a team outright canceled them. Do you think you could be more subtle?"

"Subtlety won't get the team out of San Antonio."

"True. But it's making me nervous, Vernon. I'm getting questions from other owners and the press. We all know you want out, but it's turning into a public relations nightmare."

"We agreed."

Tate leaned forward. "We agreed the team needs to move, but we didn't agree on you creating a travesty to do it."

"How else am I going to do it?" Voss asked, his voice sharpening. "I got an ironclad lease every attorney has looked at and said, 'no way out.' I need attendance to drop. My business depends on it."

"Andujar?"

"He's made it clear he's not going to let the team walk."

"Our Russian?"

"I'm working on it."

"I want the deal done. If it isn't, you need to find a local buyer."

"I'm not selling for pennies on the dollar to keep the team in San Antonio."

"What you're really saying is without the Russian, you're going broke."

Voss' eyes hardened. "Don't put words in my mouth."

"I'm well informed."

"Don't tell me you don't have a vested interest, Spencer. I pull this off and you look like a genius and get what you want."

"If you pull it off . . ."

"I'll pull it off."

"By hiring a high school coach, not drafting a single player, and signing a bunch of no-name undrafted free agents. I have no doubts." Tate's face flushed. "But this isn't Pop Warner, Vernon. No game officials are going to run the clock in the second half because they're worried you're going to get your ass whipped 76-0."

'That's not a worry. That's a dream."

"A nightmare."

"One season. Then things turn around."

"I need you to keep this under control. Do you understand?"

"Oh, I understand," Voss said.

"Vernon, pay your bills."

Voss' expression changed to a scowl. "When the team moves."

"Now."

Voss shifted uncomfortably. "You ever heard of a dry well, Spencer?"

Tate looked pained.

"I cut this deal and I'll get back on my feet, and you'll get everything you want."

"If you don't?"

Voss looked away for a moment and gritted his teeth. "I will."

"You better."

"What I need is for you to have my back."

"Have your back? The entire mess with Adams could have blown apart if I hadn't had your back." Tate shook his head. "Don't embarrass me, Vernon."

"Oh, I won't. I'll make sure Spencer Tate's little kingdom rides high."

"I mean it."

Voss's eyes grew into daggers. "You'll get what you want, Mr. Commissioner. But it will be on my terms. This time next year, you'll be sitting in that penthouse of yours sipping a glass of champagne and thanking Vernon Voss."

"You think?"

"I know."

"Don't let me down, Vernon."

Voss eyed him. "Don't forget you work for the owners. That means you work for me."

"Pay your bills."

"Oh, I'll pay them."

"Don't embarrass the League."

"You mean, you."

Tate's face reddened. He sat back in his chair. "You better strike a deal. Understand?"

"Or what?" Voss gave Tate a belligerent look, the stare he'd given thousands of times in the oil patch and across negotiating tables.

Tate paused. "I don't make empty threats."

"Have my back, Spencer." Voss started to rise out of his chair. "Remember, I still have pull."

"It's dwindling, Vernon. The other owners are getting upset."

Voss said, "They'll get what they want. You will, too."

CHAPTER 18

The players reported for Mini-Camp on a warm, overcast June day. For the first time in months, the player parking lot was full. But unlike the other teams in the League, instead of flashy, high-priced cars, there was an assortment of beat-up, dusty compacts, SUVs, and trucks pointing to a roster comprised of journeyman players barely hanging on and undrafted free agents who didn't have a dollar to their name.

Gale walked the hallways of the Complex, trying to greet players who averted their eyes when they spotted him coming. Adams had gotten to them all. It was as if Gale didn't exist and roamed the Complex as if he were a ghost. When he'd introduced himself to Abruzzi in the weight room, the second-year quarterback had turned his back and had ignored him. Gale had grown used to the coaches giving him a cold shoulder, but the players? He'd prided himself on building relationships with his teams. He was tough on them, but the players knew he cared. Now Gale was feeling like the unpopular kid at school sitting alone in the cafeteria, ignored and shunned. It shouldn't have been a surprise, but Gale was beginning to grow distraught. He'd rolled out a detailed schedule for training camp and sent it to the team. The first meeting was that afternoon after the players went through physicals. Gale knew the coaches wouldn't show up, but he and Donta Jones had worked out a plan. Gale would lay it on the line with the players about the coaching staff's dysfunction. He would lay everything on the table in hopes of gaining their trust. He would use trust to leverage the coaching staff's support with hopes of cutting Adams out.

As Gale and Jones waited for the players to arrive in the team conference room, Gale looked at his watch with growing unease. He noticed the upholstery on the seats were streaked with water stains from the sprinklers exploding.

"They're not going to show, Donta," Gale said, shaking his head, looking at his watch again, leaning against the white board.

Jones sat in one of the front row seats with a blank expression, lost in thought, his long legs extended in front of him.

"I think you're right, Coach," Jones said.

"What do you think? We can sit here and lick our wounds or go round 'em up?"

"Herding cats."

"Our cats, Donta. Not Adams'."

"Yup."

"Let's go."

Gale's heart raced as he stood for a moment outside the locker room. He took a deep breath, gritted his teeth, nodded at Jones, and pushed open the door. Gale found 90 players stuffed into the locker room with Adams presiding in front of a portable white board. Several of the players sprawled on the floor. Gale and Jones stood inside the entrance as Adams and the assistant coaches eyed them. Some of the players glanced uneasily at Gale and Jones before turning back to Adams.

Adams ignored Gale and Jones and continued addressing the team. He spoke in sharp bursts, a toothpick rolling around the side of his mouth. "Last year was a brain fart, boys. You gotta do better. You gotta play better. You gotta work harder. You gotta be smarter."

Adams paused, eyed Gale with a look of contempt, and considered his next words. "You gotta forget we hired a high school coach from nowhere who doesn't believe in punting. Imagine?" Nervously, some of the players started to laugh. "Me and Coach McClanahan," he pointed at Gale, "have it all worked out. He gets the title and big bucks, and because he doesn't know diddly squat, gets a front row seat to how it's done in the League. Right, Coach?"

Adams glared at Gale. The players turned.

Gale felt his ears grow hot.

"We got it all worked out, don't we?"

Gale's face hardened.

"I bust my ass, and he gets the glory. How does that sound?" Adams asked sarcastically. "Coach McClanahan?"

Gale took a step forward and cleared his throat. He felt his hands shaking.

"As Coach Adams says, I guess I don't know diddly squat." Gale glared at Adams and addressed him. "How many seasons did you play in the League, Coach?"

Adams' cheeks started to flush. He scowled.

"College?" Gale asked Adams, his voice started to smooth out and grow calm. Gale had read on the web how Adams had been kicked off the team at Oklahoma after his sophomore year for an undisclosed infraction.

For a moment, Gale studied Adams, letting his words sink in. Adams' face grew red and his jaw rigid.

"What he also would tell you if he were truthful, is in his twenty years in the League, he's been fired eleven times and hasn't been on a team that made the playoffs ... there's more ... I've watched tape over and over of every snap we took last year. The matchups were bad, the adjustments terrible, the lack of a coherent defensive gameplan ..." Gale's voice drifted off in disgust. He shook his head. "Worst of all. He blames you guys. What did you say, coach? 'The team has to play harder and smarter? You didn't say 'we", you said 'you.'"

LONESTAR

Gale could tell Adams was about to lash out. But he kept on, feeling stronger, more confident, knowing he had the high ground. How many times had he been in a locker room in front of teams, trying to inspire them, convince them they could do things they never imagined?

"What Coach Adams should have done today is apologize for bad coaching. Right, Buddy?" Gale asked with disdain. "But he didn't. That should tell you something." The players started to nod. Gale could feel them focusing, listening. The assistant coaches were staring at the floor, as if to say, "it's true." Gale continued. "I've never made an excuse. If I screw up, I'll tell you. That's a promise. My office door will always be open. They'll be no 'you' on a team I coach. Only 'we.' If you want to be part of what coach Adams offers, it's all yours. If you want to be part of what I offer, I'll promise you I'll work my ass off. We'll be a disciplined, smart, football team."

Silence permeated the room.

"I hope you'll give me a chance," Gale said to the players, shaking his head, his voice growing softer. "I'm like you. I want an opportunity. We'll have a team meeting in the morning before practice. 7am sharp. I hope you'll be there."

Before Adams could reply, Gale stepped out of the locker room and into the hallway. Jones followed. Before Gale could say anything, Jones smiled and shook his head. "You kicked Adams' ass, Coach. You hit him between those beady eyes."

"You think?" Gale asked, turning to Jones.

"I know. You did your homework."

"Will the players show up in the morning, Donta?"

"I hope. But we're talking about the San Antonio Lone Stars. Your guess is as good as mine."

***

A few minutes later, Gale found Rose Cutler with a large flower arrangement bursting with color on her desk.

"Who's your secret admirer?" Gale asked as he walked by to his office.

"Not mine, yours," Cutler said.

"Mine?" Gale asked, taken aback.

"That's what I said." Cutler thrust out the card attached to the vase with a knowing smile. The envelope had been opened.

He shook his head and studied the envelope for a few seconds and slipped the card out. "I was such a shit," the card read. "Can we talk? V."

Gale's thoughts flooded with images of Vanessa confronting him at Starbucks. He hesitated for a moment before tossing the card and envelope in the trash can by Cutler's desk.

"Keep the flowers, Ms. Cutler," Gale said.

Cutler smiled, a half-smile, and looked over the tops of her glasses. "V?" she asked.

"It's a long story," Gale said, trying not to sound defensive.

"It always is," said Cutler, ignoring the flowers and turning to her computer.

Gale shook his head and entered his office, trying to erase the images of Vanessa's eyes burning through him in the coffee shop. At the Mayor's Gala, the image of Vanessa wearing a sleek gown, her icy hot eyes locked in on his, coyly peering at him, while Vernon Voss' eyes grew black. Gale had told Marybeth what had happened at Starbucks. They didn't keep secrets. Marybeth had sighed and said, "That woman is nothing but trouble, Gale."

Gale knew she was right. He vowed to avoid Vanessa at all costs.

***

That evening, Gale stepped out of the Complex to get dinner. For the first time in weeks, he sensed a glimmer of hope. He knew the players had heard him and the wall Adams had built didn't seem so impregnable. The parking lot was nearly empty except for his truck sitting next to the overflowing dumpsters near the entrance to the practice field. The evening air felt warm as Gale walked to his pickup. He suddenly heard a voice call out behind him.

"Coach . . ."

Gale turned. Matt Abruzzi walked toward him. He was wearing a white t-shirt with Eastern Carolina printed across it in bold letters and gray shorts. He was nearly 6-4, with shaggy dark hair, a sturdy jaw, and a face covered with a couple of days' worth of whiskers. "You got a moment?" Abruzzi asked.

"Were you waiting for me?"

Abruzzi nodded. "We need to talk."

Twenty minutes later they were sitting in a corner booth at Grady's. Abruzzi had heaped his plate with slices of beef and a pile of steamed vegetables. Gale munched on a chicken leg and took a sip of water.

"What you said today was real," Abruzzi said, before taking a bite of tenderloin. He pulled up his t-shirt and pointed to his ribs. An ugly bruise stained his side. "Blindside hit against Miami. Seven months later, I still got a contusion and ribs that won't heal."

Gale shook his head. He vividly recalled the hit on tape, one of many Abruzzi had suffered, and wondered again how Abruzzi had managed to get up off the field.

"Last year was a disaster," Abruzzi said. "Today, it was like deja vu. Adams up there giving us crap, telling us we need to do better, the other coaches going along with his bullshit . . . I can't go through it again. I know the other returning players feel the same way." He paused. "What you said was truth." Abruzzi shrugged. "Today when you came into the weight room," his voice drifted for a moment, "I acted like a dick."

"Under a gag order?" Gale smiled.

"Adams and the staff have been telling us not to go near you. The official word was Mr. Voss and Garvin Johnson told Adams they made a big mistake hiring you but couldn't fire you until the season was over. Adams said he was going to be de facto head coach and we needed to stay away from you or Johnson would cut our asses."

Gale encouraged Abruzzi to go on.

"Coach, I've never seen a crappier organization. When I signed with the Lone Stars, I figured it was my best shot in the League to make a roster, but I never thought it would be like this. Last year, Haden had no control. Adams was always undercutting everything he did. The players didn't know who to listen to. The rest of the coaches went through the motions. The players would come into the Complex every day and put on filthy practice gear because no one was doing the laundry. I mean this is the League?" he asked with disgust. "When we complained, Johnson would step in and tell us he'd cut us, and we'd never play again. No one said anything, because all the guys on this team are hanging by a thread, trying to stay in the League. Most of them know they wouldn't be in the League if they weren't playing for the Lone Stars. I didn't think it could get any worse . . ."

"But?" Gale asked.

"It did. Our players' association rep, Trey Worrell, said he was going to file a formal complaint against the organization for practice violations. I mean we were in full pads, hitting live every day in practice. What team does that? Guys were getting injured. We were going full speed. It was like the coaching staff was trying to hurt us."

"What happened?"

"Johnson threatened Worrell. Said if he filed the complaint he'd never play again."

"Did he file?"

"No. The next day Worrell got cut and there was rumor going around the League he had a drug problem. Trey had a wife and kid and was the nicest guy you ever met. Smart, too. He was a bioengineering major at Bowling Green. He never partied. Never did drugs."

Gale shook his head and slowly chewed a piece of chicken. His mind flashed to Lorenzo and Johnson threatening to expose he'd "stolen" from the organization. He thought of Marybeth and Tilly, and he tried to erase the thought of Voss and Johnson blackmailing him.

"Everyone's scared."

Gale leaned back, his eyes clouding.

"After we beat Houston . . . I mean the only game we won, Johnson and Mr. Voss were pissed. They pulled Haden out of the locker room and went ballistic. One of the locker room attendants overheard the whole conversation. It was ugly."

Abruzzi took a bite of vegetables, swallowed, and shook his head. Gale gestured for him to continue.

"What you said to us today was the first time I've heard reality since I signed." Abruzzi put his fork down and sipped his iced tea. "I know we're going to get crushed this year. I mean what team trades its draft choices and signs undrafted guys out of colleges no one's ever heard of?"

Gale leaned back and put his fork on his plate.

"Everyone realizes Mr. Voss wants to lose. He wants to move the team." Abruzzi put his head down for a moment. "I mean I'm not afraid, Coach." He reached under his t-shirt and rubbed the bruise on his side. "But I could get killed this season."

Gale asked, "It's not a matter of winning, but surviving, huh?"

"Yeah. I want to be able to play with my kids someday," Abruzzi said, leaning back.

"Will the players show up tomorrow morning for the meeting?"

"I'm working on it."

"What's holding them back?"

"Fear."

Gale shook his head. "I told the players today I'd have their back. You tell 'em I mean it."

Abruzzi nodded.

"Matt."

"Yeah."

Gale smiled. "I promise, I'm not going to let you get killed this season."

CHAPTER 19

In the Grady's parking lot, Gale called Marybeth after meeting with Abruzzi. He recounted the scene in the locker room but didn't tell her what Abruzzi had told him about Trey Worrell. Gale didn't want to worry Marybeth more than she already was about their situation. After saying goodnight to Tilly, Gale heard Marybeth sigh when she returned to the call.

"You okay?" Gale asked.

Marybeth paused. "Your little girl misses you."

Gale went silent for a moment. "Marybeth?"

"Yes. . ."

He thought of Marybeth and Til alone in Kinney, the bills piling up, the leaky roof, the broken gutters, and the fear, anger, and uncertainty caused by his hasty swipe of a pen, a signed contract. Gale hesitated. "I'll call you tomorrow. Let's hope the players show up."

"Fingers crossed," she said, sounding distant.

When the call ended, Gale tossed his cell phone on the passenger seat. He thought about the flowers and note from Vanessa. He reminded himself, he and Marybeth kept no secrets.

***

Gale and Jones entered the team conference room a few minutes before seven. Gale's heart sank. The amphitheater-like room was empty. He walked down the steps and rested his coffee cup and thick folder full of notes on the podium. He turned to Donta.

"So much for buying Abruzzi dinner last night." Gale shook his head.

"We got a few minutes."

"I couldn't sleep last night," Gale said.

"Have you slept since you got hired?" Donta smiled.

Gale shrugged. "Not much."

Gale heard the door swing open and looked up. Matt Abruzzi entered carrying a legal pad in one hand and his laptop in the other.

Jones said, "You got your quarterback, Coach."

Abruzzi looked around the conference room and shook his head. "I'm the only one?"

"Yup," Jones said.

Abruzzi looked at Gale. "I thought there'd be more guys."

"Ten to go before we can field a team," Jones said.

Abruzzi came down the steps and sat in the front row. He placed his notebook and computer on the seat next to him.

Gale checked his watch. It was seven. It was foolhardy to think players would side with him, he thought bitterly. Their livelihoods depended on playing football. Pledging allegiance to Gale was a bad proposition considering his precarious place in the organization.

Gale was about to call the meeting off when he remembered what Jack Engle had said when Gale was a young coach. "It doesn't matter how many players show up on the first day of practice. We coach 'em."

Gale looked at Abruzzi. "Matt," Gale said, "let's talk about how to keep you alive this season."

Abruzzi grinned. "Music to my ears, man."

Gale turned to Jones. "Let's start on a positive note and watch the win over Houston."

Jones plugged a wire into his laptop and dimmed the lights. Soon, the All-22 was frozen on the white board.

Gale was about to show the first play from scrimmage when the door swung open, and a shaft of light illuminated the conference room. Gale looked up while Jones turned on the lights. Deshay Anderson, a veteran defensive end, stood at the top of the steps and peered down at Gale.

"I'm here to play, Coach," Anderson said, plopping his huge body into one of the top row seats. Anderson was a journeyman who had bounced around the League since he'd been drafted.

"Nine to go," Jones said.

"Any other players coming?" Gale asked Anderson.

"They're scared," Anderson said. "They think Adams and Johnson will cut 'em."

"How about you?" Gale questioned.

"I'm not putting up with this no more," Anderson said. "I've been pissed on enough."

Gale said, "We're watching Houston."

Anderson broke into a smile. "Starting on a positive note, Coach?"

"You got it."

"I like that."

"I only got sacked seven times in this game," Abruzzi said.

"Seven times too many," Gale answered, dimming the lights. "Roll the tape, Donta."

***

LONESTAR

They had broken down the game against Houston and had called it quits before noon. Afterwards, Gale had gone out to the field and watched from afar as Adams and the coaching staff ran practice. Despite the yelling and admonishments of the coaches, the players ran mechanically through the motions. There was little energy. The more Adams and the coaches bullied the players, the more they sank into listlessness.

Gale remembered a coaching clinic he'd gone to years earlier. Legendary coach Bill Walsh had presented in front of hundreds of high school coaches from around the country. Gale had never forgotten what Walsh had said. "If you're yelling at the players, you aren't teaching."

The first day of required spring practice was closed to the media. Gale was supposed to speak to reporters later in the afternoon. He had a hollow pit in his stomach. Thus far, the press had not latched on to the full extent of infighting between the coaching staff and Gale. Maybe it was time to put it out there, Gale thought. The media certainly understood Voss' desire to move the team and had reported with intensity after the Draft. The handwriting was on the wall. Despite the unfolding story, media outlets around town started pulling back coverage. They sensed no one cared. The city was resigned to seeing the Lone Stars crawl away, especially after several horrendous seasons, the draft fiasco, the cancellation of OTAs, and signing a bunch of no name college free agents.

Gale studied the scene on the field until Adams suddenly unleashed on a rookie defensive back, a kid signed out of Kent State, who had botched a drill. Adams ran toward the player, letting loose with a string of expletives. The kid staggered backwards, nearly tripping, as Adams relentlessly jawed away. To Gale's astonishment, Adams struck the kid in the chest with the butt of his palms. The player fell hard as the back of his helmet hit the turf, Adams continuing his verbal onslaught.

Gale's neck burned. That was his player. Adams suddenly turned and caught sight of Gale. He focused on Gale, hesitated for a moment, and started striding toward him, his thick compact arms at his side, his lantern jaw jutted out. 'What are you doing here, Boy Scout?" Adams shouted, loud enough for the players and coaches to hear. "Get your sorry ass off my field."

Gale stood his ground. Adams moved closer.

"You tell Abruzzi to get his ass out here," Adams said, his face hot and flushed.

"Hard to practice without a starting quarterback, Coach Adams?" Gale asked.

Adams drew near and stuck his finger in Gale's face. "You tell that boy if he doesn't get out here, he'll never play again."

"That's a big threat."

"It's fact."

"Like Trey Worrell?"

For a moment, Adams' eyes narrowed.

"Who else are you all going to ruin, Adams?"

95

"You tell Abruzzi what I said."

"You tell him," Gale said with contempt, turning and walking toward the Complex.

"McClanahan."

Gale stopped and faced Adams.

"You're playing with fire," Adams said.

"You've said it before."

"The little media release Johnson sent out about you not being in the room during the Draft." Adams paused. "It can get a whole lot worse."

"I bet."

"You got no clue, do you, Boy Scout?"

Gale shook his head. "I know one thing."

"What?"

"If you ever touch one of my players again, it'll be the last time," Gale said, turning and walking back to the Complex.

***

"Where are you going, son?" Garvin Johnson said to Gale, stopping him in the hallway later that afternoon. Sam Lorenzo stood behind Johnson with a smirk stitched across his face.

"Press conference," Gale said. Gale eyed Johnson, who stood in front of him, blocking his way to the conference room.

"The hell you are, not after you pulled the stunt with Abruzzi and Anderson," Johnson said, his voice rising.

"What stunt?" Gale said.

"Getting the team riled up. Making Buddy look bad. Encouraging insubordination."

"Right," Gale said, dismissing the absurdity of Johnson's accusations.

"Son, you need to take stock of where you are in life."

Gale shook his head.

Johnson looked at Lorenzo and back at Gale. "Sam's stepping in today to field questions. Tomorrow, Adams is going to meet with reporters. After today, the last thing I'm going to do is let some reporter put a microphone in your face."

"When the media asks where the head coach is, what are you going to say this time?" Gale shot back, the tips of his ears starting to burn.

Johnson flashed his teeth, ignoring the question. "You do what Adams tells you to do."

"If I don't?"

Johnson gave a thin, sugary smile. "It won't be only you who gets train wrecked, son. How about Jones, too? We've been real patient with Donta. I'm not sure why. I'd hate to see him end his career on a tragic note."

"I'm sure." Gale tried to dismiss the word "tragic."

"Son," Johnson said. "You do what I tell you. Understand?"

Gale shook his head slowly.

"Another thing. Those flowers that arrived…" Johnson's voice trailed off and his eyes turned into slits.

Gale's pulse quickened.

"I'd hate for Mrs. McClanahan to think something's happening on the side." Johnson broke into a knowing smile. "I'm guessing she has enough worries, doesn't she?"

CHAPTER 20

Gale disliked eating alone. He was tired of having dinner by himself, especially with the heartache of his family far away in Kinney. He was largely left alone at Grady's but for the occasional senior who recognized him and asked what the heck was going on with the Lone Stars. Gale's eyes drifted across the empty restaurant. A middle-aged woman was wiping down tables before closing, and an older man was pushing a vacuum near the entrance. Gale was about to get up and settle his bill, when he noticed he'd missed a call. It was an 806-area code. West Texas.

He rose out of the booth and paid. Outside, in the warm evening air, he listened to the voicemail, trying to hear the message above the noise of cars streaming by on the interstate adjacent to the restaurant. It was Grayson Wallace. "Call me," Wallace said with urgency.

Gale climbed into his pickup and punched up Wallace's number. Gale could imagine Wallace, still in his office in Kinney, a glass of whiskey on his desk, a desk lamp burning, methodically reviewing a stack of legal documents.

"Gale," Wallace said gruffly when he answered.

"What's going on, Grayson?"

"Those boys you're working for in San Antonio, I've done some homework."

Gale pulled the phone away from his ear for a moment. Puzzled.

"I knew they were trouble, Gale, but you didn't tell me the entire story."

"Who did?"

Wallace paused. Gale could feel him hesitating. Wallace said finally, "Your pretty wife. She dropped in a few days ago rightly upset. I wish you'd told me earlier, Gale. I knew when I read your contract you were working for bad characters, but I didn't know half of it."

Gale thought about Marybeth meeting with Wallace. He was surprised and relieved Marybeth had made Wallace aware of their situation. Gale had always shied away from sharing his problems, and because of his pride, hadn't even told Jack Engle how bad it had gotten with the Lone Stars. Gale had felt ashamed he'd put himself, and most of all, his family, in such a terrible place.

"After what Marybeth told me, I did some digging," Wallace said.

Gale stayed silent.

"I called one of my classmates. We suffered through Vanderbilt Law together, and there's no worse sufferin' than being a law student." Wallace gave a short laugh. "He practices in Houston and does high profile work for the oil and gas industry. He said he sued Voss a few years back after Voss stiffed the firm for over

98

a million dollars in fees." Wallace paused. Gale could hear a slight wheeze. "But that's not all. He told me about a rumor."

Wallace gave a dramatic pause. "He said Voss' son-in-law and some of the other coaches were caught betting against the Lone Stars. Not once, but the whole darn season. He thinks the entire coaching staff was involved. He thinks Voss and Spencer Tate swept it under the rug. Tate didn't want the League's reputation ruined by a federal investigation, a cascade of lawsuits from irate fantasy football bettors, and have it screw up any deals with the gaming industry or other sponsors."

"Adams?" Gale asked.

"Presto. That's the one. Imagine a defensive coordinator and other coaches influencing the point spread? It wouldn't play well, would it?"

"Who's the source?"

"My friend wouldn't tell. He said he wanted to keep his contacts close."

Gale shook his head. He thought of all the game film he had watched from the previous season and the sheer ineptitude of the coaching staff.

"My friend added that Voss has been avoiding creditors like a leper. Word has it he's been shuttling all over the world trying to keep Voss Energy afloat. It's no surprise he wants to move the Lone Stars to a more lucrative pasture. It's also no surprise you're the fall guy, Gale. He expects you to fail and is trying hard to make sure it happens. Marybeth told me you're sleeping on your office floor?"

Gale felt a sudden stab of shame.

"I'm putting $50,000 in your bank account. It'll give you a little breathing room."

"Grayson . . . no . . ." Gale's neck flushed. Charity. He thought about his father, proud and fierce, refusing to take a cent from his friends who wanted to help him save the ranch.

"My secretary's going to book you a room at The Residence Inn. They're billing me monthly."

"You can't do this," Gale said.

"The hell I can't." Wallace paused. "I don't know how you got into this mess, but I'm sure not going to see you sleeping on the floor and Marybeth buying macaroni and cheese at Dollar General. Kinney owes you, Gale. You brought this town a lot of pride and joy. Besides," Wallace said with a gruff laugh, "you always answered my game critiques on Saturday morning. If I were in your shoes, I'm not sure I would have been so generous."

"I can't take your money," Gale said. "You know that."

"Gale, I'm comfortable, and anyway, my money is the least of your worries. You're dealing with rattlers, Gale."

Gale hesitated. His stomach roiled. "I need Adams out of the picture."

For a moment, Wallace went silent. Gale could hear the wheezing again. "I learned a long time ago rumors are sometimes more powerful than facts. Use it, but carefully, Gale. My friend in Houston says Vernon Voss is the meanest cuss he's ever met. He'd castrate his own son."

Gale thought for a moment. "What you told me could bring down the whole League."

"Yes, it could, if it's true. But if you use the information right," Wallace said finally, "it might give you a chance to get out of San Antonio alive."

***

A few minutes later, Gale called Marybeth and told her about his conversation with Wallace. He felt a stinging pang for being so far away.

"Are you angry I spoke with him?" Marybeth asked. "About the money?"

Gale leaned back in the pickup and closed his eyes, fighting the urge to tell her he wasn't taking Wallace's charity. "I'm not angry, Marybeth."

"I hate where we are, Gale. I hate it," she said after a few beats. "I want our life back."

"I do, too," Gale said. "More than you know."

***

That night after canceling the hotel reservation Wallace's assistant had made, Gale tossed on his office floor. He found himself unable to sleep, fitfully thinking about what Wallace had shared, trying to sort out how he would move the chess piece to gain control of the team. In the scheme of things, the League was no stranger to misdeeds. The League found itself continually in the news for varying levels of misconduct. Yet for decades, the League had prided itself on the integrity of the game. Protect the Shield. Betting against your own team was a starkly different issue than a player getting busted for a DUI or a messy labor dispute. What Wallace had told Gale angered him but didn't come as a surprise. Gale could imagine Adams and the other coaches doing most anything, especially for money.

The next morning, Gale's heart raced when he entered the empty coaches' locker room. He'd timed it perfectly. Gale leaned up against the sink and faced the stall in front of him. He could hear a grunt.

"I'm disappointed, Buddy," Gale said after a few moments. "I knew you could stoop low, but betting against your own team?"

Gale heard a sudden shuffling and the toilet paper dispenser rattle.

"Betting against the Lone Stars for the whole season? Imagine if it got out? You'd be screwed, Buddy."

The toilet flushed and a few seconds later Adams snapped open the stall door. His face was red and his eyes sharp. "What're you talking about, Boy Scout?" He hissed.

100

Gale knew instantly what Wallace had told him was true. Gale saw a hint of fear in Adams' narrow, black eyes.

"Imagine if the players heard? Fans? All those guys playing fantasy. The Feds. It would get real ugly."

Adams squinted. "You got nothing on me."

"You want to call my bluff? You want me to walk into the *Express-News* and tell them everything I know? I got a real credible source. I knew you were dumb, Buddy, but I didn't know how dumb until a little birdie put something in my ear yesterday."

Adams cursed.

"Let me paint the scenario." Gale paused. "If this story gets out, and it will if you don't do what I say, you're not only never going to coach again, you're going to do time, Buddy. I suspect some of those guys in Huntsville or Leavenworth or wherever you end up, lost money because of you. They aren't going to be happy."

Adams took a step back. Blood drained from his face.

"It's real easy. Remember those words? Real easy, Buddy? You quit and walk away, and I keep our little secret."

Adams shifted into a defiant look. "You're full of it, McClanahan."

Gale shook his head. "Full of it, Buddy? I got the goods and nothing would make me happier than to destroy your crappy life. But I like to think I'm a better person than you, so I'm going to give you the chance you never gave me."

Adams looked away, his face bloodless.

"What's it going to be?" Gale asked.

Adams remained frozen.

Gale pushed away from the sink and turned away. "You had your chance."

"Where're you going?" Adams asked, his voice rising.

"I told you what I was going to do."

"McClanahan . . ."

Gale faced Adams.

"You're a son of a bitch," Adams said.

Gale smiled.

"You tell everyone you're resigning for personal reasons," Gale said. "If you do anything to mess with me, my family, or the team, I go to the media. Understand?"

"You're going to rue the day . . ." Adams' voice drifted off.

"I want you out now. I don't ever want to see your face again."

"There'll be payback."

Gale eyed him. "For your sake, Buddy, I hope not. Oh, and tell your cronies they're out, too."

***

Gale's mind raced as he approached Rose Cutler's desk. When she heard him approach, she didn't bother to look up. She shook her head and said staring into her computer screen, "You've done it again. Johnson wants you in his office ASAP."

"What a surprise," Gale said.

"It's been nice knowing you," Cutler said.

"Can't you give me any sunshine?" Gale asked.

Cutler turned and stared at him. Her face was blank. "Why should I?"

"Common decency."

"Don't you get it by now?"

"Get what?"

"There's nothing decent about this place. Why should I waste my time? It's a revolving door. A new coach every year. Why get attached? You're about to get fired like the rest of them. Even Haden didn't get Johnson and Voss this upset."

Gale smiled and said after a pause, "Why do I feel like we both constantly underestimate one another, Ms. Cutler?"

"Because," she said finally, "that's what I get paid to do."

CHAPTER 21

Garvin Johnson's assistant rested her nail file on her cluttered desk when she saw Gale. The smell of perfume nearly overwhelmed him. Her frosted hair glistened under the fluorescent office lights. She smiled perversely, as if a bomb were about to go off in a crowd, and she had a front row seat to witness the carnage.

She didn't say a word. She gestured haughtily toward Johnson's office door.

Gale entered and Johnson, sitting behind his desk, pointed at a chair. His face was red, and for a moment, he stared at Gale, his expression taut. Gone were the niceties.

"What did you say to Adams?" Johnson barked after what seemed like an eternity.

"You know what I said," Gale shot back.

"I got off the phone with Vernon. He's as angry as I've ever seen him. He says you've stepped over the line."

Gale leaned forward. He could feel his heart pound. He could hear Grayson Wallace telling him to be careful. "No, I'm very much on the right side of the line here."

"What you said to Adams is fiction, McClanahan. There's been no betting and no cover up. There's not a shred of evidence."

"That's where you're wrong."

Johnson eyed Gale. "Son, you're headed down an ugly road."

Gale called Johnson's bluff. "My source is credible. He's willing to go public," Gale lied.

Johnson sat back in his chair. "What do you want?"

"You know what I want. I want my own coaching staff. I want you and Voss and everyone else to quit screwing with me."

"That's not going to happen."

"Then I go to the press. I get my source to go on record. A cover up? I ruin you, Voss, and everyone else in this circus. I bring the League down."

"Ruin us?"

"That's what I said."

"Even if it's true about Adams and the other coaches, you'll never pin it on me and Vernon. Maybe I should call the FBI? This sounds like blackmail, McClanahan."

"You want to do that," Gale said, "go ahead. I told you; I have a credible source. He's willing to go on record. He's got all the facts. So go ahead and make the call."

Johnson looked away for an instant. "You think you got us by the shorthairs?"

"I know I do."

"You seem to be forgetting the stolen credit card."

"You think people are going to believe that after the media pounces on a gambling scandal?" Gale paused. "I told you what I want."

Johnson smiled slightly. "Yes, you did."

"If Adams and the other coaches aren't gone by noon, I'm going public."

"You're going to make Mr. Voss very unhappy."

"Noon," Gale said, rising out of his chair.

"You'll be coaching the team alone," Johnson said. "Because of your stunt, we're going to have a payroll full of ex coaches. You'll never find a staff before training camp."

"That's a problem I welcome trying to solve."

"McClanahan."

"What?"

"You're about to make the worst mistake of your life."

"That's not true," Gale said, leaving. "The worst mistake I ever made was when I let you and Voss sit at my kitchen table."

***

"It's been nice knowing you," Cutler said, when Gale appeared after his meeting with Johnson.

"I'm not gone yet," Gale said.

For an instant, Cutler's poker face fell away. She looked surprised. Gale sensed she was relieved. "I'm still your boss."

"God help me," she said.

"I want a players' meeting at noon. . . team conference room. Tell Donta I want to see him now."

Cutler looked astonished.

"Ms. Cutler . . ."

"What?"

"Since I'm not going anywhere, perhaps it's time we start being a team?"

***

Donta Jones' eyes clouded when Gale told him about Adams and his meeting with Johnson. Jones had a look of contempt as Gale shared what he knew about Adams and the other coaches.

"It explains a lot," Jones said. "Those skunks."

"It's you and me."

"You got your chance to walk now. They'll have to pay you. You can go back to West Texas a rich man."

Gale's eyes fixed on Jones. "They'll find another way to mess with me, Donta. There's no way out of this but to see it through. Besides, when push comes to shove, it's all conjecture. Two law school buddies sharing conspiracy theories over a bottle of whiskey. For better or worse, I'm the coach of the San Antonio Lone Stars."

"Amen."

"Whoever heard of a pro football coaching staff with only two coaches?" Gale asked, shifting the conversation, trying to shake the thought of Voss, Johnson, and the Commissioner of the League plotting venomously against him.

Jones shook his head. "It's a better scenario than what we had."

"I guess."

"What are you going to tell the players?"

"Adams and his cronies quit."

Donta smiled. "Okay."

***

The players assembled at noon. Practices had been turned on its head. While thirty-one other teams had been team building, installing the playbook, evaluating players before the start of training camp in July, and setting the tone for the upcoming season, the Lone Stars had been mired in dysfunction and strife. Ordinarily, the day would have begun with early morning meetings, players working out under the demanding eyes of the strength and conditioning coaches, practice, and more meetings. Four full days of required practices would allow coaches to evaluate the roster and players to get a feel for expectations and demands.

Instead, the turmoil had cost Gale valuable time in a league where there never was enough. When Gale confirmed Adams and the other coaches were out, the players looked at each other in disbelief. The room was silent until McCann Foster, an outside linebacker, who had played with the Lone Stars the year before, stood and eyed Gale and Jones.

"How are we gonna win with two coaches?" Foster asked. "It's crazy."

Gale glanced at Jones and turned back to Foster. "By training camp, we'll have a full staff," Gale said. "I promise you."

For an instant, Jones looked at Gale as if to say, "How are we going to do that?"

Foster shook his head. Gale had noticed on film Foster was one of the few bright spots the previous season. He was tough and smart and outspoken. He had a scar running across his chin, a shaved head, and had been drafted low out of Grambling.

"I thought this was the League," Foster said. "We're sitting here talking when we should be out on the field. Our coaching staff leaves, and we got a high school..." He stopped, realizing what he was about to say.

Gale nodded. "It's okay. You can say it. A high school coach who doesn't know lick."

Foster shook his head. "Sorry coach, but all of us are wondering how you got this job. We don't know whether to feel sorry for you or for us."

"Maybe both?"

The players started smiling.

"I've got a lot to prove," Gale said.

"Yup," Foster answered.

"This's how it's going to be," Gale said. "We have two days left of required practice. We're going to make the most of it. Coach Jones and I are going to need your help. We can't be everywhere, but we can start getting to know each other."

"I got an idea for team harmony, Coach," Deshay Anderson said from the back of the room. "How about a barbeque?"

Matt Abruzzi threw his head back and laughed.

Gale thought for a moment. Really, Deshay? A barbeque? We lost 16 games last year. He sensed a lightness in the room and an opportunity. Gale shifted gears. "You grilling for ninety players, Deshay?"

Anderson broke into a smile. "We got it, man. I been wanting a cook-out for a long time."

Jones turned to Gale. "Who's bringing the beer?"

Gale grinned, capturing the moment. "I am. You might need a lot of alcohol this year, guys. You gotta high school coach who doesn't know his ass from his elbow."

The players burst into laughter.

When the players had left the team conference room, Jones shook his head.

"How are we going to build a coaching staff by training camp?"

Gale said, "We'll have to figure it out."

"There's not a coach out there who will want to join this mess."

Gale nodded.

"Beer and a barbeque?" Jones smiled, putting his hand on Gale's shoulder. "It's going to be one hell of a season."

"We got to start somewhere, Donta."

CHAPTER 22

Practice had been hard to organize. Two coaches, ninety players. Despite the constraints, Gale had tried to run a productive and brisk session. Jones took the offense and Gale the defense. A few of the veterans helped run drills. Gale and Jones stuck to teaching fundamentals. They would get to the playbook when/if they had a coaching staff when training camp began.

Gale could tell immediately the pace had picked up from the day before and the players had more bounce in their step. There was a positive vibe. Gone was the screaming and yelling, the bullying, and the chaos Adams had rained down on the team. Gale kept his voice calm, despite a sinking feeling the roster was beyond mediocre. While player speed was a drastic change from the high school teams he'd coached, he knew from his own experience with Atlanta, and after watching hours of tape, the Lone Stars were a bad team. Even practicing in shorts and helmets during minicamp, Gale realized the players lacked fundamentals, and most of all, talent.

Gale recalled what famed coach Bum Phillips had said. "You gotta make average players good and good players great" to win. Gale wondered on a June afternoon under a cloudless sky and a hot sun, with an organization in disarray, a roster built to lose, no coaching staff, and an owner who wanted to destroy him, how he was going to get blood from a rock. He didn't have anyone to film practice but for a kid in his early twenties with purple hair and a permanent slouch, who spent most of his time mowing the field and fighting with his girlfriend on his cell phone. There was no team staff, only an old guy who purported to be a certified athletic trainer, who spent more time sneaking cigarettes under the overhang by the field entrance than he did treating the players. The team doctor was nowhere to be found.

After a series of shuttle runs to end practice, Abruzzi had trotted up to Gale, and said, "We gotta get more coaches."

Gale nodded.

"But practice was positive, Coach." He grinned. "I could feel the love."

Gale smiled.

"You really buying beer for our cook-out?"

"Yes." With a sinking feeling, Gale wondered how he was going to justify the expense to Marybeth. She disapproved of alcohol, and with only her meager earnings supporting the family, they had started to run up the credit card. Marybeth had been putting Gale's paychecks in an escrow account, not to be touched. Gale had no plans to spend Grayson Wallace's $50,000. The thought of charity shamed him.

"How about the good stuff?" Abruzzi asked.

"Such as?"

"I was thinking IPA."

Gale shook his head. "Not a chance."

"Come on coach . . ." Abruzzi said, walking alongside Gale toward the Complex. "This is the League. We don't drink swill."

"The next thing you'll be asking for is caviar."

"Maybe. We gotta start setting our sights higher around here."

"How about we start by executing plays?"

Abruzzi smiled. "The playbook's a piece of crap."

Gale nodded. "It sure is."

"What are we going to do?"

"I don't know, but I'll tell you one thing, we won't need charcoal tonight. We got enough playbooks to start a bonfire."

"I'm all over it," Abruzzi said. "I'll bring the matches and the lighter fluid."

"You do that, Matt. Like I said, I'll bring the beer."

***

Gale stepped off the field and walked toward the Complex's entrance. Three beat writers and a local sportscaster and cameraman were waiting for him.

"I thought we were meeting in the conference room?" Gale asked.

One of the beat writers said, "It's locked. Sam Lorenzo said there wasn't going to be any media access today. He said you didn't want to meet with us. That's a violation of League policy."

Another reporter faced Gale and shoved his microphone in Gale's face. "Is it true you fired the coaching staff?"

"They resigned."

"Lorenzo told us there were questions about the coaches not wanting to work for you, so they walked."

Gale shook his head. "He can say whatever he wants. By training camp, a new staff will be in place. I promise you that."

Another reporter pushed forward. "How are you going to hire a staff before training camp?"

"I'll figure it out."

"There are questions about you, Coach. People around the League are wondering if you know what you're doing."

Gale eyed the reporter. "You all can be the judge. I don't worry about what other people think."

"Why didn't Donta Jones resign with the other coaches?"

"He's an outstanding coach."

"What are you suggesting about the rest of the staff?"

Gale could feel the reporters begin to push closer, smelling blood. "I'm focused on winning. I'm not talking about the past. New season, guys."

"Are you still going to go for it on fourth down?"

"We'll see."

"What's your relationship like with Garvin Johnson and Vernon Voss?" a reporter asked.

Gale looked up and focused. "It's never been better," Gale said, trying to hide his contempt.

"Haden said the same thing. He's selling real estate now."

"Like I told you," Gale said, before walking away, "new season."

***

Johnson waited in Vernon Voss' spacious living room. Built with hardwood floors and a cavernous ceiling, and decorated with overstuffed chairs, sofas, hickory tables, and richly patterned Navajo rugs, the room embodied Voss' western roots. Johnson stared at one of a handful of Voss' priceless paintings by Frederic Remington. The vivid scene portrayed a cowboy clinging to an upright stallion while a ranch hand scrambled out of the way. Voss' 10,000 square foot ranch house sat on a 27-acre compound.

Through the large ceiling to floor windows, Johnson could see Vanessa step out of the infinity pool wearing a black bikini in the dying light. Her wet hair was slicked back behind her ears, and she slowly reached for a towel resting on a patio chair before gliding into another wing of the house. He pulled his eyes away when Voss stepped into the room.

They eased themselves into chairs facing one another. Voss smirked.

"Our boy's gone rogue, huh?" Voss asked.

"What do you think, Vernon?"

"I think McClanahan did us a favor."

Johnson leaned back.

"It's even better that Buddy and the staff are gone."

"How so?"

"McClanahan's got no coaches and no clue and less than a month before training camp starts."

"What about his threats?"

"If it comes down to that, I'll take care of him," Voss said. "Play it out, Garvin. McClanahan has what he wants now. Even if the story does break, it'll get us closer to getting out of the lease. A story about a coaching staff throwing games is going to infuriate fans. They'll stay away from the team in droves."

"It'll be a shit storm."

"Tate already called me when he heard Adams and the staff resigned."

"What did you say?" Johnson asked.

"I told him we spin it. McClanahan can't get along with anybody. He doesn't know squat. We gave him full control of the coaching staff, and he fired them against our better judgment a month before training camp."

Johnson nodded and rubbed his knee. An old college football injury.

Voss said, "Betting? Gambling? We never heard . . . if it goes public, we'll tell everyone we're shocked and appalled. We launch an investigation with the League and look pro-active."

"What about Buddy and the other coaches? They'll talk."

Voss looked at Johnson with rheumy eyes. "You think anyone's going to believe a greedy, corrupt bunch of coaches? Even if they did, it'll never be proved. There isn't a shred of evidence that we knew anything about it."

"Buddy knows. Vernon, he's your son-in-law."

"Fuck him," Voss sneered.

"How do we handle McClanahan?"

"We keep letting him fail."

"If he causes more trouble?"

"I have my ways," Voss said, rubbing his chin, his red eyes narrowing.

"I don't trust him," Johnson said.

Voss' eyes bore into Johnson's. "I don't trust anyone, Garvin."

***

In the end zone, Deshay Anderson and his teammates grilled enough hot dogs and hamburgers to feed an army. Smoke and flames billowed from the grills. Anderson wore a chef's hat and a crazy-colored, tie-dyed apron as tunes blared from the field's rickety sound system. The players sat near the end zone in the cool of the evening and inhaled cole slaw, potato salad, hot dogs, and burgers.

Gale and Jones watched them in silence. Gale's head pounded. He had a sharp, knifing pain behind his eyes. A warm, unfinished bottle of beer sat in the grass next to him. He knew he'd kicked a hornet's nest. Johnson and Voss would be gunning for him. It was going to get uglier.

When the sun had finally set, the players had left. The beer had run out.

CHAPTER 23

The absence of light made the moon and stars appear brighter and made Gale focus on the road ahead. A few miles before, a small herd of mule deer had stood in the middle of the empty interstate, caught in Gale's headlights until narrowly bolting away. Gale had left San Antonio that afternoon, and now he was making the long trek home to Kinney. For coaching staffs around the League, the period between required practices and training camp offered the only respite to a never-ending grind. Coaches spent time with their families, went to the beach, fished, golfed, and watched their children's soccer and Little League games, trying to slip into the routine of family life. The time was as close to a vacation as a coach could find. Training camp rosters were set, expectations understood, and systems learned.

As he drove across the Permian Basin, Gale knew there would be no time off. He'd already found it impossible to lure anyone onto the Lone Stars' coaching staff. He and Jones had made calls around the fringes of the League, trying to coax a handful of unemployed assistants to accept positions. With Johnson's refusal to offer salaries, Gale had no money to pay them. Making it even harder, Gale knew word had spread about the team's scarcity of talent, internal strife, and possible move to another city. No sane coach wanted to touch the organization, especially with a former high school football coach in charge.

Gale tapped the steering wheel with his forefinger. His dread grew as he neared Kinney. He hadn't seen Marybeth and Til in nearly a month. The conversations with Marybeth had grown tense as they discussed their worsening financial situation. Adding to the tension, Gale had made it clear Grayson Wallace's $50,000 would sit untouched in their bank account. He thought of his mother and father, living the last decade of their adult lives under a cloud of debt, working to the bone trying to keep the ranch from creditors. While Wallace was a good man, Gale didn't want his money. But Gale realized his stubbornness could hurt his marriage beyond repair. He'd already put his family in enough trouble.

The day before, Marybeth had snapped at Gale when she saw the credit card charge on her computer for over $700 worth of beer.

"I can barely pay the bills," she'd said. "You spend over two months' worth of groceries on booze?"

Gale had stayed silent.

"Gale, I can't keep feeding our daughter rice and beans."

As a tractor trailer passed, for an instant, Gale wished he could keep driving into New Mexico. The thought of tension with Marybeth made his stomach knot.

He knew the time until training camp would be anything but restful. He needed coaches, a new playbook, better players, and to protect himself and his family. While he was able to manipulate Adams' and the other coaches' resignations, he realized he had little leverage on Johnson and Voss. He knew they were building a fortress of deniability. It was in their DNA.

Gale's phone started to chime. The number was unidentified. He let the call slide to voicemail. After a few minutes, he realized someone had left a message. Gale listened on speaker phone. It was Catherine Reiser, Mayor Andujar's Chief of Staff.

Reiser said in a husky voice, "Mayor Andujar's concerned, Gale. He read you fired your coaching staff. Maybe that's a good thing, but three weeks before training camp? That's unheard of. Mayor Andujar can't have this thing fall apart. Understand? Remember the conversation he had with you at the Gala? He meant it. He doesn't want to see the team move, Gale. Voss can't win. He's depending on you. There's a lot riding here ..."

Gale hit delete and focused on the road. He was 110 miles from Kinney. He fantasized again about driving into New Mexico and leaving it all behind. He knew he couldn't do it. He'd never run before . . .

***

When Gale pulled up to the house, he saw Marybeth had left on the porch light. He quietly entered and set his duffel on the living room floor. For a moment, he stood in the dark. He could hear the soft whirl of the air conditioner, and from the kitchen, the clank of the ice maker in the fridge. They had been familiar sounds in a past life. He wanted nothing more than to return to what he knew.

After brushing his teeth and washing his face, he stripped down to his boxers and climbed into bed. He could hear Marybeth's soft breaths as she slept. Gale turned to her, hoping she would wake for a moment and acknowledge him.

When she didn't, he closed his eyes and tried to drift off to sleep.

***

Barbara Engle had placed several folding chairs and rectangular tables covered in checkered cloth under a large elm and Bur oak in her backyard. A country western track played in the background. On a table near the small swimming pool, a large tray of cold fried chicken sat next to an ample dish of potato salad, a platter stacked with corn, a basket of rolls, and a heaping bowl of salad. Pitchers of ice water and tea sat on the tables. On another table, a sheet cake rested. The words "Finally! Retirement!" were written in loopy blue frosting across the swath of vanilla frosted cake. The words reflected Barbara's sentiment. She'd eagerly looked forward to the day her husband retired. Now they would be free to see grandkids in

Houston and Denver. Travel. Jack could devote himself to caring for the yard and the flower beds circling the house. Barbara had grown tired of ankle high grass, dead leaves, and weeds encroaching upon her precious beds filled with an assortment of iris, mistflower, zinnias, and salvia.

She and Jack had finished the school year together. She'd taught Gale's math classes, Jack had handed the senior class its diplomas for the final time, and now they were free after forty plus years of devotion to students. It was an odd feeling. Barbara's unease grew. She knew her husband enough to know he was lost in his new world.

Of all the well-wishers who had turned out for the party, she'd watched Gale carefully. He'd lost weight and looked tired. Gale had arrived in Kinney the night before. Barbara had noticed tension between Marybeth and Gale when they had arrived at Jack's party. No words were spoken, but Barbara could tell things weren't right. Coaching the Lone Stars was turning out to be a nightmare for Gale. Jack and Barbara had gone out to dinner with Grayson Wallace and his wife, Dot, and after a few bourbons, Wallace had told them about the contract, the dysfunction, the terrible way the owner was treating Gale. It made her upset. At first, Barbara wondered why Gale hadn't told her and Jack about his circumstances. But she knew Gale well enough to know he was ashamed of how his decision to take the job with the Lone Stars had hurt his family.

Gale and Marybeth were like her own children. She'd watched them grow up, start teaching careers, marry, and raise Tilly. They were proud, grounded West Texas people who gave and never took. Now they found themselves with dwindling funds and an uncertain future. She worried about the strain on their marriage and what it might do to them.

Barbara set her eyes on her husband. He held a glass of ice water in his hand as friends and neighbors swirled around him with congratulations. After graduation, he'd seemed subdued, as if the reality of retirement was sinking in. Barbara tried to read his emotions. She sensed he was already restless. He wasn't the type to sit all morning in the local breakfast place, drink watery coffee, swap war stories, tell off-color jokes, and solve the world's problems. He didn't play golf, and he disliked hunting and fishing. She'd realized Jack and Gale had many things in common, but essentially, they were quiet, private men, who despite their public positions, had carefully preserved their privacy. As principal and football coach in Kinney, Jack and Gale had been subject to scrutiny and criticism. Now they were both in unfamiliar territory, Barbara thought.

**

The fight with Marybeth had begun before breakfast. Gale had taken Til to get a donut and had-returned to find Marybeth sitting at the kitchen table wearing a robe with her hair up in a ponytail, the checkbook and a stack of bills in front of her.

Tilly had a smear of jelly and powdered sugar on her cheek, and Gale noticed Marybeth's eyes clouding as they entered the kitchen.

"How was the jelly donut?" Marybeth asked, irritated. "Not a great breakfast for a four-year old."

Gale held a paper coffee cup in his hand from the diner and shook his head. He sat down across from Marybeth. Tilly exited the kitchen and made a beeline for the living room. Gale could hear Til switch on the television and the sound of Saturday morning cartoons.

"We can't pay these bills, Gale," Marybeth said, pointing at them.

Gale stayed silent.

"We have $520,000 in pay from the Lone Stars we can't touch. Five hundred and twenty thousand dollars, Gale. We have less than $200 in our checking account. Our savings are running out, and our credit card is near the limit. What now?"

For an instant, Gale looked away.

"Have you checked the refrigerator? We can't live on a bottle of tabasco sauce and a stick of butter."

"I'm sorry, Marybeth," Gale said searching for words.

"Sorry isn't going to pay the bills."

Gale's face flushed.

"I took a summer job," Marybeth said, her eyes penetrating his. "I'm babysitting for the Huskins." Stella and Eugene Huskins lived a few miles outside of town. They had three children under the age of twelve. Eugene was an oil and gas executive, and Stella was a pediatrician in Midland.

"What about Til?" Gale asked.

"They said she can be with me during the day. The job pays $18 an hour."

For a moment, Gale closed his eyes. He was a professional football coach, and his wife was reduced to babysitting to support them.

"I don't like it," Gale said.

"You think I do?" Marybeth snapped.

"There's got to be another way."

"There isn't unless we use Grayson's money to meet our obligations."

"We can't, Marybeth," Gale said, his voice tired and scratchy.

"Why not? He's trying to help us, Gale. This is no time for pride."

"But –"

"But what? Someone has to pay the bills," she said. "Look at us. We have no money. I never see you. You aren't around to help. Your employers are trying to destroy us. You won't take Grayson's money to make things easier?"

"I don't like it," Gale said.

"You think I do? If you have better ideas how to pay bills and put food on the table, let me know. I'm all ears."

"Marybeth . . ." Gale said, trying to control his frustration.

"You got us into this mess, you get us out." Her voice was steely.

Gale rose from the table.

"It's true."

"You know better."

"Where are you going?" she asked.

"To cut the lawn."

"There's no gas left for the mower."

"I'll clean the gutters."

"That won't pay the bills."

"No, but it'll get me outside so I can think."

"You think, Gale. In the meantime, I'll try to figure out how to keep us from going bankrupt."

***

After dropping Tilly at a neighbor's, Marybeth and Gale drove in silence to the Engle's to celebrate Jack's retirement. They were anything but in a celebratory mood. Gale thought back with regret to the morning he'd climbed on the turboprop to fly to San Antonio.

When they arrived at the Engle's, they broke apart and went in different directions. Gale found himself trying to paint an optimistic picture when folks cornered him to ask about the Lone Stars. He noticed Grayson Wallace holding court by the swimming pool. He tried to find Marybeth among the well-wishers. He yearned for her easy smile, and the playful look she would get when they were together. Like him, she looked tired and worried. The thought of Marybeth babysitting tore at him.

Gale moved away from the group of men talking about the upcoming high school football season and the team's new coach, who Jack Engle had hired a few weeks before graduation. Gale moved through the crowd and felt someone softly grab his arm. He turned and found Barbara Engle looking into his eyes with concern.

"Let's go talk in the house, Gale," she said. "I'm worried about you."

Gale shook his head and reluctantly followed.

They went into the kitchen and leaned against the counters facing one another.

"Grayson told us what's going on," Barbara said.

Gale nodded. So much for attorney-client privilege, he thought.

"While I wish you'd told us, I understand why you didn't." She paused a beat. "You know we're here to help."

Gale looked away for a moment and said, "I'm miserable, Barbara."

She smiled sadly. "So isn't Jack," she said, "if you haven't noticed. He hates retirement already, doesn't he?"

Gale nodded. "Jack's no good at doing nothing."

"I know," she said. "It's ruining my preconceived notion of the golden years."

"I watched him out there." Gale pointed at the kitchen window facing the backyard. "He looks as rotten as I feel."

"Marybeth?"

He shook his head. "I got to figure a way out of this mess."

"Take Grayson's money," Barbara said.

Wallace must have told her and Jack everything. Small town.

"I can't."

"Take it."

"It's charity."

"Look at it as a bank loan. Pay Grayson back."

Gale stared off. He thought of his parents' struggle to fight off creditors.

"Is pride worth your marriage?" Barbara asked.

Barbara's directness struck him.

"Marriages are fragile, Gale. They can unravel fast."

For a moment, Gale pondered what Barbara had said. He spotted Engle through the kitchen window drift off by himself and start picking up paper plates that were discarded on the tables. As he studied Engle, an idea flashed through Gale's mind. He wanted to kick himself for not thinking about it before. He looked at Barbara and gave a half smile.

"You're right. It isn't worth my marriage," Gale said.

Barbara's expression brightened and she nodded.

"You're going to be angry with me, Barbara," Gale warned.

"I know what you're thinking, Gale McClanahan."

"It's the best idea I've come up with in a long time."

***

In the evening, when the party had ended, and the cicadas had struck up a chorus, Gale helped Engle stack tables and folding chairs into the back of Engle's pickup. Barbara had borrowed the tables and chairs from the high school and Engle motioned for Gale to climb into the cab.

"Let's take 'em back," Engle said. "It looks like Barbara and Marybeth aren't going anywhere soon."

Gale could see Marybeth and Barbara sitting by the pool deep in conversation.

"Do you still have keys to get into the school?" Gale asked.

Engle held up his key chain. "Still do. I need to give them back."

***

They rode silently with the windows down feeling the warm breeze. The two-lane ribbon that was U.S. Highway 16 ran straight and flat past scattered homes into

116

Kinney. They drove down Main Street with its one stoplight, gas station, diner, and brick buildings until they turned off to the high school.

Engle backed up to a service entrance by the cafeteria, and he and Gale lugged the tables and chairs to a storage closet off the kitchen. When they finished, Gale said, "Do you have a few minutes to talk?"

Engle nodded.

They sat in the football stadium bleachers. With the sun setting in the hazy open sky and shadows running across the field, sprinklers swept back and forth irrigating the turf. For a moment, Gale gazed down on the field thinking about all he'd lost. When Engle broke the silence, he shifted to the present.

"Grayson told us what's going on," Engle said, shaking his head. "I wish you felt like you could have come to us."

"I don't know how to put it in words, Jack."

"Sounds like you're wrestling with bulls."

"Snakes," Gale said. Gale shook his head and turned to Engle. "I need your help."

Engle's expression shifted. He looked concerned and confused.

"I got less than three weeks until training camp."

Engle remained silent.

"I need you to be my offensive coordinator."

Engle sat back. He paused a beat. "I haven't coached football since you took over for me."

"I need you, Jack." Gale's eyes bore into Engle's. "I got to have someone I trust. I'm in a bad place. You coached for years. You played for Dallas."

Engle gave a slight grin. "I played with a leather helmet. The level of sophistication now. . . everything's changed."

"It's still football, Jack. It's still trying to put the ball in the endzone and keeping the other team from scoring."

Engle shook his head. "Even if I agreed, how are you going to hire the rest of your staff?"

"You know everyone who's ever coached in the State of Texas. We build a staff with people we trust."

"It sounds far-fetched. A Hail Mary, Gale."

"It's all I got."

"How's the roster? As bad as I'm hearing?"

"Ugly."

"How am I going to learn and teach a playbook in three weeks?"

"You're not."

Engle lifted an eyebrow.

"We start from scratch. We stick to basics, and we run our own system."

"In the League?"

"We have a team filled with cast-off veterans and rookie free agents. Expectations are low, Jack. Lower than I've ever seen. We start simple and stay simple."

"Simple doesn't win in the League."

"Right now, it's about surviving."

Engle looked off before turning to Gale. "Barbara . . ."

"Jack, if I didn't know better, I'd say she was the one who planted the idea into my head," Gale said.

Engle smiled. "I'm no good at retirement."

"You'll take it?" Gale asked.

Engle's smile grew. "I don't suppose I have a choice. Maybe we can save each other. Besides, Gale, you're like a son to me."

CHAPTER 24

As they drove home in the darkness, Marybeth broke the silence. They had barely spoken to one another the entire day and had made sure to avoid each other at Jack Engle's party.

"What did you and Jack talk about?" she asked coolly, probing to find some form of truce, looking away, staring out the passenger-side window.

"Football."

"What a surprise."

"He's going to help me, Marybeth."

"Help you?"

"He agreed to join my staff."

She turned to Gale. He could see the outline of her face lit by the dashboard. "Jack?"

"That's right."

"What about Barbara?"

"The way he's handling retirement, she'll be thrilled."

"How're you going to pay him?"

"He doesn't care about the money."

"The other coaches?"

"I haven't figured that out yet."

Marybeth paused.

"Have you thought anymore about how we're going to pay the bills?" she asked, yet unlike earlier in the day, with a hint of understanding.

"At the party, I told Grayson we're going to pay back every cent."

Marybeth leaned back in her seat, sighing with relief. She took a deep breath. "I know that was hard, Gale. I wasn't being fair this morning."

"No, you were right. I got us into this mess," Gale said, "and it's easy to see that I need all the help I can get to get us out of it."

"Even with Grayson's money, I'm still going to babysit for the Huskins."

Gale winced.

"We need every dollar we can get."

Gale shifted the conversation.

"Marybeth," Gale said.

"Yes."

Gale turned to her. His hands gripped the wheel. "We're going to be alright. I promise."

"You think?"

119

C.W. WELLS

"When Jack said 'yes,' I suddenly felt a whole lot better."

***

When they got home, Gale went into the backyard under the swath of stars dotting the jet-black sky. His face was lit by the glow of his phone, and a warm wind rustled the handful of shade trees on the property. The cicadas buzzed. He punched up Donta Jones' number.

"I found an offensive coordinator," Gale said, hearing Jones turn down the television in the background.

"No kidding?"

"Who is he?"

Gale told Jones about Jack Engle. He shifted.

"How does Donta Jones, Defensive Coordinator sound?" Gale asked.

"Like a bigger paycheck."

"Fat chance."

"You want me to run the defense?"

"I do."

"What if we give up fifty points a game?"

"I have your back," Gale said. "Will you take it?"

"I've been waiting to be a defensive coordinator for forty years."

"Well, you got it now."

"Lord, have mercy."

"Donta?"

"What, Boy Wonder."

"I figure we got to hire 10 more assistants."

"It'll be the smallest coaching staff in the League," Jones said.

"Then we better make it the smartest."

"I'll tell you what. You hired Einstein to coach the defense," Jones laughed.

"The only problem is what to do with the dumbass who took the job of Head Coach."

"True."

***

Grayson Wallace chortled as Gale and Engle read from a list of coaching candidates.

"He moved to Mexico after his third divorce. Hell of a high school football coach, though," Wallace said. A small glass of whiskey rested on his desk in his dusty, cluttered office overlooking Main Street. It wasn't noon yet. Wallace wore a bright red bow tie and suspenders, and his shock of white hair was mussed. He was relishing being part of the conversation to pick a coaching staff.

120

"He had a drinking problem," Engle said, eyeing the whiskey on Wallace's desk. "It came hand-in-hand with womanizing."

"Scratch him off the list?" Gale asked.

Engle nodded. Without hesitation, Wallace took a sip of whiskey.

"How about Billy Coyne?" Gale asked, focusing on the list of names from an outdated version of Who's Who in Texas High School Football.

"Alzheimer's," Engle said, shaking his head.

"C.J. Black?" Gale asked.

"Dead," Wallace grunted.

"Will McCoy?"

"He's a superintendent in Brownsville," Engle said.

"Clem Pratt?" Gale asked.

Engle leaned forward. "He'd be near the top of my list. Been retired for about six years."

"Worth a call." Gale wrote down Pratt's name.

"How about Rulon Alexander?" Wallace belted out. "Won more games in East Texas than anyone."

Engle smiled. "Rulon . . . I hadn't thought about him."

Gale eyed both. "Inside joke?"

"Made a name for himself in the 1974 Sugar Bowl," Wallace said. "Threw five interceptions against Alabama in the National Championship. After the game, he sidled up to Bear Bryant at midfield and bowed to the great one. One of the most famous photos in sports history. Front cover of *Sports Illustrated*."

"A character?" Gale asked.

"Funny man. Great coach," Engle said. "Need to call him."

The conversation lasted until the early afternoon. The three of them had compiled 17 names. Engle and Gale began calling after Wallace took them for lunch at a dingy BBQ joint on the edge of town. The offers were punctuated by stunned silence and disbelief. There were lots of questions. Gale and Engle explained the situation carefully. The question of salary only came up once. Retired and out of the game they loved, most of the coaches they called had long put football aside, and to be asked to coach in the League three weeks before training camp was met by skepticism, but soon the thought of coaching again at the game's highest level, even if it was the most dysfunctional team in the League, was too hard for most of them to turn down. It was an opportunity to compete again, to feel alive, and to be needed. During the calls, Gale could feel their desire to help a young, struggling head coach. A high school coach. One of them.

By late evening the next day, Gale and Engle had assembled a staff.

***

C.W. WELLS

The coaches came from all over Texas, places where the game was a religion: Pilot Point, Del Rio, Victoria, San Angelo, Cisco, Crockett, Goliad, and Big Spring. Wallace, Engle, Donta Jones, and Gale agreed the newly assembled staff would meet in Kinney, far away from the scrutiny and interference of Johnson and Voss and the prying eyes of the media. There had been calls and texts from reporters about the Lone Star coaching staff "quitting." Gale let them go unanswered. He had a plan. He had no intention of showing his cards. Barbara, Marybeth, and Wallace's wife, Dot, a force of nature in her own right, found their homes turned into boarding houses. Wallace, thrilled to be doing something away from the tedium of practicing law, wrote the check for meals. Yet the coaches were rarely present. Engle and Gale had set-up two classrooms at the high school, one for each side of the ball.

They had spent the first two days discussing how to approach training camp. Gale and Donta Jones had given the coaches an in-depth view of the roster. They had shown film of returning veterans. They had discussed the rookies and collectively had shaken their heads. They had talked about ways to organize training camp and how to squeeze the most out of each day given how far behind they were. They had discussed their strengths and weaknesses as a staff and had willingly taken on assignments with resolve. Finally, with Gale leading the conversation, they had settled upon a philosophy and planted the seeds for a playbook.

Gale had marveled at the difference. Only days earlier, he'd been butting heads with Buddy Adams, in a death struggle for control of the team, and now he was working with coaches who had long ago put their egos away and wanted only to help Gale and coach on the biggest sporting stage in America. While he was under no illusions, he felt relief to be among his own.

After the first day of meetings, Rulon Alexander had pulled Gale aside. Alexander was in his early 70's, but he still had a hint of impishness that led to him and Bear Bryant gracing the cover of *Sports Illustrated* after his disastrous bowl game. Alexander had a bald patch on the crown of his head, gray hair chopped closely to his scalp, and a deep drawl. He grew up in Killeen, and after a stint in the Marine Corps, returned home to teach and coach. The rest had been Texas high school football history.

Alexander, who had agreed to be the quarterback coach, smiled and poked Gale in the chest. "Has Abruzzi taken out a death policy?"

"Death policy?"

"You know, life insurance."

"You better ask him."

"Cause if we don't build a wall around that ole boy, he's DOA."

"Pretty bad, huh," Gale said.

"Let's hope a couple of those undrafted rookie free agents can block."

"Let's hope."

"Cause if they can't," Alexander smiled, "Abruzzi's head is going to be mounted on a wall."

CHAPTER 25

Gale arrived at the Pump and Drill Diner in the center of Kinney in the early morning to pick up donuts and coffee for the coaches. It was a few minutes past five and the doors had just swung open. The place was nearly deserted. Soon it would be full of oil and gas field hands, ranchers, merchants, and whoever else needed a jolt of coffee and a hot breakfast. In the corner, unshaven with a heft of dark whiskers sprouting on a weak chin, Jimmie Peebles sat cradling his coffee. He wore worn Dickies and a threadbare golf shirt with a Kinney High School Warrior embroidered above the breast pocket. When he spotted Gale, he broke into a sad smile. For years, Jimmie had been the equipment manager at Kinney High School before the school system had forced his resignation during a round of district-wide budget cuts. He spent his days drinking coffee and wandering on Main Street. He lived alone in a tiny apartment above the barber shop. A traumatic birth had left him with an eye twitch, a limp, and mentally impaired.

Gale went over to Jimmie's table. Jimmie's left eye fluttered up and down. He smelled mangy. Gale stepped back to avoid another whiff.

"You going to buy me a coffee, Jimmie?" Gale asked.

"You can have mine. Only took one sip," Jimmie answered, earnestly pushing the coffee mug toward Gale.

"No thanks."

Jimmie shifted in his seat. "Is it true Mr. Engle's going to coach the Lone Stars with you?"

"Yup."

Jimmie smiled. "What's it like?"

"What?"

"The League?"

"Challenging," Gale said, not wanting to go any further.

"Coach McClanahan coaching in the League." Jimmie whistled. "I ain't ever seen a pro game in real life. Bet it's fast."

"It's fast alright."

"Those guys are big."

"Yes, they are." Gale noticed Jimmie's oily hair and the grease stains on the front of his shirt. He shifted the subject. "You okay, Jimmie?"

Jimmie looked away for a moment and shook his head. "I got nothin' to do. I miss the equipment room."

"I bet."

"Was like a home to me, Coach." Jimmie's eye twitched.

For a moment, Gale thought about the slouching kid at the Lone Star Complex riding around on the mower, half-heartedly filming practice, arguing with his girlfriend on his phone. Jimmie had his limitations, but if he was told what to do, he got things done. He could film, maintain the equipment room, launder uniforms, fold and stack towels, mop the floor, and deliver a water bottle.

Gale eyed Jimmie. After a few seconds, he broke the silence.

"You ever been to San Antonio?" Gale asked.

"Nope," Jimmie said.

Gale paused.

"How'd you like to work for the Lone Stars?" Gale nearly winced when he said the word "work". There would be no pay, only long hours.

"The Lone Stars?" Jimmie's expression brightened.

"That's what I said."

"The League?"

"You join the staff and run the equipment room. You film practice, do laundry, and anything else we need you to do."

"How much does it pay?" Jimmie said, hopeful.

Gale smiled. "Nothing."

"You kiddin' me?"

"Nope."

"No pay?"

"Not a cent. Will you take it?"

"Where am I goin' to live?"

"We'll figure it out." Gale didn't tell him the coaches made the decision to sleep in their offices at the Complex. Wallace's administrative assistant had already ordered folding cots for each coach. One happy family.

"When do I gotta go?"

"Soon."

"How soon?"

"A couple of weeks."

"Is this true? You ain't kiddin' me?"

"Truer than anything I know, Jimmie."

"This ain't a joke?"

"Nope."

Jimmie flashed a smile, slapped the palm of his hands on the table, and leaned back in his chair. "I'm goin' to be in the League," he said to Nancy, the middle-aged woman behind the counter. "How about that?"

Nancy smiled and shook her head.

"Jimmie," Gale said, "you go home, take a shower, and bring your dirty laundry over to the house."

"You sayin' I stink?"

"I want you cleaned up. If you're going with me to San Antonio, I'm not riding in 100-degree heat with the windows down."

"I smell that bad?"

"Take a shower," Gale said. "Use soap. I want you over at the high school at noon."

"The high school?"

"That's what I said."

"How come?"

"You're part of the team now . . . you need to meet the coaches."

***

Later that afternoon, after Jimmie had dropped off a bag of dirty laundry at Gale's house, Marybeth had shaken her head when she'd come home after a long day of babysitting and spotted the pile of dirty clothes.

She came out of the laundry room holding her nose.

"Gale," she said.

Gale came out of the kitchen. He could hear Tilly racing down the hallway to her room. He was on his way out the door to the high school. More meetings.

"Doing other people's laundry now?" she asked, standing with her hand on her hip.

"Jimmie's."

"Jimmie?" she asked, surprised.

"He's joining the staff."

"He's going to San Antonio?"

"Equipment manager."

"Are you kidding?"

"Not at all."

She rolled her eyes. "Don't leave his laundry sitting on the floor. I can't take it."

"I won't."

"Gale."

"Yes."

"Jimmie? Don't you have enough people to take care of?"

"I felt bad for him," Gale said sheepishly.

She shook her head and gave him a half smile. "God help you, Gale McClanahan."

***

Nearly three weeks later, the Lone Star coaching staff broke camp. They climbed into their cars, SUVs, and pickups and headed east in the high summer

125

heat. Led by Gale, they'd choreographed training camp to the minute, detailed roles and responsibilities, studied hours of game tape, and built a playbook. Despite the organization and efficiency, Gale had the oldest coaching staff in the League and the least experienced. His assistants were wise, seasoned men, but they hadn't coached a down in the League.

Even with the clamoring in the press, the media prying to find out if Gale had built a staff, Gale had continued to ignore the calls and texts. In the period between required practices and training camp, he hadn't heard from Johnson or Voss. They expected him to fail, relished the prospect, and most likely imagined Gale returning to San Antonio empty handed, without a coaching staff. Gale could imagine Johnson looking forward to Gale admitting that he didn't have a staff by saying, "Well, it looks like Buddy and the boys will have to come back. How are you going to coach with no coaches?"

Gale had never been happier to disappoint in his life.

***

Rose Cutler arrived at the Complex and dropped her handbag on her desk. She looked flustered. A cup of hot coffee and a pastry sat next to her computer. She gave Gale a hard look.

"Who are all these men?" she asked. Moments earlier, she'd passed Rulon Alexander and Jack Engle in the hallway. They'd greeted her with a hearty "good morning," a nicety unheard of a few weeks before. She'd walked down the corridor and had noticed the coaches' offices were occupied, and the Complex had come to life with a working-like buzz.

"The coaching staff," Gale replied.

Gale reached into a folder and pulled out several sheets of paper clipped together. Before leaving Kinney, Gale had put together a dossier of the coaches. "It's all the information you need. I emailed you an attachment. Tell Lorenzo I've got a coaching staff. He can let the world know among all the other things he does around here."

Cutler ignored him. "Who bought this?" she asked suspiciously, eyeing the coffee and pastry.

"Compliments of the Lone Star coaching staff. Coach Alexander bought the coffee and pastries this morning."

"No one's ever done that before," she said, lifting her nose and sniffing.

"It's a new day."

"I didn't ask for it," Cutler said.

"No, you didn't."

"Tell whoever did this not to do it again," Cutler said. She hesitated. "What was his name?"

"Coach Alexander."

"Tell him to stop. He's going to make me fat," she said.

"Truly, Ms. Cutler, it's a new era. I hope you can learn to embrace it. Besides, you don't want to hurt anyone's feelings."

"Feelings won't win football games," she said with a harrumph.

***

Sam Lorenzo hovered outside the coaches' conference room. He held the folder Rose Cutler had thrust in his hand with the names and profiles of Gale's new coaching staff. He put his ear to the door and listened. There was no laughter in the room, no crude banter. While Buddy Adams was a prick, he was if anything, colorful, Lorenzo thought. Lorenzo enjoyed the way Adams had disrespected people. His coaches' meetings had been aimless bull sessions, full of profanity, jokes at other people's expense, and juvenile. What Lorenzo heard now had a far different tone. Calm. Measured. Determined. Worst of all, professional.

Lorenzo stepped away and hurried to his office. He scrambled to reach Garvin Johnson before Johnson boarded the plane to return from a General Manager's meeting in New York.

CHAPTER 26

Garvin Johnson had ignored the disdainful looks from 31 other general managers as he sat in the Waldorf Astoria Ballroom. Even though Johnson had been an all-conference tight end at Texas Tech, they had never accepted him anyway. He'd been an outsider and had been hired as Lone Star President and GM because he was an integral and trusted part of Voss' oil and gas empire. Johnson had directed fracking operations for Voss Energy in West Texas, Oklahoma, Wyoming, and as far north as North Dakota. A gas field explosion had killed seven employees and Johnson had been a key player in limiting the fall out. Voss had admired Johnson's ruthlessness and ability to thwart competitors by undercutting them at every turn. Voss had seen Johnson as the perfect fit to manage his professional football team after a series of failed GMs and dismal seasons. Then the oil and gas market had collapsed, and Voss had soon realized he'd chosen the ideal person to help him run the franchise into the dirt.

Before Johnson had stepped out of the Waldorf Astoria to catch an Uber to La Guardia, Curtis Metcalf, New York's GM had blocked his way. Metcalf's large frame filled one of the swinging brass-plated doors. One of eight children from Aliquippa, a dead steel town outside of Pittsburgh, Metcalf had been a defensive tackle for New York before working his way through the front office to become GM.

"It's disgraceful," Metcalf said, shaking his head at Johnson. "You're destroying the integrity of the League."

Johnson stuck his finger in Metcalf's chest and sneered. "You mind your business, Curtis. How many games did you guys win last year?"

New York had suffered at 5-12. Metcalf's face hardened. "I played in this league for eight seasons. I spent the next 15 working my way up so I could do the right thing and build a successful and highly respected program. What you and Vernon are doing is shameful."

"Go cry somewhere else."

"I feel bad for that coach of yours."

"McClanahan?" Johnson laughed.

Metcalf's eyes hardened. "You've put him in a world of hurt."

"You think so?" Johnson said, a cruel smile forming as he stepped around Metcalf to slide through the door.

***

LONESTAR

At the gate waiting for his plane to board, Johnson's irritation grew. Before the energy market crashed, the thought of flying commercial would have been unheard of. Now he was reduced to flying business class. He heard his phone buzz and answered the call. It was Sam Lorenzo. Lorenzo sounded out of breath, as if he'd run up a flight of stairs. The thought of Lorenzo running struck Johnson as absurd.

"Sam?"

"He found a staff, Garvin." Lorenzo sounded alarmed.

Johnson pushed the phone closer to his ear when a gate attendant started droning on about boarding procedures.

"Who did McClanahan find?" Johnson asked.

"A bunch of retired guys. High school coaches from around the state."

"High school?"

"That's what I said."

Johnson broke into a smile. "What are you worked up about, Sam?"

"I didn't think he'd find anyone to coach," Lorenzo said, flustered. "I thought he'd have to bring Buddy and the boys back."

"Sounds like he did the next best thing."

"How's that?"

"Those coaches have never seen a professional football sideline. They'll be as incompetent as McClanahan."

"You think, Garvin?"

"I know. This is a dream come true. It keeps getting better."

"You think?" Lorenzo repeated.

"We won't win a football game, Sam. The Lone Stars are DOA. That's exactly what we want and McClanahan keeps delivering."

"What if they figure out what they're doing?"

"They won't."

"You sure?"

Johnson noticed passengers lining up to board. "It's the League. It isn't Del Rio versus Harlan on a Friday night."

Johnson could hear Lorenzo wheezing. Too many cheap cigars, he thought.

"Sam," Johnson continued, cutting in front of an older female passenger to board, "it's a sure thing."

***

After the call, Lorenzo stepped out of his office into the empty hallway, thought for a moment, and tried to catch his breath. The idea of a new coaching staff had its perks. He would begin picking his spots. A wallet here, a watch there. He rubbed his hands together. He would rob them blind.

***

Deshay Anderson sat on a water bucket with a wet towel wrapped around his head. The morning sun beat down on the practice field. The temperature hovered near 100. Sweat poured down Anderson's face as he tilted his head, aimed a water bottle at his mouth, and squeezed. The team had spent the first 15 minutes running sprints. Some of the veterans were grumbling about the conditioning drills. They had never run so much.

Gale knew that a team running out of gas in the fourth quarter was a recipe for disaster.

He walked around during the practice break checking on the players. He was aware of the dangers of pushing them too hard on a brutally hot morning. He made sure to mandate frequent water breaks. It was the reality of training camp in Texas.

During the first day in helmets and pads, he'd watched Anderson attempt a bullrush and get taken down by a rookie tackle. Anderson was on the wrong side of thirty. Gale knew already his veteran defensive end was a step too slow. Time had snared him. After the play, Gale had caught Donta Jones' eye, and they both understood. Anderson was gone.

The League was cruel. Gale found himself at a loss thinking about cutting Anderson. Gale had found Anderson to be the consummate pro and team builder. Ignoring the heat, Gale looked out at the practice field. No strangers to Texas summers, the assistant coaches, wearing floppy hats, baseball caps, visors, Lone Star shorts and t-shirts, whistles around their necks, and holding laminated practice cards in their hands, walked among the players, checking the mood, asking for feedback, taking a moment or two to make a coaching point to a rookie who needed a reminder about fundamentals, or one of the veterans, who had missed a read. Rulon Alexander and Abruzzi stood talking at midfield, Jones was huddling with a group of safeties, and Engle was picking the offensive line's brain.

For now, the players had reluctantly accepted them mainly because anything but Buddy Adams was an upgrade. But Gale knew the players' willingness to be coached by the staff was fragile. He could imagine Anderson, discovering he was going to be cast off, blowing up in the locker room, sinking morale even further. Anderson had been the grill master, the one who had saved Gale with a sliver of loyalty and a sense of humor, and along with Abruzzi, had walked the team off the ledge. Where did loyalty get you?

Gale looked over and watched Jimmie and the slouchy kid with purple hair refilling water bottles. One of the players was playfully snapping the slouchy kid with a wet towel. The slouchy kid kept back peddling and shielding himself with the palm of his hand.

Gale turned to Anderson.

"We got trouble," Anderson said, pulling the water bottle away from his face and pointing it toward the Complex.

Vernon Voss, Garvin Johnson, and Vanessa stood near the end zone watching. Vanessa wore a light tank top and white shorts, her long slender legs glimmering in the sun.

"Oh, how hot she is," Anderson said, shaking his head. "Nothing but trouble, Coach. A viper. I heard she's got a serious drug problem."

Gale turned back to Anderson, trying to ignore Voss, Johnson, and Vanessa's intrusion on practice.

"Bad, bad news . . ." Anderson continued. "Ole Vernon has his hands full keeping her in line."

"Let's hope he keeps her away from us," Gale said, thinking about the large dent in his truck's side panel, her scalding eyes, roses . . .

"You got that."

"Deshay?" Gale asked, his instincts suddenly getting ahead of logic. He was going to ask Anderson to meet with him after practice to break the news. Better upfront and early. Why wait until after preseason? Why not give Anderson the slim opportunity to catch on with another team?

"What's up?" Anderson looked up and smiled.

Gale shook instinct off, at least for another day. He shifted. "I appreciate all you've done to help bring the team together."

"No worries," Anderson said. "I'm here to serve."

"You got a family, Deshay?"

Anderson broke into a smile. "Three kids."

Gale smiled. "They keep you busy?"

"Yup."

"Big responsibility, isn't it?"

"That's why I keep playing, Coach," Anderson said. "Gotta pay the bills."

Gale thought about his own broken bank account and glanced at his watch. The practice break was nearly over.

"Coach?"

Gale looked up from his watch.

"You ain't going to cut my ass, are you?" Anderson asked.

Gale felt blood rush to his temples. Caught off guard.

"Because if you do, you're goin' to make my wife a very unhappy woman."

"I wouldn't want to do that," Gale said, trying to dodge the conversation.

"They'll be hell to pay," Anderson said, before stripping the towel off his head, putting his helmet on, and standing up. "She likes the paycheck, Coach."

***

Voss eyed the practice field before glancing at Vanessa. Her face was flushed in the heat, and she had a thin line of perspiration above her lip. She wore a bored, slightly agitated expression. He knew what she wanted, and he didn't care anymore if she got it. If he supported her drug habit, she might show a shred of gratitude and stay away from hungry men, who after inhaling her promiscuous scent, found her a willing partner.

Voss turned back to the scrimmage on the field. Johnson stood next to him, wearing wraparound sunglasses, unphased by the heat. The field echoed with the thud of pads colliding, whistles blowing, and coaches peppering players with encouragement.

"0-17," Johnson said. "McClanahan's assistants are older than we are, Vernon."

A few moments later, three players jumped offside. Abruzzi spiked the ball into the turf in frustration. Gale blew his whistle and brought the offense to the middle of the field. A discussion.

"I give you credit," Voss said. "You built the worst team in League history. Look at 'em."

Johnson smiled. "It wasn't easy . . ."

"I bet. Did we sign a punter?"

"We hired a coach who doesn't punt. Remember?" Johnson smiled.

"How could I forget?"

"Anything else you want me to do?" Johnson asked.

"Let 'em implode, Garvin. Let McClanahan do his magic."

Voss turned to Vanessa. "If all goes right, you'll have your rich sugar daddy again."

Behind her sunglasses, Vanessa's expression remained frozen.

"Don't look too excited," Voss said.

"When I see it, I'll believe it," she replied before turning to walk back to the Complex, her curvy backside swishing in the heat.

"How long are you going to put up with it?" Johnson asked, when Vanessa was out of earshot.

"As long as she looks ripe and her panties come off when I tell her," Voss said. "If those things don't happen, she'll end up like the others."

"I hope you had her sign a bullet-proof pre-nup."

"The same shyster who drew up McClanahan's contract worked on it."

Johnson smiled and folded his arms.

"If I divorce her, she won't stand a chance."

CHAPTER 27

A week and a half later, Gale stood at midfield watching Arizona warm-up. The Lone Stars had arrived the day before for their first preseason game after flying on a crowded and battered Boeing 767 charter jet. Some of the players faces had turned ashen when they had climbed aboard, thinking they might never see Phoenix. After arriving, three tired yellow school buses had ferried 90 players and staff to the Blue Haven Inn, where they found rooms with stained bedspreads and the stink of cigarette smoke. The pre-game team meal had been held at a run-down Italian restaurant near the airport that served cold breadsticks and over-boiled pasta. Lorenzo served as the team's traveling secretary, and he seemed unconcerned, Gale thought angrily, with the way the road trip was unfolding when the buses to the stadium had showed up late and the players had milled around for twenty minutes in the blistering August heat.

Gale had already thrown up twice in a grimy bathroom deep in the bowels of the stadium. He threw up before every game he'd ever coached. Marybeth had gotten used to seeing him hurry into the locker room during warm-ups to vomit. His pre-game nerves had become a family joke.

It had been years since Gale had stood on the field in a pro football stadium. In college and his two seasons in the League, he'd grown used to thousands of people in the stands. But he'd forgotten. He looked around for a moment at the fans making their way to their seats, to the upper deck, to the enormous banks of lights illuminating the field and back to the Arizona players going through pre-game drills. It was surreal, as if everything was a dream. His stomach hurt, but there was nothing left but bile. He turned and focused on the Lone Stars warming up. He had to remind himself it was only preseason. A time to get better. Focus on mistakes. Fix them. Evaluate players. Gel with the coaching staff under game conditions. Put Johnson and Voss out of his mind and do what he was put on earth to do: win.

"Abruzzi said he's ready to punt if you need him," Jones said, approaching Gale, his laminated defensive play sheet clutched in his frying-pan like hand. "You sure you don't want to sign a punter?"

"Tell Abruzzi to stay loose," Gale said.

"You're a glutton for punishment."

Gale managed a wary smile.

"Whatever happens, remember Boy Wonder, the TV cameras will always be focused on you. Don't be picking your nose or scratching your balls," Jones said. "This season, you're going to be on ESPN plenty and possibly for all the wrong reasons. You don't need to have Sports Center replaying Gale McClanahan adjusting his underwear or hunting for snot."

"Got it."

"If the headsets go out, which they do more often than you think in the League, take a time-out so we can adjust to hand signals. Remember, it's preseason."

"Anything else, Donta?"

"Look over there," Jones said, pointing to the Lone Stars' bench.

Garvin Johnson stood with his arms folded, wearing a dress shirt and blazer, talking with a sideline reporter, a young, attractive woman with a helmet of blonde hair. Sam Lorenzo stood next to them, smirking, watching the pre-game unfold. Johnson caught Gale's eye and formed a thin smile.

"Johnson's got no shame," Jones said, turning away, shaking his head. "Imagine showing your face in public after putting together the worst roster in the League."

"Imagine ..." Gale said, his voice drifting.

"One last thing."

"Okay," Gale said.

"I got diapers behind the bench."

"Huh?" Gale asked, confused.

"We're gonna need 'em, Coach," Jones laughed. "Give me the high sign if you want a cyanide capsule."

***

The starters had long been pulled from the field as the game clock moved like sludge into the fourth quarter. 47-0 Arizona. There'd been more penalties than Gale could count, broken tackles, busted plays, and a stinking cloud of defeat hung over the Lone Star bench smelling worse than anything Gale could imagine. He hated it. He hated mediocrity. He hated losing. It didn't matter if it were a League preseason or a pee wee game on a Saturday morning, he hated seeing the game played poorly. He dreaded having to face the game tape on the plane ride home.

Jack Engle walked over to Gale during a TV timeout. He pulled his headset off and stuffed his play sheet under his arm.

"We couldn't beat Kinney High School tonight," Engle said. "There's only one way to go."

"Up?"

"That's right."

Gale set his jaw.

The referee blew the whistle, and Gale watched Jimmie and the slouchy kid hurry off the field with their trays of water bottles.

Engle stared hard at Gale. "If there's anyone who can do it, you can."

Engle put his headset back on and walked down the sideline. The players lined up. Another offsides. Suddenly, Gale heard Rulon Alexander, who was up in the coaches' box, bark into his headset. "What a load. . . get me a shovel, cause we're thick in it."

"A shovel?" Jones said into his headset. "We need a backhoe, Rulon."

"Whatever we need," Alexander said, "we ain't got it."

"We better find it," Gale snapped, feeling his ears grow hot.

***

Gale had refused to punt. Out of seven fourth down conversions, the Lone Stars made one first down, on a naked bootleg with a rookie quarterback from Appalachian State, who at the end of training camp, was going to be putting together his resume. A sportswriter for *The Arizona Republic* couldn't resist. It was the first question of the post-game press conference. Standing in the back, Gale noticed Sam Lorenzo smiling. Soon the rest of the media had joined the pack.

Gale stood at the podium, looking stoic and mustering patience. They grilled him until he finished the press conference with a nod and walked out of the room.

"How'd it go?" Jones asked as they walked through the bowels of the stadium to the bus that would take them to the airport.

"Ugly. I'm the dumbest SOB in the League."

"Why not sign a punter? You got enough problems."

Gale turned. "Because I don't believe in it. Simple as that."

"Stubborn." Jones shook his head. "You're making it easy for Johnson and Voss."

"Right now, they're the least of my problems."

"You think?"

"We lost 53-0, Donta. Tell me, what other problem is there?"

***

Before he stepped on the bus, Gale's cell phone chimed. Hesitating, Marybeth asked him how he was doing.

"Not good," he said. "Did you watch the game? We were terrible."

"What did you expect?" she asked, ever the realist.

"Not 53-0."

There was silence before Marybeth continued. "Grayson said he's going to call you. He has ideas. He called me twice during the game and said he was making copious notes."

Gale shook his head and moved out of the way as the players started boarding the bus.

"Gale ..." She hesitated. "The announcers. . . they were harsh."

"No surprise."

"Why don't you give in and punt?"

"Not you, too." Gale sighed and watched Abruzzi limp on the bus, his hair slicked back, and a shiny new bruise pasted on his cheek.

"They said you're way over your head."

"You believe it?"

"Gale, I don't know what to believe anymore," she said.

Gale could feel his cheeks grow hot. His own wife . . ." I got to go. The bus is about to leave."

"Don't take it the wrong way. I didn't mean to say you aren't a great coach."

"Bad timing," Gale said, not certain what to think.

"It's an awful situation, Gale. All around."

"It is," he said curtly.

"Now I've ticked you off."

"I'm not angry, Marybeth, just frustrated," he said. "I got to go."

"Gale?"

"Yes."

She paused and sighed before he hung up. "Please don't take what I said the wrong way. I'm trying to be supportive."

***

Gale stepped on the bus and heard a burst of laughter coming from the back. A group of veterans sat clumped together as one of them held up his phone showing a video. Gale stared hard in the darkened bus. The laughter grew louder and some of the other players turned their heads.

For a few moments, Gale kept staring, his neck tightening, but the laughter grew. The players started watching another video. More laughter.

Gale thought his head was going to explode.

"Turn it off," he barked.

A hush fell over the bus but for the tinny sound of the video echoing from the back. The player holding the phone paused the video and looked up.

"53-0 and you guys are laughing?" Gale asked, his voice trembling. "I'll cut you right now. You can walk back to San Antonio."

Gale tried to suppress his anger. He took a deep breath trying to calm himself. It was as if all the frustration built up since he was hired was about to pour out.

He launched, his eyes sweeping the bus. "No wonder we got our asses whipped. You think this is a joke?" He stared hard at the players in the back. "All of us," he tapped his finger on his chest, "have an opportunity." Gale paused a beat. "Who's going to take it? This is the League despite all the bullshit going on with this franchise. I don't care if we ride on crappy planes, school buses, or stay at flea-bag hotels. It doesn't matter. The only thing that matters is winning. Anyone who wants to make this roster better understand." He stared hard at the veterans at the back of the bus. "If I ever hear you screwing around after a loss, I'll cut you."

Silence.

Gale eyed the team. He could feel his temples pulse. He was about to sit down next to Jones, when he spotted Sam Lorenzo holding up his phone, videotaping. He'd taped the entire confrontation with the players.

"What the hell . . ." Gale said, stepping toward Lorenzo, who sat a few seats away. "What are you doing?"

Lorenzo gave a thin smile and shoved his phone in his pocket.

Gale repeated himself. His voice cut through the air. "What did you do?"

Lorenzo's smile disappeared. Gale knew immediately Lorenzo was going to leak the video, hoping it would go viral. A hapless coach chewing out his players after an ass-kicking in Arizona . . .

"Give me the phone," Gale said.

The players watched Gale move closer to Lorenzo. Lorenzo shook his head.

Gale moved forward, his fury building. He was only a few inches away from Lorenzo. He smelled booze on Lorenzo's breath and stale cigar smoke.

"I said give me the phone."

Lorenzo whispered under his breath, "Screw you, Boy Scout."

With a quick jab, Gale grabbed Lorenzo's ear. He began to twist it and yanked Lorenzo out of his seat. Lorenzo screamed in pain.

"Give me the phone."

Lorenzo hesitated, his eyes bulging.

"Now." Gale twisted harder.

Lorenzo sank to his knees. He shrieked, "Okay, okay, okay!" He reached into his front pants pocket for the phone before Gale could twist harder.

Lorenzo hand shook as he gave Gale the cell. Gale let go. Lorenzo rubbed his ear furiously and tried to get up.

"Get off the bus," Gale said. "Or I'll hurt you again."

Lorenzo stared at Gale. He slowly climbed to his feet and looked around, stunned.

Gale shoved Lorenzo toward the bus door. For an instant, he studied Lorenzo's phone and found the video. With a few touches, he deleted the recording. Lorenzo looked helplessly at him, rubbing his ear. Gale tossed the phone at him. "Find your own way home," he said.

Lorenzo's face turned redder.

"Get off . . ."

Lorenzo's eyes swept the bus trying to find an ally. Then he dropped his eyes and descended the stairs.

Gale turned to the players. Before he could say anything, as if there was anything to say, Deshay Anderson belted out, "Coach, you're the man!"

The players burst into applause.

Gale shook his head and found his seat. Before the bus driver could put the vehicle in gear, Jones leaned across the aisle, put his hand on Gale's shoulder, and said, "Wonder Boy, you never cease to amaze."

CHAPTER 28

On the return flight from London, Voss took special satisfaction in watching Arizona decapitate the Lone Stars. All was going as planned. The meeting with Ivan Asinov at the Savoy had surpassed Voss' hopes. Two businessmen striking a deal with a handshake in a room tucked away off the Grill over a bottle of Le Montrachet, poached oysters, roasted cod loin, and wild mushroom linguine. Voss had been struck by Asinov's dead eyes. He flattered himself that they were cut from the same cloth.

Asinov had made billions in minerals and precious metals after the fall of the Soviet Union. He'd slashed his way into the Kremlin's inner circle, and now wanted an American football team as yet another crown jewel in his international empire. He'd spent lavishly on exquisite properties in London, Paris, New York, and Turks and Caicos, a Sonoma vineyard winding along the Russian River, an island in the Caribbean, a newly renovated Southampton estate, a 240-foot yacht berthed in Sardinia, a casino complex in Macau, notable high rises around the world, and a high-performing Premier League soccer club. Voss knew what Asinov needed most was another asset to hide the billions in laundered money he'd stashed in havens like the Caymans and Isle of Man. A League team would add to his prestige, while providing a way to hide the "dark money" he'd amassed in shell companies around the world. Most encouraging, Asinov hadn't quibbled over Voss' asking price, $4.150 billion, and had agreed to make a $500 million capital investment in Voss Energy upon the Lone Stars' sale. The thought of the Lone Stars relocating to London, the League's first international franchise, made Asinov an eager buyer. After a few glasses of wine, Asinov had told Voss he'd already named his future team The London Destroyers.

Voss could feel himself relax. For a moment, he wasn't worried about the Saudi Prince or the Swiss banker's threats, the millions in debt service, or the ticking cost of flying across the world in a state-of-the-art jet. The Lone Stars would lose and lose big. Human nature being what it is, fans would stay away from The Voss Energy Dome like the plague. Attendance would drop below the coveted threshold and the deal would be done.

The Gulfstream raced across the Atlantic. Voss rested in the dimmed light, only the young Dutch flight attendant from a working-class upbringing in Utrecht sharing the plush cabin. Julia had been hired six months earlier. She'd been an au pair to a South African family in Kensington. She'd wanted to explore the world from the window of a corporate jet. Now she found herself serving Vernon Voss.

Voss gestured for Julia. She gave a stiff smile and lifted herself out of her swivel chair. Voss eyed her. Tall, curved hips, full breasts, creamy complexion, a button nose, and a cascade of chestnut hair carefully pinned back.

Voss patted the seat next to him. The young woman hesitated.

After a moment, Voss reached out and stroked her hip. She stiffened. He stared at her knowingly, then forcefully. She'd been asked to do this before. As Voss watched, she began to dutifully take off the exquisite teardrop diamond earrings he'd purchased in Paris from a jeweler on Rue Saint-Honore'. They had hours left to travel before landing in San Antonio.

Vernon Voss smiled as he watched her undress. He wasn't going to waste the night sleeping. For an instant, he thought about Vanessa. Two can play this game he thought, as Julia unclasped her bra and placed it carefully on the seat next to her.

***

The brain trust, Gale, Jones, Alexander, and Engle, sat in the coaches' conference room feeling as if they were on life support. Coffee cups littered the table along with a box of uneaten donuts. They were exhausted from their marathon flight from Phoenix that had to be diverted in the early morning hours to Albuquerque because of faulty hydraulics.

The game film from Arizona had been overwhelming. The tape flickered on the screen until Gale or another coach would say, "Stop. . . replay it." It was like that all morning. Stop, replay, curse, stop, replay, curse, stop. . .

"What the hell," Gale said after a play when the guards pulled the wrong way. "How does that happen?"

"Improvising," Jones said, shaking his head.

Engle leaned forward and eyed the coaches while Rulon Alexander bit into a donut. "We got a bigger problem."

Gale looked at him.

"If what you say is true, Gale, how do we know we won't get worse?"

"How can we get worse, Jack?" Gale asked.

Gale caught Jones eyeing Alexander, who was licking donut frosting off his fingers.

"Cuts. Final roster," Engle said.

"What are you saying?" Gale questioned.

Engle put his pen down on his legal pad. He spoke carefully. The coaches leaned forward. "I'm surprised we didn't think about this before. We have no control over the roster. Last time I checked, you weren't the GM, Gale. Johnson's going to make the final roster worse than it already is, and that's saying something. What's to stop him from cutting Abruzzi or Foster?"

LONESTAR

Against Arizona, McCann Foster had been a bright spot at linebacker. On one play, he'd stripped the ball from Arizona's tight end after relentlessly pursuing him across the field.

Engle sipped his coffee. "What's keeping Johnson from making the team worse?"

Alexander wiped the remaining frosting off his hands with a napkin. "We end up with all the stragglers. The few who can play get cut."

"Exactly," Engle said, turning to Gale. "We've been assuming that as a coaching staff, we'd make the cuts. Bad assumption."

"On top of a 53-0 loss," Gale said, pointing to the frozen play on the conference room screen, "we have no control over the roster."

"Yes," Engle said.

"That's a problem," Alexander said.

"What now, Boy Wonder?" Jones asked softly, lifting his head and staring at Gale.

Gale looked around the room. He kicked himself. He'd fallen into the trap of assumptions. The coaches eyed him, waiting for a response. They looked haggard and tense. For a moment Gale paused.

"We hide 'em," he said.

"Hide 'em?' Alexander repeated.

"We play the ones we want cut and hide the ones we want to keep. We don't give Johnson any tape to evaluate."

"How are we going to do it?" Engle asked.

"We don't play 'em. We leak a 'final roster'."

"Final roster?" Alexander said.

"That's right. We make Johnson think we want X when we want Y."

"There's no way we can hide Abruzzi," Jones said.

"No, but we can do our best to make him look bad. Bench him," Gale answered.

"Abruzzi's not going to like it," Alexander grunted.

"What about Deshay?" Jones asked.

Gale shook his head and looked uncomfortable. "We play him."

"He's the best guy we got in the locker room, Coach," Alexander said, resigned.

"I love Deshay, but his time has come." Gale waited a beat, his voice hardening. "You can't win games with guys who've lost a step."

The coaches nodded solemnly.

"We mess with Johnson before he can mess anymore with us. Sound like a plan?" Gale asked.

"A shaky one," Alexander said, reaching for another donut.

"Well, Rulon, if you can think of anything better," Engle said, "let us know."

Alexander smiled; a chunk of chocolate frosting stuck to the corner of his mouth. "If I do, I'll let y'all know. For now, we'll ride this horse, but I fear at some point, we'll have to shoot it."

"You ever shoot a horse, Rulon?" Jones asked.

"Never have. But wanted to."

CHAPTER 29

Matt Abruzzi slammed a water bottle to the ground. He flung a string of expletives into the humid Arrowhead Stadium air and collapsed onto the bench after being stripped sacked for the second time against Kansas City. Gale watched Engle peer over at Abruzzi and make the decision to leave him alone.

It had been a rough night for the second-year quarterback. A heavy, warm rain fell on and off throughout the game making playing conditions sloppy. Gale had surrounded Abruzzi with a starting team of rookies and veteran castoffs, and Abruzzi had paid the price. Besides the strip sacks and shattered plays, Abruzzi had thrown three interceptions and been unmercifully left in the game long after preseason dictated.

Abruzzi sat on the bench with a towel draped over his head. Gale ignored the tantrum and looked at the scoreboard. 56-3 with seven minutes left to play. Gale knew by the body language the top veterans and the handful of promising rookies were angry they hadn't seen any playing time. McCann Foster stood with his hands on his hips and a Lone Star baseball cap perched on his head looking with disgust at the scene unfolding around him. As the final minutes ticked, fans poured out of the stadium in droves leaving swaths of blood red empty seats.

Gale could feel confrontation brewing. He knew it was coming. He could sense it. He studied the players. Bad body language. Expressions of frustration and anger.

Defeat.

He spotted Sam Lorenzo texting behind the Lone Star bench. Since the incident on the bus, Lorenzo had stayed clear of Gale. One of the few bright spots.

Gale turned back to the field and watched Kansas City's rookie tailback dance by Deshay Anderson. Anderson had played nearly the entire game and had looked sluggish from the opening snap.

The coaches wore grim looks and stood with arms folded, talking in somber tones into their headsets. Across the field, the Kansas City players and coaches smiled. Lots of high fives. A romp. Only a couple of weeks left until the drudgery of preseason ended and Kansas City's march to the playoffs could begin.

Gale lifted his head and observed the luxury boxes ringing the field and wondered if Johnson and Voss had shown up for the game. He hadn't laid eyes on them. He could imagine both smiling with satisfaction as the Lone Stars fell hard. Had Vanessa, the ice queen, come along for the ride?

He thought about what he would say in the post-game press conference. *It was a tough loss. We need to keep working. It's preseason. Hard work will pay off. I have confidence in the team. We sat a bunch of players tonight for a reason. The best players will play. That's right, we didn't punt. I keep telling you I don't believe in it. Abruzzi had a rough night. He needs to play better, smarter.*

Gale thought about Marybeth. He wondered if she'd lost faith in his ability to coach. Worse, in his ability to be a husband and father. When she'd suggested he might be over his head, he was blindsided. The comment cut deep. It hurt him more than she could've imagined.

***

Twenty minutes later, Gale stood in the locker room. Players sat in front of their stalls, heads down, mud-caked, bloodied, bruised, and soaked with sweat. Gale could sense the storm gathering.

For a moment, Gale watched the trainer, who spent more time smoking cigarettes in the Complex's parking lot than treating injuries, and team doctor, a short, stubby man with oily strands of hair swept across his scalp, who looked bored and disheveled, hook players up to IVs and parcel out Vicodin. Stripped down to his shorts, Deshay Anderson lay on the floor with his eyes closed in front of his locker. Jimmie Peebles nervously stuffed dirty uniforms into large duffel bags. McCann Foster stared at Gale, his eyes like needles, ready to explode. Abruzzi looked away, refusing to acknowledge the coaches.

"There isn't much to say," Gale said to the players, sensing the mood. "We get back to it tomorrow."

"Screw tomorrow," Foster shot back. He was stripped above the waist, all muscle with a cross tattooed on his chest.

Anderson opened his eyes, lifted his head, and scanned the locker room.

"Tomorrow," Gale said, staring at Foster.

Foster pointed his finger at Gale. "You leave Abruzzi to get killed in a preseason game? You let him get the crap beat out of him? You play the same guys and let the rest of us sit?"

Gale knew Foster had a reason to be angry. Gale couldn't tell the team why he was doing what he was doing. It made no sense unless you were the head coach of the Lone Stars and Garvin Johnson was your GM and Vernon Voss the owner. It was absurd. Counterintuitive. Awful really.

"We play who we play, McCann," Gale said trying to stay calm as the players stared through him and the assistant coaches looked on warily, sensing mutiny.

"I don't even know why we made the trip tonight," Foster said. "What a joke."

Gale eyed Foster for a moment and pointed toward the locker room door. He needed to get Foster away from the team before he could do irreparable damage. "Let's go. Outside," Gale said.

"You can't say it in here?" Foster questioned.

"In private. Give me that."

Foster's eyes showed defiance. The other players looked on.

"I respect you, McCann. I understand why you and everyone else is angry and frustrated. I know you want to win. I do, too. That's why I'm asking you to have a conversation with me. Nothing's going to be solved in here tonight. As for you other guys, my office door is open."

Gale gestured toward the hallway.

Foster shook his head and didn't move.

"All I'm asking for is a conversation, McCann. I'll be outside." Gale could feel his heart beating faster.

Gale left the locker room and stood in the narrow corridor under a bank of fluorescent lights. He wondered if Foster would follow. A minute passed and Gale started to feel a sense of dread. Losing the players was a coach's worst fear. Once you lost the locker room, it was impossible to get it back. Gale rubbed his eyes and tried to erase the nagging doubt. Resigned, he was about to walk down the hall to the post-game press conference when he heard the heavy dressing room door swing open and Foster emerge.

"Thank you," Gale said, relieved.

Foster stared at him stone-faced.

"I'm going to be straight with you, McCann."

Foster's expression softened for an instant.

"There's a reason you didn't play tonight along with some of the veterans and rookies, and there's a reason I left Abruzzi in the game."

A look of confusion seeped into Foster's expression.

"Johnson and Voss want us to lose. Understand?" Gale said.

"Do you?"

"No… the only way Voss can move the team is for average attendance to fall below 30,000 per game. It's the only way he can break the lease with the city."

"I don't get it. I know we suck, but don't we want to avoid that by starting the best players? Even in preseason?"

"No."

Foster shook his head and looked away for a moment. "It makes no sense," he said.

"On the surface, you're right. But if Johnson sees you on the field, doing what you did last week tearing around making plays, he's going to cut you. It may be good for some other team in the League to pick you up off waivers, but not for us. I want to start the season with a chance to win. I don't want to lose you, McCann. I played Abruzzi tonight with the rookies because I wanted him to look bad. Understand? I don't want to lose Abruzzi either."

A look of disbelief crossed Foster's face. "You tanked the game tonight?"

"Yes."

"This is crazy. What makes you think Johnson won't cut us during the regular season?"

"Nothing. But I'm taking it one day at a time. I'll figure it out when I get there."

"This sucks."

"It does," Gale said. "I need you to help me. I can't tell the team what's going on. How do I tell a player he's on the field because I want to cut him? It's terrible. But I got to have your support, McCann. I need you to help me hold the team together."

Foster shifted uncomfortably. He took a deep breath and looked Gale in the eye. "If what you say is true, then they put you in a bad spot, Coach. You know what I'd like? I'd like to shove a winning season up Johnson and Voss' ass."

Gale smiled.

"What do you want me to do?"

"Go in the locker room and tell the players we worked it out. Tell 'em there's a method to Coach McClanahan's madness."

"Tell 'em I got your back?"

"Yes."

A shadow crossed Foster's face. He hesitated. "You played Deshay the entire game."

"I did."

Foster shook his head. "He's gone, isn't he?"

Gale stayed silent.

"I'm going to miss that dude."

"We all are."

"It's the right call," Foster said, turning to the locker room entrance, "but it hurts."

CHAPTER 30

Gale surveyed the Voss Energy Dome after the PA announcer announced paid attendance. Rows and rows of empty seats stretched around the dingy stadium. 16,000 fans had showed up in a venue that held 72,000 to watch Las Vegas pound the Lone Stars in the final preseason game. Down 47-6 in the last minute of the contest, Gale had taken off his headset and watched Las Vegas' quarterback take a knee as the final seconds melted away. Gale knew cuts would come in the next few days. The roster had to be trimmed to 53 players.

Gale was ready. He and the coaches had meticulously planned the ruse. He hoped Johnson would take the bait. Gale had "left" a detailed self-scouting report in the coaches' conference room the day before detailing who the coaching staff wanted to secure on the final roster. He could imagine Sam Lorenzo, drifting in and out of offices, trying to find bits and pieces of information or worse. Earlier in training camp, Rulon Alexander had told Gale $200 had disappeared from his wallet when he'd been at practice. One of the other coaches had a gold chain vanish when he'd been taking a shower. It didn't take much to suspect it was Lorenzo. It was almost a sure thing that Lorenzo would fall prey and deliver the "report" to Johnson. If he did, Johnson would discover the first two players on the list were Matt Abruzzi and McCann Foster.

The "scouting report" read:

Matt Abruzzi – Disappointing. Hasn't shown the kind of composure expected. Questionable attitude and leadership qualities. Entitled. Potentially a locker room cancer. Athletically has regressed. Has trouble reading coverages and makes bad decisions under pressure. Cut.

McCann Foster – Bad locker room presence. Limited playing time because of reluctance to do what's asked. Confrontational with coaches. Second guesses the defensive staff. Wonder how this player earned a reputation for being productive. Has an outlier personality that's not compatible with building a cohesive team. Cut.

On the list of players the coaching staff wanted to "keep" was Anderson. It had pained Gale to place Anderson front and center in a game of deceit.

Deshay Anderson – Strong veteran presence. Understands the system and can still play. Great leader. Does what he's asked and more. Can't imagine the team without him. A given to be on the final roster.

Gale shook his head as the officials blew their whistles to end the game. As players from both teams began to mingle on the field, Gale eyed Donta Jones and Engle and walked over to them.

"You think the plan will work?" Jones asked.

C.W. WELLS

Gale shrugged. "It's all we got."

"What do you think, Jack?" Jones questioned.

For an instant, Engle looked away, his eyes clouding before focusing on Gale and Jones. "Your guess is as good as mine. But if Johnson doesn't take the bait, it's going to be ugly. Uglier than anything we've seen."

"It's hard to believe it can get uglier," Jones said.

Gale shook his head and paused a beat. He thought about Johnson and Voss, Adams, the growing strain in his marriage, and a host of other existential threats.

"It will," Gale said as he spotted Las Vegas' head coach trotting across the field to shake his hand. "You can bet on it."

***

After the game, Gale tried calling Marybeth. He stood in the empty team parking lot in the shadows of the Voss Energy Dome. After a few rings, his call slid to voicemail. He wondered if Marybeth had gone to sleep after a long day of watching Tilly and Eugene Huskins' kids. He checked his watch. It was 10:30 pm. He hadn't seen her in nearly a month. For an instant a creeping doubt spread before he quickly dismissed the thought. Marybeth was as honest as anyone he'd known. If she didn't love him, she'd tell him.

Gale opened the door of his truck, tossed his phone on the bench seat, and climbed into the cab. For a moment, he thought about the angry look on the players' faces as they'd sat in the locker room and listened to Foster defiantly question Gale after being obliterated by Kansas City. Gale shivered. He was on the razor's edge. This time, he was able to reason with Foster, but what about the next? Who else would angrily question him? You gotta be kidding me coach, no punter? Gale wondered if it was only a matter of time before he lost the locker room. The regular season was about to begin and some sadistic SOB in the League office had decided to play a joke on the Lone Stars. The team would open on the road in Philadelphia. Loud and nasty. As a rookie for Atlanta, some idiot in Veteran's Stadium had chucked an AA battery at Atlanta's bench and struck Gale on the back of the helmet. For the rest of the game, Gale had stood facing the stands, in case.

Gale put the truck in drive and drove away from the stadium. Soon he was on his way to the Complex to watch tape. It was going to be another long night.

He hoped Marybeth would call him back. He missed her.

CHAPTER 31

Rose Cutler stuck out her arm Heisman trophy-like and snapped, "No!" She sat at her desk with her glasses resting on the end of her nose, and her eyes focused on her computer screen. "I don't want your kindness or your charity, Coach McClanahan."

"It's only coffee and a scone. It's not a diamond. Besides, I didn't get it for you if that's what you're worried about. Coach Alexander did. I think he likes you."

Gale had seen Alexander and Cutler speaking with one another the week before. He noticed a budding smile pursed on Cutler's lips and a hint of makeup. Alexander was telling a story, one of many he'd collected in a long and colorful life. Gale had a hard time believing Cutler was capable of love, and an even harder time believing that Alexander, a widower, could be smitten. But take away Cutler's perpetual poker face, give her a touch of makeup, a smile, and presto! There rested an attractive woman under the dour, cranky church-lady persona. Gale knew that Cutler had never been married. What would ever happen if she was alone with a man, in this case a ladies' man like Alexander, when the lights went off, Gale thought?

Cutler rolled her eyes and looked at the scone and coffee. "I don't care. Take it away."

Gale shook his head and put the coffee and scone in front of her. "Don't look a gift horse in the mouth. You're going to hurt Rulon's feelings."

"Away!" She swept her arm as if she were shooing a fly.

"Nope."

She turned from the computer and stared at him with a withering expression, her mouth scrunched as if she'd eaten a lemon. "Away," she repeated, menacingly.

"I'm going to stand here until you take a sip of coffee and a bite of that scone. Understand?"

"This is harassment."

"I'm not moving an inch."

"You'll be standing here all day."

"I can do that."

"You're impossible."

"That's probably true, but under that armor of yours lies a softy. I know it."

"A softy?" She looked incredulous.

"Deep down, yes. But it's buried, Ms. Cutler. Buried deep."

"Oh, how mistaken you are."

Gale tapped his finger on her desk. "I'm waiting."

Cutler snorted.

"By the way. The coffee's good. The scone's even better. I already had two."

"Have three." She pointed to the one on her desk.

Gale smiled. "What do you have for me this morning?" he asked, shifting the subject, turning his attention to the stack of folders on her desk.

She looked at him and pursed her lips. "You won't be smiling much longer."

"Why's that?"

She pointed to a thin folder by her computer. "Fresh off the press."

Gale's smile faded.

"Happy day," she said with a shrug, giving him the folder.

Gale opened it. He felt his stomach churn. On top of the first page, it read "FINAL ROSTER."

He quickly scanned the list. His heart sank. He felt dizzy. His hands began to shake. Abruzzi and Foster were nowhere to be seen. Cut. Anderson was at the top of the column.

"The hell . . ." Gale scowled.

Cutler said, "You should have never taken this job. A sucker is born every minute ..."

Gale's face turned red. He picked the coffee and scone off Cutler's desk and tossed them into the trash.

"Hey," she said. "Those were for me."

"Not anymore," Gale said, his neck burning, heading down the hallway to confront Garvin Johnson.

Except Gale didn't. He stopped short and took a deep breath. Confronting Johnson would play into his hands. A few minutes later Gale stood in front of Johnson's administrative assistant. She looked bored until she noticed Gale standing by her desk. Her face turned hostile.

"Mr. Johnson's busy," she said. "He told me he isn't seeing anyone today."

"I'm here to thank him," Gale said. "Tell him that."

She looked puzzled. "Thank him?"

"That's what I said."

"For what?"

Gale held out the manila folder. "The final roster."

"Ya'll aren't upset?"

"Nope. Tell him cutting Abruzzi and McCann was the best thing he ever did."

For an instant, she stared at him quizzically, her frosted hair sparkling under the fluorescent lights. Her nails were painted a startling pink. Her perfume nearly overwhelmed him. She picked up the phone on her desk, sighed, and dialed Johnson's extension.

"Coach McClanahan is out here," she said.

Gale could hear Johnson's voice on the line. After a few moments she hung up and said, "Go in. He said he'd see you."

Gale opened Johnson's door and entered. Johnson greeted Gale with a smirk. "What do you want, son?"

"To thank you."

"Whatever for?" Johnson said with sarcasm.

"Roster cuts. It's exactly what the coaching staff wanted."

Johnson leaned back in his chair and eyed Gale. His smile grew exposing his sharp teeth. "Exactly?"

"You gave me the roster I need. We're on the same page, Garvin."

"That's good to know," Johnson said. "There's nothing better than making your day, Coach McClanahan. It warms my heart. Except things have changed. What a shame."

Gale feigned disappointment. "How so?"

Johnson reached across his desk and picked up a folder. "That roster you saw, it wasn't finalized. I don't know how that got in your hands. Here's the final roster I'm about to send to the League office." Johnson slid the folder across the desk toward Gale.

Gale opened the folder. At the top of the column sat Matt Abruzzi. He quickly scanned the sheet of paper and found Foster McCann. Deshay Anderson was nowhere to be seen.

Gale forced himself to shake his head and scowl. He tossed the folder on Johnson's desk. "This isn't what we wanted."

"You don't always get what you want. Isn't that how it goes?"

"You cut Anderson?"

"Didn't want to carry his salary. It's the League. It isn't some high school football team."

"Abruzzi? I don't want him in the locker room."

"Too bad."

"Foster?"

"Get over it, son."

Gale forced a dour look and cocked his head. "The hell," he said, feigning anger and disappointment.

Johnson's smile grew. "You better get ready for Philadelphia. We don't want an ass whooping, do we, Coach McClanahan?"

"We sure don't," Gale said, before leaving.

Outside Johnson's office, Gale broke into a smile and blew a kiss at Johnson's assistant. Her face reddened.

"What are you so happy about?" she asked.

"Sometimes, darlin', you don't get what you want," Gale said, breaking into the familiar refrain, "but … "

***

151

The call with Marybeth lasted only a couple of awkward minutes. Gale caught her in the grocery store juggling four kids and a full shopping cart.

"I'm sorry we didn't connect last night," Gale said. In the background, he could hear the Huskins' children and Tilly bickering over a bag of chips.

"I didn't have it in me to stay up, Gale. I was tired," Marybeth said. She hadn't asked about the game the night before. "I'm trying to get ready for the start of school on Monday and watch all these kids."

"I miss you," he said.

"Look, I've got to go. I'll call you tonight."

Gale felt a stab of guilt.

"Okay," Gale said.

CHAPTER 32

The League's version of the Grim Reaper goes by the name of the Turk, the staff member dreaded by every player. Gale, Engle, Alexander, and Jones carried the Turk's scythe, cutting the roster as they pulled players into their offices telling them they didn't have a future in San Antonio. Releasing a player was never easy. It hurt. The conversation sometimes began with a few compliments, the outline of the process, the reasons why the player didn't make the cut. Most players took the high road, thanking the team for the opportunity before surrendering their playbook. A few didn't.

With trepidation, Gale texted Deshay Anderson in the early afternoon. A few minutes later, Anderson stuck his head in Gale's office and said, "What's up, Coach?"

Gale pointed to the chair across from his desk. Anderson broke into an uneasy smile and sat down, his huge frame squeezing into the chair. There was no easy way to do it. The League wasn't about loyalty, it was about competition. Anderson had fallen short.

"I'm releasing you," Gale said, locking his eyes on Anderson's.

Anderson's face fell. He looked at Gale quizzically. "You're joking me, man. Right?"

"It's no joke."

Anderson leaned back in the chair and for an instant closed his eyes. "Tell me this ain't true."

"I can't carry you, Deshay."

"I still got gas in the tank."

"Tape doesn't lie."

Anderson shook his head, the reality sinking in. "My wife's going to be very unhappy," he said, his voice defeated.

After a moment, Gale said, "You knew this was coming, didn't you?"

Anderson nodded. "I was hoping I could stick for one more year. I guess the game's moving too fast now."

"What are you going to do? Have you given it any thought?"

"Nope. My momma told me to save my money. I did. I didn't spend nothin' I didn't have to. I got a few mil in the bank." He gave a half smile. "But I'm gonna miss the game."

"I don't want you to be a stranger. You saved my butt."

"Now you're cutting mine."

"That's how it works."

153

Anderson smiled.

"I need your playbook."

"Okay."

***

Mike Andujar sat in his office and dropped the city's latest crime report on his broad and cluttered desk. Late afternoon sunlight washed into his paneled office, and he found himself alone in a rare moment of solitude. Catherine Reiser had left his office a few minutes before, after a conversation about the Lone Stars' deteriorating situation. The call he'd received earlier that day gnawed at him. A former law colleague at Skarp & Digby had called from the UK. Evans was now working in the London office handling merger acquisitions, corporate restructuring, and international litigation. When Evans had called, Andujar's smile had vanished. As close as he and Evans had been, two ambitious attorneys in their early thirties working insane hours together, clawing their way toward the prized goal of becoming partners, it wasn't a friendly catch-up call.

Evans' voice was low, almost a whisper as he'd told Andujar about rumors of a representative of a notorious Russian oligarch contacting the firm about a significant acquisition. Evans went on to explain. Voss and Ivan Asinov had been seen having dinner at the Savoy. Apparently, the evening had ended with a handshake.

Skarp & Digby had been contacted a few days later. The firm had handled these sorts of things before. The Russians always came with blood on their hands, looking to place offshore assets in tangible investments, usually real estate. Asinov had earned a reputation as a sinister player in the Kremlin's inner circle. Maybe Voss and Asinov had been meeting about the energy and precious metal markets, but likely not. The conversation pointed to the Lone Stars. It made perfect sense. The League wanted London to be its first international city. No secret. Asinov had money to burn, and Voss needed to sell. It would be a difficult, contentious legal transaction with the potential for huge fees. The managing partners at Skarp & Digby were licking their chops.

After the call, Andujar had asked for the attendance figure for the final preseason game against Las Vegas. He knew the Lone Stars were a mess. He knew hardly any fans had attended the meaningless preseason game, but when Reiser told him only 16,000 people had shown in paid attendance, he could feel his pulse quicken. Andujar knew losing the Lone Stars would be worse for the city than people realized, but selfishly, it would be a blight on his political aspirations. He could see himself being painted as the mayor who lost a team because he was unable to play with the big boys, and because of a shortsighted, costly deal made years before with Voss, the Lone Stars' exit would cost the City of San Antonio millions. It was no secret Andujar eyed the Governor's seat in Austin. Andujar, however, had even bigger plans. After a term as Governor, he would be in his early fifties, young enough to show youthful energy, enough gray hair at the temples to demonstrate experience, and an impressive record of legislative achievement to launch him into the White House. He realized, no Lone Stars, no Austin. No Austin, no White House.

Andujar set his jaw and vowed silently that Voss wasn't going to get his way. Not on Mike Andujar's watch. He'd liked Gale McClanahan and his pretty wife when they'd eaten together at the Mayor's Gala. But Andujar's growing doubts were being confirmed. McClanahan had seemed naïve. He'd worn a suit instead of a tuxedo and barely said a word. He was out of his element. Over his head.

Interestingly, Catherine Reiser had disagreed with Andujar's assessment. She'd said she thought that Voss was underestimating McClanahan. On the other hand, Andujar speculated, it could simply be that Reiser was attracted to the Lone Stars' handsome coach. The mayor lifted himself from his chair and walked over to the window. He looked down at the freshly cut lawn ringing the statehouse and out at the city in the afternoon light. He needed a giant like Shula, Landry, or Belichick guiding the Lone Stars. Not a lightweight from West Texas. He cursed. Voss held nearly all the cards in his hand. The only hope rested on ticket sales spurred by the Lone Stars doing the impossible: winning.

Andujar pulled away from the window. Clearly, Gale McClanahan wasn't the coach to pull off a miracle. Instead, he was a problem that could keep Mike Andujar from realizing his political dreams. He had to act. A lump formed in his throat at the thought of the television camera panning rows and rows of empty seats at the crumbling Voss Energy Dome. 16,000 fans. . . what a debacle.

***

300-1. Voss broke into a thin smile when Johnson called about the latest Vegas line. He sat in his plush office looking out the window at the street below. He could hear the faint sound of midday traffic. The odds of San Antonio winning the Super Bowl couldn't have been worse. A brash ESPN commentator on one of the evening roundtables had called for a League investigation into the Lone Stars, citing the brazen way Vernon Voss was trying to destroy the team.

Johnson turned the subject to the roster.

"Vernon," Johnson said, "you should have seen McClanahan's face when I told him the roster had changed."

Voss leaned back in his chair, put his feet up, and rested his calfskin boots on his desk.

"He walked into my office with a smile and left looking like I'd shot his dog," Johnson said.

"Has he signed a punter?"

"No."

Voss nodded slowly.

"We owe the Commissioner's Office a favor. Opening on the road against Philadelphia's going to be ugly, Vernon."

"McClanahan's going to get his head handed to him," Voss said. "Philadelphia's going to rip his heart out."

"Welcome to the League."

"Lone Star style," Voss said, his voice breaking into a deep guttural laugh.

CHAPTER 33

Gale ran the team so hard two rookie defensive backs threw up in the endzone. In the intense September heat, Gale watched as his players ran a series of shuttle runs, thundering across the practice field. Gale had realized early in his coaching career a superbly conditioned team could at times overcome lack of talent and steal a game or two. The Lone Stars might get their ass kicked, Gale thought, but he was determined they weren't going to quit.

Gale glanced at his watch and looked out at the players lining up on the goal line, while Donta Jones shouted encouragement as he twirled the whistle he held on a string between his thumb and forefinger. Two more minutes of sprints and Gale would call it a day. Gale had appointed McCann Foster as team captain, and now Foster was marching up and down the line of players urging them to work harder.

Gale studied the players. Between sprints, some clasped their hands on the back of their helmets to catch air, others stood with their hands on their hips, waiting for the next whistle. A few were bent over, struggling to finish the conditioning drill. For the few who were hurting, and the two DB's who had thrown up, Gale wondered if they'd been drinking the night before. Gale smiled to himself. If they had, they wouldn't do it again. There was nothing like harsh conditioning drills the morning after in suffocating Texas heat to make a player think twice about staying out late and partying.

During the coaches' meeting early in the week, Gale and the staff agreed the Lone Stars needed to make a statement early in the game against Philadelphia. On the opening offensive play, Abruzzi would call play action and look downfield. Engle had noticed Philadelphia's third-year cornerback, Deshaun Moss, had a habit of biting on the run and taking a half step toward the line of scrimmage. It was a subtle weakness, but one Engle wanted to exploit. Defensively, Donta Jones and Gale had agreed the Lone Stars would target Philadelphia's swift tailback, Eric Burrell, and Philadelphia's All-Pro wideout Tyreek Adams. If the defense could disrupt both player's production, the Lone Stars might keep it close. Gale knew winning was a longshot with a roster full of obscure rookies and journeyman veterans, especially playing Philadelphia on the road.

A few minutes later, after the players had circled around Gale to end practice, Abruzzi lingered on the field. He'd stripped his shoulder pads off and held them in one hand and his helmet in the other. His hair and t-shirt were soaked with sweat, and he wore a pained expression.

"You're killing us, Coach," Abruzzi said, still breathing hard from practice. "No team in the League runs this much."

157

"We do," Gale said, his voice hardening.

"Are we training for a marathon?" Abruzzi asked, his face glistening with sweat.

"Maybe."

"The guys are bitching."

"Too bad." Gale looked down for a moment.

"It's a long season, man. It's not high school. We gotta save some gas in the tank."

Gale spit and looked up. "You want to go 1-16 again?"

Abruzzi took a step back. "Of course not."

"What's the problem?" Gale asked, staring hard at Abruzzi.

Abruzzi shook his head and hesitated. "Nothing."

Gale set his jaw. He pointed at Abruzzi. "We play Philadelphia in three days, and you better be ready."

When Gale turned toward the Complex, he noticed a large figure standing at the far end of the field by the security fence. It was Deshay Anderson. Anderson wore an untucked t-shirt and shorts. His eyes were hidden by wrap-around sunglasses. Gale waved and Anderson nodded his head. It was the third day in a row Anderson had watched practice. He missed football, Gale thought. It sucked getting old.

***

"What do you mean, Sunday?" Gale asked, standing on the tarmac at San Antonio International Airport in the shadow of the team's charter jet. Gale felt a bead of sweat on his forehead. The team itinerary had the Lone Stars arriving in Philadelphia that Friday afternoon, 48 hours before kick-off as the League dictated. After a loud popping noise from one of the turbines, players and coaches slowly streamed out of the Boeing 767's cabin door down the portable stairway and stood by the empty baggage carts, some with cell phones pressed to their ears under a blinding sun.

The plane's captain shrugged and gestured toward the starboard engine. "The jet blew a camshaft."

"What does that mean?" Gale asked.

"It means the whole engine has to be repaired."

"It's going to take nearly two days to fix it?"

"That's what I told you, Coach. It's nearly impossible to get parts for a jet this old. We've got to order the part and have it flown in from Seattle."

"Get another plane," Gale said in disgust.

The pilot shook his head. "There isn't another plane. This is it. The team knew that when it hired us. We're a small charter company."

LONESTAR

Gale turned to Sam Lorenzo, who was hanging in earshot of the conversation. Lighting a cigar, Lorenzo smirked and shrugged, as if to say, not my problem.

"Get another jet," Gale said, turning to Lorenzo. "This breaks every League rule. You know we're supposed to be in Philadelphia today. No team travels on gameday."

"No can do. Mr. Voss isn't going to pay for another charter. Too bad."

Gale looked over at Engle and Donta Jones. They both shook their heads and began walking toward the terminal entrance to escape the heat. Jimmie Peebles stood near the wing, looking confused. Rulon Alexander, the former Marine, sipped a warm Diet Coke and eyed Lorenzo, as if he were contemplating tearing him apart. The rest of the coaches stood with hands on their hips or arms folded across their chests listening to the conversation between Gale and the pilot.

"We play at 1 p.m. on Sunday. That means a 4 a.m. departure," Gale said.

The pilot nodded.

"So the players get a bad night's sleep and spend the whole morning on the day of the game traveling?"

"Look at it this way," the pilot said. "Isn't it better the engine blew out on the ground than in the air?"

Gale met the pilot's comment with silence. He looked over the pilot's shoulder at the plane. A relic, it sat broken in the midday heat. He turned toward the players.

"Go home," Gale said angrily. "Get some rest. We'll have a walkthrough tomorrow. Maybe by then, I'll have figured out how we're getting to Philadelphia."

***

The rock hit the bus windshield like a gunshot. Some idiot had hurled it from an overpass as the lead team bus rambled from the airport to the stadium. The day had already been a nightmare. The team charter had departed San Antonio at 4:30 a.m., half an hour late, players had found it impossible to sleep on the cramped plane, and making things worse, they had circled Philadelphia for nearly forty minutes as the team ate stale bagels smeared with cream cheese, waiting for a thunderstorm to pass. Now some moron had shattered the buses' windshield causing the driver to pull over on the side of the highway nine miles from Lincoln Financial Field.

Gale surveyed the damage. The driver, who barely fit in his seat and looked unscathed, had rolls of flesh around his shirt collar. He kept muttering "Lordy, lordy" as he carefully brushed shards of glass off his lap. Gale noticed a small, red splotch on the back of his own hand, where a piece of glass had embedded itself. He pulled the tiny shard out and sucked on the wound to stop the bleeding. In a few minutes, they were moving again. Gale felt the growing, sour roil in his stomach. He fought the feeling like he had before every game he had ever coached. He knew

159

he was going to vomit. It was only a matter of time. Kick-off was less than three hours away, and the team found itself caught in traffic.

***

Abruzzi overthrew the ball. His high arcing sideline pass from the Lone Stars' twenty-five-yard line sailed past the fingertips of Javon Ellis, a rookie wideout from Ellerton State. In frustration, Engle slapped his game sheet on his thigh while Gale cursed. The first play from scrimmage had nearly gone exactly as the coaching staff had imagined. Deshaun Moss, Philadelphia's defensive back, had bit on play action and Ellis had sailed down the sideline on a fly route. The play was an opportunity to strike first. It would have silenced Philadelphia's toxic fans, who made it known from the opening whistle how much they were going to enjoy watching the Lone Stars be disemboweled. Two plays later, San Antonio faced fourth and six, and Gale heard Donta Jones on the head-set telling him to punt.

"Boy Wonder, you're going to have 80,000 people clawing at your ass," Jones said. "Tell Abruzzi to punt."

Gale gritted his teeth. "No."

The crowd was beginning to chant, "Go for it. . . go for it!" Word had spread . . .

Abruzzi looked at Gale and raised his hands, palms up, as if to say, decide, will you? The play clock ticked.

"Go for it," Gale said, swallowing hard, nodding at Engle, who stood a few yards away. Out of the corner of Gale's eye, he saw McCann Foster, fiery and emotional, slam his helmet down in disgust as if to say, *"Going for it on fourth down on the road against Philly? Really? . . ."*

Engle called a slant to the slot receiver. The play was designed to pick-up enough yardage for the first down.

The stadium exploded when the Lone Stars broke huddle and Abruzzi stepped to the line of scrimmage. The noise was deafening. Gale felt as if the world was crashing down. His pulse beat wildly, his bowels churned, and his legs weakened as Abruzzi frantically tapped both sides of his helmet, trying to communicate the snap count in the rising furor. In a blur, a half-full beer can sailed past Gale's ear and struck the field in front of him. He had felt the whoosh but his mind was numb. He quickly glanced at the play clock. Three seconds . . . snap it, he heard himself say. Snap the ball!

Abruzzi took a three-step drop, sidestepped a blitzing linebacker, and threw a bullet to Sammy Moore, a short, stocky slot receiver who had played for four teams in his three-year pro career. Moore caught the ball in traffic and hit the turf before the safety could slice him in two. Suddenly, a hush fell over the crowd. Gale felt the weight lift from his shoulders. Engle broke into a smile. Foster shook his head, retrieved his helmet, and walked to the bench to sit with the defense. Gale heard Jones say over the headset, "Boy Wonder, you live another day."

Eleven plays later, the Lone Stars scored on a 12-yard pass from Abruzzi to Ellis.

After the touchdown, Gale would have thought the Lone Stars had won a world championship. With Abruzzi leading the charge, the players piled on Ellis, and the San Antonio sideline burst into euphoria. For an instant, Gale caught a glimpse of what it could be. For months he had been wallowing in the Lone Stars' sewer. In this moment, he emerged from the slime and stink to see blue sky.

Three quarters later, the excitement had vanished. Philadelphia had worn the Lone Stars down and put their foot on San Antonio's throat, 35-7. Gale walked off the field to a chorus of boos and taunts. He was bone tired. The sleepless night, the insane gameday travel, the bus windshield exploding, and the frantic rush to the stadium had left him as tired as he'd ever been. But there were glimpses. The team hadn't quit. Abruzzi had shown composure. Led by Foster, the defense had demonstrated cohesion and toughness despite the score. The offense had converted three times on fourth down.

Still, they weren't a good football team. Gale needed to figure out how to make them better. If Gale had any chance to survive professionally and personally, the Lone Stars had to win.

Gale noticed a spot above his temple hurt. As he walked toward the tunnel, keeping his eyes locked straight ahead with two police officers escorting him off the field, he winced when he touched his scalp. He pulled his fingers away and noticed blood flecked on them. He touched the spot again and rubbed. He felt a sharp, painful pinprick. It dawned on him. A tiny shard of glass had embedded itself from the shattered windshield. He touched the spot once more and cursed.

***

Voss stepped from the TV after the final whistle. He looked out the living room sliders to see Vanessa lying on her stomach by the pool on a lounge chaise wearing an Emilio Pucci bikini. Her tanned skin glistened in the afternoon sunlight and her perfectly cut ash blonde hair spilled across the pillow. Next to her sat a highball glass topped with vodka and cranberry juice.

Voss turned away. 35-7. An ass kicking. Yet, something didn't sit right. Voss felt a tightness in his throat. Something tugged at him, an uneasiness he fought. The Lone Stars had played hard, harder than he had seen them compete in years. He tried to shake the uneasy feeling. He didn't want the Lone Stars to lose. He wanted them to be crushed. He wanted blood. 35-7 wasn't enough. *Blood . . . give me blood, he thought.*

***

161

Surrounded by flickering television screens, Spencer Tate stood off to the side in the crowded League Command Center. Jonathan Colvin, a former All-Pro safety and the League Director of Football Operations, stood next to him watching the last seconds tick off the clock in Philadelphia. His sleeves rolled up, Colvin sipped a cup of coffee and turned to Tate.

"They didn't stand a chance," Colvin said. "When was the last time a team traveled on gameday?"

Tate looked past him toward the television screen and smiled thinly.

Colvin shook his head. "It could have been a lot worse."

Tate hid a feeling of elation. 35-7. The perfect score. Lopsided but not a slaughter. The game might quell the shouts for an investigation into competitive practices. At times, the Lone Stars had appeared competent.

"Have you seen ticket sales for the home opener?" Colvin asked.

Tate had not only seen them, but he had been checking them daily.

Colvin continued. "It's going to be ugly. If there's more than 30,000, I'll be shocked."

"A bad situation," Tate said, shaking his head, feigning concern.

"I got a call during the game," Colvin said, taking another sip of coffee, as League officials sat in large swivel chairs in the darkened room and began to focus on upcoming West Coast games.

"A call?" Tate asked.

"Mike Andujar. He was livid."

"What about?"

"He said he wanted next week's game blacked out in Texas."

"Did you tell him we don't do that anymore?"

"I did."

"What'd he say?"

"He said televising the game would be a travesty. He's worried about empty seats."

"He's worried about his poll numbers," Tate said. "What'd you tell him?"

"I said we televise all games. Attendance doesn't matter."

"Good."

"But he said something that worries me, Spencer," Colvin said. "He threatened a lawsuit."

"We get sued every day, Jonathan," Tate said, dismissively.

"His threat wasn't garden variety. He told me he knows about a meeting in London. He said he'd launch criminal proceedings if he discovers a deal has been made." Colvin looked at Tate. "What went down in London?"

Tate turned away from Colvin to one of the large HD screens and ignored his question. Tate had warned Voss not to meet with Asinov in public. If the Lone Stars abandoned San Antonio, there would be the usual lawsuits. Yet Tate knew if Voss wasn't careful, a case could be made for several transgressions: breach of contract, fraud, and illegal enrichment to name a few. That could mean the Feds. Tate had enough lawyers orbiting him to know Voss' recklessness could endanger the League and Tate. Tate needed to tell Voss to keep his mouth shut and do what Tate told him. Asinov was another story. No one told the Russians what to do. Tate knew taking the game permanently to the UK would be the crown jewel in his legacy.

Tate took a deep breath and reassured himself. There was no paper trail. There was no way he could be implicated, he reassured himself. Let the FBI snoop all day. If there was a culprit, it was Vernon Voss. Spencer Tate was the Commissioner of the League and above reproach. He would keep pounding on the talking points: San Antonio was a bad situation that the League was monitoring carefully. It was unfortunate. He felt for the Lone Star fans. He would do everything he could to keep the team in Texas. The integrity of the League came before all else.

CHAPTER 34

Rain fell on the streets of Zurich. An early September cold spell made the evening air raw. Max Hartmann, the prim Swiss banker, made his way to the parking garage across from his office building on Lagerstrasse, his coat collar pulled to his throat, his leather briefcase swinging mechanically in the dying light. It wasn't unusual to work on Sundays, but Hartmann had planned to take the day off until Rasheed had called. The conversations with the Saudi Prince were growing longer and more heated. Rasheed had made bad bets across the globe. People owed him money. They weren't paying. He owed money. He wasn't paying. The energy sector had squeezed him as it had others, the blood money running out.

Rasheed's extravagant lifestyle had caught up with him. The gambling, the nightlife, the women . . . it all added up to an extraordinarily precarious balance sheet.

Now anger. What did Rasheed expect, Hartmann asked? He'd warned Rasheed about his lifestyle, his business decisions, and ultimately, his vanity. Now the Swiss found himself unsettled, the focus of the Prince's ire.

The conversation that afternoon had struck a dark note. Rasheed had hinted at violence. He'd ranted about the American. Still humiliated by the bourbon thrown in his face, the Saudi Prince wanted blood.

***

Twelve coaches sleeping in their offices made the Complex smell like dirty socks. Stale food and coffee mingled with sweat permeated the air. As much as Jimmie Peebles emptied the trash, vacuumed the floors, scrubbed the bathrooms, and worked with the slouchy kid with purple hair to keep the dressing room and training facility clean, the building had been neglected for too long. Carpets were stained from years of spilled fast food, soda and coffee, leaking ceiling pipes, chewing tobacco, and soiled shoes. Jimmie cleaned in the late afternoons while the large industrial size washers and dryers whirred and tumbled with loads of practice uniforms, towels, and assorted laundry. Jimmie slept on a cot in the cramped equipment room. At night, he would sit in the corner of the coaches' conference room listening intently to Gale and the staff plan practices and tweak gameplans. He would lean forward nervously, his eyes fluttering, focused on every word, until Rulon Alexander would turn and say lightly, "Jimmie, don't think so hard. I'm gettin' a headache watchin' you concentrate."

LONESTAR

While the Complex was being given attention, Rose Cutler did everything she could to express her dismay at grown men living in and adding to what she considered a rodent infested, foul-smelling dump. She sniffed the air frequently, grimaced, and complained to Gale. He would shrug. What to do?

"Grown men, sleeping on mattresses on the floor," Cutler said on a Tuesday morning with contempt. "Don't you have wives?"

"They're football widows, Ms. Cutler. They're used to it."

"You mean to tell me your wife puts up with it?"

Cutler hit a nerve. Gale thought for a moment. Grayson Wallace had booked plane tickets for Marybeth and Tilly for the home opener against Detroit. In fact, nearly the whole town of Kinney was traveling to the game. There had been no problems securing tickets. The opener was less than a week away and only 19,000 tickets had been sold. Gale wondered if Marybeth really wanted to come. Their conversations had been muted. They talked about Tilly, the weather, Marybeth's students, but she didn't want to hear about the Lone Stars. Gale could feel the slow, painful drift in their marriage away from any sort of intimacy.

"I miss my wife," Gale admitted.

Cutler leaned forward and asked with sarcasm in her voice, "Does she miss you, Coach McClanahan?"

"Why don't you ask her?"

"She's a mystery woman. With all that money you make, you could at least have your wife and child in town."

Gale looked away. "She has a life in Kinney."

Cutler sat back in her chair. "You have one here?"

Gale thought about the flowers Vanessa Voss had sent and Cutler's suspicious tone. He turned back to Cutler and searched her eyes. Thankfully, Cutler shifted the subject.

"Deshay Anderson's looking for you."

"What does he want?"

"I'm not a mind reader," she said.

Gale's ears grew hot. He wanted to say, "maybe not, but you sure do a good job probing mine."

"Have you typed the practice schedule for tomorrow?" he asked.

"Demands, demands. Always demands."

"I really should have fired you a long time ago, Ms. Cutler."

She smiled. "Then who would keep you honest?"

***

The next day, Gale walked out of the training facility and into the furnace-like heat. Donta Jones was leading warm-ups. Jimmie stood high in the tower ready to film practice, his video camera focused on the rows of players stretching near

165

midfield. Engle scribbled notes with a pencil on his practice sheet. Rulon Alexander, wearing his battered Marine Corps campaign hat, squatted like a catcher next to Matt Abruzzi, telling him a war story from his days at Arkansas. Abruzzi kept throwing his head back to laugh. The other coaches walked among the players, checking in, making sure that they were ready for practice.

Earlier in the morning, the players had groaned when Gale told them they would be practicing in full pads. In the League, players loathed contact during the week. It was an unwritten rule: avoid injuries at all costs, even if it meant limiting blocking and tackling, areas where the Lone Stars needed repetition the most. At this point, Gale didn't care about unwritten rules. He demanded the Lone Stars be better conditioned and tougher than any team they would play. The tape had confirmed the team had surprised Philadelphia, despite the score, by playing hard until the bitter end. Gale wanted practices to be tougher than games. He wanted game day to be a welcomed relief.

When he had played for Atlanta, in the days before the Players' Association bargained for practice restrictions, it wasn't uncommon for full pads to be worn on Friday, and for players to be hitting full speed. That was the League before collective bargaining, CTE, and a new generation of players. Gale understood times had changed, but it was Thursday, and the Lone Stars were going to hit. In team meetings, he'd drilled down to the basics: blocking, tackling, limiting turnovers, avoiding penalties, and completing assignments. Despite his misgivings about the team, Gale put his doubts aside and pounded the message home, especially the week before the home opener against a struggling team like Detroit. While players still had their doubts about being led by a bunch of high school coaches, they kept opinions to themselves, even McCann Foster, who wore his emotions on his shirtsleeves.

Thirty minutes later, Abruzzi threw a ball into double coverage. It was the second time in practice he'd tried to force a pass into a tiny window and had the ball picked-off. Gale stood with his hands on his hips and his head cocked. Abruzzi slapped his hands together, angry at himself. Gale had seen enough. "On the line," he shouted. The players started cursing under the blinding September sun. Abruzzi said, "Shit."

Ten minutes later, after a grueling series of shuttle runs, the players sucked water and cooled off under the two dilapidated water misters that sputtered and coughed. Gale walked over to Abruzzi, who was sitting on one of the benches, head down, trying to catch his breath.

"It rides on you, Matt," Gale said. "Simple. On you. You make bad decisions, we don't stand a chance. Understand?"

Abruzzi stared at the ground and spit.

"I want better decisions."

Abruzzi looked away and nodded. Pissed. But that was okay. Gale could see that Abruzzi was mainly upset at himself.

Gale stepped away. Out of the corner of his eye, he spotted a lone figure at the far end of the field. Gale turned to Jones and Engle and said, "Give 'em another minute, then get practice going."

"Got it, Boy Wonder," Jones answered.

Gale broke into a jog until he reached Deshay Anderson, who stood along the security fence.

"I heard you were looking for me," Gale said. "Can't get enough?"

"I miss it, Coach."

Gale couldn't see Anderson's eyes beneath his sunglasses, but he could sense Deshay's body language. He wasn't the brash player Gale had met during OTAs. Anderson's shoulders slumped. He bit his lip.

"What's going on?" Gale asked.

"Nothin'."

"What's your wife saying, Deshay?"

"She don't like me at home durin' the day. 'Get off your ass,' she says."

Gale smiled.

"I get up early and check the weather. I feed the kids breakfast and take 'em to school. Then I sit my ass in a coffee shop and stare at my phone. Look at this . . ." Anderson squeezed his stomach with both hands. "I'm gettin' fat. Fatter than a hog to slaughter."

"How about getting a job, Deshay?"

"I don't want a job. I want to be part of the team."

Gale shook his head. "I can't do that."

"Not as a player. A coach. I got things to offer. I can help you." Anderson took off his sunglasses. His eyes misted. "I can help Coach Jones on defense. I'll do whatever you ask. I can help turn this thing around."

Gale shook his head. "You don't think you're too close to the players, Deshay? There has to be separation."

"I can separate. I'm older than all of 'em. I want to coach, Gale."

It was the first time Anderson had called Gale by his name. It struck a chord.

"I can't pay you," Gale said.

"I know."

"The hours are terrible. Your wife might not like putting the kids to bed alone."

"Naw. She's tired of ole Deshay mopin' around the house."

"If we don't win, we'll all be looking for jobs next season."

"Yeah, but maybe I'll get one that pays."

Gale smiled and gave Anderson a long look. He could see the sadness, but also the fierce pride.

"I'm not askin' for charity."

"Can you help coordinate special teams?"

"Can do." Anderson's voice rose.

"Help coach the defensive line?"

"Piece of cake."

"The hours are brutal."

"You said that." Anderson smiled.

Gale grinned and tossed Anderson his whistle.

Anderson matched his grin, even through misty eyes. "You're not gonna regret this coach."

"Let's go tell the team," Gale said. "After the practice we just put them through, they need some cheering up, and you're just the man to do it."

CHAPTER 35

The call came in the late afternoon and Voss' administrative assistant reluctantly told her boss that Mike Andujar was holding on line one. Voss grunted and pulled his eyes away from the stack of financials detailing Voss Energy's demise. Adding to the bleak picture, earlier in the week, a faulty harness had snapped, sending a derrickman plunging to his death in the Parshall Oil Field. Five years earlier, seven field workers had been killed in North Dakota when an explosion had ripped through a Voss Energy gas line. The families had refused to settle and hired Carabin Ohnstad, a well-known Fargo attorney who'd made a bundle specializing in wrongful injury claims. Voss' had tangled with Ohnstad before. Worried that other workers would bring to light a host of safety issues, Voss' lawyers had fought the suit and won with a payoff to a dirty judge.

Now Andujar. "What does he want?" Voss barked into the speaker phone.

"He didn't say."

"Tell him I'm in a meeting."

Thirty seconds later, Voss' assistant buzzed again. In a timid voice, she said, "The mayor told me that he wants to talk about your meeting with Ivan Asinov in London."

Voss' eyes narrowed. He hesitated. Meeting publicly with Asinov had been a risk, but the Russian had insisted on dinner at the Savoy. Voss was in no position to refuse.

"Tell Andujar to go screw himself," Voss snapped.

***

Twenty-four hours before kick-off, Gale stood in the terminal waiting for Marybeth and Tilly to arrive along with a plane full of friends and townspeople who climbed aboard a Southwest flight in Midland to watch one of their own coach in the League. Gale's chest grew tight when he glanced at the monitor and saw that the plane had landed. He hadn't seen Marybeth and Til in weeks, and recently Marybeth's aloofness had frightened him.

Twenty minutes later, when the Kinney contingent made its way led by Grayson Wallace pulling a small, black suitcase on rollers, Gale's heart rose when he spotted Marybeth and Tilly walking behind Wallace with a crowd of well-wishers, but when his eyes locked with Marybeth's, he knew her smile was feigned. A cloud of uncertainty hung between them. Before Gale could say anything to Marybeth or hug Tilly, he found himself engulfed by friends and well-wishers who had piled off the plane to watch Gale coach the San Antonio Lone Stars. He tried to pull away to greet his wife and daughter, but the crowd wouldn't give him a chance.

***

That evening, after team meetings and a walkthrough at the Complex, Gale had driven to the Residence Inn where he, Marybeth, and Tilly were staying for the night. He'd missed the dinner that Grayson and Dot had hosted at Biga's on The Riverwalk. When he arrived at the hotel, he found Tilly curled into a ball, asleep in one of the queen-size beds. Marybeth rested on top of the bedspread next to Tilly, her floral-patterned sundress bunched around her thighs, her head propped up by pillows. When he entered the room, she'd placed the magazine she'd been reading on her lap and looked up. Her eyes were distant, and she gave little effort to greet him. He could tell she was tired. The color had drained from her face.

"How was dinner?" Gale asked, trying to break the ice.

"Grayson drank too much. Dot and Barbara worked hard all night to make sure he behaved."

"He likes his whiskey."

Marybeth sighed and put her magazine on the bedside table.

Gale studied her for a moment. "And?"

"I'm having a hard time. You realize this, don't you?"

Gale nodded.

"It's terrible, Gale. I keep thinking that these people are going to ruin our lives."

"I know."

"For what? We had a good life. We didn't need this. I'm alone, Gale. I wake up in the morning alone and I go to bed alone. I can barely keep it together. Every time we talk, I'm reminded of the mess we're in. Your daughter doesn't even know you anymore."

Marybeth paused, and for an instant, looked away.

"I can barely sleep. I lie in bed at night thinking about what we had and where we are. These horrible people have entered our lives and are trying to destroy everything we have, including our marriage."

Gale felt a stab of fear and wanted to lie next to her, hold her close.

She continued. "I'm struggling, Gale. I've thought about asking Grayson to cut a deal with Voss. I've thought about walking away and taking Til to Colorado to live with my parents . . . but I can't," she said, her voice resolute.

Gale felt chills move up his spine and didn't speak.

Marybeth kept on. "If I'm thinking this way, I can't imagine what's going through your head. I know I've beat you up for signing the contract, but now looking back, I don't see how you couldn't." Tears welled. "The humiliation you've experienced. The hand you've been dealt . . . no one deserves that."

LONESTAR

Marybeth wiped her tears away with the back of her hand. "So here's the deal, Gale. Whatever happens, I'm with you. There's no turning back. We have to make sure these bastards don't win."

Gale walked silently across the room, sat on the edge of the bed, and kissed her, feeling her warm breath and damp cheeks. His voice broke. "You have my word."

"I know," she said, hungrily pulling him to her, as if they were seventeen again in the flatbed of a pickup on his parents' ranch under a pile of blankets and an ensemble of stars.

CHAPTER 36

For the first time in his coaching career, Gale didn't throw up before a game. He scanned the multitude of empty seats, the scattering of fans, the Kinney contingent in the second deck, and guessed attendance fell under 20,000, not close to the 30,000 average needed to keep the Lone Stars in San Antonio. There had been no fanfare for the opener. A tinny recorded rendition of the National Anthem, a skimpy honor guard, a long-discarded state senator taking part in the honorary coin toss. For an instant, Gale imagined Johnson and Voss smugly gazing down on the field from the team's luxury box, knowing that their scheme was working. Gale turned back to the players.

Gale pulled the team together before the opening kick-off. A surge of adrenaline hit him. He locked in on the players, sweeping his eyes across the huddle. His voice was fierce. As fierce as it had ever been. The words poured out, unrelenting and defiant.

"There's no way we lose today, understand? No way. You're better conditioned, you're tougher and there's not one person in this world who believes we can beat Detroit but us. Not one." He paused. "Everyone thinks we suck. A bunch of shitty players and coaches. Everyone thinks we're going to lay down and let Detroit kick our ass." He paused. "No one believes in us, understand? But we know better, and we know better because we believe in one another."

Gale turned to Abruzzi.

"You ready to play, Matt? It's time for you to step-up."

Abruzzi nodded.

"McCann?"

McCann's eyes were red and war-like, and his eye black had already started to run down his cheeks from sweat. "No one beats us in our own house. Get that? No one," McCann said, his voice hard. "On the count of three . . ."

The players started lining up for the opening kick-off when Engle cupped his hand over the microphone on his headset and put his arm on Gale's shoulder.

"You know why we all signed up to coach with you?"

"Why?"

"Because you're a helluva coach, Gale."

Gale looked at Engle surprised, but Engle turned to the field. A few seconds later, the opening kick soared high in the Voss Energy Dome air.

***

172

LONESTAR

At halftime, Detroit led 14-7. Gale had never seen his players hit with the velocity they showed during the first two quarters. The anger was fueled by a blitzing Detroit linebacker who'd broken Abruzzi's nose on the Lone Star's opening drive. The defender had swung his arm like a hammer, earning an unsportsman-like conduct penalty and a chorus of boos from the smattering of fans. Flags had rained down on the field as Abruzzi woozily pulled himself off the turf and tried to staunch the blood streaming from his nose. Three plays later, he'd trotted back in the game after passing concussion protocol, taking a painkiller and having a bandage taped across the bridge of his nose.

***

After the half, as the players jogged into the tunnel, Gale knew something was different. The Lone Stars had attitude. The first half had convinced them that they could play with this team. Gale knew that success wasn't all about talent. It was about desire. He could smell the fear on the Detroit sideline. He could practically hear Detroit's coaches. *Are you kidding me? Up only a touchdown to San Antonio? Shit . . .*

During the first quarter, when the Lone Stars had converted a fourth and seven on their own 36-yard line and had scored five plays later, Gale realized his team had a chance. If the Lone Stars were expecting a speech during halftime, they were wrong. After he quieted the players, Gale stared at his team and his one word reverberated through the locker room: "Win."

When the players had streamed out to the field, Donta Jones pulled Gale aside, his eyes alive. "We got a chance, Boy Wonder. Sweet Jesus . . ."

"We do," Gale said. "It's right in front of us."

"I want to see Johnson and Voss' eyes when we take Detroit down."

Gale grinned slightly. "Thirty minutes, Donta. We need to play hard."

***

Javon Ellis took a quick screen pass and raced twenty-seven yards to Detroit's 23-yard line. Before the snap, Gale noticed blood pouring once more out of Abruzzi's nose. The front of Abruzzi's uniform was covered in red blotches as he tried to stop the bleeding by pinching his nostrils and tilting his head upward.

Ellis' run after the catch was stunning. He broke from the line of scrimmage and beat the cornerback who'd over-committed trying to pick-off Abruzzi's throw. Down 21-14, the Lone Stars were on the verge of tying the game with 12 seconds left. It had been a slugfest. McCann Foster had left the field early in the fourth quarter with a deep shoulder contusion. Gale watched him stalking the sideline with a large ice pack taped to his shoulder.

After the Lone Stars took their final timeout, Engle calmly spoke into his headset as the referees spotted the ball. "We need to take a shot, Gale. A fade?"

"You think we got it, Jack?"

"I think so. . . Matt," Gale said to Abruzzi on the sideline. "You look like a stuck pig with all that blood. Having fun yet? Let's take a shot. How about a fade? 52 Rain Maker Z right. If you miss, miss out of bounds. Okay?"

Abruzzi nodded and trotted to the huddle. Gale felt his stomach contract and a lump grow in his throat. The few fans who showed up were trying to fill the cavernous Voss Energy Dome with noise. It was a game no one expected. The lowly Lone Stars, the team every pundit picked to lose, in striking distance of tying Detroit.

Abruzzi leaned over center and belted out the snap count . . . 71 Redzero. . . Green . . . As the play clock ticked down, Gale put his hands on his knees and went into his familiar coaching stance, trying to get a better angle on the play. Abruzzi barked hut, hut . . .

For an instant, the stadium froze.

***

Vernon Voss stood behind Vanessa in the owner's box. His black eyes were locked on the field as he drank his bourbon with a shaky hand and squeezed the tumbler until it nearly shattered. He'd watched with growing fury as the Lone Stars marched down the field. Garvin Johnson stood next to him. Johnson watched silently, not daring to speak, staring with disbelief as Abruzzi stood over center.

Vanessa looked bored as she drank her third vodka tonic. She watched the final minutes with seeming disinterest. For an instant, she focused on Gale, her cold blue eyes settling on him until Abruzzi took the ball from center and dropped back to throw.

***

Grayson Wallace found himself on his feet surrounded by the contingent from Kinney. He chewed his knuckle as Abruzzi dropped back in the pocket. "Come on,"
he said under his breath. "Score."

***

Mike Andujar's eyes were glued to the television. He watched silently in the mayor's mansion as Abruzzi set to throw. He watched Detroit's linebacker coming hard from the edge and Abruzzi's arm snap forward . . .

***

LONESTAR

Marybeth held Tilly in her arms and bit her lip while Abruzzi's pass arced high in the air as Ellis sprinted toward the corner of the end zone. She felt her heart race. "Oh, my god," she whispered as the ball spiraled toward Ellis.

***

Ellis ran the fade the way Engle had taught him. Ellis fought off the cornerback as the two sped into the endzone. The spiral was tight, nose down, and Ellis caught it over his left shoulder. The referee raised his arms as the Ellerton State rookie tumbled into the corner of the end zone, the ball tucked safely away.

As the referee raised his arms, Voss shattered the glass of bourbon in his hand. Johnson swore and kicked the chair sitting in front of him. Vanessa smiled. Her eyes suddenly alive with a satisfied glow.

***

The stadium fell silent. Stunned. Gale held up two fingers. He was going for the win. He wasn't putting the game in the hands of a shaky rookie kicker from Millsaps College who looked stricken with fear.

"Are you kidding me? You got big balls, Boy Wonder," Donta Jones said into his headset. "Kick the extra point."

Gale shook his head. Once more, he held up two fingers.

Rulon Alexander smiled. "Gale, how about showing a little courage?"

With no time left on the clock, Gale focused on the two-point conversion. Engle called the play. A quarterback draw. Abruzzi nodded, blood trickling out of his nose, and went to the huddle. A few moments later, he barked out the snap count, took the hike, and dropped back before racing toward the line of scrimmage. He leapt over the goal line and landed on the back of his helmet. He felt disoriented. His nose stung. He was covered in blood, but as his teammates began leaping on him with huge smiles and shouts of joy, Abruzzi said to himself under his breath, feeling the weight of his teammates as they piled on, "We won! We fuckin' won!"

As Abruzzi landed, Gale put his head down and fought back tears. Donta Jones and Deshay Anderson tossed their headsets and hugged him. Rulon Alexander, frozen on the sideline, watching the celebration unfold, said to no one in particular, "I'll be a son of a bitch."

***

Gale met Marybeth and Tilly under the stadium after a fawning and boisterous press conference. A forklift near one of the entrances moved large containers of bottled water. Whenever the driver backed into reverse, a shrill warning alarm

175

beeped on and off. When Tilly saw Gale, she held back for a moment before racing into his arms. He embraced his daughter, kissed her over and over on her forehead, and told her he loved her very much.

"You won, Gale," Marybeth said, her face bright with joy.

Gale pulled Marybeth toward him. The three of them hugged.

For a few moments, Gale was unable to put his feelings into words. He said finally, "We beat Detroit."

"You did," she said.

"No one believed we could."

Marybeth shook her head and gave him a playful look. "I even thought you were in over your head, Gale."

He looked into her eyes. "Really?"

"The winning touchdown was caught by a kid from Ellerton State."

Gale broke into a grin.

"Who ever heard of Ellerton State?" She laughed.

"I guess," he said. "How about now?"

"You beat Detroit. Doesn't that tell you something?"

CHAPTER 37

Spencer Tate shook his head in disbelief when Jonathan Colvin told him the news. The Lone Stars had released Abruzzi and Ellis two hours after beating Detroit. Vernon Voss had panicked and put Tate in a precarious position. Tate's anger grew as he thought about the media backlash and the calls for an inquiry into the League's integrity. Tate not only feared the Feds, but he continually kept a wary eye on the rabid politicians who licked their chops hoping to dissolve the League's antitrust exemptions.

Tate eyed Colvin and lifted himself out of his office chair. Red Zone flickered on the large HD screen in Tate's office. The West Coast games were in full swing.

"Those stupid SOB's," Tate said.

"It's a bad look, Spencer."

"Have the transactions hit the wire yet?"

"No. Johnson just filed them."

"Kill the waiver deals."

"Kill them?"

"You heard me."

"How?"

"Call Johnson."

"What am I going to say?" Colvin asked.

"Tell him that he and Voss have gone too far. Tell him to find another way for the Lone Stars to lose."

"Lose?" Colvin's eyes clouded.

"Forget I said that."

"What's going on, Spencer?"

Tate turned away from Colvin and stared out at the darkening Manhattan skyline. "You don't want to know. Believe me. You don't want to be anywhere near this."

***

Gale heard the news from Sam Lorenzo, who caught Gale in the empty Voss Energy Dome parking lot before Gale climbed into his truck to drive to the Complex. Lorenzo gleefully told him Johnson was cutting Abruzzi and Ellis.

Gale's ears grew hot.

"They're gone, McClanahan. Released."

"Gone?"

"That's what I said, Boy Scout."

Gale stared hard at Lorenzo. He wanted to punch him between the eyes.

"You tell Johnson and Voss they'll never get away with this."

"Why don't you tell 'em?"

Gale grunted and climbed into his pickup. He slammed the door. His conversation with Lorenzo had left him feeling hollow, alone, and angry. Marybeth and Tilly had flown home to Kinney. Now with news of Abruzzi and Ellis being waved, the joy of beating Detroit fell away.

He'd had enough.

***

The drive to Voss' estate had taken 40 minutes. Gale had found the address online and plugged it into Google maps. The route took him into the hills as the sun set and shadows spread across the winding two-lane road. When Gale arrived at the estate, two imposing stone pillars greeted him along with a sliding iron gate stretching across the entrance. A key card sensor was attached to the driver side pillar along with an intercom system.

Gale pushed the intercom button and a few seconds later heard a Hispanic woman ask what he wanted.

"Tell Vernon that Gale McClanahan wants to see him."

"Is he expecting you?"

Gale paused. "He'd better be."

"What's your business, Mr. Gale?" she asked, flustered.

"The San Antonio Lone Stars."

Gale heard static on the other line. Nearly a minute passed until he heard the sultry and cool notes of Vanessa's unmistakable voice. "I'm letting you through," she said.

Gale pulled up to the house in the dying light. It was immense. The home was built out of Austin Stone with gas lanterns flickering on each side of a massive, varnished mahogany door. It had a high pitched, slate roof, copper gutters, and neatly trimmed shrubs and flower beds lit by landscape lighting along the front side of the house. A flagstone walkway led to the entrance.

Gale pushed the buzzer and waited. Nearly a minute passed before a tiny woman wearing an apron opened the door.

She frowned and without hesitating said, "This way."

She led Gale through several large, high ceiling rooms with expensive artwork, plush furniture, and richly woven Navajo carpets until they entered a room with large sliding doors opening to an infinity pool, and on the horizon, the glow from San Antonio's skyline.

He'd never been inside a house like Voss'. The oil and gas men in Midland had impressive homes, but he'd never seen a place which felt so luxurious.

LONESTAR

Gale heard a voice say, "What a shame, Vernon's not here." He turned. Vanessa Voss stood in front of him wearing black leggings and a white crop top. Her stomach was taut and tanned, and her thick blonde hair was freshly brushed. She held a drink in her hand and wore a half smile.

She continued. "He's gone. You've made him very unhappy, Coach McClanahan. Beating Detroit? What a naughty boy. I imagine he and Garvin are somewhere crying over a drink, plotting your demise."

"How about you?" Gale asked.

"You gave me reason to celebrate." She held up her drink, as if to say "here's to you," and took a sip.

"Celebrate?"

"That's what I said. Whenever Vernon loses, I celebrate."

"A happy marriage."

Vanessa smiled. "What's happiness have to do with it? I grew up with nothing. Vernon gave me a way out and as long as I don't screw the pool boy, he gives me what I want . . . great clothes, jewelry, a beautiful house, travel, and," she held up her glass, "what I need to live with a man I detest."

She paused.

"You want to know something? You're the first man I've ever sent flowers to. The day I smashed your pickup, I was out of my mind. I couldn't find my Percocet. I don't often feel remorse, but when I looked into those brown eyes of yours at Starbucks, I felt sorry for you, and I wanted you."

"I'm a married man."

"So, I guess you're a man who'd never sleep with someone like me. An addict. A tramp. . . or in Vernon's words, a 'slut.'"

"Divorce him."

"A divorce?" She laughed. "With the prenup, I'd be waiting on tables at Denny's again. In fact, that's where I met Vernon, waiting tables at the Denny's down the street from the Complex. He told me who he was, and I smiled, wiggled my ass, and screwed him that night in this house while wife number three was on a shopping spree in New York. When it all comes down, I'm not a good person. I'm a shit." She paused. "So, it doesn't matter that you're the first person I've sent flowers to?"

"Am I supposed to feel good about that?"

"Feel whatever you want. I don't tell people what to feel. I can't sort out my own feelings if I have any. How am I going to be in charge of yours?"

Vanessa continued. "I'm a lot of things. But I'm honest. I like beautiful homes and private jets. If I need Percocet and Gray Goose to put up with Vernon, it's a deal I'm willing to make."

"I've got to go," Gale said. The conversation left him unsettled.

"You're not going to have a drink?" Vanessa smiled. "We could have so much fun, Boy Scout."

179

"I've got a coaching staff breaking down today's game. I'm late."

"You know, Vernon's going to win, don't you?" She paused and sipped her drink. Her full lips caressed the glass. "Especially when his business is on the line. He's going to find a way to ruin you, like he's ruined everyone else. You know what?"

"What?"

"In the end, you'll be like me. Sitting on Vernon's trash heap. We won't have fun together then?"

Gale stayed silent.

"Do you have kids?"

Gale hesitated. "A daughter."

"Don't let her wait on tables."

"She's four-years old."

"Watch her closely. Before you know it, she'll be sixteen."

"Tell Vernon I'm looking for him," Gale said, turning to leave.

"I don't tell Vernon anything. But don't worry. You met Mrs. Herrera. She'll tell Vernon a man came to see him tonight. She'll tell him we talked. Maybe had a drink. Vernon will interrogate me. I'll tell him what I know."

"What's that?"

"That you're dangerous. That he'd better destroy you."

***

On the ride back to the Complex, Donta Jones called. Gale had told Jones about Abruzzi and Ellis after Lorenzo had shared the news. Lost in worry about Abruzzi and Ellis, Gale turned down the radio and flipped on Bluetooth as he sped down the highway, passing cars on his way into the city. It was dark and Gale's headlamps illuminated the smattering of vehicles in front of him.

"Abruzzi and Ellis are still with us, Coach," Jones said.

"What happened?" Gale asked, relieved.

"I called a buddy of mine at the League office. He heard the Commissioner squashed it."

"A buddy?"

Jones paused. "Franklin Washington. Head of League Security."

"Friends in high places?"

"We played together at William and Mary. He joined the FBI after graduation and the rest was history."

"Do Abruzzi and Ellis know they were cut?"

"Nope. Word never got out."

"I guess we live another day, Donta."

"We do, Boy Wonder. We sure do."

CHAPTER 38

Sitting behind his desk, Vernon Voss held the sheet of paper with the most recent attendance figure. It was Friday. In two days, the Lone Stars would be hosting Seattle. Still angry about the Lone Stars beating Detroit and upset at Spencer Tate for refusing to allow Abruzzi and Ellis to be released, Voss set his black eyes on Garvin Johnson.

"Do you know what this says," Voss said tersely. "27,542. That's paid attendance so far for Seattle."

Johnson shook his head. "It's only a marginal increase, Vernon. Even if attendance breaks 30,000, it's only one game. Seattle's a 28-point favorite."

"So was Detroit."

"Last week was an aberration."

"It better be."

For a moment, Johnson looked away from Voss' harsh glare.

"Our Russian was very unhappy to see Sunday's score. I'd assured him we wouldn't win a game this season."

"Like I said, an aberration," Johnson said.

Voss leaned back in his chair. "Screw with McClanahan, Garvin. Do everything you can to make his job impossible. Understand?"

"I've been doing that, Vernon."

"Not good enough," he said with the wave of his hand.

Voss stood up. Johnson reluctantly followed.

The meeting was over.

When Johnson left, Voss picked up his phone. He studied it. Max Hartmann had called him again, the third time in a week. The banker's voicemails were tinged with subtle threats. Very Swiss. Polite and threatening all at once. Rasheed would have to wait like the rest, Voss thought. Voss imagined the Saudi Prince growing frantic in his palatial office with its sweeping view of the Dubai skyline and Persian Gulf as he tried to reconcile his debts. Voss stared at a folder on his desk. It was the most recent balance sheet for Voss Energy. The numbers were growing worse. Voss cursed. His life depended on the Lone Stars tanking. Like the Saudi Prince, Voss wasn't averse to extreme measures. *The deal with Asinov was going to go down. No one was going to stand in Voss' way, especially Gale McClanahan.*

***

After the meeting with Voss, Johnson called Lorenzo. The conversation lasted less than a minute. Johnson couldn't have been clearer. Lorenzo said he would come up with a plan. He assured Johnson with smarmy swagger that Seattle would trounce the Lone Stars.

***

Saturday morning's walkthrough ended with a pizza delivery van pulling into the Complex. Standing in the endzone, Deshay Anderson smiled at Gale as the players walked off the field, and said, "Looks like lunch is served."

Anderson and Jones had begun to be a force to be reckoned with coaching the defense. Anderson was making a smooth transition to coaching. He drew a clear line with his former teammates in his role as defensive line and special team's coach. When a handful of players asked him if he wanted to go out for a beer, Anderson laughed and said, "I'm no candy ass player no more. I got work to do."

Gale had felt that it had been a spirited and confident week of practice. The team was getting better. He'd warned the players about letting down after beating Detroit. They'd listened.

"You order lunch, Coach?" Anderson asked, as the delivery man, paunchy and unshaven, unloaded a stack of pizzas and carried them into the locker room entrance.

Gale noticed Jimmie follow the delivery man into the Complex. "Did you?" Gale turned to Donta Jones, who had walked over to Gale and Anderson.

"Nope. But I'm hungry."

Gale shouted at Rulon Alexander, who was talking with Engle and Ellis several yards away about a new curl route they'd installed for Seattle. "Rulon, did you order pizza?" Alexander, who loved every conceivable type of junk food, said, "No. But I'll be first in line to eat it."

Gale watched the delivery man going back to his van to grab more boxes of pizza. Gale walked over to the van outside the security gate. "Who ordered this?"

The delivery man squinted in the midday sun. "I don't know," he said. "Someone called."

"Do you remember?"

"Look. I deliver the pizza. I don't take the orders."

"Open a box."

The delivery man looked confused.

"Open it." Gale pointed at one of the cardboard containers.

The delivery man shook his head and opened one of the boxes. Gale took a slice and smelled it.

"It doesn't smell right," Gale said. "How long has the pizza been sitting?"

"Look, buddy. It's fresh. We don't deliver stale pizza."

Gale noticed a thin, gray hardened crust on top, as if the pizza had been left on a counter overnight.

"Put it back in the van," Gale snapped.

"What?"

"Take it back."

"Are you kidding?"

"Now." A bolt of fear hit Gale. He found himself sprinting toward the locker room entrance. When he entered the locker room, he saw the players opening the stack of pizza containers that were sitting on a large fold out table in the middle of the room. McCann Foster was about to bite into a slice of pepperoni. "Put it down!" Gale yelled. Foster looked at him and shook his head. The rest of the players pulled away from the table.

"You gonna eat it all?" Foster asked, tossing the slice back in the box.

"Where's Jimmie?" Gale asked, ignoring Foster.

"He's in the equipment room," Abruzzi said, his eyes and nose swollen and blackened from the flagrant foul against Detroit.

Gale sprinted out of the locker room and found Jimmie, sitting on top of one of the dryers, munching a slice of pizza.

"How much have you eaten?" Gale asked.

"What?"

"How many slices, Jimmie?"

He began to stammer. "Two. I thought the pizza was for all of us. . . I didn't know. . . I was hungry."

"Put the pizza down. It's bad."

"Bad?"

"It'll make you sick."

"How do you know, Coach?"

"Trust me, Jimmie."

Later, Gale could hear Jimmie heaving in the bathroom next to the coaches' conference room. He'd been throwing up for nearly 30 minutes. Gale cursed. It was getting uglier. Open season on the Lone Stars.

CHAPTER 39

Gale ran off the field as 29,411 fans in paid attendance cheered. He had a feeling of disbelief. The Lone Stars had beaten Seattle. It had been a ferocious game, and Donta Jones' defense had made the difference when they stuffed Seattle on a goal line stand late in the fourth quarter to seal a 17-10 victory. Gale even broke from his go-for-it mentality on fourth down and during the second half instructed Abruzzi to punt three times deep in their own territory.

A half an hour later, Gale stood in front of the media as beat reporters flooded him with questions. He hid his giddiness and answered with a sober, flat cadence. *Yes, the defense had played well. Yes, the Lone Stars were improving. Yes, on any given Sunday in the League one team could beat another. Yes, he felt punting today in the second half was a better strategy. Yes, he knew the Lone Stars had been nearly a 30-point underdog. Yes, he realized that the team's winning record, 2-1, was the first time in five years the Lone Stars found themselves over .500. Yes, he realized that he and his coaching staff had been ridiculed. No, he didn't have any comment about Buddy Adams and the team's other former coaches. Ancient history. No, he wasn't worried about Voss relocating the Lone Stars. It was his job to coach, not worry about things out of his control.*

The press conference lasted for nearly twenty-five minutes. Afterwards, Gale noticed voicemails from Marybeth and Grayson Wallace as he made his way to the Lone Star locker room. Wallace had called Gale a half dozen times after the team had beaten Detroit. He'd given a litany of advice. Wallace was at it again.

As Gale walked underneath the stadium, his phone dinged with a text. He read the message and felt his pulse quicken. He was about to delete it but pulled away. It was from Vanessa. It read: *Naughty, naughty boy! You won again. Vernon's out of his mind. You grow more interesting every day. V*

***

Mike Andujar stood in front of a new affordable housing project in the late afternoon sunlight about to make a self-congratulatory speech. He hoped for a boost in the polls from his efforts to create homes for low-income families. He was about to launch into his script when Catherine Reiser whispered in his ear. A few seconds later, Andujar smiled. The Lone Stars had pulled off another miracle beating Seattle. Gale McClanahan's star was rising.

***

Three days later, in the early morning, Rose Cutler failed to raise her head when Gale walked by her desk. Doing her best to ignore him, she focused on her computer, her glasses perched precariously on the tip of her nose.

"You won't like this," she said, failing to look up.

"What?"

"The practice field."

"What about the field?"

"Jimmie Peebles, that strange man you brought from your hometown, said it's ruined."

"Ruined?"

"That's what I said." Cutler turned and faced Gale.

"What happened?" Gale's mind began to spin. Practice was starting in an hour.

"I don't know."

Gale went quickly outside and found a bewildered Jimmie looking like a wet dog as sprinklers pumped water onto the field. There was nearly an inch and a half of standing water. A lake had formed despite the field's subtle crown. Gale ran over to the irrigation control box and tried to cut off the flow, but the switch was sabotaged. He stepped back and swore. There was no way practice could be held. Gale envisioned broken ankles and torn ACL's. It would take at least a week for the field to dry and that was if the turf survived the drowning. How could they possibly get ready for Pittsburgh?

"What happened?" Jimmie asked, shaking his head.

"I have a good idea. Get Coach Alexander and Jack," Gale said. "Now."

"Will do, Coach Gale."

"Jimmie . . ." Gale said with urgency.

"Yup."

"Tell Abruzzi and Foster they need to meet me in my office in fifteen minutes."

***

Jack Engle and Rulon Alexander watched the sprinklers whir back and forth, spraying plumes of water onto the field. The day before, Gale had caught Alexander hovering over Rose Cutler's desk. A box of chocolates had sat in front of Cutler as she peered upward at Alexander with a coy smile pursed on her lips. As the sprinkler drenched the field, Alexander turned to Engle and Gale, put his hands on his hips, and said, "How about a swim meet?"

Engle turned. "We won't practice on that field anytime soon, Gale."

Gale shook his head. "What now?"

"How about the parking lot?" Alexander said ruefully. "I've had teams practice on far worse."

"How about the Dome?" Gale asked.

"Monster truck event all week," Alexander answered.

"Who do we know?" Gale questioned.

Engle and Alexander stared at each other.

"Know?" Alexander asked.

"Is there a coach at one of the area high schools? Can we use their field?"

Engle and Alexander thought for a moment.

"Tom Parsons," Engle said, finally. "Thomas Jefferson."

"A good man," Alexander said. "Played at A&M."

"Call him, Jack," Gale said. "Tell him we got a problem. Tell him we need to use his field."

"Got it," Engle said.

"Jack," Gale said.

"What?"

"Tell Parsons we may be using the field for a while."

"What if the high school wants to charge rent?"

"Tell him we don't have a pot to piss in."

"That might not play."

"It has to," Gale said, shaking his head. "Can you imagine McCann Foster tackling someone on a parking lot?"

***

Abruzzi and Foster met Gale in his office and sat across from him. Abruzzi wore a gray Lone Star t-shirt and practice shorts and a Houston Astros' cap propped backwards. Foster sipped a Red Bull, his muscles rippling through a dark blue, long sleeve workout shirt.

"How are we going to get across town to practice?" Foster asked after Gale explained the situation.

"Drive your own cars."

"You're kidding me?"

"Nope."

"Drive across the city wearing full pads?"

"Carpool," Gale said.

Abruzzi shook his head. "You gotta be kidding me."

"How long are we doing this?" Foster asked, a scowl forming.

"For a while," Gale said. "The field's ruined."

"The players are going to be pissed," Abruzzi warned.

"No one likes it, Matt," Gale said, leaning forward in his chair, for an instant studying Abruzzi's mangled nose.

"Just one more obstacle," Foster said, giving Gale a knowing glance.

"What happened to the sprinkler system?" Abruzzi asked.

Gale thought about the way Sam Lorenzo lurked around the Complex. No doubt Lorenzo had his hand in the ruined field.

Before Gale could answer, Foster interjected, "The sprinkler system's broke, Matt. It's like everything else around here. A joke."

"They need to fix it," Abruzzi said.

Foster lifted himself out of his chair to leave. He'd clearly had enough. "Fat chance. We'd have better luck fixing it ourselves."

CHAPTER 40

They found themselves losing to Pittsburgh 24-3 at halftime. Walking into the tunnel, Gale was boiling. Missed tackles, botched plays, lack of energy. A coach's nightmare. Without hesitating, he followed the players into the cramped dressing room. He turned to Foster and said, "You aren't doing squat out there, McCann. And you," he turned to Abruzzi, "I've never seen you look this bad." He faced the rest of the team. "24-3? I thought we were better than that?"

The players stared blankly at the floor.

"I thought we were done being embarrassed. What's it going to be? Get the snot knocked out of us for the next thirty minutes, or come out and kick their ass?"

Gale fought his growing exhaustion. The trip to Pittsburgh had been a mess. Another delayed flight, a bad hotel, a fire alarm ringing at 3 am, a greasy pre-game meal at a self-serve cafeteria, and a bus driver who happened to get "lost" driving to the stadium. Lorenzo hung around the team like a jackal, scheming and plotting with Johnson, always on his phone, trying to find ways for the Lone Stars to stumble. Abruzzi and Ellis waived, rancid pizza, a ruined practice field . . . what next?

Gale left the locker room and stepped into the stadium tunnel; its concrete block walls were painted Pittsburgh team colors. The other coaches followed. Deshay Anderson pulled Gale aside.

"How about an onside kick, Coach?" Anderson asked. The Lone Stars were kicking-off to start the second half. "We got nothin' to lose."

Gale thought for a moment. After a few beats he said, "Do it."

Anderson broke into a toothy grin. "Maybe it'll shake up our dudes."

"Maybe," Gale said. "If it works."

***

A hush fell over the crowd. Jaquon Temple, the Lone Stars' rookie special teamer, recovered the onside kick after diving into a pile of bodies. After untangling himself, Temple jumped in the air and punched the sky, before running off the field with the ball tucked under his arm. A keepsake. Anderson hugged him and Rulon Alexander said into his headset, "Here we go . . ."

McCann Foster walked over to Gale and said, "Playing like crap? Wait and see."

Gale ignored him and suppressed a smile. He loved Foster's fiery nature, his will to win, and the visceral way he approached the game.

LONESTAR

Over the course of the second half, the Lone Stars ate Pittsburgh's lunch.

With 00:46 remaining in the game, the Lone Stars trailed Pittsburgh by a field goal, 24-21. The offense had clicked. The defense had shut Pittsburgh down and made a statement early on when Foster nearly decapitated a slot receiver on an incomplete pass. Pittsburgh fans sat uneasily on the edge of their seats as the clock ticked while Abruzzi drove the Lone Stars down the field. After two completed passes to Javon Ellis, San Antonio found itself in field goal range with nine seconds left.

"Kick it," Alexander said into his headset.

"We got time for one more play, Jack?" Gale asked Engle, knowing he had one timeout left.

"Kick it, Gale," Engle said, staring at the game clock.

Gale nodded at Anderson. The kicking team ran onto the field. A thirty-seven-yard attempt. There wasn't a lick of wind on a beautiful early October afternoon. Perfect kicking conditions.

"I got my rosary beads," Alexander said.

"Kiss 'em," Jones said.

Pittsburgh iced the kicker with a timeout.

Gale turned to Anderson, standing next to him. Gale put his hand over the mic on his headset and said, "I hate kickers, Deshay."

Anderson broke into a grin. "Scourge of the earth."

Gale shook his head. "Especially on the road."

When the game official blew his whistle to resume play, Gale took a deep breath. He felt his stomach knot. It came down to a field goal.

***

Voss sat up in the Gulfstream's master bed, his rage growing. As the jet shuttled him to Moscow for a meeting with Asinov, Voss glanced at Julia for an instant before turning back to the HD screen. The flight attendant's breasts, covered by a silk sheet, moved up and down as she slept as far away from Voss as the bed would allow. He'd relaxed during the first half and had her while the Lone Stars fell further and further behind. When the second half began to unfold, Voss watched in horror as the Lone Stars clawed back against Pittsburgh. When the Lone Star kicker ran onto the field in the final seconds to tie the game, in his rising fury, Voss knew he needed to take matters into his own hand. The stakes needed to be raised before it was too late. Johnson was failing. The thought of being forced to meet with Asinov in Moscow made Voss angrier. He hated Moscow with its drab, Soviet-era buildings, and government bureaucrats. Most of all, he hated Russia, with its massive energy reserves and penchant for global meddling. Voss tried not to think about the meeting with Asinov, especially if the Lone Stars won. He clenched his fists and took a deep breath as San Antonio's kicker waited for the snap.

C.W. WELLS

As the play clock ticked down, Gale closed his eyes for an instant. The kicker, Jerome White, an undrafted free agent, nervously swung his arms back and forth as the long snapper gripped the ball.

It was a perfect snap, perfect hold, and imperfect kick. The ball spun end over end and hooked away from the left goal post. Pittsburgh players and coaches struck their fists in the air and hugged each other. 70,000 fans roared. Gale kicked the dirt and felt his heart sink. He caught Anderson's eye and said into his headset, "I hate kickers, Deshay."

At midfield, as Gale shook hands with Mike Thompson, Pittsburgh's veteran coach, Thompson leaned over and said, "You're doing a helluva job, Gale. It's impressive. I'm rooting for you guys."

Gale nodded.

The Lone Stars found themselves 2-2. As Gale walked off the field with the noise from the crowd ringing in his ears, he'd already begun trying to turn the page. The Lone Stars' next game was against New York at home. A tough matchup but winnable. Losing to Pittsburgh stung especially in the final seconds. *Losing always did.*

***

Voss breathed a sigh of relief as the kick sailed wide. For a moment he relaxed and felt a youthful desire to have Julia again. Then he thought about the upcoming meeting with Asinov, the upcoming home game against New York, and his worsening financial woes. He felt his ardor recede. He reluctantly let Julia sleep until over the intercom, the pilot said they would be landing soon. A few minutes later, Voss thought he heard Julia crying in the Gulfstream's custom-fit shower. He shrugged, picked up his phone, and punched up Johnson's number. The stakes were growing higher, and Voss had everything to lose.

***

The call came while Gale rode on the team bus from the stadium to the airport. Caller ID pegged the number as spam. Gale let it slide. A few minutes later, he noticed a voicemail. He tapped the message and listened. After hearing the recording, Gale scratched his head and turned to Donta Jones.

"You ever had an endorsement deal?" Gale asked.

"No," Jones laughed. "Why?"

"Billy Evans called me. He wants me to be the face of his car dealerships. Says he's amazed with the Lone Stars and wants a clean-cut young man to pitch his cars."

190

"How much, Boy Wonder? Speak to me."

"$500,000 and a new Ford 150."

"You jokin'?" Jones thumped his hand on the vinyl seat.

"I could pick-up the tab again at Grady's."

"You could pay the bills. Make your wife happy."

Gale sat back in his seat as the bus rumbled along the freeway. "What do you think, Donta?"

"It'll make Johnson and Voss happy to see your face on late night TV."

Gale tried to muster a smile. The loss to Pittsburgh was still eating at him.

"Next thing you know, you'll be hawking blenders."

"We could do a lot with 500 grand."

"We?"

"The team. You don't think I'd spend it all on myself?"

"Not you, Boy Wonder," Jones said, rolling his eyes.

"The players can start eating right, and we can pay out coaching bonuses. Pay Jimmie, too."

"Most people would take the money and run."

"You think?"

Jones sat back. "I know. This is professional football, Boy Wonder. Greed drives all."

Gale stared out the window for a moment as the bus pulled onto the airport exit. "I want to win, Donta. It's the only thing that matters."

"Not the money?"

"If we win, the money will take care of itself," Gale said, his voice drifting off for an instant. "For now, I'll pay bills at home and make things better for the team."

"What about the new truck?"

"It's yours, Donta."

"Mine?"

"You had my back when everyone else bailed."

"You're giving me a new Ford 150?" Jones said, shaking his head in disbelief.

"That's what I said." Gale paused. "You're my friend, Donta. Friendship means everything to me."

CHAPTER 41

Gale called Marybeth when he landed in San Antonio. It was late and the terminal was empty. He had called Billy Evans before he'd left Pittsburgh and had agreed to the deal, and he wanted to get some things squared away.

"I'm real sorry about the game," Marybeth said.

"I'll be sending you a check for $125,000," Gale said. His voice was tired and hoarse.

"What are you talking about, Gale?" she asked with astonishment.

"An endorsement deal."

"Endorsement?"

"A guy who owns a bunch of car dealerships in Central Texas called. He wants me to be the face of his business."

"Are you kidding me?"

"I'm not. The deal pays half a million dollars."

There was silence. A deep breath. "My gosh. . . I never expected that."

"I'm going to pay the coaches and Jimmie with what's left. Help the team."

"That's generous of you."

"Please write Grayson a check to cover his loan. And Marybeth . . . we play New York at home on Sunday."

"I know. I have every home game highlighted on the refrigerator."

"It's going to be a huge game. We got to win. I've got to get people in the stands."

"I know."

Gale felt his heartbeat quicken. He hated the loneliness. "Would you and Til fly in for the game?"

Marybeth paused. Her hesitation made Gale's heart sink.

"I can't, Gale," she said, finally. "I promised the Huskins I'd watch the kids this coming weekend. They've been good to us."

"I get it," Gale said, feeling a hollowness growing in his chest. "Marybeth?"

"Yes."

"Make sure you pay Grayson back. I don't want to owe him or anyone else anything."

"I will," she said. "Are you okay, Gale?"

"I'm trying to keep my head clear," he said, watching a few travelers file by. "We play New York in seven days, and I'm bone tired. Kiss Til for me."

***

192

LONESTAR

Gale walked toward the airport exit with his duffel slung over his shoulder when he heard shouts come from the lone bar still open in the terminal. A group of men in their late twenties yelled, "Hey, Coach McClanahan!" They had had a few.

Gale turned. They waived him toward the bar. People were starting to recognize Gale since the wins against Detroit and Seattle. He wasn't certain how to feel. He realized he wasn't a high school coach anymore, but he didn't like the prospect of signing autographs while trying to eat a meal at Grady's.

"You gotta have a beer with us," one of the men, unshaven and grinning, implored.

Gale didn't see a way out. Besides, a beer might ease the pain of losing to Pittsburgh. "Only one, fellas. I got work to do tonight."

They bought him a beer, slapped him on the back, told them they were diehard football fans, and took numerous selfies. After nursing a Budweiser, Gale said his goodbyes and found his pickup. Twenty minutes later, Gale noticed blue lights flashing in the rearview mirror. He pulled over on the side of the highway and cursed.

The officer edged up to Gale's pickup and asked for Gale's license.

"You were weaving," the officer said. "And driving over the speed limit."

Gale knew it wasn't true. He was driving 65 and straight as an arrow. Gale turned his eyes away from the high-powered beam of the officer's flashlight as the policeman took the license and walked back to his cruiser.

Gale waited. A steady stream of traffic raced by on the highway. It seemed to take forever for the officer to return. When he did, he said, "Mr. McClanahan, I need you to get out of your truck."

"For what?" Gale asked.

"I smell alcohol."

"I'm not drunk." Gale fought the urge to tell the officer who he was. But for all Gale knew, the policeman wouldn't know or care. "I drank one beer in the airport."

"Out of the pickup," the officer said.

Gale shook his head and reluctantly climbed out.

"Against the vehicle," the policeman ordered.

"You're kidding me, right?"

"Now."

"What have I done?"

"Now," the officer repeated.

It struck Gale. It was like a thunderbolt. *Voss . . .*

The officer pushed Gale against the truck. Gale had an urge to lash out. Instead, Gale put his arms out and spread his legs. The officer frisked him before pulling Gale's hands behind his back and cuffing him.

"Drunk and disorderly conduct, driving to endanger, resisting arrest," the officer said. "Not pretty, Mr. McClanahan. We're taking a drive."

"How much is he paying you?" Gale asked, seething.

In one swift motion, the officer punched Gale in the stomach. Gale bent over gasping. He couldn't get air. He tried, but his lungs failed him. It was like a blindside hit by a linebacker. His eyes rolled into his head as the officer pushed him into the cruiser.

***

The concrete block holding cell had a dented stainless-steel toilet and sink. Two scroungy looking men shared the space with Gale. One had greasy long hair and a jagged scar across his forehead. The other stood over 6-5, had arms the size of tree trunks, a nervous tick, and menacing eyes. He kept staring at Gale as Gale sat on a metal bed with a thin foam mattress. Gale had asked for a breathalyzer test and to make a call, but the officer in charge had refused. Gale figured it wouldn't be long before the press discovered he'd been arrested. His mind raced. He was about to call for one of the officers again when an overweight man dressed in a shirt and tie approached the cell. He was bald, and his eyes were set too close together.

"Having fun?" he asked Gale. He flashed a smile. "Officer Recco said you pushed him."

"Officer Recco is full of it."

"Maybe. But you're in a load of trouble."

"I want my lawyer. That's my right." Gale desperately wanted to call Grayson Wallace.

"Is it? Resisting an officer. Driving under the influence. You got no rights."

The prisoner with the scar running across his forehead began to laugh. He brought his fist to his mouth as he broke into a hacking cough.

Gale paused. "Tell Voss this isn't over."

"I don't know what you're talking about." The plain clothed police officer smiled.

"I bet."

"Oh, and just so you know, the press is starting to call. What should I tell them?"

Gale looked away.

"Have a good night's sleep, Coach," he said, grinning. "Sweet dreams."

***

Before dawn, an officer came to the cell for Gale. Gale hadn't slept. He'd kept his eye on his cellmates all night. He'd been ready for trouble. His ribs hurt, and he wondered if he'd broken one from being sucker punched by the cop. The officer led him away from the holding cell and walked him into a dingy conference room and left. Gale looked up as Catherine Reiser, the mayor's Chief of Staff, entered the room. Her strawberry hair was tied up in a ponytail and her green eyes looked tired and wary. She wore jeans and a cream-colored blouse. Reiser said, "The mayor sent me to get you out, Gale."

"Thanks," Gale said wearily.

"No thanks needed."

"This is ridiculous."

She eyed him. "I know. That's why I'm here."

"Can we go?" Gale asked.

"Free and clear."

"How about a cup of coffee? You know a place that's open?" Gale didn't want to be alone. He was too tired to ponder the fallout from his arrest. He missed Marybeth, yearned for company, and a woman's voice.

Reiser broke into a tired smile. "I do."

***

"I was an assistant prosecutor with the state's attorney's office," Reiser said, sitting in a booth across from Gale in an empty all-night diner, "then Andujar called. I worked with his law firm for eight years before joining him in the mayor's office as Chief of Staff."

Gale watched her as she stirred the sugar into her coffee. She brushed a few wisps of hair from her forehead. She was pretty, with a smattering of freckles across her nose, and the subtle crow's feet at the corners of her eyes painted her as no one's fool.

"Two kids and a divorce later," she said with a tired smile, "I'm bailing professional football coaches out of jail."

Gale gave a half smile and poured cream into his coffee.

"I'm sorry that you had to deal with those cops. The officer who arrested you has an ugly track record. He's under investigation for misconduct. It's one of Mayor Andujar's goals to clean up corruption and make the city a more just place."

"Sounds idealistic." Gale tried to take a deep breath. His ribs burned.

"Maybe. But worthwhile."

Gale leaned back. "Vernon Voss set me up."

"I know. We have our eyes on him. He's enemy number one at City Hall."

"Am I going to be prosecuted?"

"No."

"How'd you pull that off?"

"As you can imagine, the mayor has clout."

"It won't help with the media."

"I'm afraid not. They love a scandal."

Gale took a sip of coffee and hesitated. He imagined the swarm of reporters. A few beats later, he asked, "Tell me, is there more to this than San Antonio losing the Lone Stars?"

For a moment, Reiser cast her eyes on the mug cupped in her hands. "Lots."

"What?"

"Voss hasn't met his lease payments to the city in over two years. We could fight him in court on that if he tries to move the team, but the case won't fly."

"Why not?"

"It won't. It's not enough. The lease agreement is clear. Average attendance has to be over 30,000." She paused for a moment. "But there's a hidden clause."

"What's that?" Gale's eyes hardened.

"If the city doesn't support the team, and the Lone Stars are sold, the sale triggers debt forgiveness and Voss gets even bigger prizes."

Gale looked quizzically at Reiser.

"He gets free of the millions he owes the city, and he gets rewarded to boot."

"The reward?"

"Years ago, when he bought the team, the city was excited. With a successful and hard driving owner, San Antonio was going to be put on the map. Voss knew how high the stakes were for the city so he did what came naturally. He negotiated hard and cut a deal. The agreement said that if the Lone Stars weren't supported and forced to move, Voss would get a payout."

"A payout?"

"This is where it gets interesting." Reiser leaned forward. "No one thought in a million years the Lone Stars would leave. Shortsighted politicians."

"What does he get if the team is sold and moves to another city?"

Reiser leaned back in the booth. She pushed her coffee mug away. "125 million dollars and rights to the largest undeveloped land tract in the city. What adds more drama is that the payout and land rights for Voss expire in January."

"When the season ends."

"The mayor's been holding his breath for Voss' rights to sunset. When the city made the deal with him, nobody wanted that land. It was an old industrial site. Now it's gold."

At that, Reiser leaned forward and put her elbows on the table.

"Voss is up against the clock," she said. "Mayor Andujar's been approached by a developer who wants to create a retail, hotel, and casino complex. Texas doesn't allow legalized betting, but that's going to change soon like everywhere else. The tax revenue alone would be enormous. Imagine if we lose the team and the city loses the land, the revenue stream from the development, and has to pay-out $125 million to boot. The mayor's got bigger ambitions. It's no secret. He has his sights set on Austin. Voss bankrupting the city would sink Andujar's political career."

"So, Voss walks away smelling like roses. Sells the team, makes billions, covers his losses, and has San Antonio by the short hairs."

She smiled. "Well put."

"All he has to do is make sure we don't put fans in the seats."

"Yes. From what I hear, you've made him very upset the past few weeks. You're not supposed to win games, Coach."

Gale shrugged.

"The mayor wants you to know he's got your back, but to be careful. Honestly, he had his doubts about you, but he doesn't anymore."

"And you?"

Reiser's eyes brightened for a moment, and she smiled. "I know very little about football, Coach. But you have the look of someone who doesn't like to fail."

Gale nodded and sipped his coffee.

"The mayor told me he'd do damage control on your run-in with the police, but he's walking a tightrope. It's dicey aiming accusations at law enforcement."

"Thanks."

"This will give Voss a reason to fire you," she said. She reached over and patted his hand, concern growing in her eyes. "But it's hard to fire a coach who can win in San Antonio."

Gale smiled and set his coffee on the table.

"Be careful, Coach McClanahan. Now you know how high the stakes are."

Gale signaled the waitress, who was sitting at a booth across the diner scrolling on her phone. He caught her eye, and she reluctantly pulled away from her cell and delivered the check.

"Thanks for the coffee," Reiser said.

"It's the least I can do."

CHAPTER 42

Billy Evans severed his relationship with Gale with a text. Gale's face reddened as he read the car dealer's message and walked to his office in the mid-morning. He'd had a chance to ease his money pressures, make things right with Wallace, and pay his coaches, but Voss had stolen another opportunity. For once, Rose Cutler read Gale's mood. Without a word, she handed him a print-out. Gale entered his office and closed the door. It was a statement from the San Antonio Police Department.

Gale McClanahan, 39, was stopped at approximately 10:40 PM yesterday after he appeared to be driving erratically and with excessive speed. The vehicle was traveling southbound on US 281. After holding McClanahan overnight and interviewing both the charging officer and the subject of the investigation, no charges were filed. For press inquiries, contact San Antonio Police Department Media Services.

Gale crumpled the statement and tossed it into the trash can. Word had spread. He had his regular Monday morning press conference coming up and already ESPN, Fox Sports, and a host of other media outlets had contacted him for comment. His endorsement deal was up in flames and Marybeth and Grayson Wallace had left repeated voicemails. Earlier that morning, Rulon Alexander had met Gale at the Complex with a smile and said, "You could have at least invited me to the party."

Gale checked his watch. He dreaded the press conference then felt his sore ribs. He was about to leave for the conference when his office phone rang. It was Garvin Johnson's assistant. Her voice was full of venom. "Mr. Johnson wants to see you NOW, Coach McClanahan."

Gale itched for a fight. He opened his office door and found Rose Cutler giving him an uneasy look.

Gale moved swiftly past Cutler, cut down the hallway, and blew by Johnson's assistant. She jumped out of her desk chair and said, "Hey, you can't go in there without Mr. Johnson's permission."

Gale ignored her and flung open Garvin Johnson's office door. He found Johnson sitting behind his desk, with his phone pushed up against his ear. "I'll call you later," Johnson said and hung up.

"What do you want?" Gale asked, his voice hard.

"Reckless driving? Driving under the influence?" Johnson said coolly. "That's unbecoming of a Lone Star employee." He smiled thinly and paused. "We've put up with a lot, son. I could go into detail, but it isn't worth my time. Bottom line, Mr. Voss and I agree that you're a blight on this storied organization."

"Storied?"

"We're letting you go. We're bringing Buddy and his boys back to coach."

Gale's eyes clouded.

"Clear out your office."

"Buddy and his boys?"

"That's what I said."

"That won't happen after I tell the world about Adams' little gambling habit."

"You think they're going to believe you after being arrested last night? We're firing you for cause."

"I'll tell them everything, Johnson."

"You think we care?" Johnson shrugged and broke into a smile.

"Everything."

Johnson leaned back in his swivel chair. "It's all rumor and innuendo coming from a desperate and angry man."

"We play New York on Sunday, and I'll be on the sideline, or this 'storied' organization and the scumbags who run it are going to be in a world of hurt. You can bet on that."

Johnson rose out of his chair and waved his hand. "I hope you saved your money, son, cause you're going to be writing Vernon Voss a mighty big check."

***

Hazel Dinkins, a clerk for the San Antonio Police Department, had been at her desk when they'd booked Gale McClanahan, the boyish and handsome coach of the Lone Stars. For years, Hazel had been bitterly disappointed with the Lone Stars' performance. Before her husband, George, had died a few years earlier, they'd held season tickets, the one splurge in their lives, high above the field in the Voss Energy Dome's cheapest seats. They rarely missed a game. Now George was gone, and Hazel had given up the season tickets, but watched every game on TV with fervor. For an older woman who weighed only 105 pounds, her love of football and loyalty to the Lone Stars were ferocious. She often wondered why. Before Gale McClanahan had shown up, there wasn't any reason for undying loyalty. The Lone Stars were finally exciting, and Hazel firmly believed the new head coach from West Texas was the reason. She was alarmed that McClanahan sat in the empty booking room. So when that terrible Officer Recco and his bald and overweight supervisor, plain clothed Lieutenant Furst, unabashedly recounted the false arrest a few feet away, she'd heard it all and kept her mouth shut. But she'd had enough. Furst and Recco had crossed a line. They'd falsely arrested her football savior, Gale McClanahan, and were laughing about it as if she didn't exist.

C.W. WELLS

Little did Recco and Furst know that Hazel had carefully and discreetly pushed the record button on her phone. She didn't care anymore about her job or the backlash. She was a faithful parishioner at her Baptist church, and what she'd witnessed between Recco and Furst was evil incarnate. Oh, the accusations she could make from all that she had heard over the years. She was ready for retirement, for her modest pension, and for her Lone Stars to win.

Hazel prayed about what to do with the recording. As she walked to her car in the early morning with the pale sun rising behind City Hall, she was determined to be a servant of God and save McClanahan.

***

Sam Lorenzo stood in front of the press conference room door. Lorenzo smelled of cheap cigars and a hint of liquor. He grunted when Gale bulled by him.

"You live another day, Boy Scout," Lorenzo said.

A few minutes earlier, Donta Jones had told Gale about the recording. It was spreading like wildfire on the news feeds and social media. Already there was a cry for an investigation into police corruption. Officers Recco and Furst were in the crosshairs. The media smelled blood.

As Gale pushed open the press conference room door, he set his jaw. He had made up his mind. The season was no longer merely about winning. It was about bringing Voss down. When he reached the podium, a dozen cameras clicked and TV lights nearly blinded him. Gale had never seen so many reporters.

***

Hazel Dinkins watched the press conference from her small apartment. She, Hazel Dinkins, had saved Gale McClanahan. As the press conference unfolded, she had a growing realization that McClanahan would deliver the Lone Stars to the promised land. Years and years of futility would end. If only her beloved George were here to witness it. It made her sad for a moment to think of her late husband. She brightened. Officers Recco and Furst were going to jail. She had put them there.

***

The next Sunday, as Gale stood on the fifty-yard line, he recalled reading about a Hall of Fame coach who toward the end of his career coached the Chicago Blitz in the struggling upstart USFL. The coach would gaze at the Soldier Field stands before kickoff with the hope the stadium held enough fans to make payroll.

Gale wondered if the crowd broke thirty thousand. He wasn't sure. He heard the side judge say, "Here we go, Coach." A few seconds later, New York's kicker belted a high, soaring kick into the arms of Javon Ellis.

LONESTAR

***

Vernon Voss, Garvin Johnson, and Vanessa watched from the owner's box high above the field. Voss cursed when he'd seen Gale during warm-ups. The two police officers hadn't said anything about Voss' role in having McClanahan arrested. While Voss felt sure that Recco and Furst wouldn't talk, he had made it clear what sort of accidents might befall their families if they did. Still, Voss seethed. Spencer Tate hadn't returned his calls, and now Andujar had launched an investigation into police department practices. Johnson had failed to remove McClanahan and McClanahan was now the center of media attention. A darling. A victim of police injustice and a hero to cop haters. Worse, he was a winner to boot. It was going to be nearly impossible to fire him, Voss thought.

Or was it?

Voss' eyes settled on Vanessa as she yawned and raised her vodka tonic to her lips. He thought for a moment. He had to leverage her somehow in case his plan for the Voss Energy Dome failed. Max Hartmann had called again full of threats. This time not so subtle. Asinov had texted full of demands. Voss turned to the luxury box attendant, who'd served them for years. He pointed at Vanessa, and whispered, "Cut her off, Sally."

The attendant blinked and looked confused.

"No more booze," Voss said.

"Are you sure, Mr. Voss?" Sally asked.

"Not a drop."

"Your wife's going to be very upset."

"Let her be," Voss said. "She needs to know who's boss."

CHAPTER 43

Marybeth sat under a shade tree and kept her eyes on Tilly and the Huskins' children. On a Sunday afternoon, the playground on the outskirts of Kinney was empty. Beyond the park, the desolate plains surrounding the town were stark and gray under the cloudless October sky. The children took turns going down a tube slide and climbing on a wooden castle.

Marybeth tried to focus on the kids, but sadness overwhelmed her just as she thought she could stop the scrimping and saving. Gale's run in with the police, the endorsement deal crumbling before her eyes, and the constant chafe of worry weighed on her. For all the years she'd been with Gale, she'd never doubted him. Like all married couples, they'd had their moments, but then the Lone Stars. After Gale's parents had died and the ranch had gone into foreclosure, she knew Gale had grown restless and sad, wondering if there was more to his life than coaching the Kinney Lions. Yet, Marybeth's life was in Kinney, and it scared her to think that she'd been forced into a world of treachery and deceit. When she stripped everything away, she had only Gale and Til. He was in the middle of the fight of their lives, and she was alone watching children on a dusty, deserted playground, while her husband was coaching against New York. What did she have to show for it? A growing bank account they couldn't touch. Debt. A despotic owner trying to ruin them. A deep wound in their marriage.

Marybeth glanced at her phone. Her heart began to race. 17-0 San Antonio in the second quarter. My god, she thought. They're winning. She was about to call Barbara Engle when she heard Tilly cry out. Marybeth looked up and found Tilly sitting in the dust at the bottom of the slide while the Huskin's kids circled her. Tilly sobbed and held her arm out for Marybeth to see. Marybeth knew right away. Tilly's forearm was bent at an odd angle. The rest of the day would be spent in the emergency room. Marybeth grabbed her handbag and hurried over to Tilly.

"It's okay, honey," Marybeth said with growing concern. "We're going to get some ice on that."

"It hurts," Tilly managed between sobs.

"I know it does," Marybeth said, carefully picking her up.

"It hurts, Mama."

"You're okay," Marybeth said. "Everything will be fine. I know it."

"I want my daddy," Tilly whimpered.

Marybeth held her daughter close. She bit her lip to keep from crying. She knew in her heart she couldn't live like this much longer.

LONESTAR

***

"We got a real team, Gale," Engle said, walking off the field after the Lone Stars defeated New York, 27-17.

Gale nodded. He wanted to feel elation, but his ribs hurt like fire each time he took a breath. His mind drifted. "How many people were in the stands, Jack?"

"I don't know. I thought there'd be more."

"31,000?"

"Maybe. All you can do is coach the team, Gale. You can't worry about anything else."

Gale stopped and turned to Engle. "We have to keep winning, Jack. There's no choice."

"You win and there'll be other teams who'll hire you. You know that."

"I made a commitment to this team, to this city, to myself. I got to see it through."

Engle studied Gale. "It's more than winning on the field, isn't it?"

Gale stayed silent.

"This is about Voss."

Gale's expression turned cold.

"Be careful," Engle said, putting his hand on Gale's shoulder. "Men like Voss rarely lose."

***

Ivan Asinov hated Kremlin receptions. Attendants swirled around Georgeievsky Hall, serving dollops of caviar on wedges of dry toast and flutes of delicate champagne. Asinov had little time and patience for desultory gatherings, but He had requested his presence, and Asinov learned never to refuse Him. Without Vladimir's support and loyalty, would his financial empire collapse? If Asinov was perceived to have taken a disloyal turn, the stakes could grow deadly. Volkov had been poisoned in Hyde Park while his young daughter watched as he choked to death. Petrov's plane had mysteriously disappeared over the Indian Ocean traveling to the Seychelles. Oligarchs lived by His grace. One had to be careful in Russia and beyond.

Earlier at the party, Vladimir had cornered Asinov. He'd heard about the prospect of Asinov's pending acquisition. Unsurprisingly, Vladimir had known everything. Vladimir relished judo, hockey, and an occasional soccer match. He'd focused on Asinov, his pale blue eyes empty and sinister. Vladimir had no interest in American football, but he needed a place to hide his flow of stolen money. As Vladimir had shoved caviar and toast into his mouth and had taken large sips of champagne, he'd bullied Asinov into a partnership. Asinov had hidden his anger and had agreed. Vladimir had twirled his champagne flute in his thumb and forefinger as he pronounced the team's name, The London Destroyers. London was, after all, one of his favorite killing fields.

Asinov's watch buzzed. He cocked his wrist and glanced at the dial. He felt a flash of anger. The Lone Stars had beaten New York. *Voss had promised they wouldn't win.*

Asinov placed his half-empty champagne glass on a table with cherry inlays and left the reception. He might have to take matters into his own hands. Voss was a fool and Asinov had made his displeasure known earlier in the week when the two had met over drinks in a private room at Café Pushkin. Now that Vladmir was involved, Asinov's life depended on the team moving to London. Who was this new coach named McClanahan? He would need to be dealt with before things grew out of control.

***

On Monday morning, Spencer Tate sat at his desk while his administrative assistant placed a folder in his hands with the latest attendance figures and digital platform ratings. The League's shift to a high tech, paperless world had not influenced the Commissioner. He liked his coffee with milk and sugar and his reports printed on paper.

He opened the folder and poured over the figures. As usual, Dallas led the League in attendance and an estimated 19.4 million viewers had watched Sunday Night Football the evening before. Tate smiled. He buttered his bread with TV ratings. A few months before, the owners had given him another long-term contract and a guarantee of $57 million for the coming year. Tate scanned to the Lone Stars and frowned. 31,253 fans had attended the game against New York. He leaned back and swore. Voss was making a mess of things. The Lone Stars were winning.

***

Vanessa ransacked the house. Her Percocet had vanished, and the liquor cabinet was bare. When she'd tried to access money from an ATM at a nearby shopping plaza, her card was rejected. As she sat in her Range Rover, she felt her hands trembling and a bead of perspiration form on her forehead. She suddenly felt dizzy, flung open the door, and vomited as tears streamed down her cheeks. Vernon had cut her off. He'd never done this before. Of all the things he could do to her . . . no money, no drugs. Vanessa began to grow hot and claustrophobic. She felt a stab of fear. Vernon wanted something from her. That much was clear. And she knew she would have to give it to him.

CHAPTER 44

Gale's plane landed in Midland early Monday afternoon. He flew home after breaking down film with the coaching staff and holding team meetings with the players. The night before, he'd received Marybeth's anxious call from the emergency room. Tilly needed surgery. The surgeon had scheduled the operation early Tuesday morning.

Grayson Wallace met Gale at the airport. Gale spotted Wallace's shock of unruly white hair in the crowded terminal and met him near one of the baggage carousels.

"Did you get my email?" Wallace asked.

"Which one, Grayson?"

Wallace smiled. "Ah, what did Polonius say, 'Give thy thoughts no tongue' . . . you should have punted in the fourth quarter."

"We won, Grayson."

"Yes, but it could have been fatal."

Gale changed the subject. "How's Marybeth?"

"I'm worried about her," Wallace said. His eyes grew uncertain. "Your wife's sad. Sadder than I've ever seen."

Gale nodded. "I know."

Wallace shrugged. "You both are good people, Gale. You have a lovely daughter. If I could get you out of this mess, I would."

Gale turned away before facing Wallace. "Where are you parked, Grayson?"

Wallace smiled. "In a no parking zone."

"Figures."

"Are you coming?" Wallace asked.

Gale's face turned grim. "Let's go."

***

Marybeth and Gale put Tilly to bed. Tilly's arm, wrapped in an air cast, was propped on a pillow to keep the swelling down. Earlier in the evening, she'd asked Gale to place her stuffed animals on the bed and had asked Gale to read a few of her favorite stories. Tilly's surgery was scheduled for the early morning. The pediatric orthopedist, a former center at Texas before attending UT Medical School, told Marybeth the surgery would be no more than an hour and a half.

Gale and Marybeth quietly stepped into the living room and looked at each other. Gale didn't know what to say. Marybeth stood in front of him, her hair clasped in a ponytail, wearing jeans and a Kinney High School Homecoming t-shirt.

Marybeth looked around the living room, frowned, and shook her head. "Can we go outside?"

Gale nodded. They put on coats and went to the backyard. High above in the chilly autumn sky, the stars clustered in a milky swath. Marybeth faced Gale and took his hand. Gale felt her squeeze and let go.

"I'm scared," she said.

"I am, too," Gale answered, his eyes adjusting to the darkness. He could see the outline of Marybeth's cheekbones.

"I'm a small-town girl, Gale. I never married you thinking we'd live anywhere else than Kinney or be anything else than teachers."

For a moment, they studied each other in the faint light.

"I watched Tilly lying in the dirt with a broken arm and felt fear like I've never felt it before."

Gale moved to her and took her in his arms and touched her cheek with the back of his fingers. Marybeth rested her chin on his shoulder.

"I'm afraid we'll never get our life back," she whispered.

Gale felt Marybeth shiver. He wrapped his arms tighter around her, stood in the darkness, and peered upward at the stars.

"I'm frightened, Gale," she said, finally. "More frightened than I've ever been."

***

The next morning, Catherine Reiser entered Mayor Andujar's office. The mayor rose out of his chair when Reiser walked into the room. She wore a thin wool skirt, a white blouse, and pearls. Andujar had always thought her attractive, and her divorce had caused a stir in City Hall as rumors persisted that she and Andujar had been having an affair. Untrue. But Andujar didn't dispel the notion. He thought about her at times, especially when they were alone together working into the late hours. He imagined holding her, kissing her long slender neck, and feeling her against him.

This morning, however, Andujar knew something was wrong.

"You're not going to like this, Mike," Reiser said.

"What happened?"

"I got a call from the *Express-News* a few minutes ago. There was an explosion in the Voss Energy Dome."

"Explosion?"

Reiser shifted. "Two workers were seriously injured when a transformer burst into flames. There's wide-spread damage. They're struggling to put the fire out."

Andujar's expression clouded.

"I'm trying to get confirmation from the stadium authority and fire department."

"I need more facts, Catherine."

"I know. I'm working on it, Mike."

He shook his head. "Do you think Voss is behind it?"

Reiser stood in front of his desk. "Of course."

The blood drained from Andujar's face. "Well, we're going to have to prove it or we're screwed."

"I know," she sighed.

***

Engle and Gale looked out at the Lone Star practice field. Brown, parched, and ruined. They'd been shuttling to Thomas Jefferson each day. The only good news was that Tilly's surgery had gone smoothly the day before. Now the Voss Energy Dome was a charred hulk. The turf field and plastic seats had melted and created an inferno.

Despite having no stadium to play games, after beating New York, the players were starting to believe in themselves, the team, and the coaching staff. When Gale spoke, they listened. He was no longer a high school coach from an obscure West Texas town. The Lone Stars were winning. He'd earned his stripes in The League. Doubt ebbed away and players like McCann Foster reminded teammates that something special was happening and not to piss it away.

"Have you spoken to Abruzzi?" Engle asked.

"What's up?"

"He caught a finger in his car door."

Gale's pulse quickened, and he turned to Engle. "Throwing hand?"

Engle nodded. "The trainer's checking him out."

"Broken?"

"Not sure."

Later that afternoon, they would be traveling to Los Angeles. Controversy once again swirled around the Lone Stars. The media fell into a frenzy about the blaze at the Voss Energy Dome. City Council members were calling for an investigation and pointing fingers at each other and the mayor. There were rumors swirling that the team would finish the year playing at the University of Houston or the ancient Cotton Bowl in Dallas. Gale understood Voss had scored a victory in his quest to sell and move the team.

"I'm going to go check on Abruzzi," Engle said, about to turn away from the ruined practice field.

"Does Rulon know?" Gale asked.

"He's already working on another game plan if Matt can't play."

"Let's hope it doesn't come to that."

CHAPTER 45

The evening before playing LA, Deshay Anderson had pinned Sam Lorenzo to the wall by the soda fountain. When Anderson saw where Lorenzo had booked the team dinner for the Lone Stars, he'd cornered Lorenzo and was about to rip his head off, when Gale said, "Don't do it, Deshay. Leave him alone."

The restaurant, The Palms, sat on a tawdry commercial strip near LAX. Planes flew low overhead, the thrum of jet engines drowning out any chance for conversation. The restaurant smelled of stale cigarette smoke and the tables hadn't been wiped down.

When Anderson backed off, Lorenzo said defiantly, "Wait til Johnson and Voss hear about this."

Anderson groaned. He turned to Gale. "We can't eat here, Coach."

Gale looked out one of the dirty windows. McDonald's sat across the street. "Let's go," Gale said to the players, who were milling around in the filthy restaurant.

"McDonalds?" Anderson asked.

"They have vegetables, Deshay."

Anderson smiled. "That's a reach, Coach. But it beats this dump."

As the players and coaches walked across the busy intersection, Abruzzi came up behind Gale and said, "I'm playing tomorrow, Coach."

"You think?"

"The team doc said he'll shoot the finger up and tape it."

"Can you throw?"

Abruzzi shrugged. "Maybe not deep routes, but I can get the ball to people."

"Let's see how it goes in warmups."

"Coach?" They walked to the entrance of McDonald's. "Do you think any team in the history of the League ate its team dinner at The Golden Arches?"

"Doubtful," Gale answered.

"I heard when Dallas plays LA they stay at the Conrad."

"Fancy?"

"Five star."

"Tell that to Vernon Voss," Gale said as they entered the restaurant.

Abruzzi shook his head and studied the long line of players and coaches waiting to be served and the perplexed look of the manager, who was scrambling behind the counter to sort out the orders. "I'm not telling that SOB anything."

***

Gale finally closed his laptop. He'd studied hours of game film, trying to keep from thinking about Marybeth and Tilly. He knew the coaching staff had created a solid plan and hoped that Abruzzi could play. He could hear planes flying overhead from LAX as he lay on the thin, frayed bedspread. The hotel room was cramped, hot water was in short supply, and the toilet didn't flush properly. Gale sighed.

He was about to strip off his clothes when he heard his phone ping. He picked it up. His heart started to beat harder.

"Please. I need your help. I'm staying at the Wilshire. Room 1206. V"

Gale studied the phone. He debated whether to return Vanessa's text. He remembered what Deshay Anderson had said. *Viper.* But Gale knew Voss was capable of anything.

Gale texted: *"What's going on?"*

"It's about Vernon . . . I'm scared . . . Now"

Gale tried calling her. The call slipped to voicemail.

He texted Vanessa again. Nothing . . .

Gale cursed and checked his watch. Nearly midnight. He'd be a fool to put himself in harm's way. He heard the ping of another text.

"He's going to kill me, Boy Scout. Please ..."

Gale shook his head and cursed. With apprehension, he put his jacket on and left the hotel room.

***

Gale's Uber dropped him in front of the Beverly Wilshire, one of LA's most historic, grand hotels, and a far cry from the team's dingy, run-down accommodations on the doorstep of the airport.

Gale entered the deserted lobby with its arched entrance way, grand crystal chandelier, and polished marble floors, then found the elevator. He hesitated for a moment and closed his eyes for a second before pushing the button. This was a bad idea, but here he was. He wouldn't be able to live with himself if something happened to Vanessa after he'd ignored her texts. A few moments later, the elevator climbed. Gale's ribs hurt, and he desperately needed rest. In the League, for a coach, sleep was a precious commodity.

The elevator door slid open, and Gale walked down the carpeted hallway and found Vanessa's room. He took a deep breath and knocked. After a few moments of silence, he heard a woman's unsteady voice say, "It's unlocked."

Gale found Vanessa wrapped in a white, terry cloth robe, lying on a lush, king-size bed in a suite furnished with a set of stuffed chairs, couch, and a sweeping view of LA at night. Her face was pale, washed out, and a nearly empty glass rested in her hand. Her ice blue eyes were tinged with red. She didn't bother to get up when Gale entered.

"You made it, Boy Scout," she said, slurring her words. "I didn't think you'd rescue me."

"Why'd you text me?" Gale asked, studying her.

"I need you."

"What's going on, Vanessa?" he asked with a flash of anger.

"Vernon's cut me off. He threatened me. I'm dying, Boy Scout. I need my Perc. This isn't enough." She stared at the drink in her hand. "I'm sick."

"What do you want from me?"

"I need you to get me into rehab. I need someone to support me. I need you . . ." She lifted herself unsteadily off the bed. Gale noticed the outline of her breasts, the way her hips flared, and her long, tanned legs. She moved toward him, tears starting to streak down her cheeks.

"Forgive me, "she said. "I'm a shit. An absolute shit."

She grabbed the collar of his shirt and pulled him toward her so that he could smell the vodka on her stale breath. Her face pressed close to his. He could feel the weight of her breasts as she leaned into him. Her tears dampened his shirt.

"I'm sorry," she repeated.

"For what, Vanessa?" Gale asked, confused, wanting to push her away, but feeling the crush of her abdomen.

"For this, Boy Scout," Vanessa said, dropping her robe and clasping her hands behind his neck as she kissed him hard with her soft, full lips.

***

Thousands of city lights fell away as the team plane climbed above LA and rumbled east toward the desert. Gale closed his eyes hoping to sleep, but the adrenaline from the game and the images from the night before played over and over in his head. Abruzzi had played. With his finger taped and Toradol running through his veins, he'd thrown for 247 yards and two touchdowns, propelling the Lone Stars to a 17-10 victory over Los Angeles. San Antonio stood at 4-2, the team's best start in a decade.

Gale should have felt elated, but there had been Vanessa, pushing him onto the plush sofa, her breath hot and fetid with alcohol, her frantic kisses, and hand finding his crotch before he could push away. When he'd left, the image flashed again and again of her splayed on the floor next to her crumpled robe, face in her hands, breasts heaving as she struggled to catch her breath amidst sobs.

When he left the Wilshire, he'd replayed the scene and started to feel exposed and uneasy. "Forgive me," she'd said.

There was something wrong. Contrived. Vanessa sitting on the bed, lifting herself toward him. Her eyes smeared with a cloudy film. The way she clutched his shirt collar, violently pulling him toward her as if she'd rehearsed it. The kisses forced and mechanical. The whole time there was nothing but despair etched on her face, as if she'd planned it all.

He'd fought a moment of desire when she'd begun kissing him. He'd nearly clasped her hips and guided her toward the bed. He hadn't felt another woman's body pressed against his since he'd met Marybeth. But he'd pushed her off and left the hotel room. As the plane ascended, he shook his head to try to erase the image.

As the plane flew toward San Antonio, he finally fell into a fitful sleep. When the team flight touched down in the early morning darkness, Gale turned his phone off airplane mode and watched the emails and texts pop up on the screen. Gale felt a stab of fear and stared at his phone. His hand began to shake. It was an email from a Gmail account tagged Cheater. He wanted to hit delete, but he noticed the link. With trepidation, he clicked on it.

CHAPTER 46

Grayson Wallace was an early riser. He relished the morning, puttering around his office with a steaming mug of coffee before his administrative assistant arrived and started admonishing him for having a whiskey before lunch. He looked out his window in the dawn light and saw pickups lined along the street in front of the Pump and Drill Diner. Breakfast was being served to oil field workers and ranchers. It was Monday with a long week ahead.

Wallace loathed the ring of a cell phone, so he kept his ringer on mute. But he pulled away from the window when he noticed his phone vibrating on his desk. He reached for it and answered.

Wallace listened as Gale told him what had occurred. He asked Gale to forward the link, promised to call him back, and replayed the video half a dozen times. There would be no doubt. Despite Gale's insistence that nothing had happened, the video was damaging. A beautiful woman rising off the bed, pulling Gale toward him, kissing him, her robe slipping to the floor as she fell on top of him on the sofa before her hand darted to his groin. The scene ended there, but anyone who watched would let their imaginations run wild about what ensued.

Wallace set his coffee down, sighed, and opened his desk drawer. He pulled out a bottle of Henry McKenna and poured himself a bourbon. He'd handled numerous tawdry affairs in his life as a small-town attorney. Most clients lied. It wasn't Wallace's position to ask if they were guilty. Gale was different. He'd always been careful, smart, principled, and faithful to Marybeth. Wallace fought the doubt creeping into his thoughts. Gale had always been honest, yet the video had even made Wallace wonder.

What now?

Wallace watched the tape again. The woman's muffled words caught his attention.

He replayed the video and listened carefully. It was as if she wanted to cast doubt on the seduction, Wallace thought. A disclaimer.

Wallace knew the damage the video would cause Gale. Gale had fallen into Vernon Voss' honey trap. The outcome was clear. Wallace was going to call Gale back and advise him to tender his resignation before the tape was made public. Wallace prayed that Marybeth would never see the tape.

Voss had won.

***

212

LONESTAR

The hardest thing Gale had ever done was bury his parents beneath a stark, winter sky. He lost them in a flash of scorched tires and twisted steel. The last year had muted the memory but not eased the pain of their deaths. Telling Marybeth what had occurred in LA would be hard. Harder than Gale imagined. Gale listened as Wallace wheezed into the telephone.

"I can call Voss and try to negotiate an agreement," Wallace said. "We don't want the video seeing the light of day, Gale."

"But it was a set-up, Grayson," Gale said, sitting in his pickup at the airport as the sun rose.

Wallace paused. "The one thing I've learned in my tawdry life is that perception's truth."

Gale grunted. "I'm not signing anything."

"Play it out. Voss releases the video. The tape goes viral. You lose your job and maybe your marriage. Your explanation will fall on deaf ears. No one will believe you."

"Do you?"

Wallace paused. Silence.

"Grayson?"

Wallace sighed. "I do. I know you and what you're up against."

"I'm not signing any agreement," Gale repeated.

"Then what?"

"I'm going to tell Marybeth."

"Do you think she'll believe you?"

"I don't know."

"Even if she does, the rest of the world won't." Wallace, as always, was matter of fact.

Gale's jaw tightened. "I don't care about anybody else, Grayson."

Wallace paused.

"Gale . . ."

"What?"

"Let me call her."

"Why?"

Wallace's voice grew low. "Haven't you learned by now? If there's anyone who's the voice of truth, it's yours truly."

"I forgot," Gale said with a hint of sarcasm.

"Besides, people always believe a small-town lawyer." Wallace grinned.

Gale started to smile despite himself. After a few moments, he said, "Not a chance, Grayson. I'd never be able to live with myself."

"I'm going to prepare a non-disparagement agreement in case you change your mind."

"It's a waste of time."

"Maybe," Wallace said, "but after your conversation with Marybeth, you may see the handwriting on the wall."

***

After speaking with Wallace, Gale drove to the Complex. When he arrived, it was still too early to call Marybeth. She'd be climbing out of bed, going to the kitchen to pour her first cup of coffee. After showering, she'd fix breakfast for Tilly and review her lesson plans at the kitchen table until it was time to leave for school.

Gale thought angrily about Vanessa. He wondered if she'd returned from LA. Voss had been absent at the game against Los Angeles, and Gale had overheard Lorenzo mention that Voss was overseas. Gale leaned back in his office chair and rubbed his eyes. He wondered what she knew. Was she privy to Voss' dealings? He knew he didn't have much time. The clock was ticking.

Gale bolted from his office and took off down the hallway. He hurried past the coaches' offices and entered the training room. He spied the locked medicine cabinet hung on the wall near the whirlpool tubs and yanked on the knob. The metal cabinet refused to open. He scanned the room and found nothing to snap the lock. He went into the equipment room and found a tired Jimmie stuffing soiled uniforms into the washing machines.

"You got a screwdriver?" Gale asked.

Jimmie opened his desk drawer. "Lots of 'em," he said.

"I need that one," Gale said, pointing.

Jimmie handed Gale the tool.

"Will that work?" Jimmie asked.

"Perfect," Gale said and went back to the training room.

Gale wedged the screwdriver between the medicine chest's two hinged doors, and with a grunt, forced open the cabinet. For a few seconds, he scanned the row of prescription drugs which included Hydrocodone, Vicodin, Fentanyl patches, and vials of Toradol. Soon he found what he was looking for: Oxycontin. As he grabbed one of the pill containers, he noticed Jimmie standing behind him.

"You can't take them pills, Coach," Jimmie said, alarmed. "You'll get in big trouble."

"You never saw me do this. Understand?"

Jimmie looked confused.

"There's a reason for everything, Jimmie," Gale said, turning to leave. "Trust me."

CHAPTER 47

Gale didn't announce himself. He ignored the intercom at the gate. He parked his car on the uneven gravel road running outside the estate, looked around to make sure no one was watching, and swung himself over the fence guarding the property. He heard a buzzing sound and realized a camera attached to a tree had swiveled and focused on him. His morning arrival would not go unannounced.

After he made his way to the house through a maze of Live Oaks and clumps of sage, he went around to the back of the home by the pool. He tried the slider door. It was locked. He walked around to the kitchen entrance and came face to face with Mrs. Herrera, who stood outside the door. She held a heavy skillet in her hand and regarded him fearfully.

"I need to see Mrs. Voss," Gale said.

Herrera shook her head. "She's not awake."

"Wake her."

"I can't do that."

"I'll wake her," Gale said, and despite Mrs. Herrera's protests, he pushed past the small woman into the house.

When he found Vanessa, she was drinking vodka in the study, wearing a sheer red silk robe. Gale could see the outline of her bra and panties. Mrs. Herrera followed, frantically shouting in a high-pitched voice for Gale to leave.

Vanessa looked up when he entered and waved Mrs. Herrera away with the flick of her hand. She said coldly, "It's okay, Isabella. I've been expecting Coach McClanahan."

"Are you sure?" Mrs. Herrera asked.

"I am," Vanessa said. "You can leave us now."

Herrera hesitated, then turned and left the room, softly closing the door behind her.

"Do you have no feelings at all?" Gale asked, standing in front of Vanessa, who stared back at him with frigid eyes. Her face was pale, her skin clammy. Her hair fell to her shoulders in a stringy tangle.

"Not in withdrawal. Vernon's cut me off. Soon I'll be selling my diamonds." Her hand shook as she brought the vodka to her lips. She tried to steady the glass with her other hand. "Do you know how this feels? I'd kill my firstborn for a hit of Perc."

"I can lose my family, Vanessa," Gale said. "Do you understand?"

"Oh, I understand. The question is, 'do I care?'"

"What's it going to take?"

Vanessa shook her head. "What do you think, Boy Scout?"

Gale pulled the pill container out of his coat pocket. He held the bottle in front of her. Vanessa's expression suddenly shifted, her eyes grew big, and she looked hungrily at the pills.

"Oxycontin. A month's prescription," Gale said, putting the bottle on the coffee table in front of her. "You won't have to kill your firstborn."

Her face hardened. "What do you want for it?"

"What do you think?"

"No one will believe me if I say the video was staged. They'll think we were doing something kinky or that Vernon set-up a camera in the hotel room to catch us on tape."

"I know."

"Then what?"

"Information."

Her eyes refused to stray from the pills. Slowly, she looked up. "About Vernon?"

"Who else?"

"What kind of information? That he's an asshole, and he treats me like crap?" A sudden tear rolled down Vanessa's cheek and with a shaky hand, she wiped it away.

"What's he done, Vanessa? What can you give me so that he doesn't ruin my life or anyone else's?"

"What's he done?" She laughed bitterly and wiped her eye. "What hasn't he done?"

"Help me. Give me something I can use."

She leaned back in her cushioned chair and shook her head. "I don't even know where to start."

"Start somewhere."

Her face was contorted by need. "You and I know what he's doing to the Lone Stars. That's nothing. . . there's so much shit. . . there's North Dakota," she mumbled.

"North Dakota?"

"It was terrible. Vernon didn't care. That's when I knew he would do anything to get what he wanted. It blew me away."

"What happened?"

"Five years ago, a rig blew up. It killed oil and gas field workers. There were safety violations. Not run of the mill. Serious ones. You'd think Vernon would care about the men and their families? All he cared about was making sure the whole thing went away. You see, he has people in his pocket."

"How so?"

"Vernon bought off a judge. He practically bought off the state's whole legal system. It was a travesty."

Vanessa paused.

"Now give me the Oxy," she said. "I gave you what you wanted."

"Not yet. I need more than that."

"I'm dying," she said. "Please. . ."

"I need a paper trail."

"I haven't got one."

"Get one."

"How am I going to do that? Even if there's a trail, you think Vernon's going to let me go into his computer?" She laughed coldly. "Don't be naive."

"Proof, Vanessa."

"I need the Oxy," she said. "Understand?"

"You get me what I want, and the drugs are yours."

"Vernon's too smart. You think any of this is documented?"

"Who was involved? Any names?"

Vanessa shook her head. "I don't know."

"Think harder."

Vanessa put her head in her hands and rocked back and forth before looking up. "It was in the papers. The accident. The lawsuit. Everything but the truth."

"That gives me nothing, Vanessa."

Vanessa started to sob. "Please."

"When's Vernon going to release the video?"

"Soon," she said, trying to catch her breath.

"Soon?"

"I don't know. Today. Tomorrow. Friday."

"If I resign?"

She lifted her head and flashed a grotesque smile. Her hair fell in strings across her forehead and tears smeared her face. "Oh, you think he's going to keep the video locked away if you quit, Boy Scout? Not a chance. He wants to destroy you. You made him look bad. You won. Besides, it doesn't matter. The Voss Energy Dome's toast. He's meeting with Asinov and Tate on Thursday to sell the team. There's nothing you can do about it."

Gale's mind raced. He reached out and took the pills off the table. He looked at Vanessa and instead of seeing a beautiful young woman, he saw a cadaver. "I'll take you to a rehab place. Right now."

She shook her head violently. "The Oxy. You promised!" Her teeth looked like daggers as she spoke.

"They can help you at a rehab place, Vanessa. They can make things better."

"The pills," she whispered.

Desperation was stitched across Vanessa's face. Gale lifted himself out of the chair and went to the door.

"You promised!" She shouted.

He turned, faced her, and looked at the container.

"Don't be a prick, Boy Scout. Please . . ."

He tossed the pills to her. It was her life, and he had, after all, made a bargain. The bottle fell at her feet and burst open. Pills scattered across the hardwood floor. She fell to her hands and knees and scurried to collect the Oxy, her hands moving furiously.

As Gale left, she didn't look up. She was like a starving dog hunting scraps.

***

Twenty minutes later, Gale pulled into a shopping center. He parked his truck next to Tom Thumb as a few morning grocery shoppers made their way into the supermarket. He googled Voss Energy North Dakota derrickmen case and found a stream of articles spanning nearly five years. After reading, he punched up Grayson Wallace on his phone.

"Fargo?" Wallace's voice sounded dubious.

Gale explained.

"I need to find someone who's credible and has dirt on Voss. I need to go to North Dakota."

"Who represented the field workers?" Wallace asked gruffly.

"Carabin Ohnstad."

"Ah, Carabin."

"You know him?"

Wallace laughed. "We've tangled before. The oil patch is small." He paused. "I heard about the mishap, but workers get killed. Dangerous work."

"Does Ohnstad hate you, Grayson?"

"Hate doesn't even begin to describe our relationship," Wallace laughed.

Gale shook his head.

"Have you ever been to Fargo?" Wallace asked with a grunt.

"Never."

"Hell on earth, my boy. Hell on earth."

***

The hollow feeling in Gale's chest grew. After speaking with Wallace, he took a deep breath and checked his watch. Marybeth would have playground duty. She'd be able to talk. They'd always been honest with one another. The dread grew as he stared at the phone in his hand. He took another breath, tried to control his breathing, and tapped Marybeth's number.

"Gale?" she answered. He could hear children playing in the background.

With his pulse racing, he told her what had occurred. Afterwards, there was silence.

"You have to believe me," Gale said finally.

"I have to go," Marybeth said, sounding stunned. "Recess is over."

"Marybeth . . ."

"We'll talk at another time. Understand?"

"When?"

"Another time."

"I'll call tonight."

"I've got to go."

"I don't want to end the call this way."

"Tonight," she said angrily.

CHAPTER 48

The short, stubby team doctor with strings of oily hair pasted across his scalp eyed Jimmie and pointed toward the broken lock on the medicine chest. The doctor's face reddened, and a vein protruded from his forehead. Stolen opioids was a felony, and because of a much-publicized malpractice suit where he'd replaced the wrong hip of an elderly patient, his medical license hung by a thread.

"Who stole the Oxycontin, Peebles?"

"I got no idea," Jimmie said, shifting his feet, staring at the floor.

"I bet," the doctor said, his round face hardening.

"Honest." Jimmie shrugged.

The doctor pointed his sausage-like finger. "If I discover you're lying, you'll be in big trouble, Peebles. More trouble than you can imagine."

***

League coaches hated Mondays. Win or lose, there was always bad news. Today, the injury report was bleak. Abruzzi had taken a flagrant hit against LA. His knee was swollen to the size of a grapefruit, and his broken finger on his throwing hand had turned purple. There was speculation that he'd need his fingernail removed. Javon Ellis had pulled a hamstring on a fly route in the fourth quarter, five other players started the practice week doubtful for Sunday's game against Atlanta, and Edgar Hillman, a rookie guard from James Madison had dislocated his ankle and was out for the season.

When Gale returned to the Complex, Donta Jones met him in the hallway outside Gale's office. Rose Cutler ignored them as she typed at her computer.

"I got no clue where we're going to play on Sunday," Jones said.

"Find out," Gale said before pulling Jones aside and sharing what Vanessa had told him.

Jones sighed and leaned against the wall.

"It's not about football anymore, Donta. I have a score to settle. I need you, Jack, and Rulon to run the team for a couple days."

"A couple of days?"

"I'm going to North Dakota."

"North Dakota?" Jones stared at him.

"Fargo."

"Lord."

"Keep things under control."

Jones paused and studied Gale's face. He said, finally, "You, too, Wonder Boy."

"I'll try," Gale said. "But I can't promise."

***

A few minutes later, Rose Cutler knocked on Gale's office door. She wore a concerned look on her face. Gale had never seen her this way.

"North Dakota?" she asked.

"Yes."

Her eyes softened. "Be careful, Coach McClanahan."

Gale nodded. "I will."

"I've grown to like you, you know." She blushed.

Gale gave a half smile. "I always knew you did."

"Don't let Voss win."

"I won't."

"Promise?" Cutler asked, reaching out tenderly and touching his elbow.

"I promise, Ms. Cutler."

***

Catherine Reiser found herself doing damage control. The media wolves were circling the mayor's office. The Voss Energy Dome was a total loss. There were rumors the stadium's fire suppression system had failed and a neglected transformer had led to the blaze. Even if Reiser's suspicions about Voss were correct, the possibility of the Stadium Authority ignoring years of engineering reports made her head spin. There was never enough money and accountability. She knew city governments lived on the edge. All it took was an egregious safety issue to leave a trail of ruined political careers. All it took to bring the Lone Stars crashing down was Vernon Voss lighting a match. Only a few weeks before, a condominium had collapsed in Florida, killing nearly two-dozen people. Investigators had found a litany of structural concerns that had been ignored by local officials and the condominium board.

Reiser closed her eyes for a moment and tried to think beyond the growing shouts and accusations as the politicians pointed fingers at everyone but themselves. As a former litigator, she prided herself on being a step ahead of opposing counsel. She knew the situation was dire. The Lone Stars were lost without a miracle. Plans were undecided where the Lone Stars would play the rest of the season. Regardless, there'd be no way for the team to hit attendance targets. Reiser had poured through the League by-laws. A city unable to maintain a safe, suitable venue for contests would open the door for a franchise's sale and relocation.

Reiser thought about Mike Andujar. She'd attached herself to his rising star after she'd been tired of the endless grind and terror of private practice litigation. She had two small sons to raise and an ex-husband to navigate. She accepted the pay cut to be Chief of Staff in the hope of more. Austin? The White House? Reiser knew Andujar was attracted to her. There were times when she could feel it when the two of them were in cabinet meetings, and she would catch Andujar gazing at her while she addressed the staff. Reiser, however, wasn't about to screw her boss. At heart, Andujar was like the rest of them, a political animal. Now his career in public office hung in the balance.

For some reason, certainly part of it attraction, she thought of Gale McClanahan. She hadn't spoken with him since the morning he'd been released from jail. She replayed their early morning conversation over coffee. The moment she'd met him, she knew immediately McClanahan was everything her former husband wasn't. She'd been smitten by his tired, honest brown eyes, rugged looks, and quiet resolve. Reiser sighed and sat back in her desk chair. Her ex had the boys for the week. It was a good thing they were with their father with hell breaking loose in the mayor's office.

Reiser decided to call McClanahan. In the aftermath of the stadium fire, she wanted to see how he was holding up and wanted to hear his voice. She picked up her cell phone and called. A few moments later, he answered. He sounded exhausted. She probed. He finally told her about the video, his conversation with Vanessa, the dead oil and gas field workers, the trip to Fargo, and the meeting on Thursday in New York with Voss, Asinov, and Tate and how they were about to orchestrate the sale of the Lone Stars. Impulsively, she said she'd meet him at the airport. She could help. After hesitating, Gale had agreed without protest. As she grabbed her purse to go home and throw together enough clothes for a couple of days, she convinced herself that if there was the chance to save Andujar, the Lone Stars, and the city, this was it.

CHAPTER 49

They rented the last car in the lot. When Gale and Reiser pulled in front of the Holiday Inn Express in the darkness, a late October snow was dusting the tops of cars and grassy strips along the road. The clerk laughed when they asked for two rooms and told them they were "lucky" that he had one. A sudden cancellation. Hundreds of ranchers had convened for Fargo's Annual Stockman Association Convention. Hotels were packed.

Gale turned to Reiser and shook his head. "It looks like I'm sleeping in the car."

Reiser smiled. "Nonsense. One of us can sleep on the floor. Don't worry, I won't bite, Gale."

"I'm skittish about hotel rooms," Gale said, breaking into a soft smile. "For obvious reasons."

Before Gale could put a credit card on the counter, Reiser moved past him and slid her Visa card toward the clerk. Gale protested. A few minutes later, they stood quietly eyeing the king-size bed.

"This is awkward," Reiser said finally.

Gale nodded. Her strawberry hair fell above her shoulders and freckles dotted her nose. She wore jeans and a light sweater and moved gracefully. She placed her travel bag on the dresser next to the television.

"Are you hungry?" Gale asked.

"Not really. Just tired."

Gale nodded. "I'll sleep here." He pointed at the floor.

Reiser shook her head. "We're both tired. The bed's big enough for two. I'll keep to my side. Promise." She smiled.

"You take the bathroom first," Gale said.

"Okay."

Soon Gale could hear Reiser showering, the water beating against the curtain and tub. Gale checked his phone. Nothing. It was only a matter of time before the video was released. Voss wasn't going to give Gale the opportunity to resign. He was going to destroy him. The tape would go viral and the Lone Stars would shoot out a press release, stating that because of unacceptable behavior, Gale's employment would be terminated. Making matters worse, Gale had tried calling Marybeth when he'd landed in Fargo. The call went unanswered.

A few minutes later, the shower stopped, and Gale could hear Reiser brushing her teeth. Soon, she stepped out of the bathroom wrapped in a towel, smelling like soap, her toenails painted a crisp red.

"Your turn," she said, pointing.

When Gale came out of the bathroom, Reiser was propped up in bed under the covers, wearing a long sleeve t-shirt, reading glasses, with her laptop resting on her thighs. Gale wore a Lone Star t-shirt and boxers.

"I think we start with Ohnstad in the morning. I have a sneaking suspicion he's not a Voss fan," Reiser said.

"You think?"

"If we can get someone to talk, Voss could be looking at federal prison."

"If . . ."

Reiser nodded and placed her laptop on the bedside table.

"Anything yet?" she asked, her expression darkening as she pointed to Gale's phone resting by his duffel.

"Nothing. Voss is playing coy."

"That's good."

"For now."

"Did you ever reach your wife?"

Gale shrugged. He'd tried calling Marybeth upon his arrival in Fargo. She hadn't answered. He shifted the subject. "How old are your boys?"

"Five and seven."

"I bet they miss you."

"Their father's doing his best to make sure they don't."

Gale shook his head.

Reiser looked away for a second. "Divorce is no fun."

"I bet."

"But we survive."

"That's what it comes down to, doesn't it?" Gale asked.

"Unfortunately." Her eyes crinkled, and she gave a sad smile. Gale thought her pretty.

"I'm an early riser," Gale warned, changing the subject.

"How early?" she asked.

"I'm usually watching game tape by 4:30 am."

"Oh, god."

"I'll go to the lobby when I get up even though by then I might be unemployed."

"Please do."

"What do you take in your coffee?" Gale asked.

"Low fat milk and sugar."

Gale hesitated for a moment. Reiser smiled and patted his side of the bed.

"It's okay," she said. "I'll behave."

When they turned off the lights, Gale couldn't fall asleep. He knew Reiser couldn't either. He could tell by her breathing that she lay awake. He could feel her body heat as she curled next to him. He thought of Marybeth, angry and alone. Gale had never felt lonelier.

"Gale," Reiser whispered, startling him.

"Yes."

"I'm not sure I can sleep."

"I'm not sure I can either."

She rolled over and he could feel her rise on an elbow, her face above his, her hair falling at an angle across her cheekbones, her breath sweet and hot. She touched his cheek softly with the tips of her fingers, tracing his jawline.

"I promised to behave," she said.

"You did."

"Now I don't want to."

Gale paused. He took a deep breath. "Goodnight, Catherine."

"Are you sure?" she asked.

"I'd never forgive myself."

***

Carabin Ohnstad sat across from Reiser and Gale. In his late fifties, he had a handlebar mustache, shaggy brown hair with a touch of gray at the temples and was dressed like a caricature of the celebrity western lawyer. Bolo tie, calfskin boots, pressed Wranglers, and office walls adorned with hunting and fishing prints and photos of himself with rodeo stars.

"We had the case in the bag," Ohnstad said, twisting his mustache with his fingers, "and the only thing that stood between a good verdict was a dirty judge."

"You never could prove it?" Gale asked.

"Never." He leaned back. "Voss got to him. A year or so after the case, I heard the judge bought himself a ranch west of Amidon. Put it this way, Mr. McClanahan, unlike a pro football coach, the judge wasn't drawing a big paycheck."

Gale winced. If only Ohnstad knew.

"We need your help," Reiser said.

"There's nothing I can do. It was five years ago. Ancient history. The families' appeals fell on deaf ears. The case is dead."

"You sure?" Gale asked.

"We had Voss' oil and gas field supervisor prepared to testify as a star witness. I got him on the stand, and after the first question, I knew they'd gotten to him. He lied through his ass."

"Is he still around?" Reiser asked.

Ohnstad nodded and tugged at his mustache. "Last I heard he lives in Wilton."

"Does he still work for Voss?" Gale questioned.

"I don't know. Like I said, ancient history."

"What's his name?" Gale asked.

"Maynard Bremmer."

Ohnstad paused.

"We had a private investigator digging into some of the people surrounding the case. He was killed in a single car accident near Manning. No one knows what happened."

"But you do," Reiser said.

Ohnstad leaned back in his chair. "I have my suspicions."

"Who was being investigated when the accident occurred?" Reiser asked.

"Several Voss employees," Ohnstad said. "Bremmer was our primary witness. But the investigator was killed, and the families of the deceased were getting anonymous threats. I assume Bremmer was warned. The case died when I called him to testify."

Ohnstad paused before continuing. "Those men who died in the explosion, died through negligence. They cut a gas line they were told was shut down. Anyone who tells you anything else is a liar." Ohnstad pursed his lips. "Voss never set foot in the courtroom. But he was the master puppeteer."

"We need to visit Bremmer," Gale said, shifting in his chair.

"Good luck," Ohnstad said. "And be careful."

Gale glanced at Reiser.

"You're from West Texas. Kinney, right?" Ohnstad asked Gale as he and Reiser lifted themselves out of their chairs.

Gale nodded.

"Tell Grayson Wallace he's a son of a bitch." Ohnstad smiled.

"Will do," Gale said.

"I'm sure that'll make his day."

"He loves compliments."

"I'm sure he does, especially from an old nemesis."

***

Leland Skees had seen the man and woman come into Ohnstad's office. He overheard them talking to Ohnstad's secretary about wanting to see Ohnstad about the Voss Energy case. Skees had moved closer to hear the conversation while he emptied trash cans. During the trial, he'd been paid good money to feed information to Voss' lawyers. He'd bought a new pickup and ATV. For three years during the trial and appeals, he'd hunted through the garbage each night and rifled through folders in file cabinets and on desks. He hung near offices. Anything he found and overheard, he passed along. It had been a lucrative time for an office park janitor without a high school degree making $14.35 an hour. After the final verdict, the payouts had stopped. It had been a bitter moment when Skees had realized the gravy train was over. What did he have to show for his work? He'd totaled the ATV when it had flipped one night on a drunken ride. His pickup now had 111,000 miles, a faulty transmission, a cracked windshield, and a set of threadbare tires. Finally, a new opportunity. He listened more closely. When the two of them disappeared into

LONESTAR

Ohnstad's office, Skees walked outside to the parking lot and dialed his contact at Voss Energy. A few minutes later, he'd told the man on the other end of the line everything he knew.

***

In the late afternoon, after a six-hour drive from Fargo, Gale and Reiser found Maynard Bremmer's trailer on the outskirts of Wilton. The insanity of the oil and gas boom had died, leaving the town's sudden prosperity a painful memory. Gale noticed the telltale signs. Storefronts on Main Street shuttered and oil rigs idle in overgrown fields, derricks frozen beneath the cold October sky. As Gale and Reiser climbed out of the car, Gale noticed a pit bull chained in the yard and an old, battered Chevy Malibu, sitting tireless on cement blocks. The dog tugged on its chain, barking menacingly.

"Lovely," Reiser said. "Home sweet home."

Gale shook his head and stepped between Reiser and the pit bull. "If that dog breaks loose, he'll tear us apart."

"I hope that chain holds," Reiser answered.

Gale and Reiser went to the trailer and knocked. The aluminum screen door was chipped and bent, and the battered trailer was smudged with mold streaks on the rotting lattice that extended to the ground.

No one came to the door. Gale knocked again.

Finally, a man with patchy gray whiskers, pinched eyes, wearing a torn flannel shirt and stained oil field Dickies, cracked open the door. When the pit bull spotted him, the dog stopped barking, and with a whimper, sat belly down in the dirt. Gale figured the man was in his mid-sixties. He smelled like cigarette smoke.

"Maynard Bremmer?" Gale asked.

"Depends," the man said. His eyes shifted from Gale to Reiser.

"I need to speak with you."

"What's it about?"

Gale shifted. "Vernon Voss."

The man cursed and started to shut the door, but Gale reached out and grabbed the door handle. Gale glimpsed an older woman behind Bremmer before she ducked away.

"Who sent you?"

"Carrabin Ohnstad."

"I got nothin' to say."

"We think you do," Reiser said.

"Well, you'd be wrong."

"I don't think so," Gale said. "Tell us about the men who died."

"Go away."

"Tell us," Gale said. "What kind of deal did you cut with Voss and the judge?"

227

The man tried to pull the door shut again, but Gale's grip on the door handle was too strong.

"There's more than you know riding on you coming clean," Reiser said. "Besides grieving families."

"I told you what I know. Nothin'."

Gale looked at Reiser before turning to Bremmer. "Vernon Voss is trying to destroy my life. He's trying to destroy my family. I'm not going to let that happen. Understand? You know why the gas line exploded. Negligence. Whatever Voss gave you wasn't enough." Gale studied the shabby trailer and shook his head. "You got nothing to show for it."

"Get off my property."

"Or what?" Gale asked.

Bremmer glanced at the dog. "I'll set him loose."

Gale grabbed the man by his shirt collar and pinned him against the doorframe.

"Gale," Reiser yelled. "No!"

Gale pulled the man close, his face red and ears hot. "Tell me what happened."

Bremmer's eyes showed defiance. "Hell, no."

"I'll hurt you," Gale whispered before shoving Bremmer against the door frame and freeing him. Gale turned to Reiser. "Let's go."

'That's a good idea," Reiser said. "You're already in enough trouble."

***

An hour outside of Wilton, Gale noticed a vacant Voss Energy oil and gas complex stretching alongside the deserted interstate. Someone had spray painted graffiti across the corporate sign. Weeds grew around the empty parking lot and the entrance gate was closed. Gale thought about Bremmer. If Voss had paid him off, it didn't show. Unlike the judge, Bremmer hadn't purchased a ranch. Reiser and Gale had ridden in silence. Their only lead had refused to talk. But what had they expected? It had been a longshot. Gale had lost his cool and made matters worse. Reiser looked stonily out the window, watching the flat landscape pass by.

"I lost it," Gale said finally.

"He'll never talk now."

Gale shook his head. "I can't understand how Bremmer could be living in dirt after testifying for Voss."

Reiser shrugged. "Maybe Voss had something on him?"

"Who knows? A guy like that could have pissed it away."

"You think?"

Reiser turned to Gale. After years as an attorney, she didn't pull punches. "Any chance we had of getting the truth ended when you grabbed him."

"Frustration."

Reiser broke into a mischievous smile. "Maybe if we'd done what I wanted last night your blood wouldn't have been running so hot?"

Gale almost smiled. "Think so?"

"You missed a golden opportunity," she said.

"I'm married."

"You keep telling me that."

"It's true," Gale said, thinking about his unreturned calls to Marybeth and the growing pit in his stomach. He took his eyes off Reiser and turned back to the road. "I think."

***

A few minutes later, they pulled into a deserted rest area and parked the car by a small, wooden building. Reiser slid out of the car to use the facilities while Gale stretched and checked his phone. The video of Gale and Vanessa hadn't gone viral. He had a few texts from Donta Jones and Jack Engle about the plan for the upcoming game against Atlanta, and nothing from Marybeth. Grayson Wallace had sent him a long email about a non-disparagement agreement with Voss. With a violent shake of his head, Gale deleted it. A moment later, his cell chimed with a number Gale didn't recognize. He answered.

Gale's heart started to beat hard when the woman spoke. She was older with a clipped accent who spoke in hushed tones. He saw Reiser come out of the building and put his finger to his lips when she noticed the phone pressed against his ear.

"How'd you get my number?" Gale asked.

"Ohnstad's office. The secretary didn't want to give it up, but I told her I had information."

"You heard us talking to your husband?"

"That's right. You need to come back to Wilton."

"We're an hour away."

"I'll meet you at The Pour House."

"Why are you doing this?"

Her voice grew edgy and cold, full of revulsion. "Cause I hate Vernon Voss as much as you do."

CHAPTER 50

Maynard Bremmer's wife had puffy bags under her eyes and a cigarette hanging from her lips. Her dyed hair had grown out and left her with a gray streak along her part. She rested her heavy arms on the table, and before looking up at Gale and Reiser, took an ample sip from the bourbon sitting in front of her. Her voice spoke of whiskey and cigarettes. Gale realized as soon as he sat down in the darkened bar, she'd been the woman in Bremmer's trailer.

"Maynard got screwed," she said.

"How so?" Reiser asked. A glass of white wine sat in front of her. The wine glass looked out of place in a bar full of hard drinking, out of work oil and gas field workers.

"You think he wanted to testify against those families? Voss threatened him. Told him if he didn't, he'd never work again. Told him he knew Maynard stole drilling equipment and sold it."

"Did he?" Gale asked, sipping a beer.

Bremmer's wife picked up the glass of bourbon and raised it to her lips before taking a long drag on her cigarette. "He didn't do nothin' more than what anyone else was doin'."

"So, he did," Reiser said.

"It was nothin'. Ninety, a hundred thousand worth of equipment. A drop in the bucket for Voss Energy."

"Voss blackmailed him?" Gale asked.

Bremmer's wife nodded.

"He lied on the stand to keep from being prosecuted," Reiser said, leaning forward.

"What was Maynard's options?"

"Why didn't your husband try to strike a deal with prosecutors?" Reiser asked.

"He don't trust law enforcement. Do you?" She sneered.

"What happened after the trial?" Gale asked.

"Voss fired Maynard anyway. Said if he ever said anything about the gas line exploding, he'd destroy him."

"What do you want from us?" Gale asked.

Bremmer's wife eyed Gale.

"I want a deal," she said. "I want you to help us get back on our feet. We got no money and no prospects. Maynard testified in one of the biggest trials in North Dakota and got nothin' for it. Only misery."

"You said you don't trust the authorities?" Reiser asked, glancing at Gale.

"We got no options."

"Your husband would come clean?"

Bremmer's wife nodded. "For a million bucks and a plea deal."

Gale glanced at Reiser. She rolled her eyes. A million dollars?

"What happened? Why'd the gas line explode?" Gale asked, ignoring Bremmer's wife's demands.

Bremmer's wife took a long drag on her cigarette, raised her head, and blew a cloud of smoke toward the ceiling. "The rig operations were shoddy. Cement and casing failures. Contamination. Unmarked lines. Those workers died cause of carelessness and greed."

"Your husband?" Reiser asked.

The woman looked away for a moment. "He'd been sayin' there were live gas lines all over the field. It was only a matter of time."

"Why didn't they shut them down? He was the supervisor."

The woman gave a thin smile and coughed. "He couldna if he wanted to. The only thing that matters at Voss Energy is profit."

"Your husband will testify?" Reiser asked.

"Like I said, for a deal. No prison time and a payout."

"Okay," Reiser said, turning to Gale, her voice resolute. "We'll see what we can do."

***

Outside in the bar's parking lot, Gale and Reiser stopped before climbing into their car. Darkness had settled and Gale could see his breath shoot out in plumes in the freezing air. Illuminated by a lone streetlight, a few flakes of snow drifted down. Reiser sighed.

"No State's Attorney or Federal prosecutor is going to give Bremmer a payout," Reiser said. "Maybe a reduced sentence, but we're talking about lying under oath, obstruction of justice, bribery in a case where seven men died. . . no way."

Gale looked away, for a moment lost in thought.

Reiser added, "We're wasting our time. She's not going to budge without a deal —"

"Catherine," Gale interrupted.

"What?"

Gale's mind raced. "I got an idea. I need to call Donta Jones."

"What are you thinking about?" Catherine reached out and touched his arm.

"I'll explain on the ride back to Fargo."

"They'll be plenty of time. It's a long drive."

***

231

C.W. WELLS

Grayson Wallace's phone blew up. A flood of texts and a persistent ring made his cell shake and shiver. Wallace peered at the phone and took a shot of bourbon. He knew immediately the video had gone viral. He ignored the flood of texts, googled "Gale McClanahan," and found the internet trending with scandal. He took the hard copy of the non-disparagement agreement he had drafted for Gale and tore it in half. It wouldn't be long. A statement would be coming from the Lone Stars.

Wallace picked up his phone and replayed the video. He had to admit, with the shake of his head, Vanessa Voss was a beautiful woman.

***

Vernon Voss put his cell phone on the table in front of him. He barked at Julia to fix him a drink as the Gulfstream banked away from the Irish coast. The video had gone viral. Voss didn't care if people saw him as an old man with a young wife who'd betrayed him. There'd be other women. Maybe Julia? All that mattered was selling the Lone Stars to Asinov, getting out of debt, and saving his crumbling oil and gas empire. It had always been simple. Anyone who stood in the way would be dealt with. And by any means necessary. Wives were expendable commodities, after all.

Voss watched Julia as she fixed his drink before turning back to his phone. Before he could pursue his line of thinking, he noticed an incoming call. Voss tapped accept and pushed the phone against his ear.

Ten minutes later, he ended the call with a curse. McClanahan was snooping around North Dakota with Andujar's Chief of Staff. They'd met with Carabin Ohnstad and driven out to Wilton to ask Maynard Bremmer questions. Voss began to feel his rage build. *Vanessa had talked.* The team was on the brink of being sold. He'd had enough.

***

Sam Lorenzo brought a hard copy of the press release to Garvin Johnson. Johnson sat in his office with his boots on his desk and read the statement. He broke into a smile. After the video had gone viral minutes earlier, his phone had flooded with texts and calls. The media jackals wanted McClanahan's blood and Johnson was going to spill it.

Johnson said, "Send it, Sam."

Lorenzo held his phone up in his nicotine-stained fingers and smiled. The statement was terse. It said it all: *"Gale McClanahan is no longer coach of The San Antonio Lone Stars."*

***

232

Gale called Jones and listened on Bluetooth as Jones asked him about the video and told him what Gale had just discovered: that Gale had been fired. Gale grimaced as he drove toward Fargo, the car's headlights illuminating the snowflakes that were blowing in swirls across the road.

"Why?" Jones asked. "I told you she was poison."

"It's not what it looks like, Donta. I got set-up. Voss again. Same story."

Jones went silent for a few moments. "How can I help?" he asked. "I love you like a brother, Boy Wonder."

Gale looked at Reiser who nodded.

Gale tapped his forefinger on the wheel. "I need you to make a call, Donta."

Gale sensed Jones hesitating on the phone.

"I'm going to need more than that," Jones finally said.

Gale explained.

"You do need Batman after all. Seriously, even if I could talk him into it, we could end up in big trouble," Jones answered.

"Maybe. It's all I got in my playbook. Think about it."

Jones sighed. "For anyone else, no." He paused. "You're going to owe me bigtime,"

"I know."

"You'll be buying me lunch at Grady's the rest of your life."

"Let's hope. I hear prison food isn't good."

"I wouldn't know," Jones said. "I don't intend to find out."

After the call, Reiser reached over and took Gale's hand. She pressed it softly.

"I'm sorry about everything, Gale," she said, turning to him. The glow of the dashboard lit her face.

"It's okay."

"He must be a great friend."

"The best."

"What now?"

Gale turned and tried to smile. He tried not to think about what people were saying about him. He tried not to think about Marybeth and the consequences if his plan failed. His mind raced. It was nearly impossible to concentrate, and he felt a sharp pain building behind his eyes.

"Let's find a hotel with two rooms," Gale said.

"That would make things easier."

"It would."

She pressed his hand one more time before pulling away.

"If we can't?" she asked.

Gale turned to her. "I'll sleep on the floor."

"The floor's hard."

"Not as challenging as the alternative," he said as they continued toward Fargo.

Twenty minutes outside of Fargo, Gale noticed a vehicle quickly approaching in his rearview mirror, its headlights on high beam, nearly blinding him as he drove. For over a minute, the SUV clung a few feet away from Gale's bumper and finally fell back before charging ahead and nearly striking the rental car.

"We've got a friend," Gale said, trying to shield his eyes from the blinding headlights penetrating the car.

"He's going to kill us, Gale," Reiser said, bracing her hands against the dash.

Gale sped up. The SUV dropped back then shot once more toward Gale and Reiser's vehicle. As the SUV was about to collide with the car, it swerved and hurtled down the highway, its taillights disappearing in a flurry of snow showers.

"A drunk?" Reiser asked, leaning back against the headrest, and closing her eyes for an instant.

"I'm not sure. That was close."

"Voss?"

"It could have been anything."

"You think he knows we're in North Dakota?"

"Maybe."

"I hope your plan works, Gale."

Gale nodded.

"I want to see my boys grow up."

Gale thought of Tilly and wondered if Marybeth would ever speak with him again.

"Let's get to a hotel," Gale said.

"Please."

CHAPTER 51

Franklin Washington was used to late night calls. 1,696 active players made up League rosters, and five percent of them found themselves in trouble. Drunken driving. Domestic disputes. Drug possession. Illegal firearms. Nightclub brawls. Washington had seen it all as Director of League Security. He'd witnessed even more as a 32-year-veteran of the FBI.

In his role, Washington had kept close tabs as well on the thirty-two owners. He didn't like what he saw, especially with Vernon Voss. Then there was Spencer Tate himself. Washington knew more about the Commissioner's sordid world than Tate imagined. Washington hadn't survived as a federal agent without understanding how the game was played. *You protected yourself. You learned about who you worked for. You found dirt on someone and held it close until you needed to use it.*

Earlier in the evening, he'd watched Voss' wife peel off her robe and push Gale McClanahan onto a couch. Washington wasn't surprised that the Lone Stars had fired McClanahan within minutes of the video going viral.

But there was something wrong with the scene. The woman's actions seemed almost staged. For months, he'd been following the Lone Star situation closely. He didn't like it. Donta Jones had given him the inside, and there were several times that Washington thought about approaching Spencer Tate, but his internal shit detector told him to stay away. Washington learned early on to pick his moments. The League was a powerful and dangerous animal, capable of anything. And if Tate was an animal, he would be an eel. Slippery as they come.

When Donta Jones called and woke Washington, Washington wasn't surprised. He and Jones were fraternity brothers. They'd played football together at William & Mary. They were best men in each other's first weddings, consoled each other during their divorces, married strong second wives, and watched each other's back. Hence, Washington's timely call to Jones earlier in the season about the League killing waivers on Abruzzi and Ellis.

"You know what time it is, Bro?" Washington said, clearing his throat when he answered his cell. His wife's eyes opened briefly before she rolled over with a sleepy murmur. She was accustomed to late night calls.

"Time to get your ass out of bed," Jones said.

"What's going on?"

Jones told him.

"You want me to do what?" Washington asked, sitting up in bed, when Jones finished explaining.

"You heard me."

"I could get my ass fired. That's just the beginning. It's a felony to impersonate a federal agent."

"I can't let my man McClanahan have his life destroyed, Bro."

"North Dakota?"

"That's right."

"I don't like it."

"Neither do I."

"Pack your bag," Jones said. "I'll see you in Fargo."

***

Early the next morning, Gale watched Reiser pour herself a cup of coffee in the hotel lobby. Gale had tried calling Marybeth the night before. The call had clicked to voicemail. He pulled his cell out of his pocket and tried again. After several rings, Marybeth answered. Her voice was cold and distant. Gale could tell she was trying to get Tilly ready for school.

"I need to withdraw $1,000,000 from our account," Gale said bluntly.

"For what?" Marybeth shot back in disbelief. Gale's untouched, accrued compensation thus far was just over a million dollars. The funds sat in The First National Bank of Kinney.

"You're going to have to trust me."

"Trust you?"

"That's right."

"You're going to take a million dollars from our account and do what? That's money that we're going to have to pay back to Voss along with everything else. He's ruined us, Gale."

"Not yet."

"What do you mean, 'not yet?'" she asked doubtfully.

"Like I said, you'll have to trust me." Gale could hear his voice growing more determined.

"You're all over the internet. People think you cheated on me."

"Do you?"

Marybeth went silent.

"I didn't cheat on you. It was a set-up. I've never looked at anyone else in my life, Marybeth." Gale's voice hardened. "You think I'm going to sleep with a drug addict? Give me a little credit."

Marybeth's voice broke. "Oh, Gale. I'm so ashamed. People don't know what to say when they see me."

"I don't care what people think right now. Understand? Either believe me or not. I need the money, Marybeth. Understand?"

Marybeth paused. "Where are you?"

"North Dakota."

"Jesus."

"I got a shot at getting us out of this mess."

"Look, I got to get Tilly ready for school. I haven't got time for this."

"You'll have to trust me."

"Did you sleep with that woman, Gale McClanahan?"

"No."

Marybeth stayed silent for a few moments before she said fiercely, "If I find out you're lying, I'll shear your balls off."

Gale caught himself almost smiling.

"I mean it. I'll come after you with the biggest pair of scissors you've ever seen."

Gale shifted the subject. "The next few days are going to be rough, Marybeth."

"Rough? How can it get worse?"

"It can."

"That's hard to believe," she said, sighing.

***

Gale put his phone back in his pocket and rubbed his eyes. His head was beginning to pound. He watched Reiser cut gracefully across the lobby holding a cup of coffee and a muffin on a paper plate.

"How'd it go?" she asked.

"As good as it could." Gale shrugged. "I'm going to wire the money when Donta sends me an account number."

"When are they leaving?"

"This morning."

"You're going to make Maynard Bremmer a rich man."

"No. I'm going to take Voss down."

"That's a better way of looking at it."

***

Jack Engle surveyed the conference room. The coaches were assembled early, as usual. The smell of coffee permeated the room and a box of untouched frosted donuts sat in the middle of the table. Rulon Alexander and Deshay Anderson along with the rest of the staff wore glum faces, trying to make sense of the leaked video and Gale's firing.

"Where's Donta?" Alexander asked.

"He's gone for a couple of days," Engle said. "Personal matter, Rulon."

Engle continued. "Deshay, you got the defense today."

C.W. WELLS

Anderson nodded and picked up his pen off the table and stuck it behind his ear. "Full pads?"

Engle shook his head. "Shells. Too many guys nicked up."

"I give Coach credit," Alexander said about the video, "at least he picked a stunner."

"A viper," Anderson added. "I warned him."

Engle cut off the conversation. His eyes bore into the staff like he was about to admonish a handful of wayward students. *Once a principal, always...*

"We got a game to play," Engle said, feeling his heart sink. He thought about Gale, Marybeth, and Tilly. He'd called Barbara before the meeting to make sure she checked on Marybeth. Barbara had called. Marybeth hadn't answered. Earlier, when Engle had called Grayson Wallace, Wallace had told him what he knew. Gale was in North Dakota. Seven men had died. Voss had orchestrated a bogus trial. Gale was digging around, trying to unearth the truth. Slim odds.

"How we gonna handle the team? There'll be lots of questions," Anderson asked.

Engle leaned back. He looked at Alexander. "What do you think, Rulon?"

"We tell 'em the truth. They know as much as we do. We tell 'em our thoughts and prayers are with Gale and his family. That he got a raw deal. That the video is garbage. That we need to beat Atlanta and win one for Coach McClanahan."

"They're going to be pissed," Anderson said. The other coaches nodded.

"That's right, Deshay," Alexander said. "A hornet's nest."

"Okay," Engle said, getting up. "I'll see you on the field in thirty minutes."

"Have you seen, Jimmie?" Alexander asked.

"He wanted to tell me something real bad, Rulon," Anderson said. "But I told him I had to get to our meeting."

"Bad?" Engle questioned.

"He was fidgety. Scared," Anderson said.

"Go tell him things are going to be okay." Engle paused. "We don't want Jimmie tanking on us."

"Hell, no," Alexander said. "Who's gonna do my laundry?"

***

Engle left the coaches' room and was met in the hallway by Sam Lorenzo. Lorenzo wore a smug look and as usual, looked disheveled and bleary eyed. He had a large foam cup of gas station coffee in his pudgy hand and his phone in the other.

"Johnson wants to see you," Lorenzo said with a smirk.

"He can wait. We got practice."

"I don't think so." Lorenzo broke into a smile.

"Tell him I got other things to do." Engle started to edge by him.

Lorenzo stepped in the way. "Big mistake, coach."

238

Engle shook his head and focused on Lorenzo. He wanted to say something but bit his tongue.

"Where is he?" Engle asked.

"In his office," Lorenzo said.

"Tell him I'll be there in a couple of minutes."

"You don't want to keep the big man waiting, Coach. Believe me."

"I said a few minutes," Engle repeated, pushing past him to go to the team room.

***

Engle refused to knock. He was a proud and loyal man, but his loyalty rested with Gale McClanahan, the coaching staff, and the players, not this vulture. Engle knew in his heart Gale hadn't cheated with Voss' wife. He would tell Marybeth that, too. Garvin Johnson and Vernon Voss fell into the category of lowlifes in high places. Engle had seen it before. As a teacher, coach, and principal, he worried about the smart, devious kid with no moral compass. That kid often grew up to be ruthless and conniving. A dangerous outlier. A Garvin Johnson. A Voss.

When Engle entered Johnson's office, his lips grew numb, and he took a step back. With a toothpick rolling in his mouth, Buddy Adams sat in a chair across from Johnson with a grin. Johnson sat behind his desk, leaning back in his swivel chair, with a 'I got you expression.'

"This I'll be quick, Coach," Johnson said, pointing at Engle. "You and McClanahan's staff are out. Buddy and his boys are in."

"So," Engle said, kicking himself for being surprised, "this is how it's going to be?"

Johnson turned to Adams and gave him a half smile. "You bet your ass," he said.

"The team won't play for him." Engle looked disdainfully at Adams.

"You think Vernon cares?"

Adams grinned.

"I want you and the other coaches out of the Complex along with the half-wit, Jimmie."

"Half-wit?" Engle felt his chest tighten.

"That's what I said, Coach Engle," Johnson barked. "Ole Buddy and his boys have a practice to run, and I don't want you or anyone else getting in their way."

CHAPTER 52

In the late morning, Gale spotted Jones and Washington as they pulled into the empty rest area outside of Fargo. Gale quickly checked his phone. Engle had texted him saying Johnson had fired the coaching staff and Adams was back. Gale cursed under his breath. He showed the message to Reiser. She swore. What did he expect? Given the video with Vanessa, Gale had no credibility. No one was going to believe an allegation from him about Adams and his coaches betting against the Lone Stars, especially since he didn't have any proof. His bluff was called, and he had nothing. He thought about his only way out and about the money he was about to wire. The funds might be disappearing into thin air. *A million dollars. God help him if his plan fell apart. Then he would have nothing. Nothing at all.*

Jones and Washington pulled up in their car and hopped out. Gale shook hands with Washington and hugged Jones. Gale introduced Catherine Reiser.

"We ready to go?" Gale asked.

Washington nodded. "What we do for our friends." He looked at Jones and shook his head.

"Thank you, Franklin," Gale said, "for putting your butt on the line."

"See you in New York," Jones said. "I can't wait to see Voss' face when we ruin his party."

Gale nodded. Thanks to Washington, they knew the details about Voss, Tate, and Asinov's meeting. Washington's source in the League office had given them the time, date, and location.

A few moments later, Gale and Reiser watched Jones and Washington pull out on the highway and make the long drive to Wilton.

***

In the mid-afternoon, Jones and Washington parked their rental car next to a deserted, overgrown playground on the outskirts of Wilton. A chilled wind blew across the flat landscape as the sun began to lower in the sky.

The two had arrived in the mid-morning, called Maynard Bremmer, who after nearly hanging up, agreed to meet after Washington had briefly outlined the reason for the meeting and confirmed the dollar amount. They had made the long drive from Fargo and now listened to a staticky, AM country western station. They sat silently in the car. Jones was seething at the thought of Buddy Adams' return. Engle had called him with the news of their firing when Jones had stepped off the plane in Fargo.

"Remember," Washington said. "You let me do the talking."

"You afraid I'm going to screw it up?" Jones asked, shoving a pretzel into his mouth.

"Yup."

"That's what I love about you, man. You believe in me."

Washington turned and smiled. "You think I survived three decades in the Bureau by letting someone else do the talking?"

"A pickup is coming," Jones said. He folded his bag of pretzels and tossed it in the back seat.

"Follow along and make sure your phone is recording."

"Got it."

The pickup approached and pulled into a spot a few yards from their sedan. A pit bull rode in the flatbed untethered, came to attention, snapped its jaws and barked when it spotted Jones and Washington sitting in the car. An older man and woman parked, shut the engine off, and slowly climbed out. They were poorly dressed, smoking, and looked suspiciously at the two men parked next to them.

"Let's go," Washington said. "Remember, not a word."

Washington approached Maynard Bremmer, introduced himself and shook his hand. He tried to shake the heavyset woman's hand, but she refused. Jones shook Bremmer's hand but didn't bother with the woman. She pulled on her cigarette and stared at Washington and Jones with a scowl. Washington pointed to the two benches sitting under a lone tree and said, "Let's talk."

After they sat, Bremmer said, "I want to see ID. I'm not talkin' until I got proof who you are."

Washington pulled his worn FBI badge from his coat pocket and handed it to Bremmer. Bremmer studied it before the woman snapped, "Let me see that."

Bremmer handed her the badge.

Washington leaned forward. "We have reason to believe several federal laws were violated before and during the trial. "Extortion." He looked hard at Bremmer. "Wire fraud, which is a federal offense. Bribery of a judge overseeing an NTSB case, which also falls under Federal jurisdiction."

"NTSB?" The woman asked, pulling on her cigarette.

"National Transportation Safety Board. It's the governing body that helps oversee the oil and gas industry."

"What about him?" Bremmer asked, pointing at Jones.

"Mr. Jones is a Field Agent. He's assisting me."

Bremmer eyed Jones. Jones hoped they wouldn't ask for identification. All he had was his driver's license.

Bremmer took Washington's badge from his wife, glanced at it one more time, and handed it back to Washington. "I don't say nothing until I see the money and you promise me no prison time."

"I told you to bring your bank's wiring information and your account number. Do you have it?" Washington asked.

Bremmer slowly handed him a slip of paper. Washington handed it to Jones.

"If you agree to have your testimony recorded, you'll be treated fairly by the Federal Government and state and local authorities. A million dollars will be wired into your account right after this meeting. There will be no prison time. You have my word."

"We want the money upfront. Understand?" The woman interrupted, waving a cigarette nearly burnt to the filter. "No games."

Washington nodded at Jones. "You can make the call now, Agent Jones."

Jones lifted himself off the bench and walked to the center of the park with his cell pushed to his ear. Gale had given him the wiring information from the bank in Kinney. Fifteen minutes later, Jones sat down again on the bench as Bremmer and his wife silently took deep drags on their cigarettes.

"Is the money in our account?" the woman asked greedily.

Jones nodded.

She pulled her phone from her handbag and pulled up her bank account. After a few agonizing minutes, she finally nodded at Bremmer.

"Okay," she said.

"Let's get down to business," Washington said, ignoring her. He turned to Bremmer. "Do you agree to have this conversation recorded under the jurisdiction of the Federal Bureau of Investigation?"

Bremmer nervously glanced at his wife. She nodded.

"Okay," Bremmer said.

"Field Agent Jones," Washington said. "Please record the testimony."

Jones tapped the video record button on his phone. He held the phone so Maynard Bremmer was framed in the video.

"Will you swear under oath that what you tell us today is true?" Washington asked.

Bremmer nodded.

"Will you agree under oath in a federal court of justice that you will tell the truth and nothing but the truth?"

Bremmer mumbled, "Yes."

"Please state your name, date of birth, social security number, and residence."

Bremmer hesitantly recited the information.

"Tell us your association with Voss Energy Corporation."

Bremmer complied.

"Tell us why seven oil field workers died on the afternoon of July 14 . . . ?"

Bremmer glanced at his wife. Despite the cold, beads of sweat formed on his temples, with a halting voice, he began.

An hour later, when Jones and Washington were about to leave, Bremmer's wife pulled a thick manila envelope out of her handbag. "Insurance," she said, dragging on her cigarette before giving the envelope to Washington. "I got copies. You make sure Maynard don't get screwed."

As darkness descended and the air grew colder, Washington and Jones drove away from the park.

"You got the whole interview, Donta?"

Jones patted his phone.

"The file?"

Jones nodded and fingered the envelope Bremmer's wife had given him. "Lord knows what's in it."

"Bonus material?"

"Hope so."

"If we were real, we could nail Voss to the wall," Washington said.

"If ..."

Washington turned the car onto the main road and headed out of town. "Spencer Tate ain't going to like it. His director of security impersonating an FBI agent, bringing a load of dung to his door."

"How you feelin'?"

"Queasy. Real queasy, Bro. Your man better come through on his end."

"He's got it."

Washington nodded. "Let's get to New York. This place gives me a real bad vibe."

"Amen."

***

Gale and Reiser sat in a booth at the bar at Hyatt Place, the hotel a stone throw from La Guardia. They had landed a few hours before, and now Gale had barely touched his meal. His mind raced. No call yet from Donta Jones. No updates. He'd tried Marybeth again, but she didn't answer. Reiser quickly finished her salmon avocado salad. She was starved. She was working on her second glass of white wine while she checked her phone.

"The mayor is on the warpath," she said after reading a text from Andujar. "He's livid. He wants to know where I am." A smile crossed her face. "I never told him I was headed to North Dakota."

Gale put his fork down after poking around his plate. The waiter came over and started refilling water glasses. With a look of concern, he eyed Gale's untouched fish tacos as Gale's phone began to chime. Gale answered. It was Donta Jones. Reiser leaned forward.

"Game on," Jones said. "Bremmer talked."

Gale gave Reiser a thumbs up as the waiter moved to another table.

"Franklin found out through a contact at League Headquarters that the meeting will take place in the Hamptons at Asinov's estate," Jones said. "I'll call you about the details when I get 'em."

Gale shifted.

"Send me the interview with Bremmer, Donta."

"The video's safe with me."

"Not if the plane goes down."

"Thanks for that cheery thought. I got something else, too."

"What?"

"A present from Bremmer. Serious bonus material. I'll send you screenshots."

"Okay," Gale said. "Donta. . ."

'What?"

"Be careful."

"No worries, Boy Wonder," Jones said. "I got Batman with me."

CHAPTER 53

He'd followed them, taking the same flight from North Dakota. He sat at the crowded bar and nursed a beer while the man and woman sat tucked away in a corner eating dinner. For years he'd roamed North America doing Vernon Voss' dirty work. He lived in Minot and rose out of the oil patch as one of Voss' trusted henchmen. He'd help snare Maynard Bremmer, had busted a few heads, and orchestrated a fatal single-car accident to ensure a "clean" resolution to the trial. While the work now wasn't steady, Voss had him on retainer to protect Voss Energy's fading interests. When he'd received the call from Voss about McClanahan and Reiser, he'd tried to scare them, nearly running them off the highway to Fargo. Now he'd followed them to New York. He could tell by the way Voss had spoken to him earlier in the day: edgy, cold, urgent. Voss had been menacing. His orders were simple and clear. *Do whatever it takes . . .*

***

Ivan Asinov gazed into the darkness as the rollers broke against the beach. Valued at over $120 million and built in the 1920's by a famous New York heiress and socialite, his renovated Italian Renaissance Southampton estate sat majestically behind him in the damp, chilly air, the lights from the house casting shadows across the marbled patio and double-tiered infinity pool, which was designed by the same architect who'd imagined the Hanging Gardens in Bali. Asinov smiled. Voss had finally met his promises. The meeting with Tate and Voss would take place the next day. A secret letter of agreement would be signed. The London Destroyers would be born.

Most Russians ignored American football. Not Asinov. He was drawn to the game's violence. He wanted the glamor and power of owning a League franchise in London. The downside was Vladimir. Asinov shook his head. The Russian President would be an untrustworthy and dangerous partner. Asinov sighed and pulled his phone from his back pocket and tapped out a text. It was short and to the point, the way Vladimir demanded. After staring at the text for a few seconds, Asinov scowled, pushed send, and disappeared into the house.

***

Spencer Tate watched Ashley Henninger slip off her clothes in his luxury penthouse at The Pierre on Fifth Avenue. He'd met her a few years earlier when she began working in the League's Digital Entertainment Division in Burbank, and they'd managed to keep their affair secret from the 32 owners who cut his paycheck and from Tate's wife, who spent most of her time shuttling between homes in Palm Beach and Martha's Vineyard. For the first time in months, Tate felt buoyant. The next day's meeting with Asinov and Voss would set the stage for the League's expansion to London. While dealing with Asinov and the Russians would be challenging, Tate relished the thought of Voss disappearing into the night and taking his dysfunction and empty checkbook with him. Tate had had enough of Voss' mismanagement, his threats, his penchant for tarnishing the League. The London Destroyers would give the League even more power and fuel American football's international ascent.

Henninger climbed into bed and nestled close to Tate. Tate felt her smooth skin against his and her hand slide across his abdomen. For an instant, he closed his eyes and took pleasure in her warm hand. There were moments when life offered perfection, Tate thought, opening his eyes as Henninger kissed him softly on the chest. He made $57 million a year, he was making love to a striking woman, and he presided over the most powerful professional sports organization in the world. *And tomorrow his legacy would be secure.*

***

At two-forty-five in the morning, Gale's phone rang. He reached over groggily and stabbed in the darkness at the bedside table until he found his phone. When he heard Engle's voice, he took a deep breath.

"Jimmie?" Gale asked.

"They arrested him at the hotel tonight. We were set to drive back to Kinney in the morning, but the police showed up."

"Stealing Oxy?" Gale asked, feeling the familiar pang of guilt.

"With intent to distribute."

"Where's he now?"

"They took him away."

"Call Grayson."

"I already did," Engle said.

"It wasn't Jimmie."

"I know."

"It was me."

Engle went silent.

"I took the Oxy, Jack," Gale said. "I needed Vanessa Voss to talk."

"Not good, Gale. We got to get Jimmie out of jail. The bail isn't going to be cheap."

Gale closed his eyes and paused. He was growing more miserable by the second. He took a deep breath and opened his eyes.

"I'll pay you back," Gale said. "How much?"

"They set bail at $25,000. I'll cover it," Engle said.

"Thank you."

Engle paused.

"Where are you, Gale?"

"New York."

"You okay?" Engle's voice grew more concerned. "I'm here if you need me. I'll do my best to help Jimmie."

"Thanks."

"Gale?"

"What?"

"Whatever you're about to do, is it worth it?"

"It's our one shot, Jack."

"Okay. I trust your instincts."

"Take care of Jimmie, and I'll see you in a few days."

After the conversation with Engle, Gale looked over in the darkness at the outline of the empty side of the bed. He desperately wished Marybeth were beside him. Then he imagined Jimmie sitting in a San Antonio jail. Gale knew Jimmie would be out of his mind. Gale tried hard to not succumb to his feelings of guilt so he could drift off.

***

Gale had never seen Catherine Reiser look so pale. She hurried across the parking lot carrying only her handbag. The thunder of planes taking off from LaGuardia reverberated in the air. When she climbed into the car, she was out of breath and distraught.

"What's going on?" Gale asked.

"Someone trashed my hotel room," she said, her tone revealing a mixture of anger and fear. "They broke in when we were eating breakfast."

After breakfast, Gale had gotten the car and Reiser had gone back to her room to gather her things.

"Anything stolen?"

"I don't know," she said. "It was like they were looking for something or messing with me. The whole room was turned upside down. I got out fast."

Gale shook his head and looked away for a moment.

"The SUV near Fargo. Now this," he said.

"I was thinking the same thing," Reiser echoed, trying to calm herself with deep breaths.

"Are you okay?" Gale asked.

Reiser closed her eyes for a moment. "I think so."

"You don't have to do this, Catherine," Gale said.

"I know," she answered, looking out the passenger window before turning. "I just keep thinking about my boys."

"You're out. I'll call Donta and see if I can figure out another way to make this work."

"No," Reiser said. "I'm with you. Too much is at stake. I just got spooked."

"You sure?"

Reiser looked determined. "You bet," she said before sliding out of the car to catch the waiting taxi to Manhattan.

CHAPTER 54

In the early morning, Donta Jones and Franklin Washington shook their heads at the departure screen. As they looked out the terminal windows, sleet fell in heavy sheets on the tarmac and runway beyond. Their flight from Fargo to Minneapolis was delayed. It would be impossible to catch their connection to New York in time to meet Gale.

Jones reached for his phone and punched up Gale's number. When Gale answered, he told him the news.

***

Voss' Gulfstream circled Westhampton before settling into the approach. The flight from San Antonio had been smooth. Voss was exhilarated about the meeting with Tate and Asinov. He'd been given assurance that McClanahan would be taken care of. Intimidation was a useful weapon, Voss thought. He'd lived his life delivering fear. Thankfully, the night before, Bremmer and his wife had been taken care of. When Voss' men had called him a few minutes before midnight, they had a signed affidavit in their hand. They'd left Bremmer with a broken nose, a few cracked ribs, and a pit bull with a bullet between its eyes. He checked his phone and ignored the Saudi Prince's most recent voicemail. The last few weeks, Rasheed had been the one uttering threats. The Swiss, Max Hartmann, had predictably drifted off into the background as Rasheed had hinted of violence. Screw them. They'd get theirs soon enough, Voss thought.

For a moment, Voss gazed at Julia. She was strapped in her seat, her eyes closed, dozing, her long, slender legs carefully tucked to the side. She would be a suitable replacement for Vanessa, Voss thought. Beautiful. Young. Obedient. He made note to have his attorney begin preparing divorce papers. Two days before, Vanessa had broken down. She'd confessed about her conversation with McClanahan. Voss had eyed her coldly and later, had found the stash of Oxy McClanahan had given her tucked away in a tampon box. He'd flushed the pills down the toilet. Before he'd left for New York, he'd found Vanessa lying on the bathroom floor in a pool of vomit.

***

The black limousine sat at 445 Madison Avenue in front of League Headquarters. Freshly waxed and streaked with rain, the limo waited in the midday as Spencer Tate, shielded by an umbrella, stepped onto the sidewalk and ducked into the car. He carried a briefcase with a sheaf of documents, including a letter of intent which would begin the process of selling Asinov the Lone Stars and relocating the team to London. Tate had made the decision to attend the meeting alone. He didn't trust Voss or Asinov. Better to leave the League's phalanx of attorneys behind, at least in the initial conversations. Tate hadn't prospered by being careless. The sooner Voss was out of the picture, the better. As the limousine pulled away from the curb, Tate thought about the night before.

***

Gale made the drive from LaGuardia to Southampton in two hours. Rain pelted the windshield and gusts of wind blew from Long Island Sound as he turned off Route 27 and drove on a cold, gray autumn day through the nearly deserted upscale village with its trendy restaurants and boutiques. He headed toward Coopers Beach and passed several large estates behind immaculately trimmed hedges until he pulled into a parking lot by the ocean.

He parked his car and stared beyond the dunes at the gray, windswept Atlantic. White caps rolled offshore, while large waves topped with foam crashed onto the beach. Blowing rain struck the car. He glanced at his watch. He'd arrived nearly 30 minutes early. He checked his phone for messages and called Reiser. The phone rang, and she didn't pick-up. He called Jones and the call went straight to voicemail. Gale assumed that Jones and Washington were finally enroute to Minneapolis to catch a connecting flight to New York. But he worried about Reiser. She should have answered. A few seconds later Reiser called.

"Sorry I missed your call," she said.

"You okay?" Gale asked. "You scared me."

"Sorry."

"All set?"

"All set," she said.

"Catherine . . ."

"What?"

Gale paused and took a deep breath before he said, "Thank you. And be careful."

***

A sudden, final realization struck Gale as he peered at the ocean. He was alone. It was his fight and had been since the moment he'd signed a contract to coach the Lone Stars. He'd put himself and others in a terrible position through his own misguided ambition, naivete, and hubris. Likely, he'd forfeited his family and good life in West Texas. He'd been born with a gift. He could coach. He'd proved he

250

could win in Kinney and in the League. But now that gift seemed flimsy and insufficient. He wondered what his father would have said to his only son. It was a painful thought. He needed to make things right.

He checked his watch again.

Gale was about to start the car when he heard a tap on the driver side window. A man stood in the rain with a bewildered smile. He wore a nylon windbreaker with the collar pulled up. His sandy blonde hair was soaked and unruly. He made a motion for Gale to roll down his window. Gale wondered where he'd come from. There was no other car in the parking lot. The man kept smiling and making a rolling motion with his hand. Finally, after several taps on the window, Gale depressed the window button.

The man's smile vanished as he threw himself at Gale. His fist caught Gale square in the face, hard, deliberate, striking him flush in a brilliant concussion of stars. A wave of pain and shock hit Gale as the man seized him by the throat and struck him again on the side of the head. Gale felt the door swing open and the man drag him out of the car onto the wet gravel and begin kicking him. Gale felt a searing pain in his ribs, already cracked from the traffic officer's blows in San Antonio, and closed his eyes in agony as the man hammered away. After a few moments, Gale lay curled in a fetal position, blood streaming from his nose, trying to breathe. The man kicked him hard one more time and slowly knelt beside him.

"A gift from Vernon Voss," the man hissed. "Don't screw with him. Understand? If you do, next time we won't be so nice."

Gale grunted.

"You climb in your car and drive back to La Guardia. You and your friends say anything about Bremmer, Voss Energy, or our little meeting here, and it'll be your family next. Understand? I hear you got a pretty wife and a sweet little girl. Don't be stupid."

Gale tried hard to breathe. He could feel the fury build in his chest. With the ocean pounding in the background, the man leaned close in the pouring rain, his breath shooting out in plumes in the raw air. Gale noticed the man had relaxed. He'd erased Gale as a physical threat. Gale needed to muster any remaining strength and make a move before the man rose to his feet. Gale gathered himself for an instant as his high school wrestling instincts came racing back. Gale grabbed an ankle and pulled. His assailant fell backward on his haunches and landed on his back. Despite the fire in Gale's ribs and the blood streaming from his nose, he leapt on top of the man, flipped him over in one motion, slid his arms under the man's armpits and linked his hands behind the man's neck in a devastating full Nelson. Without hesitation, Gale placed enormous pressure on the man's arms and heard the sickening pop of shoulders dislocating. The man howled in pain. Gale's heart beat hard as he lifted the man off the ground and pushed him toward the beach. He pressed on the man's arms, pulling them further out of their shoulder sockets. As Gale shoved the man toward the ocean in the pounding rain, he noticed how

251

grotesque the man's arms appeared, as if they were hanging by a thread of sinew beneath his windbreaker.

When they reached the ocean, Gale let go and kicked the man's legs from under him. He stumbled into the wet sand. Gale kicked him hard in the stomach.

"You touch my family, and I'll kill you," Gale said, catching his breath and wiping the blood off his face with the back of his coat sleeve. "Understand?"

The man's eyes blinked in recognition.

"Whoever you are, you crawl back under the rock where you came from. If you don't . . ." Gale's voice drifted off. Gale wheeled and kicked the man in the balls. The man's face turned purple. When Gale pulled away from the parking lot, the man had dragged himself a few yards from the water's edge and had curled into a lifeless heap.

CHAPTER 55

Vernon Voss sat in a plush Antonlini oversized chair and eyed Asinov and Tate. He'd imagined this moment when he'd strike a formal deal with the Commissioner and the Russian and staunch the gaping wound of his crumbling financial empire. He smiled to himself. He'd done what he always had done: win. When he'd left home after barely graduating from high school, dirt poor and angry, and began as a field worker in the Anadarko Basin, he knew someday he could be more than a roughneck. He was smart and he was mean. He had risen in the ranks because he got things done and didn't care about how he did it. After a few short years, he was able to buy a stake in the oil and gas venture, and it wasn't long before he'd owned it all. Voss Energy was born. Voss had found himself sitting on oil and gas rights across the Woodford Shale at the forefront of fracking.

Now he was sitting across from Tate and Asinov. Tate with his finely tailored suit, perfectly combed hair, prep school manners, and thirst for money and power. Asinov with his distrusting eyes, flat forehead, broad nose, meaty hands, and heart of a wolf. Voss flashed back to the rotted house where he and his siblings had fought over food each night. Winters with no heat and running water. Filthy clothes and the smell of piss.

Voss would sell the team and survive another day. He would pay his creditors and wait for the price of oil and gas to come roaring back, and then he would destroy those who'd tried to destroy him. Now he was sitting in a lavish ocean estate with two of the most powerful men in the world. He'd come far, and he wasn't going back.

***

Franklin Washington had given Spencer Tate's personal cell number to Gale. The iron gates and towering hedges protecting Ivan Asinov's estate blocked access to the Russian billionaire's oceanside mansion. Gale sat in his idling car next to the gated entrance and punched up Tate's number. The front of his coat and his face and hands were smeared with blood. He'd managed to stop his nose from bleeding, but his head pounded, and his ribs burned with every breath. After a few rings, his call went to voicemail. Without hesitation, he tapped out a text: *"I'm going to call again in a minute. You have one opportunity to answer. Gale McClanahan."*

Gale hit send.

A few seconds later, Gale's phone pinged.

"Or else?"

Gale texted: *"I go to the media."*

Gale's phone immediately chimed. He answered.

"What's going on?" Tate snapped, annoyed.

"Right now, I'm outside Asinov's estate sitting in a pool of blood. One of Voss' goons is lying unconscious on a Southampton beach, and I have enough evidence to send Voss to prison and implicate you and the League in a whole lot of shit. That's what's going on."

Tate hesitated before shifting his tone. "Okay, Gale," he said, his voice growing calm and even, ever smooth. "We'll buzz you in."

The gate opened with a grinding sound, and Gale drove down the tree and hedge-lined driveway to the estate. The sprawling stucco villa finally appeared with its hipped and tiled, low-pitched roofs, arched entrances, and crowned windows peering out to sea. The mansion looked as though it should have been perched on the Mediterranean. A dark limousine, a Maserati, and a Bentley sat parked in front of a six-car garage. Wearing a yellow rain slicker, the limo driver leaned against the vehicle with a phone pushed against his ear, smoking. A member of Asinov's security detail stood near the front door wearing a dark rain suit. Gale swung the rental car between the Maserati and Bentley and grimaced from the sharp pain in his side as he climbed from his seat.

He stood in the rain for a moment to catch his breath.

The security guard followed Gale menacingly as Gale walked to the elaborate arched entrance and pushed the doorbell. Gale stood with his hands on his hips, bloodied and bruised. He wanted to tear Voss apart.

An older man opened the door. He was dressed in black shirt and slacks, eyed Gale up and down, and with a sigh led Gail and Asinov's rain-soaked bodyguard through a series of ornately decorated rooms into a light paneled study. Gale found Tate, Voss, and Asinov waiting for him. With a quick wave of his hand, Asinov dismissed the guard who stepped out of the room and closed the study door.

Voss' black, demonic eyes settled on Gale. "To what do we owe the pleasure, Coach McClanahan?"

Gale noticed Tate's expression harden. Blood dripped on the tile floor from a small gash on Gale's hand.

"I won't make this any longer than it needs to be," Gale said, staring at Voss. He pulled his phone from his back pocket. "I have taped testimony from Maynard Bremmer, a former Voss Energy employee, detailing how you blackmailed him, set him up for perjury, and illegally influenced a trial where seven men died because of your negligence."

Voss leaned back and flashed his teeth. "You believe Mr. Bremmer?"

"I do."

"Well, Coach McClanahan. I have an affidavit, signed last night by Maynard Bremmer, that any testimony he gave to you and your associates was false and given under duress. In fact," Voss turned to Tate, "Franklin Washington's impersonation of a federal agent could land him in prison."

Tate responded with surprise and alarm. "Washington?"

"That's right. What Coach McClanahan's failing to reveal is that he sent Donta Jones, an assistant coach with the Lone Stars, and your Director of League Security to North Dakota to obtain false and misleading testimony from a former Voss Energy employee."

Tate's eyes sharpened. He stared at Gale. "Is this true?"

Gale said, "The testimony isn't false or misleading. Voss Energy's negligence killed seven oil field workers. Voss not only covered up the crime, but he bribed a federal judge."

Asinov leaned forward in his chair, his confusion growing. "What's this to do with our meeting today?" He looked at Tate and Voss.

"Everything," Gale said.

"Actually, nothing," Voss barked.

"If Vernon's telling the truth, the testimony you received isn't admissible," Tate said.

Voss said dismissively, "We've heard enough, Coach. It's time for you to drag your sorry ass out of here."

Gale felt his ears grow hot. He took a few steps toward Voss. "There's something else I need to say." Gale looked at the three men. "Catherine Reiser, Chief of Staff for Mike Andujar, is sitting in a coffee shop across the street from *The New York Times*." Gale held up his phone. "If she doesn't hear from me in the next 10 minutes, she spills everything."

"You son of a bitch. You've got nothing." Voss rose from his chair. His face was red, and he stepped toward Gale pointing a finger.

"The testimony's inadmissible," Tate said.

"You've always underestimated me," Gale said, still looking at Voss. "Reiser will spill everything."

"Spill what?" Asinov asked.

Gale said coolly, "Bremmer not only gave testimony, but he gave Washington something else. It seems bribing judges wasn't the only thing Voss did."

"What else?" Tate asked uneasily, glancing at Voss.

"How about fraud and racketeering. Is that enough?" Gale paused and looked at Voss. "You violated antitrust laws. You orchestrated a conspiracy where your oil and gas company colluded with another to purchase leases. I have the hard copies of every document Bremmer kept."

Voss glanced at Asinov and Tate and turned to Gale. "What do you want, McClanahan?" Suddenly, Voss' voice was unsteady.

"It's simple. The Lone Stars stay in San Antonio. The League takes custody of the team until it's sold. My coaches and equipment manager get rehired and paid, and I never have to see Garvin Johnson or you again."

"If I don't?" Voss asked with a glance at Tate, who had suddenly gone quiet.

"We go public." Gale tapped his phone. "Catherine Reiser tells everything. Buddy Adams' gambling ring, how you colluded with Tate on tanking the season, how you covered up the deaths of seven men, and rigged oil and gas leases."

"Sounds like all hearsay," Tate interjected.

"How about your affair with a subordinate?" Gale asked Tate. By the sudden look on Tate's face, Gale's threat had struck a chord. Washington's information was proving useful.

Tate's face reddened.

"Forget about how much your wife will get in a hefty divorce settlement. You'll lose your job. Sleeping with an employee? The owners won't protect you, not with everything else you're trying to dismiss as 'hearsay'. What happens to Spencer Tate's bright and shining legacy?"

"Blackmail."

"Justice," Gale shot back.

Asinov looked at Tate and Voss and said coldly, "We have an agreement."

Tate stared at Gale.

Voss said through gritted teeth, his fists tightening, "We have an agreement, Spencer. He's bluffing. He's got nothing."

"What's it going to be?" Gale asked Tate.

Tate hesitated. He glanced again at Voss and paused. "No deal," he said finally. "Unless you want to go to prison, Vernon. I have the integrity of the League to think about."

Voss swore, his eyes black, turning into slits. "Integrity? I'll ruin you, Tate. We had a deal."

"Not now."

"You son of a bitch," Voss lashed out.

"There's two more things I forgot to mention," Gale said, ignoring Voss' outburst.

Tate's face grew angrier. "More?"

"They're not negotiable, Mr. Commissioner," Gale said, bloodied and smiling, pointing his finger at Tate. "They're deal breakers."

EPILOGUE

The battered taxi pulled onto the gravel road and parked next to the corrugated shed. The January night was pitch black but clear and star-filled. A sharp wind cut across the West Texas plains. Gale paid the taxi driver and climbed out of the cab into the frigid air. The season had ended the day before. Gale hadn't told Marybeth he was coming home. He felt his heart race, took a deep breath, and walked toward the house.

Gale noticed a light flip on in the kitchen, followed by the porch light, and before he could get to the entrance, Marybeth opened the door. Her thick hair was mussed, and her robe was pulled tight. She looked careworn.

"Gale?" she called.

Gale stood a few feet away in the shadows and said, "I needed to see you." He stepped closer into the light.

She studied his face, her expression softening. "I thought you were coming home next week."

Since Gale's reinstatement as the Lone Stars' coach, Gale and Marybeth had spoken regularly. A few times during the season, she and Tilly had flown to Dallas with the Wallaces and Barbara Engle to watch the Lone Stars play at the Cotton Bowl. While the Voss Energy Dome remained an unplayable hulk, there'd been signs of a new stadium rising on the site. Bulldozers loaded debris into an endless line of dump trucks and a few cranes stood positioned as plans moved forward for a new home for the Lone Stars.

Gale and Marybeth had promised each other they wouldn't discuss the future until after the season. "I need to make sense of all this," Marybeth had told Gale after she'd learned of his confrontation with Voss and Tate. Those moments together, they'd focused their attention on Tilly. Gale realized Marybeth needed time to process and heal.

When the League had taken custody of the Lone Stars until the franchise could be sold, the team's road accommodations had vastly improved. In Dallas, the Lone Stars had stayed at the Ritz-Carlton and had eaten team meals on white linen in one of the hotel's chandelier-draped banquet rooms. One of Gale's first acts in the post-Voss era had been the firing of Sam Lorenzo. Johnson's office had been cleaned out, and his administrative assistant had been replaced by a young woman with a Texas-size smile, a can-do attitude, and ability to master sophisticated data bases and type 75 words per minute. Voss Energy had filed for bankruptcy, and Voss, still under pressure from Gale's threats of exposure, had sold the Lone Stars to a local owner at a fraction of what Asinov had agreed to pay. For a moment, Gale thought about Vanessa. Despite his pleas for her to get into rehab, Vanessa had vanished. Gale figured she'd found a new sugar daddy and was lying nearly naked in the sun on a yacht in the Caribbean, vodka and Percocet in hand.

***

A few minutes later, Gale and Marybeth sat across from each other at the kitchen table, the same table where, eleven months prior, Gale had signed the contract to coach the San Antonio Lone Stars.

Gale had known what he was going to do when he'd driven away from Asinov's estate with caked blood on his clothes and broken ribs.

Gale felt the words spill without regret. "I'm quitting," he said.

Marybeth's face clouded. "What?"

"The only thing that matters are you and Tilly."

"You're going to quit the Lone Stars?" she asked in disbelief.

Gale nodded. The Lone Stars had finished the season 9-8, narrowly missing the playoffs. Gale was going to be an easy pick for Coach of the Year. Unlike seven of his brethren who'd been fired earlier in the day on what the League called Black Monday; he'd orchestrated the Lone Stars' astonishing ascent.

"You're going to walk away?"

"That's right."

Marybeth shook her head. "Why now of all times?"

"I want a life with you in Kinney, Marybeth. That's all that matters. If there's anything that I've learned throughout the last year, it's how much you mean to me. I'll give up ambition and the spotlight and everything else that goes with it to recapture the life I gave away."

"And quit coaching?"

Gale smiled.

Gale reached over and took Marybeth's hand. She accepted it. He noticed the subtle lines at the corners of her eyes.

"You'd quit for me?" she asked.

"Yes."

"The job of a lifetime?"

Gale nodded.

She choked back tears and for a moment looked away. "I've missed you so much. I'm sorry I doubted you. I was overwhelmed. You have to admit, you gave me a lot to absorb," she said, smiling through tears.

Gale rose from his chair and approached Marybeth. She stood as he pulled her gently to him. "I'm sorry for all I put you through."

She nodded and rested her chin on his shoulder.

After a few moments, Gale whispered, "I need to tell you something."

Marybeth looked into his eyes.

"I put a down payment on my parents' ranch."

Shock spread across her face. She pulled back. "With what? Even with the rest of your salary, it's not enough."

"I didn't want to tell you until the season ended and we worked things out," Gale said, a smile spreading across his face. "The Lone Stars owe us $25 million."

Marybeth's jaw dropped.

"A settlement."

"Does Grayson know?"

"Who do you think negotiated the terms? I plan on making sure the coaches and Jimmie get taken care of. They deserve it. The rest goes to us."

She leaned back and eyed him suspiciously. "What else haven't you told me?"

"I'm going to teach Tilly how to ride. She'll be a rodeo star before long. Barrel racing is in her future."

Marybeth frowned. "Her arm's still healing, Gale. Horses?"

Gale grinned.

Marybeth stepped back for a moment. "Ranching's a hard life."

"My father loved you, Marybeth. He'd say with that woman you can do anything."

"He was always so kind to me. But Gale, are you going to miss coaching? It's in your blood."

"Jack tells me Midland Senior High needs a defensive coordinator."

Marybeth smiled. "Would that really make you happy?"

"You bet."

"You mean that?"

Gale pulled her close. Marybeth's face lit up. Her breath was warm and inviting.

"After this past year, do you even need to ask?"

***

The line of senior citizens at Grady's moved sluggishly. As usual, the crowd gathering around the salad bar seemed paralyzed by the choices. Cold peas or beets? Gale spotted Donta Jones across the restaurant, waved his hand, and slid into the booth opposite his assistant coach.

"No food?" Jones asked, taking a bite of meatloaf.

"Not for me."

"You ready to talk about next season? We're gonna be better, Boy Wonder. Playoff bound," Jones said between bites.

Gale ignored Jones and watched him take a sip of iced tea.

"Hear about Rulon?" Jones asked, eager to share the news about Alexander.

Gale nodded with a knowing smile. Alexander and Rose Cutler were headed to the Hill Country for a weekend escape.

"There's sunshine in that woman," Jones said, shaking his head. "Rulon figured out how to part the drapes."

Gale smiled.

"I have some news myself," Gale said.

"What's that?" Jones asked, dipping his fork into a hunk of mashed potatoes.

"Big news."

Jones leaned forward and rested his elbows on the table. "Spill it."

Gale paused and took a breath.

"I'm looking at the new head coach of the San Antonio Lone Stars."

Jones slowly put his fork down. "What are you talking about, Boy Wonder?"

"It's official. The contract is waiting your signature."

"What are you saying?"

Disbelief crossed Jones' face as Gale explained. What Gale didn't tell Jones was he'd threatened Tate he'd go public with the Lone Stars' sordid narrative and Tate's affair if Jones wasn't named head coach and given a five-year contract.

Jones sat back in the booth, stunned.

"You got this, Donta," Gale said. "No one's earned it more than you."

"Boy Wonder, I was happy being your Defensive Coordinator. Are you sure you won't come back? We're going to make the playoffs this year."

"I've had enough of the League to last a lifetime. I'm like Dorothy. I'm clicking the heels of my boots together as we speak."

"Are you sure?"

"Surer than I'll ever be," Gale said.

"I owe you, Boy Wonder."

"No. I owe you. More than you'll ever know."

* * *

Approximately 20 miles southeast of Terlingua, Texas, on a July afternoon, a sheriff spotted an abandoned Mercedes sitting in the desert. The car rested in the heat and dust about two hundred yards off a dirt road amidst low-growing cactus and scrub.

The sheriff had stumbled upon it. Whoever had driven the Mercedes had ditched the car in the middle of nowhere.

The sheriff, a veteran law enforcement official, was no stranger to the shenanigans that went with living along the border. He had seen it all. That was until he drove his SUV toward the Mercedes and noticed that something was resting on the car's hood, pushed up against the windshield like a heavy sack.

A man had been stripped and duct taped to the windshield, his hands and legs bound and his body secured by swaths of tape wrapped across his chest through the open cab. His face was charred, like those grotesque pictures of burn victims, their faces distorted and pulled tight, like cadavers with crepe skin. The desert sun had cooked him. It was surprising that the turkey vultures weren't onto the carcass yet.

The sheriff moved away from the dead man, and with his back turned, radioed the Sheriff's office in Alpine.

When the other officers arrived, they stood under the mid-day sun and agreed they had seen nothing like it.

A day later, after combing through dental records, the authorities identified the body of a man in his late sixties. A few days earlier, they had received an anonymous call that he was missing.

His name was Vernon Voss.

Acknowledgements

I'm deeply grateful for the following people who have championed my writing and provided valuable feedback: Arnie Holtberg, Brian Fidler, Kevin Colby, Tom Helming, and Merritt Grover, who by word of mouth, single handedly turned my first novel, Eight-Man Cowboy, into a local bestseller.

I am indebted to my friend and editor, Wright Abbot, who has devoted untold hours to LONESTAR and supported and guided me through the ups and downs of writing a book, and to Dan Edwards of Creative Texts, who gave me a chance. In particular, I am fortunate to have a loving family who supports my writing obsession: thanks to Annie, Trevor, and Jen, whose love and encouragement have been amazing.

And to high school coaches, who are some of the finest educators I know.

About the Author

C.W. Wells began his professional life as an award-winning sportswriter before turning to a career in education. He coached high school football in Texas and grew up in a small town. C.W. encourages readers to write a review of *LONESTAR*. He would appreciate your feedback. He can be contacted at cwwells97@gmail.com.

About the Publisher

Creative Texts is a boutique independent publishing house devoted to high quality content that readers enjoy. We publish best-selling authors such as Jerry D. Young, N.C. Reed, Sean Liscom, Jared McVay, Laurence Dahners, and many more. Our audiobook performers are among the best in the business including Hollywood legends like Barry Corbin and top talent like Christopher Lane, Alyssa Bresnaham, Erin Moon and Graham Hallstead.

Whether its post-apocalyptic or dystopian fiction, biography, history, true crime, science fiction, thrillers, or even classic westerns, our goal is to produce highly-rated customer preferred content. If there is anything we can do to enhance your reader experience, please contact us directly at info@creativetexts.com. As always, we do appreciate your reviews on your book seller's website as well.

Finally, if you would like to find more great books like this one, please search for us by name in your favorite search engine or on your bookseller's website to see books by all Creative Texts authors. Thank you for reading!

Find us on Social Media

Made in the USA
Monee, IL
22 May 2023

34306629R00154